S0-EKO-267

BROKE BUT NOT BUSTED

Wild Horse Shorty's line of blarney could move a dead Indian. He thought fast and talked even faster. But he only had eighteen cents left to his name, and sixteen hungry horses to feed. In short, Shorty owed money all over town.

To keep his belly filled, Shorty would go round to the old hotel that had been in its prime when the Earps and their hell-swearing posse had found reason for stopping, but had since gone to seed. The present landlord was a gambling man and had staked him many a dinner.

But Shorty went there one time too many. Ben, the owner, met him one night with a pistol, drawing back the hammer till it hit full cock, saying, "You been getting away with plenty, pardner, but you ain't getting away with the eighteen dollars you owe me."

He raised the barrel and pointed squarely at Shorty's chest. "Pay," he said without smiling.

Here are two exciting novels starring the fastest-talkin' horseman of them all—

WILD HORSE SHORTY

Wild Horse Shorty

AND ITS SEQUEL

Blood of Kings

Nelson Nye

Selected and Edited by Keith Deutsch

ZEBRA BOOKS

KENSINGTON PUBLISHING CORP.

ZEBRA BOOKS

are published by

KENSINGTON PUBLISHING CORP.
21 East 40th Street
New York, N.Y. 10016

Wild Horse Shorty copyright © 1944 by Nelson C. Nye
Blood of Kings copyright © 1946 by Nelson C. Nye

This edition copyright © 1978 by Nelson Nye

All rights reserved. No part of this book may be reprodueed in any form or by any means without the prior written consent of the Publisher, excepting brief quotes used in reviews.

First Printing: June, 1978

Printed in the United States of America

WILD HORSE SHORTY

1.

PLENTY OF ELBOWROOM

The unlovely collection of weatherbitten structures where the Hilvitia Trail had once joined hands with the Greaterville trace to cross a roaring Santa Cruz River, still clung to its faded glories and was known as the Horsehead Crossing. But the Santa Cruz River •hadn't run for so long there was not one frog in its entire length which had ever learned how to swim.

The COLLOSSAL MERCANTILE—Geo. Provencher Prop.—now creaked with a loose-shackled misery, every plank a-rattle, every barrel braced door a-squeal on its hinges, a-moan to every wind that blew; its insides dim with the must of years, aromatic with sorghum and strong yellow soap and the gunny-sacked fertilizer piled by the counter.

There was a dust devil romping the Helvitia Trail and old Jack Williams, coming out of the mill, took one hasty look and sprinted for the Mercantile. "George!" he panted. "Bolt your doors quick—he's a-comin' again!"

"Coming? Who's comin'?"

Young Provencher, poking his head out the door, raked a roundabout look through the broiling glare and ground his teeth on a cuss-word. Old Jack, who had seen them come and go, chuckled.

"Sure brings back the past, watchin' that feller—y' would almost reckon he ackshully had *business.* Lookit him shovin' them broncs! Lookit 'em come! Jus' burnin' the sand up!"

"I'll burn *him*," young Provencher rumbled, "if he tries any more of his tricks around *here!* The gol-rammed fool! Tearin' around like a pea in a pitcher—spurrin' an' yowlin' an' a-pitchin' up dust! Who's he—"

"I dunno," Williams said; "but don't be too hard on him. He's a good lad at heart—he don't mean nothin' by it; all this borryin' an' chargin's on account of his horses—he's a natural born horse lover. He jest can't help it."

"Well, *I* can!" snarled Provencher acidly. "Hard up or not, he ain't chargin' no more up at *my* counters! He ain't goin' t' spend no more of *my* money on 'em! Why, all that chewin' t'baccer he bought, he went right out an' give it to them crow-baits! Bad enough if he *bought* it—but he don't. He don't buy nothin'! *Charge! charge! charge!* Everything he gets here goes down on the cuff!"

Jack Williams nodded. "Fed 'em off my place long's the Missus'd stan' fer it—like to plumb ruint old Pete Hague's pasture. Pete never said nothin' about their eatin'; Pete never opened his mouth till that shad-bellied stud took t' chousin' them mares around the fenceline. Why, they tromped out the grass in that pasture till 'twas drun nigh as smooth as Lute Dickerson's racetrack . . . *Shh!*—here he comes—"

"An' wantin' to borry somethin' sure as I'm standin' here!"

WILD HORSE

Wild Horse Shorty and his sixteen bangtails took up a lot of room when they visited; and it seemed like visiting was all they did. Shorty's line of blarney would move a dead Indian. It had taken the townsfolk a while to get onto him, but all knew him for a man to bear watching.

His horses weren't much. You had the straight of it there. They were jug-headed critters, narrow chested and spavined, too long through the barrel, too short in the leg—a ring-boned, roaring, pot gutted bunch. And he always came shoving them hellity-larrup like they was off to a rummage sale of Tiffany's diamonds.

The occasion in hand proved to be no exception. He came streaking the nags at a headlong gallop, enveloping the porch like an exuberant zephyr.

"H'are you, boys?" he yelled, yanking his stud straight up on its hind legs just like they do in the moving pictures. "Still beatin' yore wife these days are you, Provvy?"

But George, by now, had moved his barrels. He slammed the doors shut and made off after Williams who was fading away around a far off corner.

Wild Horse cuffed back his hat and stared. "Well, fan my saddle!" he said, peering after them. "What you reckon has got into them two?"

He stood awhile, frowning, quite baffled and curious, entirely forgetting that Bill Hart look which he always had taken such pains to cultivate. Even his mares, fanned out at the hitchrail, snorted and pawed at the ground, disgruntled.

It was enough to make a guy look himself over to see if he had what the magazines advertised.

Had he been a dang tramp, a drifter or whatnot, he would not have felt peeved at such Philistine treatment.

But heck! Here he was, the best dressed sport at this end of the cactus. He was clean and close shaved, and his five-foot-seven was clothed in rare splendor; a real work of art by any guy's say-so. His big San Fran hat, white-and-red striped shirt and the cowhide boots with that dilly of a cactus hand-painted on each, were brand new and straight from the shelves of Provencher's Mercantile. His vest, with the gaudy-gay flowers whipped on in gold thread, he had got from L. Ernenwein, the sheriff's deputy, who in turn had acquired it from a late sporting gentleman. And good as new, by grab! The blood didn't show — it had spilled on a rose; and the bullet had gone through a Black Eyed Susan. Shucks! don't talk about clothing! Old Rodeo Ben couldn't hardly show better — and not one cent had Shorty paid for anything. Even his saddle and spurs had come free, by the grace of "Doc" Wallace who vetted for the ranchers and, times between, did a modest business in firearms and leather goods.

It wasn't as though Shorty aimed to be spongy. A horse has to eat and horse eats cost money; and money was something dang hard to come by. You couldn't expect a plain four-legged horse to know anything about the high cost of living. Only Mr. Babson understood that, and his prognostications always left Shorty bug-eyed. But on this one thing Wild Horse stood mighty firm; if there were just so much, he saw his broncs always got it.

He gave a hitch to his chaps and climbed into the saddle.

"Devil with *them* guys!" he grunted and, whistling up his mares, struck off down the road toward Cramp Fritchet's saloon. "C'mon, Figure 8," he beseeched his saddle stud, "pick up yore feet an' put 'em back down again. Yonder stands Fritchet's and Fritchet's stands treats—sometimes, anyways. Special when Miz Baisy's round. *There's* a gal, dang you—easier t' look at than a stack of gold eagles!"

He took down his big tin-plated guitar and reeled off a good-sized chunk of his talent, which was plenty loud to say the least for it.

" 'Twas onct in the saddle
   I used t' go dashin'
'Twas onct in the saddle
   I used t' be gay,
I got mixed up with drinkin'
   Then took t' card-playin'
Got shot through the belly;
   I'm dyin' t'day . . . ."

George Provencher, distantly watching him, nodded. "He'll git shot, all right, if he messes round there!"

But Shorty's thoughts were far from shooting as he fanned out his cavvy before the saloon. He hung his guitar to the saddle horn and left Figure 8 on grounded reins; because Figure 8 was a genteel horse and didn't need tying no more than a zipper.

Wild Horse was thirsty—but not for what Cramp sold at the bar. Nor was he thinking of anything so mild as well water as he clanked up the steps with spur chains jangling. Mr. Fritchet himself stood blocking the doorway, thumbs in his galluses, a frostbitten stare looking out of his eyes.

Shorty did not see him until he almost ran into him. He shrugged, then smiled. He said, 'H'are you, Fritchet?

How's the National Thirst holdin' up?"

Fritchet's face was like a board. He didn't open his mouth, even. Nor did he make any move toward unblocking his doorway.

Wild Horse sighed. This was the dangdest country! You just couldn't get yourself a glad hand no way—except from Miss Baisy, the saloonman's daughter. *She* was all right! Knew how it was with a roving cowpoke—had given him her hand in warmest greeting; passionately, in fact. Right square on the cheek that time he had kissed her.

'Course, she had only *made out* to be mad. But just the same, Shorty thought, this was the rebuffingest country he had ever come into. Plumb hos-tile.

But he had his horses to think of so he fetched up a smile and clapped Fritchet's shoulder.

It was just like clapping the rib of a mountain.

"You know . . ." Wild Horse said, clinching up his will power, "I b'lieve I'll shove my roots down here. The's somethin' about this dawgone country. More a man sees of it, more it gits him. Big! That's what it is. Plenty of elbowroom. Know of any outfit I could buy in cheap?"

"With what?" Fritchet said, very bleak and unmoving.

"Why—with money, of course."

"*Whose* money? Not mine, by grab, 'cause you ain't goin' to git it!"

Wild Horse registered reproach, but Fritchet had seen that look before.

"You heard me," he growled. "Git along with you now before you curdle my custom. You know there won't nobody come while *you're* here—wouldn't have no place to tie up if they did—"

"These horses is tired, man. They got t' rest *someplace*—"

"Go'on," Fritchet said—"git that vulture bait outa here!"

"I could move 'em—"

"You're *goin'* to move 'em—an' you can just move yourself along with 'em. Git a wiggle on now before I call the sheriff."

"Which one?" Shorty said.

Fritchet glared. "Sheriff Potter—"

"You'd be wastin' your breath. Potter wouldn't come— No he wouldn't! He druther set on his fanny an' scratch up the taxpayers' property with them shiny gold-inlay spurs he's been sportin'—them ones he comfiscated off Bob Lowndes. Potter'd jest keep a-settin' an' tell Ernie t' come. An' you know dang well Ernie wouldn't come neither."

"Wouldn't come!" Fritchet gasped. "Why the blue hell wouldn't he?"

"Not if he knew it was me, he wouldn't."

The saloonkeeper's eyes showed a kind of glazed look. "He would dang well come if the sheriff sent him!"

"No he wouldn't," Wild Horse muttered doggedly. "He's a man of conscience an' his conscience wouldn't let him."

"What's his conscience got to do with it?"

"Well—" Wild Horse said, "the facts of the matter is he owes me some money; owes me forty-seven dollars an' eighty-five cents an', natcherly, he ain't got it. Ain't even got no more'n you could stuff a gnat with. This county don't pay its— Anyway, owin' me all that money you won't catch Ernie comin' anywheres near me. Go ahead— call 'im! Look here—I'll bet you forty-five dollars you can't even git him t' cross the street!"

Fritchet passed a hand across the line of his stare. His face had a queer look, like maybe he was empty.

11

Wild Horse hastened to lend him assistance. "Ain't you et—"

"Keep away—don't touch me," Fritchet muttered. He took hold of his head with both hands and shook it. But the queerness still looked out of his stare.

He drew a long breath and seemed to freshen up somewhat. "Would you mind," he said with an elaborate politeness, "explaining why it is Ernie owes you that money?"

"Full house."

"How's that?"

"Full house ag'in' two pairs—he had the pairs," Shorty mentioned.

"So you got him into a card game—" Fritchet suddenly stiffened. "Mean t' say you had that much money jest in one pot?—that much money *apiece?*"

"Uh-uh. Matches."

"What?"

"We was playin' with matches," Wild Horse sighed. "Potter was out an' Ernie couldn't find where he kep' his chips at. So we played with matches. Took dang near all of 'em t' build that pot or—"

"Too bad," Fritchet said. "Forty-five—"

"Forty-seven dollars an' eighty-five cents—that's a mort of money," pronounced Wild Horse wistfully. "I could do a heap with a pile like that."

"Well, you've still got the money you started with. Now if—"

"Uh-uh. We was playin' with matches."

Fritchet stared blankly. "You never had nothing to *start* with?"

"Ernie," Wild Horse explained, "didn't know that."

Fritchet did not say any more. A kind of strangled gulp

came out of him. He wheeled away, kind of staggering across his sawdust-strewn floor, and went through a door which he shut behind him.

Wild Horse heard the key in the lock.

He shrugged when he caught the bartender watching him.

"Looks kind of bad, don't he?— hev them spells often? Looks t' me like it might be a spot on his kidney." He shook his head. "You kin make mine bourbon, pal. I always say—"

The barman jerked a curt thumb toward the wall, tipped back his head and took a swig of cold tea.

Wild Horse spelled out the large new sign. It said:

IN GOD WE TRUST—
ALL OTHERS PAY CASH

Shorty sniffed. "I don't guess you make any charge fer leanin' ag'in' the bar here, do you?"

The apron shrugged, industriously wiped up a wet spot.

Wild Horse brought out a blue-and-gilt package. He seemed to be in the grip of a selfish impulse. But charity won. He reached it across to the interested barkeep. "Hev one?"

The apron looked at them. Frowned; kind of hesitated. He took a look round and decided to try one. Wild Horse scratched him a light and the bartender took a deep drag and coughed. He kept on coughing.

Shorty's face showed concern. He stretched over the bar and slapped the man's back. "It's that tea, I reckon. Lots of them tea drinkers got that cough . . . They tell me

13

the whole town of Boston's got it. Some kinda lung condition. You ever consider goin' up t' Denver?"

The barkeep wiped his streaming eyes, ran a shaky hand round his collar. "Whadda y' call them things?"

"Them is cigarettes, pard."

"Damndest cigarettes ever *I* smoked!" The barkeep wiped cold sweat from his forehead, "What they got in 'em—isinglass?"

"Got in 'em—Oh! you mean that smell?" Wild Horse shook his head. "I ain't never been able t' figger it out. Must be the medicine in 'em, I guess—"

"Medicine!" The bartender's eyes stood out big as a hen's eggs. "You put *medicine*—"

"Uh-uh. Not me. They come that way, pal. Already dipped. I smoke 'em reg'lar—for my health," Wild Horse added. "Say—you ain't seen nothin' of Miz' Baisy, hev you?"

But the apron didn't seem to hear him. With a dazed, kind of all-gone look on his face he put up a trembling hand to his head and, with the other hand catching quick grips on the bar, he lurched its length and stumbled out the side door.

"It sure beats hell," Wild Horse muttered, looking after him. Then a sound of high heels out front grabbed his notice. Miss Baisy favored a high kind of heel. . . .

He grabbed up his asthma-aid cigarettes and made for the porch. His glance was excited—triumphant, too.

It *was* Miss Baisy! With her eyes all lit up like a Christmas tree.

What a picture! Hurrying along with her free-wheeling stride, cheeks the color of health, smiling teeth all pearly —cute as the pup under Provencher's wagon.

It made Shorty's heart drum hard on his ribs to see her

come loping up to him that way. Because it proved he'd guessed right about her real deep-down thoughts of him, that slap and that fuss she'd kicked up notwithstanding. She had only made out to be mad, like he'd figured. Inside, like enough, it had tickled her frantic to think of being kissed by a man like Wild Horse.

He clanked down the steps to the roadway to meet her.

"I thought you were *never* going to come," she cried; and Shorty's heart like to shook the shirt off him. There wasn't no girl like Baisy in miles. She was the pride of the Crossing and the belle of Tucson—more handsome than a steak plumb smothered in onions!

"Shucks," he said, with his Bill Hart look; then his jaw dropped down till he almost stepped on it.

Miss Baisy had sailed right on past him.

2.

"THE DICKERSONS *IS* THE LAW!"

Wild Horse flung around and a wilt hit his look. For there, right behind him with a fine looking pair of horses in tow, hat off and dimpling, stood Luther K. Dickerson, the greatest horse breeder in five hundred miles.

And was Baisy giving him the come-hither smile! Rushing right up to him—giving her hands to him!

It was enough to cramp rats, and no kidding.

Had it been anyone else Shorty reckoned he could have stood it. But *Dickerson!* Honest to Pete, he looked just like one of them toothpaste ads. Not quite so young, maybe, but curly yellow hair combed back like a marcel, a great big grin and that yellow mustache with its sharp waxed ends— Honest to Jonah! it made Shorty squirm just to past him one.

It had likely made a lot of folks squirm, but danged few had done any pasting. Lute Dickerson had this town in his pocket—and all this country, clean up to the Whetstones. He was a Hereford raiser and a breeder of horses that sold for prices never less than four figures; he was reputed to be a heap richer than Croesus. They called his spread the Roman Four, and his sleek palominos were Arab and thoroughbred crossed on Quarter.

"Oh, Lute!" Baisy cried. "What *beautiful* horses—they're simply *gorgeous*! Are they Galab's get or—"

"You guessed it first off," laughed Dickerson, pleased. "I don't know how you do it, Baisy; there isn't another woman in the country knows as much about horses as you've forgotten."

It was Baisy's turn, and she glowed quite enchantingly.

Then Dickerson said, "I presume you noted the Arab characteristics. Like gets like—fine heads, aren't they?"

"Oh, Lute, they're *grand*!" Baisy praised.

It made Wild Horse sick just to hear such foolishness.

It made him sicker when Dickerson, with his toothpaste smile, said:

"Why, hello, Shorty—didn't see you. How do you like this gelding I'm giving Miss Baisy? Think—"

"Oh, *Lute*!" Baisy cried. "Not *really*?"

"Sure," Lute smiled. "You don't suppose I make it a practice to go loping around with a led horse, do you?" He gave Shorty's mares a slanchways smile; and Wild Horse savvied the point all right. "No," Lute said, "I brought him in just for you, Baisy. His name is Valhalla, and he's double registered. PHBA and in the Half-Bred Stud Book. Had a chance to sell him only yesterday—fellow from Montana wanted me to take twenty-five hundred for him—"

Shorty said: "He ort t'hev his head looked at," but Dickerson paid him no notice.

"I told this fellow 'you're just wasting your time, I'm giving that horse to my girl for her birthday.' That's what I told him, but he couldn't believe it. He said 'It's that

17

horse or nothing!' I just told him politely I was sorry he'd had his long trip for nothing. He went tearing off mad as a hatter.

"But shucks," Lute laughed, "my girl don't have a birthday every day, and when she does there isn't anything too good for her."

So of course Baisy blushed and lowered her eye-winkers, but Shorty noticed that she got hold of the lead rope; and it sure made him grind his molars to think of her taking presents from a whifflestitch like Dickerson. Honest to Pete, he felt downright ashamed for her.

"Well," Lute said, "guess I got to be going. Got a big deal on—"

"But I haven't even *thanked* you," cried Baisy. "Surely you'll stay for dinner, won't you?"

Dickerson's look said he would mighty well like to; but aloud he said regretfully, " 'Fraid I just plain can't today, Baisy. I've got that deal set for two o'clock—"

"Oh—but how utterly silly of me! I should have said 'lunch'. I keep forgetting you have your 'dinner' at night. You'll stay for lunch, won't you? Father never hears enough of your talk about horses—he'll be *so* put out."

"Well . . . I suppose . . . I wouldn't want to offend Mr. Fritchet—Hi! Not leaving, are you, Shorty?"

But Wild Horse had heard quite enough of that gassing. With his Bill Hart look sticking out all over, he whistled his mares and jumped into the saddle, just like he'd seen them do in the movies.

"Regular back-country brush popper," he heard Lute tell Baisy; and after that wild horses couldn't have held him, because if he had stayed any longer, he would have popped Lute sure.

Feeling plumb disgusted with the ways of the world, Shorty started up the trail to get shed of this country. That, leastways, is what he told his mind, and he sure enough took the old Greaterville trace that led off through the dun, broiling miles toward the mountains. There was a boom on up at Greaterville and those hairy-chested miners werer making big stakes, and Shorty was of a mind to get some of it. But when he came to the SIGN OF THE HAPPY HARP — to which some bright soul had added a Y — he recollected it was eating time and discovered that he was ravenous.

The Happy Harp was an old hotel that had been in its prime when Heck was a pup. Curly Bill had used to carouse in the place, Virgil Boucher had taken a bed there and the Earps and their hell-swearing posses had found frequent reason for stopping. But the beds were lumpy and creaky now and the entire place had a gone-to-seed look. The present landlord, a gambling gentleman with a very sly eye, was known very simply as "Ben". He had a hate for work that few could equal and did not care whether school kept or not. He maintained an interest in just three things: the hotel, suckers, and personal comfort. But it took the second to support the first, and the entire gross proceeds of both to permit his meager measure of the latter. To augment this system he served good meals, very easily worth three-fifths of the price, which was arbitrarily fixed at one dollar.

So Shorty climbed out of the saddle again and left Figure 8 to keep an eye on the mares. But he took his guitar in with him because Ben had a red-haired hasher; and if there was one thing that girl disliked more than her name, it was to have somebody get fresh about it. Her name was O'Grady and her handle was Rose, so every time

Shorty came within gunshot of her he took down his tin-backed guitar and roared *Sweet Rosie O'Grady* at her.

He went in roaring it at her now; but it looked like he'd got the girl used to it finally. She did not even look up at him. She had her bare arms on the counter and her head poked into a newspaper; and that was where she kept them.

Shorty hung up his guitar on the hat tree, clanked over and plopped himself down on a stool. "Hello yoreself!" he said glumly. "Times is sure gittin' fierce when even a hasher won't give you a tumble."

That fetched her — brought her head up in a hurry. "An' what's wrong," she said, "with bein' a hasher?"

"Not a thing," Shorty grumped, "if you like it."

"Then I'll thank you to keep your bright cracks to yourself. If I didn't like it I wouldn't be doin' it."

Her look kind of dared him to call her a liar; but Wild Horse, recalling past arguments, was not to be drawn into further hostilities. He had gotten his rise and now he wanted his dinner.

"If you'd pass me over that bill o' fare—"

"Got any money in your pockets?"

Shorty broke out his Bill Hart scowl. "Would I be here else?"

"You've been here before. Times without number, and I've yet to see your first cent on the counter."

Shorty looked halfway minded to get up and go out, but it did not appear to discomfort her any. "I've got orders," she said, "not to feed you no more. That Ben went over the tickets last night and like t' took my head off." She colored up a little and her look got tight like what she remembered were better forgotten. "Cash in advance or the plates stay right where they are—in the kitchen."

Shorty's scowl got darker. It took a mort of conniving to

get your dang bills paid if you were trying to keep horses within gunshot of Tucson. "I come in here," he growed. "t' git things settled up with you—"

"About time you did. You're into us eighteen dollars right now and Ben says meals hereafter, to you, will be a dollar two-bits—"

"Then I'll eat someplace else!"

Shorty shifted his weight to slide down off the stool; but the O'Grady wench just curled her lip at him.

"Suit yourself," she said; and Wild Horse paused.

"Two bits extry! What's the big idear?"

"Ben says them broomtails of yours eat two-bits worth of wood off the place every time you anchor them here—"

"That's nominal wear an' tear," Shorty scoffed. "If he thinks he's goin' t' slap such stuff on his custom—"

"Ben doesn't consider you 'custom'. If you want the plain facts he calls you a 'blight'—and he usually says it with some adjectives added. Claims our poorest days are the times you stop here—"

"Enough!" Wild Horse said like the thought of it choked him. "I ain't a-goin' t' set here an' git called rotten names by no bald-headed toad of a dang hotel leech! I'll take my business somewheres else. Some place where they know how t'—"

"Fine!" declared a husky voice just behind him. "That will suit me plumb right down to the ground. This bald-headed toad of a dang hotel leech will be almighty gratified to see the last of you."

Shorty jumped from the stool with his face shut so tight it looked like he would bust his nut-crackers sure. He made for the hat tree to get his guitar.

But Ben was not without notions himself. "Just a minute," he said. "You ain't throwing no dust till you pay that bill.

"*What* bill?"

"*Your* bill!"

Ben lifted a pistol out of his pocket and drew back the hammer till it hit full cock. "You been getting away with plenty, pardner, but you ain't getting away with my eighteen dollars. Just count it right out on the counter."

Wild Horse stared at the gun snout eyeing him. A kind of all-gone feeling hit the pit of his stomach. The look of that gun, and Ben's hard eyes back of it, were pretty good proof Mr. Ben meant business. And Shorty did not have so much as eighteen cents.

"Come on," Ben said; "start counting, bucko."

Wild Horse wished he had gone to Greaterville.

"Look—" he said nervouslike. "Let's not do anythin' we'll be sorry for. I'm goin' t' pay that money—"

"That's the unvarnished truth," Ben said. "Start paying."

"But—but I ain't got it with—"

"Where is it?"

"Well—uh . . . you see—"

"I see," Ben said, and there was a baleful light shining out of his eyes. "You plain ain't got it—"

"Don't git me wrong," broke in Wild Horse hastily. "I'm goin' t' pay you—I didn't hev no idear of beatin' you out of it. It's only that I ain't got it . . . just now . . . right at present. I done spent m' last cent t' git grub fer them horses . . ."

He saw the O'Grady lips curl scornfully.

Ben said acidly: "If them damn old skates was worth anything I'd have them skun for their hide and tallow— But I'll think of something," he added ominously. "Meantime you can shuffle out in that kitchen and start washing up them pans and things you'll find cluttered round there. Roll up your sleeves and get right at it. Here! I'll take that fancy vest. Time you get things slicked up, dinner'll be over an' you can wash the dishes. Hump now — *mosey*!"

It was an almighty come-down for a man like Wild Horse. A plain old pot licker for Ben, the hotel leech. It was enough to make a man hang up his saddle.

Shorty sure felt low.

And it did not lift his spirits any to have that snub nosed hasher standing over him; you would think they was married to hear her jaw at him. "Don't do it *that* way! My soul! ain't you never washed dishes? *This* is what we scour them with— Great Hannah! if you don't *wreck* the place! Put the *clean* ones over in that cupboard. Why don't you roll up your sleeves?"

Wild Horse said, plumb fed up with her clatter: "Why don't you hesh up fer awhile? Bad enough hevin' t' do yore work fer you without bein' forced t' listen—"

"Humph!" she sniffed. "It would kill you to do one *half* of my work! Just look at that skillet! Here—wash this fork again and get that egg off!"

"If you don't like the way I'm a-doin' you kin git over here an' do it yoreself!"

"I might just as well," she said tartly. "I'll probably wind up by having to, anyway. Look at the sugar in the bottom of that cup—look at it, durn you; it ain't going to bite! Put your hand in and scrape it out. If you had to *work* for a living—Have you ever done a day's work in your life?"

Before Wild Horse could decide what remark would flatten her proper she had to dash out and wait on some customers. But after awhile she was back and right at it; she always came back. She was bad as a gadfly.

"Why don't you get a job at something? You want to be a saddle tramp *all* your life? Don't you ever get a hankering to *be* somebody?"

"I'm *goin'* t' be somebody!" Wild Horse shouted, banging a plate down so hard he broke it. "I'm a-goin' t' git me a ranch an' raise horses, by thunder!"

"Thunder never raised no horses round here." Rose curled her lips at him, plainly contemptuous. "Why don't you quit all this helling around? Whyn't you get you a job and act respectable? I sh'd think you'd be ashamed, a grown man like you, flyin' all over with that bunch of scrub horses—I sh'd think you'd have more *pride* about you! Folks'll be sayin—"

"If they do," Wild Horse snarled, "it ain't no skin off *yore* nose! Jest keep yore freckled mug out of it! An' don't make no more cracks about my horses!"

That held her. She went slamming out of there hellity-larrup and Wild Horse wasn't bothered with her again for the rest of the evening. He washed the rest of the junk in peace, and if he chanced to miss a little egg now and then he did not get fussed up about it. He either left it stay or wiped it off on the towel!

Afted he'd got the supper things done Ben came out to the kitchen and said, "I was fixing to pare fifty cents off your bill for the afternoon's work, but you broke two plates, a cup and a saucer so I guess we'll just call it square for the work. Which leaves you owing me eighteen dollars: I'm afraid it'll cost me too much to work it out of you so I'm holding your silver plated saddle, your fancy vest and that tin-plated music box till you come in like a gent, and pay your account here. If you don't pay it off by the end of the month I'm going to sell that stuff for whatever it'll bring me."

Wild Horse shut his mouth like Bill Hart, because it looked mighty plain if he let himself go he would have all hell to pay for. He grabbed up his hat and Ben said nastily: "You don't have to drag your spurs through the restaurant; you'll find your broomtails in the corral out back. That hitch rack out front is for customers."

Shorty clapped on his hat and slammed the door behind him. ·

He found his mares all right but still unfed. So he lugged them a sack of oats from the barn and figured, by grab, he had earned it. Might be a good idea though, he thought not to bust it open till he was off of Ben's property. And when he saw how Figure 8 had been putting in his time he danged well knew this was a place to get shed of. Ben had hitched the stud to the two-post back porch, and the way Figure 8 had been sharpening his teeth it looked like a sneeze would blow the thing over.

Wild Horse got right out of there.

He never pulled up till he got to the livery.

The best thing about the Horsehead Livery was the stuffed bronc's head mounted over the door. George Kerley, the owner, was standing just under it.

"Well, I swear," he said, looking Wild Horse over. "What have you done—gone an' hocked that saddle?"

"I lent it t' Ben," Shorty grunted gruff-like. "Hellbound around?"

"Like enough you'll find him here somewheres. Look over in that feed box yonder. If you don't find him there he's prob'ly up in the loft—or it might be he's gone off to feed his face. I don't seem to hear him. Make yourself right to home. He'll be back before long I shouldn't wonder."

Kerley went off and Wild Horse broke open the oats he'd brought with him and the mares came crowing like flies to a honey pot, nickering and nipping and pawing the ground up. But as he shoved his way clear of his manada, Shorty heard a cracked voice singing "No place is so dear to my chi-ild-hood" and he knew it was Hellbound come back.

Hellbound Hank was a tall, cadaverous sort of a jigger who was built like a bed slat and had to stand twice to cast one shadow. He was the town's "bad example" and was mostly shunned by those who had any pretentions to anything. Hank had two buck teeth in the front of his mouth which gave him a kind of rabbity look—or would have if it had not been for the twelve lank hairs, seven on one side and five on the other, which he pridefully cherished and called a "moustache". These, like the thinned-out locks he spent the bulk of each morning arranging artfully, were of a shade most resembling a henna-rinse red. There was a strong smell of horse about his person and he was—to quote Mrs. Sheriff Potter—a "lazy, shiftless, good-for-nothing old fool which Obe would of shut up long ago if it wasn't for getting the jail contaminated."

"Hurry up!" Wild Horse hailed him. "Got a question t' ask you."

"Be there in a minute, son—there in a minute. I got t' rub bacon grease on this critter's tail first."

Wild Horse strode into the stable, overlooking operations with some curiosity. "What's the big idear? If you're tryin' t' git his tail slicked up—"

"I c'ld shine up his tail without haff this work," the old man grunted, keeping on with his scrubbing. "I'm a-treat-in' this critter fer lampers." He turned his head to tell Wild Horse critically, "All a horse's ailments comes down to his tail—remember that, son. Work on the tail—always work on the tail. The's all kinds of cures fer horse troubles put up by the quacks in them Eastern factories; but all you got t' remember, son, is t' work on the tail an' you kin cure 'em of anythin'."

Wild Horse showed Bill Hart's thoughtful look. His nod bespoke an entire agreement. "But about this question . . . It has come t' me I ain't what you'd call real popular round here."

Hellbound nodded complacently. "Nobody is ef they talk much t' me. You'd best keep away from me, son— plumb away from me."

Wild Horse snorted. "I'll be danged if I do—"

"You'll be danged ef you don't," Hellbound grunted. " 'F you keep augurin' with me the's on'y two ends I kin see fer you. Either you'll be cast out or you'll be a outcast."

He leaned against the horse he'd been greasing; took off his hat and studied it. He smoothed the tattered crown on an elbow. "Now look at it reas'nable. This town's got one outcast a'ready; a fella what's spent his whole lifetime at it . . . what knows every wrinkle, every prop of the business—you might say, in fack, I've made a projeck of it. Now see here, son," he said, peering down at Wild Horse. "You wouldn't wanta do a ol' man out of his trade, would you? You're young—got yore whole life's span stretched ahead o' you. You go on, son; you go on over the hill an' keep ridin'."

Wild Horse mulled it over with himself; but he finally shook his head and said bleakly: "I jest can't do it, Hank. This town's done give me a challenge. I couldn't never look at my face 'f I was t' go ridin' off like a dang whupped cur. No sir! I've got t' hang on here; I've got t' show these folks that Wild Horse Shorty—"

"Yeah—I know," Hellbound sighed. "I was young an' had great idees m'self onct. But you can't cut 'er, son; it jest can't be done. You're up ag'in' the clannishest town you ever heard tell of—Why, the folks yere *brags* of the guys they've busted! Time an' ag'in I've heard 'em say 'He rolled in yere with a heap o' coin but he never took none of it outa yere with 'em!' You can't beat 'em, son," Hellbound said, frowning sorrowful. "They'll hammer you down an' they'll th'ow you out—"

"Oh, they will!" Shorty said, rearing up indignantly. "I'll show them bobcats! By grab, I'll squat right here an' make 'em like it! I'm goin' t' git me a ranch an' I'm a-goin' t' raise horses—the bes' dang horses that money kin buy!"

Hellbound stared at the mares outside and turned a pitying eye on Shorty. "With what?" he said, like it was Fritchet speaking.

"Never you mind! I'm goin' t' do it, *see?* I'm goin' t' pitch right in! Alls I'm wantin t' know is this: If I git me a place will you take on a job with me?"

Hellbound smoothed his hat dubiously. "Who you figurin' t' buy out, son?"

"I ain't figgerin' t' buy out *no*body. There's places t' be got—there's land, anyway—"

"I'd admire t' know where."

"What's the matter with Banjo Springs? There's five-six sections bounds the south of that water—"

"Banjo Springs—Did you say *Banjo Springs*? Lord God!" Hellbound said, and looked around nervously. His eyes looked like they would jump from their sockets. "Banjo Springs . . . I—I can't believe it."

"Can't believe what?"

"That anybody'd make right out t' commit sewerside thet way— Why, Jesus in Heaven, son! Don't you know them Dickersons hez been usin' thet country fer up'ards of twenty-five years? Thet was Ol' Man Dickerson's winter range. When Lute took t' runnin' things he switched over t' horses—but I ain't never heard he aimed t' let thet place go. Ain't you seen thet horse camp he built in there?"

"I seen," declared Shorty, "it was on state land. If he wants t' go decoratin' land he don't own—don't even *lease,* with a lot of fah-de-lah buildin's an' whatnot, I don't consider it no skin off'n *my* nose. Anyways, the law—"

"Boy," Hellbound grunted, "don't say a nother word— the Dickersons *is* the law around yere!"

3.

JUST A HINT, SO TO SPEAK

When Wild Horse got off the Nogales-bound train next evening, he had to jump quick and take his chances because the freights didn't stop at Emery Park any more. He had been up to Phoenix getting acquainted with the folks in the State Lands office. Traveling, like he had, just above the cinders, had not improved his appearance any. He looked like a pretty rough customer, but the gent who hopped off with him had the look and the air of a Deacon. This man gave his name as McGee—Nels McGee. He had just come down from Dakota, he said, having sold his big ranch on the Rosebud. He had just about got himself lubricated when Shorty had picked him up at a bar; and, seeing as how he claimed to know horses, Shorty had straightaway hired him—because you never could tell when that roll might come in handy. That is to say, of course, if there were anything left of it.

This McGee was no spring chicken. He was seamed and wrinkled as a Kansas prune. Angular, wiry—a sandy-haired man who looked to be into his middle sixties but who might have been at least a score of years less, any continued exposure to Dakota climate being uncommon likely to erode a man some.

He was entirely sober as he picked himself up and stood staring around. "Awful crowded," he mentioned with his eye on the ten or twelve houses off yonder. "What's them?"

"Hen farms." Shorty's tone, too, was a trifle disparaging. He was a horse raising man and hadn't much use for those who tried to raise eggs for a living. "We got three or four at the Crossin', too—but thank Gawd we ain't got no weed-benders there! She's a horse ranchin' country with a tatter of cows humpin' round on the edges."

"I should think," McGee said, "they'd have t' hump considerable to get any eatin' off this kind of desert. How we goin t' get over to your place?"

"Expect we'll hev t' walk—it ain't far," Shorty hastened to assure him. "Not over six mile at the outside, hardly—"

"Six mile! You expect me t' walk six mile in these boots?"

"Little walk won't hurt you. Be good fer yore kidneys."

McGee put his hands on his hips kind of violent. He looked Shorty over clean down to his bootheels. "When I said I was a foot specialist I wasn't describin' myself as no walkathorn! I thought you said you was a horse-raisin' outfit! Why ain't you got a couple broncs here t' meet us?"

"T' tell you the truth," Shorty said, "I ain't had the time t' make no arrangements. I ain't been round this locality long—fact of the matter, I'm jest gittin' started. Only got one hand outside of yoreself."

McGee said less crustily, "That's all right. Two hands is a-plenty. Lots of high-class spreads these days ain't got more'n that to run 'em. How you fixed for horses?"

"Wait'll you see 'em."

"Well—come on; let's git started," Nels said; so they picked their way across the S.P. tracks and struck out through the broomweed and greasewood.

When Shorty told McGee he had one other hand, he was really doing a lot of tall hoping. There hadn't been anything settled for sure when he'd hopped that freight last night for Phoenix. The town's Bad Example wouldn't pin himself down. All he had said to Shorty's offer Wild Horse thought all-fired vague and rambling. "Expect I'll hev to," old Hellbound had said, "ef I aim t' hang hold t' my standin' round yere." Way he talked you would think he was *proud* of it!

The scattered lamps of the village hadn't yet come on when, footsore and dusty, they limped past the Mercantile. They still had better than two hours till dark and McGee, gazing round, began to look sort of grim. "If there's a eatin' house—"

"Hotel," Wild Horse told him—"Happy Harp. You'll find 'er right down the road there a piece. I'll go on over to the Livery—"

"Ain't you goin' to eat first? Gosh sakes, ain't you *hungry?*"

"Well . . . uh . . . no—not right now."

"Hell! I'll pay fer my own."

But Shorty knew durn well he would if he aimed to get in any eating. But he did not say anything of this to McGee. "Come over to the Livery when you're finished," he said; and with his Bill Hart look he tramped off and left him.

Arrived at the Livery, Shorty found Hellbound puffing a smoke whose smell was familiar. The old hostler said, "I sure admire yore taste in terbaccer. These yere things would

32

curl a gnat's toe nails. How'd you make out?"

"I'm all set to go. Hired me a hand an'—"

"Yeah. I seen the pair of you limpin' in. I got yore stud all saddled."

It was the saddled stud that Shorty was staring at; not so much at the horse as it was at the saddle.

Hellbound, seeing his look, let loose of a cackle. "It's yore'n, all right. Bein's you was outa town I knowed Ben couldn't never prove it ag'in' you. I got yore whole outfit—yere's yore vest an yore guit-tar."

Shorty put on the vest and stood holding his instrument. "I— Much obliged an' all that, but—"

"Now don't you git skeered of Ben or thet sheriff. Onct we gits t' be millionaire horse raisers they'll be glad ef you th'ow 'em the crumbs off yore table."

Shorty shrugged. He hung the guitar's strap over the saddle horn. "So you've made up yore mind t' take that job with me, hev you?"

"I figgered we'd gotten thet all ironed out. When we leavin'? Them mares is all fed an' plumb rarin' t' go."

"Then you figger I done right, eh? They sure looked me over up there to the Capital. You'd go ahead with it, would you?"

"Son," Hellbound said, "I ain't no hand fer givin' out ad-vice. All my born days I've been a misfit—a square peg in a round hole—a fella what was borned too late fer his own danged good. But one thing I've found: When a fella comes up an' he asts fer yore ad-vice, that ain't what he's a-wantin' at all. Like enough he's come with his mind made up. Alls he wants outa you is a go-sign—backin'. He wants t' hear you tell him thet's the on'y thing he *could* do; an' ef you count yoreself a real friend t' thet fella, thet is what you are goin' t' tell 'im."

"Humph. Then you reckon—"

"Son, I've done told you. I'm ridin' with you," Hellbound said.

"Okay," Shorty said, and reached for his guitar; then he chanced to remember old Ben might hear him. There wasn't no sense inviting Ben's notice.

McGee drifted up, still chewing what food he could dig from his molars.

"All set?" he said. "Got some broncs hired for us?" Then his eye fell on Hank. "Who's this?"

Shorty said: "Ain't you heard of *him*? That's Hellbound Hank, the Bad Example."

Hellbound's rheumy eyes fired up. He reached out and pumped McGee's hand solemnly. "Well," McGee said, "ain't you hired the horses yet? Damn' if I'm goin' to *walk* any further."

"What does he wanta hire horses fer? He's got his own right yere," Hellbound told him.

"I ain't got no saddles," Shorty cut in hasty like. "Anyways, my stuff's breedin' stock. I don't ride 'em much—"

But McGee said, grunting, "If there's any of your stock here trot it out. I can ride anything with hair on it."

"Well, you can't ride *them*," Shorty told him; "leastways, not all that far piece. I don't ride my stuff out like some spreads does. I gentle 'em. A horse has got feelin's jest like anyone else. Treat 'em right an' they'll do the same fer you. There ain't a nag in my outfit won't foller me round like a dog."

"Humph—*pets*!" McGee said. "Don't you know the most dangerous horse every dadburned time is a *pet*? Show me a pet an' I'll show you a mankiller." He looked at Shorty as though he might be readjusting his opinion. "You got any *sweets* in your cavvy?

"Sweets?"

"Yeah—sweet this or sweet that; *names* I'm talkin' about. Don't you savvy the English languige?"

"Oh!" Wild Horse said. "Yeah, I got one sweet; but, mostly, my mares ain't named much of anythin'—"

"Did you say *mares?*" McGee's gritty tone held a cowhand's temper. But Wild Horse said, flaring up himself:

"If you know any way t' breed horses with*out* mares—"

"Where are these mares? What're you hidin' 'em for? Where's the stud you're figurin' to cross on 'em? How many you got an'—"

"Right there," said Hellbound, waving a hand at them. "There's the whole bunch—the stud's got the saddle on."

McGee just stared. He stared three full minutes before he looked at Shorty.

"Which one's the sweet?"

"Sweet Columbine's the gray," Shorty said. "That one over there with the shed-off tail—"

"That sway-backed one?"

"No, that's Columbine's sister—expect I rode 'er too quick. Columbine is the chunky one; the *other* one with the shed-off tail—see 'er? I can't figger what's got at them tails. They used t' hev nice—"

Wild Horse went stiff and stopped talking sudden like.

There was a hand on his arm and it was not his own hand. It was not McGee's—he could see McGee's hands; and it sure wasn't Hellbound's because Hellbound was over feeling Columbine's tail.

So whose was it then, and where did it come from?

He turned his head very carefully. Abruptly saw, and shivered.

It was Rimfire Logan, the Dickerson hard case.

"They tell me," Logan said with a sneer, "you been off up-state, pokin' round at the Capital. They tell me you're fixin' to git in the horse business."

Shorty's Bill Hart look didn't make much impression. But his voice said in spite of him: "You got any objections?"

"If I had," Logan said, "I wouldn't be talkin' to you." He tapped the gun butt that peeped from his waistband. "Just keep yore horsin' away from *our* place. Git as far off from us as you can. Do you savvy?"

"Yes, sir," Wild Horse said to him meekly.

"That's all," Logan nodded, and swung off through the cottonwoods.

4.

ADVICE FROM A NEIGHBOR

Shorty guessed that settled it.

He couldn't swing this business alone, and nobody else was like to stick out his neck after hearing that Dickerson hard case.

He leached a quick look at Hellbound. The old man was fingering Columbine's tail, much as if it were a harp or zither, with a faroff look in his faded eyes, as though Mr. Logan had not come within miles. And Nels McGee was hunkered nearby teaching Columbine's sister how to shake hands.

Wild Horse widened his eyes and stared.

Had he been in a trance and imagined that visit? There were people, he had heard, who imagined things regular; there was a place up to Phoenix that was all fixed up for them with mattressed walls and bars on the windows. Maybe they'd be sending the dog-catcher after him . . . .

He felt of his head and it was kind of damp. He removed the tailormade smoke from his mouth, looked at it queerly and pitched it away with a visible shudder.

He looked again at the others.

Just like before. It was plumb uncanny. He would have sworn he had just finished talking with Logan, but he couldn't find anything round him to prove it. McGee, it was true, might have missed the significance, being a stranger and all and not knowing about Rimfire; but old Hank, you'd have thought, would be white as a bedsheet because Rimfire Logan was the only man in Cochise County with the guts to ignore the local firearms ordinance.

Then it came to Wild Horse that a man left tracks. He looked at the ground and saw Logan's plainly.

There was only one answer. Old Hellbound was bughouse. Nobody but a loony tick would stand there like Hank was, fingering a critter's tail like he owned it.

McGee stood up and dusted off his knes. "Any buildin's on this 'ranch' of yours?"

"Huh?—Oh!—Yeah—*sure*. Buildin's. Plenty of 'em. Corrals an' chutes. A squeeze an' breedin' pens. Haybarn. Bunkhouse—even got a 'fraid hole under it. Why?"

"I just wondered," McGee said, and changed the subject. "How long you been in the horse breedin' business?"

Because he was still a bit flustered Shorty gave him the truth. "As a matter of fact, I'm jest gittin' started."

"An' this here's your stud, eh?"

That disparaging tone brought Shorty to in a hurry. "Now you look here!" he bristled. "I won't stand fer no slurs bein' heaved at that horse! Figure 8 has got a heap more to him—"

"I won't argue that; but he won't help your mares to find them no colts."

"He won't?"

"He sure won't. If you're figurin' to set up in the horse breedin' business you better not do no countin' on *him.*"

A hard blow to take, and Shorty's look showed it.

"But I think," McGee said, "I can find you a stud. There'a a place down near Hereford—"

"A *good* stud?"

McGee looked like that talk was an insult. "This outfit don't raise nothin' but good ones. One I'm thinkin' of's a palomino—a half-Arab. 'Course, if you don't want no Arab blood . . . There's a three-year-old Apaloosa near Billings that would make you a pretty fair studhorse—"

"Could I get 'em cheap?"

"Now see here, boy," McGee said sternly. "It costs just as much to feed a plug as a *good* horse. You got all the plugs one outfit can stand."

That was plenty reason to make a mule roar; and Shorty reared up handsome. "Don't you dast call them mares of mine 'plugs'! I'll hev you know them janes has got Thoroughbred scattered all through 'em! They kin trace straight back t' ol' Steel Dust himself, an' don't you dast say they can't, by jingoes! Hell's fire!" he said gloweringly. "Them mares—"

"You want another stud or don't you?"

" 'Course I want another one—I'll take 'em both, dang you! But don't you heave no aspershuns on them mares, by grab, or you'll dang well find out who's boss around here!"

Wild Horse bristled like an angry bantam. "Go over t' the Mercantile an' send off yore letters, an' don't say another word about them mares. Go on—time you git back we'll be ready t' ride."

It was a longish trip to the Dickerson horse camp, a long ride and a silent one. But the night was fine, rightly cool and starry; and if you've never traveled by the back of a horse across the desert's thirsty miles with a gay moon dancing through the clouds above you, you have missed one of the simplest joys attainable. There is a real satisfaction to be drawn from a horse, and to fork one by moonlight is to heighten the pleasure. What stauncher friend has man than this animal that will go to his death still accepting your guidance?

The camp at Banjo Springs, when they reached it, was found to be an extensive one. McGee's eye showed a quick glint of approval. "How long have you owned this layout, Shorty?"

The night must have worked its mood on Wild Horse, for he said quite truthfully: "I don't own it, Nels. It belongs to the state—or the land does, anyway. That's Roman Four land to the north of them springs. Dickerson country. Lute Dickerson put this horse camp in here; seems like he had a big colt crop that year and his regular equipment jest couldn't handle it. Guess he felt safe enough puttin' money on this place. His family'd been usin' these sections fer years. But it's still state land and open for lease, if a guy don't mind buckin' up ag'in Dickerson."

"An' who," McGee said, "is Dickerson?"

"Lord God!" cried Hellbound; but Shorty amended:

"He only *thinks* he is—by grab, I'll show 'im! Stealin' my girl an' always runnin' it over me! You'd think he owned the whole Earth t' hear 'im; but alls he's got title to is ten or twelve sections. S' gol-rammed smug you couldn't melt butter on the seat of his pants!—but I'll show 'im!"

"The local big-bug," McGee observed thoughtfully.

WILD HORSE

"Big palomino breeder. Like t' think palominos ain't worth a whoop in the hot place without they got Arab or Thoroughbred blood in 'em. Oh, he's got a big spread an' a heap o' real pull, I reckon; but you kin see how he is by the way he does business—never gits less'n four figgers fer a horse, an' so tight he won't even pay a nickel fer all this land he's been hoggin'.'"

"What if he orders us off?" McGee asked.

"I'll tell him, by grab, t' hop a hitch to the hot place!"

"But if he's big, like you say, he may come down hard on us—"

"Let him come!" Shorty glowered.

"He can force the state to put it up for sale an'—"

"Not while somebody else is leasin' it, he can't!"

"Just the same," McGee said, "he can probably make us powerful uncomfortable."

Wild Horse snapped: "If you're gittin' cold feet you kin roll yore cotton!"

A wintry gleam lit McGee's dark glance and it looked for a minute like he would do just that. Then he said very calm, "How much money have you got in the bank? Have you *any*?"

All the fierceness left Shorty. He said reluctantly, "No."

"How you going to pay for them studs I just ordered?"

"I'll hev the money time they git here."

"You better. An' afterwards? What'll you do for cash till your colt crop's ready? It takes hard money to run a horse ranch, mister."

"I'll cook up somethin'—I'll git the money," Shorty growled. "I know what I'm doin'!"

"I sure hope so!"

Wild Horse glared and McGee glared back. It was

Shorty's glance that finally shifted. "I'll tell you, dang it. I figger t' grease the skids as a dude ranch—savvy?"

McGee just stood there. But Hellbound's mouth fell completely open. "A—a *what*?"

"You hear me," Shorty said truculently. "A glory-eyed horsetorium."

Hellbound shook his head, plumb speechless.

But McGee appeared to look well on the notion. "That's smart figurin'—but there's a catch to it though. You can't get dudes without you've got somethin' t' offer them."

"I got somethin'—I got *plenty* t' offer 'em," Wild Horse sniffed. "Got m' ad all writ an' in the papers a'ready. It's what I borried that money off you fer." He fetched a sheet from his pocket and smoothed it out with a noticeable pride. "Listen:

" 'Horse ranch in historic Southwest to entertain limited number cash-in hand guests for balance of season. Excellent opportunity for people with means to see big horse breeding establishment in actual operation; also chance to use guns on really Big Game—participation optional. Not responsible for accidents. Hot and cold water, mild climate; permission to hunt, fish and shoot at no extra cost. Forty minutes from Tucson. RATES: $50. per day, $120. per week, or $300. per month—payable in advance. Address all enquiries: WILD HORSE SHORTY, WHS Ranch, Horsehead Crossing, Arizona.' "

"Lord deliver us!" bleated Hellbound, and braced a hand against the side of the bunkhouse.

McGee eyed Wild Horse admiringly. "Guess I been kind of underratin' you, Shorty. Where are them fellas going to fish?" he said.

"We ain't goin' into that," Wild Horse grinned. "We don't give a whoop *where* they fish. All we're doin' is givin' permission."

"Three hundred dollars!" groaned Hellbound; and "Forty minutes to Tucson! Good Lord! Never in my palmiest days—"

"Well, they *might* make it that quick," Wild Horse argued. "Depends a heap on what they gallivant in."

"You're all right, Shorty," McGee said fondly. "Jest spin me over t' Boston, will you?" And he went off laughing fit to burst his breeches.

The WHS Ranch, as Shorty now called the place, was situated on land sloping south from the Banjo Springs waterhole in the shape of a wedge; only the apex abutted the springs. All land north and east of the springs was Dickerson property, duly patented, with the headquarters layout some four miles east among the tree clad slopes of the Santa Rita foothills; a fine horse country, well watered and shaded and with rich grass plentiful. To the left of Shorty's—to the west, that is—lay the Morgan horse ranch of the saloon man, Fritchet, much smaller than Dickerson's and, being well in the desert, demanding constant irrigation to produce *any* grass. Most of Shorty's land needed water, too, but Dickerson had been farsighted enough to install on the place a gasoline pump with a forty foot tank of stored petrol handy; indeed, McGee, after viewing the stored food in the cook shack, had said the Roman Four boss reminded him of "one of them birds in the Bible, kind of."

Shorty and the boys made themselves right at home. They cleaned out the tool shed, the blacksmith shop and harness house, and hand-moved the stuff to an empty corner of the big horse barn. Shorty told them he aimed to put guests in these buildings and, to that end, they commenced building bunks for the prospects to sleep on. These, when finished, they covered with some Navajo blankets snatched from the walls of the bunkhouse yonder. "Because," Shorty said, "these things ain't no use to us fellas nohow, an' we might jest as well give them dudes *some* comfort."

The guest shacks were made of laid-up adobes; but the long log bunkhouse was where the boys slept; and the second day of their occupancy, just after noon, Phil Cinch, the Dickerson foreman rode over. He was a tall man, and handsome, but there was blood in his eye. And his voice, when he spoke, was like a West Texas wind.

He didn't let any moss grow under him. "What do you reckon you're doing here?"

"Raisin' horses," McGee said mildly.

"Well, you can't raise them here—this is Roman Four property. Belongs to Lute Dickerson."

"You better talk to the boss," McGee said, and beckoned Wild Horse. "This guy—" McGee's thumb jerked at Cinch, "claims this spread don't belong to us. Says it's Dickerson property."

Wild Horse said, "It mighta *been* Lute's property, but it sure ain't *now*. You tell him, Nels, t' take a run up t' Phoenix—"

"I ain't taking no run up nowhere. I'm telling you plain to get off this place."

"Tell again," McGee said; "the boss don't hear you."

Phil Cinch's cheeks colored. He stood very still. "You get out of this camp before dark tonight."

WILD HORSE

5.

HELLBOUND WITH COMPANY

"Bound t' come," old Hellbound said when they told him of Phil Cinch's visit. "Bound t' come," he said, shaking his head. "Well, I guess I better go round up the pasture—"

"What for?" Wild Horse growled.

"You ain't figgerin' t' leave him yore horses are you?"

"I ain't figgerin' t' *leave*."

Hellbound stepped back like a snake had bit him. "You ain't?" He peered at Wild Horse amazedly. "Y' mean yo're cal'latin' t' stay right yere an' let 'em *bury* you?"

"Humph!" Wild Horse said. "They ain't buryin' nobody. They're jest runnin' a bluff an' I'm goin' t' call it."

Hellbound's eyes held unbounded pity. "I recollect Mac Jones sayin' thet twenty year ago—but where is he now? I'll tell you! Come Fourth o' July they burned him out! 'Course they told it around it was the fireworks that done it, but there was plenty of head-waggin' I kin tell you; an' Mac, he up an' got out of the country. A man don't go off an' leave his land—"

But Wild Horse impatiently waved him quiet. "You can't

45

git away with that stuff no more. Folks is civilized now. There'a a law in this country—"

"What good's the law," Hellbound scoffed, "to a dead man?" He waggled a finger before Shorty's nose. "You listen t' me! Them buckos mean business an' they ain't t' be trifled with. You take my ad-vice an' git t' heck outa yere."

"You kin quit if you want," Wild Horse snapped, "but I'm stickin'. I'm goin' t' show them squirts which pole t' git off at! By grab, I kin bluff it as good as they kin."

And, as the days sped by, it began to look as though Wild Horse had called the turn. Nothing untoward came from Cinch or the Dickersons.

They found some wire and some posts laid away in the barn and Wild Horse told the boys to string a new fence. When they got done they had two pretty fair looking twenty-acre pastures in addition to the old one Lute Dickerson had fenced. The original pasture bordered the springs; but the water had lowered since the fence had been built and Dickerson, rather than reset his posts, had put in a gate to let the stock through to water. It was evident why he had not enclosed the springs in the pasture to start with; to the north, east and west the land was too rough and rocky to afford safe footing for such high-priced stock and, rather than risk any broken bones, he had set his fence to get the seep in his pasture. But three years of drought had receded the waterline till now it was thirty feet outside the fence. So Shorty was forced to drive his broomtails through the gate as, evidently, Lute had done. There was a tank in the circular adobe corral that was fed by an intricate system of underground piping. But it was too much bother to water a cavvy there, so he got in the habit of using Lute's gate.

But one morning they got up to find the water cut off quite completely. Dickerson's hands must have worked all night. There was a brand new fence clean around the water-hole.

Dickerson was within his rights in thus protecting his property. The waterhole was on his patented land, McGee reminded them, and he could fence it forty times if he cared to. "There ain't nothin' we can do about it."

Shorty chewed his lip. Then he clamped his teeth and grabbed up a piece of six-by-eight. He strode for the fence belligerently. He knocked down the three posts nearest the gate and the taut wires jerked them into the water. Shorty strode after them and heaved them farther.

He said, "It's amazin' what stray stock'll do." He wiped his hands off on his pantslegs. "C'mon," he growled, "let's eat."

"You're askin' fer trouble, son, pullin' thet fence down."

"Bluff," Shorty said, and hit out for the cook shack.

The others tramped after him, Hellbound frowning, McGee coolly taciturn.

"We ort t' hev a cook fer this outfit," Hellbound criticized grumpily. "I'm a-gittin' plumb weary o' waitin' my turn at thet stove ever' mornin'."

"All right," Wild Horse said. "Take at it, pard. From here on out you're cook for this—"

"*Me!*" Hellbound stared aghast at the notion. "Now you looky yere—"

"Don't argue," McGee said. "You heard the boss, didn't you? Git in there and cook."

Hellbound looked kind of mad about it. "Mebbe them dudes won't keer fer my cookin'—"

"We ain't got no dudes yet. An' if they can put up with the other things they can stand your grub, I reckon."

So Hellbound started slamming pots and pans around. Shorty and McGee sat outside smoking. Through the bang and the clatter they could hear the old man's cracked voice singing:

"Oh, love that will not let me go —"

And, after breakfast, McGee told Wild Horse he did not know which was quite the worst — Hellbound's food or Hellbound's singing.

Later in the morning, it was discovered that Columbine's sister, the other rat-tailed gray — the swaybacked one — had cut herself on the fence somehow. "What we need," Hellbound said, "is some axle grease for the flies —"

"Axle grease nothin'!" Shorty blared, indignant. "You ride in t' town an' git that vet out. That mare has got t' hev the best of care. She may be in foal —"

"To what?" McGee said. "Not to that shad-bellied stud I'll bet."

"Now you hesh!" Shorty said. "I won't hear no more o' that. Matter of fact I wa'n't thinkin' of Figure 8 noway. These mares was out at Pete Hague's fer awhile an' one of his studs — I think it was that Alla Bin Ghaszi, got in with 'em one day. He took quite a shine t' that mare. You ride in an' fetch Doc Wallace, Hellbound."

After the old man had left, McGee, looking over the stock with Wild Horse, said: "Whyn't you get rid of that sweet, Shorty? After she up and kills some-body —"

"Columbine wouldn't hurt a gnat — why, that mare's s' gentle you could stake her to a hairpin. Honest, Nels, that mare's got attributes —"

"Then the sooner she's shot, the better," McGee said. "Never heard of one yet that got that an' lived —"

"Attributes," Wild Horse explained, "is jest a high-fangled way of sayin' she's got a lot of desirable things about her—"

"Like them hips, you mean?"

"She's unusual," Wild Horse said carefully. "Absolutely gentle. Fine disposition. Strong conformation, yet sensible —dependable. Even a child could ride her an' handle her. She'll ride single or double, with or without a saddle, an'—"

"I'd hate," McGee said, "t' see two saddles on her."

"An she's fine with the studs," Shorty went on, ignoring him. "Never kicks 'em or bites at 'em—stands right up there jest like a lady; an' she'll give you colts of good color every time."

"How do you kow?"

"I've seen 'em, ain't I?" Shorty slapped at a fence post. "She's had five already. All of 'em horse colts."

"Five? Where are they?"

"She had 'em all in one litter. Unfortunately," Shorty admitted, "they didn't none of 'em live over eight or ten seconds—but they was good horse colts, every one of 'em."

Doc Wallace came out after lunch with Hellbound. He showed a big happy grin and shook hands all around like he was welcoming a Bible tract bunch to rehearsal. "Lovely day—lovely," he beamed. "Exceptionally nice for this time of year, isn't it?"

Shorty gave him a knock-down. "This here's McGee—shake hands with him, Doc. He comes from the Rosebud up in Dakota. Foot specialist. Guess you fellas'll hev a lot in common."

They did not appear to have, but the Doc gabbed on until Shorty said, "Did you bring any medicine?"

49

"I . . . ah, yes—certainly. Where is the patient?"

"I put her in the pole corral," Nels McGee mentioned; so they all trooped over to have a look and find if the mare had bled to death yet.

She hadn't. She looked pretty much as she always had, which was a matter of opinion how that was. About the only apparent change in her condition was the ugly slash the wire had given her, and this looked a lot worse than it actually was.

The Doc was a man who took his trade seriously. He eyed the mare with a professional frown. He said. "Hmmm" and rubbed his red neck contemplatively. "Hmmm," he repeated, and looked at her teeth awhile. "How long has the patient been suffering with this?"

"If you mean them cuts, she got 'em last night, I reckon. Don't seem t' be drainin' much. 'Course the flies—"

"That's the catch," the Doc said. "Can't be too careful," he added fussily and, after conducting a search through the pockets of his vest, finally brought forth a vial which he shook with some vigor. Then he held it up to the light, squinted a bit, and shook it again—several times, in fact, before handing it over to McGee to hold while he went on a search through the pockets of his coat.

"It's the flies you've got to watch out for—infection, you know. Screw worms and maggots. Take a high-strung, nervous animal like this— Ah! Was sure I'd brought it along with me someplace."

"It" was a tuft of none-too-clean cotton which he finally had dug from a bulging hip pocket. Old Hellbound watched admiringly as the Doc rolled a wisp about the end of his pencil. This he handed to Wild Horse to hold while he got out a rectum thermometer and gingerly proceeded toward the gray mare's rear.

"I don't know," Wild Horse said, "if she'll care for that thing. Mebbe you better get her used to it gradual-like . . ."

"She don't kick, does she?"

"Well—not usually."

" 'Course she don't," McGee grinned. "You could stake her to a hairpin. Ask the boss. She's just a good old usin' horse. Mild as May—he wouldn't have a kickin' horse round here. Step right up to 'er Doc—"

"Maybe I had better let you take her temperature," the vet said to Hellbound. "You're more familiar with her habits than I am."

So Hellbound shoved the thermometer in her and the mare looked round with a trembling lip and blew a long sigh as though she wished this were over.

"How do you like your new ranch?" the Doc asked Shorty with his big-toothed smile. "You've certainly got fine neighbors. One of the most progressive men in the state, Lute Dickerson. Fine chap. Done more for the breeding of palominos—"

"Don't you reckon I kin take that thing out of her now? I think," Hellbound said, "she's gettin' a little mite oncomfortable. Mebbe—"

"Here—I'll take it," the veterinarian said. "That should be quite sufficient . . . Mmm . . . Yes. Quite sufficient." He shook the thermometer, thrust it back in his breast coat pocket. "Just pass me that vial, will you, Mister McGee?—and that swab, please."

"You reckon," Shorty said, "that cold water paint—"

"That's not paint!" the good Doc said indignantly. "That's a drug we describe as 'Pyketyne blue'—very essential in a case of wire cut; as a matter of fact, I find it quite useful in most equine ailments."

He dipped the cotton-wrapped end of his pencil. "Hold

her head," he said; and when he stepped back he nodded, satisfied.

"Don't you reckon it might be a good stunt," Hellbound said, "if I rubbed some grease on her tail ever' mornin'?"

"You mean for that baldness?"

"Fer them cuts," Hellbound said; and the Doc kind of laughed the way doctors do usually and did not commit himself anyway further. He looked over at Wild Horse and kind of rubbed on his hand, but Wild Horse had never been bothered by hints. "Much obliged, Doc," he said, and tramped off toward the house, saying over his shoulder; "Be callin' you ag'in some time, I shouldn't wonder."

"Any time—any time," Wallace said wryly.

After Doc had left and they were setting their teeth into Hellbound's chuck, Shorty bemoaned the dearth of mail they were getting. "Seems like that ad ort t' be gittin' some action."

"Dudes is peculiar," McGee reflected. "Mebbe take months before you'll drag down a answer. Lots of them wouldn't think of goin' to a place which hadn't run full-page ads reg'lar in all the big journals ever sinct they was kids. Then there's the kind of dude which won't go noplace his friends haven't been. There's a heap of 'em got to be met at the train with a station wagon—your ad didn't say nothin' even about *meetin'* 'em. All that tribe'll pass you up sure. Then there's some that insists on their golf every day, an' a few that has to have their tickertapes handy—"

"They expect t' git all that in the wilds?"

"An' then some! Some of 'em even expects taxi service. "Hell! you don't know them dudes like I do. Wyomin' an' the Dakotas used t' be plumb over-run with 'em—Montana's getting a heap of them nowadays. I don't know what it is, but—"

"When you're dealin' with dudes," old Hellbound declared, "you're askin' fer trouble anyway you spell 'er. Ef thet Doc wa'n't a dude he'd uv had some respeck fer bacon grease. Some of the bes' dang horse raisers in this yere country wouldn't ever dast dream of usin' anythin' else. They wouldn't no more sop 'em with thet colored water than . . . than . . . Hell! than anythin'!"

"I've always found," McGee tucked in, "a lot can be done with a horse's feet . . ."

The days dozed on. No mail appeared for the WHS. No rain came down and the sun and the termites worked together to denude the range of the last speck of graze; the sun killed the grass and the termites ate it off short at the roots and Shorty's horses got gaunter and gaunter. The pump folded up one day and quit, and all Hellbound's puttering failed to revive it.

"I don't know what's goin' to become of this stock," McGee said one afternoon. "If we don't get a rain or some money—one, they're goin' to lay right down like that pump pretty soon, boy. I don't know what she's been findin' to eat, but Columbine's sister is down with the scours, an' Hellbound's been ridin' Columbine so steady—"

"He's got to quit it," said Wild Horse. "I can't hev him—"

"Here he comes now. Got company with him—looks like that Happy Harp hasher."

"Now what's *she* wanta come out here for?"

"Mebbe she's come to answer that ad."

"What ad?"

"Hellbound's."

"Hellbound's!"

"Sure—that one he's been runnin' in the *Tucson Citizen*. I s'posed you knew all about it. '*Cook wanted. WHS Ranch. good· pay to right party.*'" He grinned at the look on Shorty's face. "That hasher can cook—I'll say that for her."

The pair rode up in a nervous silence. Hellbound shifted his weight uncomfortably; cleared his throat. "Miz' Rose yere," he said, "hez come out fer thet job. Thet frisky Ben give 'er the sack this mornin' an' I told her as how you'd allowed we could sure as hell use a good cook on this dude ranch. I—"

"Wild Horse," Rose said, "I couldn't accept your charity. If I thought you were just making a place for me—"

"If I didn't need you—"

"Well," she said, "it's a real Christian thing for you to do, anyway—especially after all the harsh things I have said to you. I want you to know I appreciate it and— Well," she said, with a wry little smile, "I'll do my best to see you don't regret it."

"An' fairer words was never spoke," old Hellbound said, like everything was settled. "We're almighty lucky t' git her. The dudes is a-comin' in droves—I kin feel it. 'Fack, one of the tribe hez already write you—come in this mornin' by RFD."

The letter he tossed Shorty was addressed to the ranch in a crab-wriggle scrawl. "Got a Floridy postmark," Hellbound said.

Shorty ripped open the envelope and, sure enough, old Hellbound proved right. It was from some dude at Oneco. The dude said:

Dear Mr. Shorty:

My wife and self will arive at your place about the 23rd. Have no kids and are coming by car. If we like the place and can stand the climate my wife says we might stay maybe two or three months. I don't know where the Horsehead Crossing is, but I expect it is out on the desert someplace. My wife ain't very crazy about deserts. She comes from Vermont and likes things green.

Yrs. Respectfully,
F. E. Farrar.

6.

A MATTER OF VIEWPOINT

Wild Horse, with a quite unlooked-for chivalry, made Rose O'Grady welcome. He said, "I hope you'll like it an' kin be real comfortable. Like enough there'll be a heap of things these dudes'll want that they ain't goin' t' git on the WHS—but you jest leave us worry about that. Folks'll put up with a heap of things if the grub slips down easy an' there's plenty of it. So that's your job, ma'am: keep their bellies full."

After which delivery they all rolled up their sleeves—all but Hellbound, and commenced getting ready for the influx of trade. Rose scrubbed till she was blue in the face, McGee pruned the yard's droopy cottonwoods and took a sickle to what few weeds the mares and the termites had still left standing, and Hellbound rode Sweet Columbine soapy while Shorty went in and jawed with Provencher, trying to wrangle himself a bill of goods.

No one expected he would have much luck because George was known to be tight as a clam shell. He must have been feeling expansive that day because the last time Shorty had seen him the storekeeper had made it real plain he did not want Shorty's shadow on his doorstep. Wild Horse must have talked fast and convincingly. He got six gallons of paint and two bulging feed sacks filled with such tinned cowboy luxuries as peaches, blackberries, pears, loganberries, beets, apricots, asparagus, tomatoes and corn. In addition he talked George out of two big jars of strawberry jam, three gallon jars of pickles and four packages of radish seed which Rose had said he must be sure to get. And every last bit of it went on the cuff.

When he had all these things securely lashed to the roller-coaster back of Columbine's sister—who was usually called by whatever came handiest: mostly adjectives banned by the printers' code—George Provencher said, "What are you doin' for meat out there, Shorty? Ain't took to cuttin' them horses up yet, have you?"

"Nope," Wild Horse stated; "as a matter of fact, there's usually some stray beef hangin' round that water an' they're all the time gettin' stove up, it seems like. It's a act of charity t' kill the poor critters."

The storekeeper grinned. "I'm glad my stock don't stray out your way. You got a new cook out there, they tell me."

"Yeah," Shorty said, and changed the subject. "If the's any stray dudes comes by here askin' fer me, jest send 'em right along an' don't delay 'em. It's cash in advance out at my place, an' the first ones come I'll drop by an' square you. Any time you an' the Missus wants t' take a rest, jest come on out. We know our friends an' we'll treat you right, George."

"How much you figurin' to charge them dudes?"

Shorty told him and Provencher whistled. "You must be

feedin' 'em out of gold painted plates."

"Nope. They don't git no diff'rent from the rest of us, George. That's where most of these dude outfits makes their mistake. Always givin' 'em too much—all this 'modern convenience' stuff. That ain't what dudes wants— they come out to the West huntin' atmosphere. They kin git all the convenience they want at home. Everybody tells 'em the Old West is dead; they come out here an' stop at one of these highpowered *motel* places an' quick's they git home they tell all askers: 'Hell! you ain't missed a thing. You git the same thing out there you kin git right here without hevin' the cost of it tacked on extra. We never even seen a cow!' "

"Nope," Shorty said with an air of wisdom, "we don't give 'em no trimmin's out t' *my* place, pardner. They come out here t' rough it an' I give 'em a bellyful. They wanta see cattle an' horses an' real workin' ranch hands, an' if they come t' my place they're goin' t' see 'em, dang it."

The storekeeper chuckled. "They may get to see a heap more than they bargained for. Special if Lute gets his mad up proper. I hear you tore down one of their fences."

"Twice," Shorty said, "an' I'll do it again if they don't git wise to theirselfs."

"But that water's on patented Dickerson land—"

"On account of the drought. But, in ordinary years the's a good two feet of that water on *my* side. I know, because I've checked with the records up t' Phoenix."

"I don't know about that, but you better keep your eyes skinned. That Rimfire pelican—"

"Hoo hoo!" jeered Wild Horse; but his eye had an uneasy tinge to its coloring.

"Goin' to run anything in the annual sweepstakes?"

"What's that?"

"Ain't you heard of it? The Tucson Sweepstakes? Why, I s'posed the whole world had heard about *that* meet. The Tucson bunch holds races every season—mostly Quarter stuff on a quarter-mile course, or a little better; then, at the last of the season, they have their annual Sweepstakes. Big affair. Up near Sabino Canyon—horses shipped in from all over for it. Half-mile course an' twenty-five hundred bucks to the winner. One of Dickerson's horses—that palomino stud of his, San Felice—has copped it three times hand-running. You ought to get in on it. It would be the chance of a lifetime."

"I dunno," Shorty said, not noticing George's grin. "Mebbe I will, at that. I could use it."

Back at the ranch there were eager exclamations as Shorty unloaded. He handed Rose the radish-seed packets and paint and brushes to McGee and Hellbound. Old Hellbound kind of looked down his nose, but Wild Horse put the facts bluntly: "A little present fer you, boys—ketch hold an' fly at it. That dude said his wife likes t' see things green an' the WHS sure aims to oblige."

So the days rolled by. The skies stayed unremittingly clear and the distant hills waved and shimmered in the heat and everything else turned brown and baked and the sun got so hot you could almost taste it. But the Dickerson horse camp renewed its hold on a sliding life and blossomed out like a carnival under the paint-slinging hands of McGee and Hellbound. The whole place gleamed with green and white trim. McGee had the green and worked the fastest, though Hellbound piddled with the white here and yon till McGee caught him at it and took the roof off. "You nizzy old fool!" he shouted. "Quit slappin' that white all over my green! If you think

59

I'm sweatin' the seat off my britches—"

Wild Horse came running and took old Hellbound firmly in hand. He toured him over to the horse barn. "Git a hoe an' a shovel an' clean this place out. When you've got it clean take that white paint to it, an' don't stir out of it till every board's painted."

That took care of the old man nicely and the place fairly glistened when Hellbound quit. Gay blue-an-white signs hung above the doors to the long line of stalls, each sign emblazoned with the name of its former occupant; Doc Wallace had done them for Luther K. Dickerson; but Hellbound hit the nail on the head when he mentioned they weren't any use to Shorty. They talked it over with the Doc next time he dropped by.

"You'll jest hev t' paint 'em over, that's all," Shorty told him. "We can't use them names nor that color, neither. They got t' be white an' green like everythin' else here—*these* are the names they got t' hev on 'em."

Off over the hills in their mountain fastness the Dickersons seemed to be biding their time or, perhaps, like Achilles, they were merely sulking. If they were, Shorty prayed they would keep on doing it.

The Doc came, regular, to look at the horses. He came with such frequency McGee told Hellbound, "I swear you could dang near set your clock by him. If he ever quits comin' it won't seem natural; be the same, pretty near, as gettin' lost from your shadow."

And then one day, while the boys were nooning, a wagon rattled past under the hard-eyed escort of three cow-punchers. It pulled up at the springs and the men pitched off a lot of rolls of new wire and a couple of arm-fuls of stout cedar posts; and while this was going on, Dickerson, himself, and his shadow, Phil Cinch, rode into the yard and sat in their saddles in the shade of the cottonwoods.

McGee saw them first and put down his fork. "Comp'ny," he said, calmly wiping his mouth off.

Some of the ruddiness faded out of Hellbound's cheeks, and Wild Horse pushed back his chair and got up.

Dickerson showed them a conciliating smile.

"How are you, Shorty? You're looking pretty good. I've been doing some thinking," he said, kind of meaching like. "There don't seem much sense to the way we've been acting, so I've come over like a neighbor to settle our differences. I'll admit you have a certain standing here. Due to an oversight I neglected to look up the title to this land before I began erecting these improvements. My fault entirely. I don't hold it against you for knowing a good thing and trying to take advantage of it. But," he said, smiling, "you'll have to admit I've some money tied up here."

"How about gettin' to the point," said Wild Horse.

Dickerson regarded him tolerantly. "I can see you haven't changed much," he said. "Still fighting the bit. Then a calculant glint briefly touched his glance and he said as though he were just thinking it over, "You *could* go, I suppose . . . there isn't much here to hold you. You could pull out right now—and well heeled, if you cared to. Everybody's got their price—*some* kind of price. What'll you take to move out of this, Shorty?"

"I'm pretty well suited right here," Wild Horse said; and Phil Cinch's lips tightened ominously.

He picked up his reins as though he'd heard a-plenty.

But Dickerson said, "Let's quit sparring, Shorty, and get down to cases. Let's get down to cash business. It's plain enough you've reached the end of your rope. I don't *have* to pay you to get out. You made a pretty slick play but the weather has licked you. You're just about out of the last of your grass, your pump's broke down and you haven't any money or the credit to fix it. If I fence off the springs you won't have any water. What's the use stalling? I've just to sit back and in another two weeks this drought will finish you."

"That all you rode over to tell me?"

"No," Dickerson said, plainly nettled. "I pride myself on being a gentleman." He cleared his throat; his look suggested there was a proper procedure for these things, a proper order, a proper style of establishment. "I came over here solely out of Christian charity if you want the plain facts of the matter. I just can't stand by and see dumb animals suffer. I knew," he said in a diferent tone—"I knew what your game was as quick as you moved in here. To cut a long story short—and on account of your horses, I've decided to oblige you."

"Good news," Shorty said; and McGee smiled fatuously.

"How much do you want?" asked Dickerson.

"For what?"

"For getting out of here an— For your lease," Dickerson said, getting hold of himself. "Go ahead; name your price and I'll write you a check for it."

"You've missed the boat," Shorty told him. "I didn't come in here t' hold you up—I come in here t' ranch; an' I'm goin' t' do it."

"Now look here," Lute said, and his smile quit entirely. "You know well as I do how long you can stick it. No point going over that again. Name your price and I'll pay it and you can take your stock out of here. If you figure you can peddle that lease—"

"I ain't in the peddlin' business," Shorty snapped. "The

lease ain't fer sale—is that plain enough?"

"Then you flatly refuse to get off my property?"

"I ain't on your property. It belongs to the State—"

"I ain't here to quibble or bandy words with you! I want you out of here—"

"You kin keep on wantin'. As fer my bein' licked— Hell! I ain't even started!"

"Come on," Cinch said. "Don't waste breath on the fool. I know how to deal with the likes of him."

"You're right," Lute nodded. "He don't understand kindness."

7.

E-QUINE-OTICS

Full of gusty oaths and chill foreboding, Wild Horse
watched the Roman Four finish their fence—the fence that
was to cut his stock off from water and make him repent
the stand he had taken.

Old Hellbound's face was fit for a funeral. "You can't
beat 'em, son," he said over and over—"you jest can't beat
'em. They kin law you ef you pull down that fence.
They've give you your two foot of shoreline this time an'
ef you kick the thing down they kin put you in jail fer it."

"It's a bluff," Wild Horse scowled, but his tone was not
confident.

"Bluff!" Hellbound said. He looked Shorty over with a
downright pity. "You think it's a bluff with thet Rimfire
left there? Ef you think thet feller is the kind thet bluffs—"

"If he fires that gun we kin lam him in jail!"

"But where will *you* be whilst he's coolin' his heels there?
You'll be deader'n salt herrin'—"

"Hoo hoo!" jeered Wild Horse— "he ain't shot me yet!"
But just the same his look was uneasy and he did not dis-

play much of an appetite at supper that night.

Rose said practically, "What are you going to do about water for the stock?"

"He craves t' pull down thet fence," Hellbound told her. "An' quick as he does we're goin' t' see the last of 'im."

"He'll be famous, though," McGee pointed out. "Get his name in the papers an'—"

"I ain't honin' none t' see my name in *that* column!"

"Why, shucks," McGee said, "it's a real opportunity. You'll be a seven days' wonder if Rimfire salivates you. Folks'll know your name clean from here t' 'Frisco."

Rose was indignant. "I don't see how you can sit there and joke. That man is a terror—"

"Amen," declared Hellbound. "He shorely is. He's a tripple tipped terror. Kilt thirty-three Injuns up in Wyomin'—leastways nobody ain't never heard him denyin' it. Ain't got no more conscience than a bull in ruttin' time. An' shoot— My God! I seen him put five shots through Mac Jones' hat onct without even aimin'; an' a quarter woulda coverd all five of 'em easy."

"Well, we can't hev water long as that fence stands. It's gotta come down," Wild Horse muttered doggedly. "Unless—" He stared, real intent, at the beans he was eating.

Ready to fly off the handle, Rose said: "*Now* what's the matter? If you don't like the way I fixed those beans—"

"Them beans're— By grab! I b'lieve I've got it!" Shorty cried excitedly; and Hellbound scraped his chair back hurriedly.

"Got what?" McGee said.

"Water, dang it! We're goin' t' git us that water an' we ain't goin' t' hev t' rip that fence down, neither!"

"I'd admire t' know how," Hellbound stated, sourly seating himself in his chair again.

"Pipe," Shorty said "Jest like fallin' off a log. There's a carload of pipe buried round this place an' nothin', that *I* know, t' stop us from usin' it."

"Nothin' but Rimfire," McGee said, and grinned at him.

"Ahr—that hyena! He can't watch forever kin he? He's gotta sleep *some*time. When he sleeps we move pipe. You boys dig me a hole this evenin' out back of the barn where he can't git his eye on you. Coupla feet deep by about twenty wide; an' shelve the edges so's the broncs'll hev footin' when we git it t' workin'."

Hellbound said: "*When* is right!"

But Shorty grinned. "You dig the hole. I'll take care of the rest of it. The angle's good, it'll run by gravity. All we gotta do is connect them springs t' the hole you're goin' t' dig. We'll run the pipe in through that brush at the west edge an', the chances are, they'll never get next to it."

"But supposin' that hard case don't sleep?" McGee said.

"You jest leave that t' me. I'll keep him so busy—"

"Mebbe they'll send someone else out t'morrow."

"Well, it's a idear, of course; but I don't look for 'em to. They're bankin' on Logan's rep t' stop us from pullin' that fence down again. 'F I keep him busy all night he will sure as heck hev t' sleep tomorrow."

"So will you," Rose said; and Wild Horse gave her a scowl for her trouble.

Rose made a face at him. "If we had some liquor—some whisky or . . . Lute might have left a bottle or two around here. He was always throwing wild parties, they tell me. . . ."

The ranch was a busy place that day. All afternoon the

boys kept digging. Wild Horse, back of the barn, dug the hole for his tank while McGee and Hellbound spaded up ground and planted the radish seed—this latter being done with malice aforethought directly in line between the barn and the waterhole. It was two hundred yards from the spring to the barn. They would dig for a little bit, drop in a few seeds, then back to their shovels and turn up some more. From the shade of his covert Logan watched and guffawed; he had never in his born days seen such foolishness. From the barn, in rows set two feet apart, with the ground in between carefully spaded and mealy, the radish patch ere they got it finished—by planting each seed a good foot from its neighbor—stretched almost up to the Dickerson fence.

"Like takin' a lollypop away from a two-year-old," Wild Horse declared when they quit at dark and tramped in for their supper.

McGee said, "We better take turns proddin' Logan tonight; an' I hope you got plenty of liniment handy. I could sure use a bucket-load on my back."

Rose had dished them up a rip-snorting dinner of beans and hot rolls and pie from canned peaches. When it was time for the pie, Shorty said, "Jest save my piece an' when he gits done, Hellbound kin take it out t' Logan."

Out of a hard, shocked silence Rose said indignantly: "And what is the matter with that pie, I'd like to know?"

"Not a thing," said Wild Horse hastily. "It's only I'm such a Christian gent I can't stand t' think of pore Logan without none."

McGee's glance was shrewd. "What have you got up your sleeve?"

"Well," Shorty mentioned, "Rose has dug up a bottle of Lute's coffin varnish an', 'stead of foolin' round all night tryin' t' keep that guy up, I think I'll jest give it to 'im an' git the ball rollin'. Time he gits that bottle drunk up he won't care *who* killed Cock Robin. By sun-up we kin hev that pipe laid an' the water runnin'."

McGee slapped his thigh and old Hellbound snickered. "But where does that pie come in?" Rose said.

"Well, if we *gave* him the whisky he prob'ly wouldn't drink it. Figger the' must be somethin' wrong with it. But if Hellbound takes him out that pie an', accidental like, a bottle of rotgut falls outa his pocket, Logan'll down the stuff plenty pronto case Hank should miss it an come back huntin' for it."

And so it turned out; and when the morrow's sun got up the pipe was all buried, with its end in the spring, and the dug tank back of the barn filling rapidly with good clean water straight and fresh from the source of supply Logan was supposed to be guarding. The boys tumbled into the bunkhouse and slept.

When they got up at noon they found the tank overflowing and running all over the adjacent adobe. "Damn!" Wild Horse said. " 'F we don't git that capped an' shut off in a hurry, that Dickerson waterhole won't be nothin' but a mem'ry!"

They had just got it capped when Doc Wallace rode up.

"Lovely day!" the Doc beamed, looked round like he was manna dropped straight out of heaven. "Doesn't that air smell good though? Mmmmm! Makes me think of when I was back in New Mexico. Bet you didn't know I used to raise beans for a living—yes sir! Many's the bushel I've packed to Mountenair— Say! What's this? An artesian? That's quite a tank you've got. Something new, isn't it?"

"It ain't very old," McGee told him dryly; and Wild Horse said: "We was forced to it, Doc. 'Druv' is the word;

that hound of a Dickerson fenced the springs off an' put Rimfire Logan to guardin' 'em."

"He wasn't doing much guarding when I came by. Stretched out in the sun and sounding like an iron horse getting up steam."

Shorty changed the subject. "I reckon you come out t' look at the mares, didn't you? How much you gettin' fer these visits, Doc?"

The corners of the Doc's lips pinched in a little. He said, "Not enough to worry anybody."

"Seems like you're droppin' round almighty reg'lar—"

"Didn't you tell me that mare was to have the very best of care?"

"Well . . . mebbe I did—but you don't hev t' care for her EVERY DAY, do you?"

"Every time I've been out here I've found some new cuts on her. Why don't you keep her *away* from that fence?"

"An' you claim t' know horses!" Hellbound said. "If you knowed the first thing about the e-quine mind you'd know thet any spirited horse or mare looks on a fence as a deliberate challenge; an' any individual with a ounce of git-up is goin' t' assert hisself; he's a-goin' t' git his feet on t' other side if he hez t' rip hisself naked t' do it!"

"Of course," Wild Horse said. "Hell's fire! *Any* coot oughta know a pasture looks greenest jest beyond the fence."

Rasping his jaw he eyed the Doc testily. "Now git this straight," he said blunt like, "I ain't no walkin' gold mine an' I sure can't keep no horse doc in diamonds."

A touch of fire warmed the Wallace cheeks. "I don't re-collect ever fetching a carpet bag to lug away any payments in. If it comes to that, I don't recall any payments."

Wild Horse waved that aside. "Mebbe not. But if you keep pilin' up the bills this way—"

The Doc smashed a fly on his shirt-cuff, absent-mindedly wiping it off on Hellbound. "All I'm charging is two bucks a call. If you can't pay that you've got no business raising horses. *Most* vets would knock down at least twenty dollars coming way out here—"

"Not off *me* they wouldn't, by grab!"

"If you dispense with me you'll have to pay it. You can't get a vet in Tucson to go anyplace outside the city limits—"

"I ain't hirin' no vet from Tucson!" Shorty said irascibly: "I wouldn't hire one of them t' git me rid of the *gophers*!"

Then a sheepish grin broke through the scowl of him. "Never mind what I say; you suit me plumb right down t' the groun', Doc. Trouble with me is I'm hard up fer cash—can't afford t' pay a doc every whipstitch. But—"

Hellbound was tugging at Shorty's arm.

Wild Horse shook free of the bothering hand. "Tell you what, Doc. You send me out a gallon of that stuff—"

Hellbound was not of a mind to be further ignored. He grabbed Shorty's arm and shook it violently. "Look here! Gol dang it, we got comp'ny comin'."

Wild Horse sent a harassed look gateward and, of a sudden, his eyes lit up plenty pleased like and he said, "Jest a minute—" and departed forthwith.

There was a big, shiny car driving through the front gate and, surer than hell, it looked like business.

8.

"KEEP SETTIN'!"

The car drove into the yard and stopped.

A wiry little man was slouched back of the wheel. He wore a blue serge suit and a ten gallon hat. "I'm looking for the WHS Ranch," he told them.

"You're a-settin' right on it," Wild Horse hailed him heartily. "Tie yore bronc to the hitch rack an' heave out yore bedroll."

There was a woman in the front seat, meek appearing and quiet. The rear seat was hidden under a pile of luggage. The woman wore a veil wrapped around her head, and she suddenly spoke up to say through its folds: "This looks like a real nice place, Fred — of course there aren't many trees; but just see how pretty and green everything looks, and how quiet it seems and restful."

Wild Horse sneaked a quick look at the waterhole, but Rimfire Logan was still sleeping his booze off so it looked like things would stay quiet for a little while.

"Yes, ma'am," Wild Horse said, taking his hat off.

"I was under the impression," the man declared gruffly,

"your ad said something about there being a chance to use guns—"

"Be a mighty good chance," McGee said, "before long."

Wild Horse gave him an indignant glance, but the little man cut off his motor. "Well—pile out, Mary. What are you waiting for?"

While she was getting the door unfastened on her side the man climbed out of the car on his; and stood looking around while he munched his tobacco. After a prolonged inspection he walked over to Shorty and stuck out his hand. "I see you got my letter. Farrar's the name—F. E. Farrar; better known in some parts as 'Flip'n-Shoot—"

"Fred!" the woman said, put out like. "Why do you want to tell such lies?"

Doc Wallace hid his mouth.

Mr. Farrar did not say anything. He and Wild Horse looked about of a height, and his pale blue eyes studied Shorty unwinking while he gummed his tobacco in silence. He gummed it because he hadn't any teeth. To be real precise, he *did* have a few; he had three sets of store teeth, but they could usually be found where he had them now—joggling around the inside of his pocket.

"Yes sir," he said, his pale eyes piercing Shorty, "Ol' Flip'n-Shoot Fred I was knowed as in them days. Here—have a chaw?" He dug out a packet of Redman and passed it.

"Uh-uh. That stuff don't agree with me," Wild Horse said; so Farrar hastened to cram the hollow of his own mouth.

His companion—a pretty good looker now she'd got her veil off—wrinkled her nose with a show of distaste. "I don't see why you can't wait until you've spit out what you've got before you stuff any more of that horrid stuff into you. Aren't you going to make me acquainted?"

"Well, Mary," Mr. Farrar said testily, "I can't until I know what their names are. I don't even know that much myself yet—"

"Pardon *me!*" blushed Shorty. "I got too much on m' mind t'day, seems like. I'm boss of these diggin's. Wild Horse Shorty, himself—in person; an' at no extra cost to the audience. This gent's a horse doc—Wallace, his name is. That coot over there is Nels McGee—made a study of feet on the Rosebud, he tells me. This bow-legged jigger is Hellbound Hank. Hellbound," he added gratuitously, "is by way of bein' a tooter; folks round here points him out to their kids as a walkin' delegate of what they might come to if it weren't for the guidance of p'rental dictates."

Old Hellbound fetched up his orneriest look, made a leg for the lady and allowed he'd just as lief try some of that "senorita tobacco" seeing as how it was being passed free. "Sure," the dude said—"a real disinfectant." Then he said in an aside to Shorty that the female woman with him went by the name of "Mrs. Fergie" and was by way of being his wife. "She has finally got the other leg in my pants, but I still make out to tell the dog where to go, and that takes care of all my surplus energy."

Hellbound did not seem to know how to take that.

Then the dude said, "Now what about this good hunting you mentioned? I've done a heap of gun-firing in my time. I can shoot from seven angles, and I've brought all my weapons along. I have a shotgun, a pistol, a .22 rifle and a jint-crickey air gun—that last bein' mostly my speed these days. I am uncommon handy with it if I do say so myself. Been takin' all kinds of prizes luggin' 'er round to the county fairs. I would sure like to try 'er on some really Big Game. How far do you have to go to shoot around here?"

"Just wait till along about mealtime t'morrow an' you won't have to go a dang step," McGee said.

"Who does the cooking?" Mrs. Fergie asked; and Wild Horse said:

"We got a hasher here what kin really sling it. Got a garden, too—see where that ground's busted up over there? Them's radishes—planted 'em yesterday."

Mr. Farrar said, "Radishes?"

"Sure—don'tcha like 'em?"

Mrs. Fergie said: "Fred wouldn't touch a radish. He thinks they're bad for his kidneys—"

She broke off sudenly, intently staring toward the Dickerson waterhole. "Isn't that a man over there?"

They all swung to look and Wild Horse said, "Yes, ma'am. He mostly manages to pass fer one. That's Rimfire Logan, the Dickerson hard case."

"But what is he doing all stretched out that way? Look at those flies on his face!—is he sick or something?"

McGee said: "He will be."

And Hellbound told them, "He's takin' a sun cure—"

"This will be the very place for you, Fred," said the woman. "Don't you think we ought to stay for the season?"

Mr. Farrar looked at Shorty. "Usually I charge things," he mentioned, "but I suppose you would like a little money in advance."

"If you don't mind," Shorty said. "I could git better use from it that way."

"Check or cash?"

"Better make it cash," Wild Horse told him. "Nearest bank is in Tucson and my car is broke down."

Mr. Farrar extracted his wallet and cocked a dubious

look at his lady. "You reckon you can stand it here more than a month?"

"Why, Fred—it's your health we must think about. We could stay here forever if you think it would help you. Pay him for a couple of months and if you see no improvement we'll go somewhere else."

Mr. Farrar munched away at his Redman and counted out six hundred good dollars while the boys looked on like vultures watching a calf's last gasp. Shorty passed a handful over to the Doc. "I've give you some extra so's you kin afford t' come out when I holler. Meantime, don't fergit t' send me out a gallon of that coldwater cure for wire cut."

After the Doc had pumped hands and departed, Wild Horse showed the folks their new quarters. He called it a "guest cabin" but it was only the remodeled blacksmith shop and it still had somewhat of a cold-iron smell to it. He said: "You kin fetch your luggage in any time."

"Don't you have another bed we could use?"

Mrs. Fergie had sat down rather hard on the pine slat bunk Shorty had covered with a blanket. She was vainly trying to get some bounce from the thing. She gave them a rather melancholy smile. "It doesn't seem to have much *give*; and anyway, it is much too narrow for the both of us."

"You might take turns," suggested Hellbound.

"Oh, but Fred has to have his rest," she said; "and I know *I* couldn't ever get to sleep on it. Why, our beds in Vermont—"

"Now Mary," Mr. Farrar put in nervously, "the man isn't interested in a history of our belongings. Very probably he hasn't ever heard of Vermont—"

"Never heard of Vermont! Where has he been? I supposed everyone knew about Ethan Allen!"

"Trotters," Shorty said, "ain't in much demand around here, ma'am. Cramp Fritchet, our neighbor, has got a few Morgans, but ... Well, make yoreselfs right to home, folks."

Mrs. Fergie looked just a little bit blank, but she was not one to be put off the subject. "We have to require another bed." She looked indignant. "Why this isn't hardly big enough for Mitzy."

"Mitzy's the dog," Mr. Farrar translated—"the other dog."

Hellbound said, "All the dogs I've knowed hez allus slep' on the ground—"

But Shorty said practically, "I'll hev McGee build in another one for you—'twon't be no trouble, ma'am. We kin put it where that wash stand is—"

"But where will we put the wash stand then? Fred has to have some place he can spit."

"We could put it outside the door—"

"You leave it right where it is," Farrar said. "I can't spit that far without my teeth an' I ain't goin' to wear them teeth for nobody!"

About the time Wild Horse was establishing the dudes, Sheriff Potter, over in his office at the back of the Mercantile, looked up from his littered desk with a scowl. During his first three terms he had been quite active, but an excess of leaf lard had slowed him down. Time had endowed him with two extra chins and the horn of the saddle got in the way of his stomach. Quite assured by now of the Dickerson patronage, he had given up riding and had hired L. Ernenwein to conduct such chores as required any movement not negotiable afoot.

Time, however, had done little for his temper. Nor had it greatly improved the caliber of his judgment. He considered the Dickerson power impregnable and anyone running counter to the notion could expect little mercy from Obediah Potter.

"You're too easy goin' fer any damn use," he told his deputy irritably. "Didn't I tell you to move that squatter out? Why ain't you done it then? Go turn him out or turn in your badge."

Chief Deputy Ernenwein rubbed one leg with the boot of the other. He was a big-boned gent who had run to lankness. He had a blond mustache and bright twinkling eyes; but right now the eyes were not doing any twinkling. He had hoped, in time, to fill the sheriff's boots, but the sheriff's tone was not reassuring. Ernie said uneasily: "But I told you, Obe—"

"I know what you told me! You said this guy was on a state lease. What's that got to do with it? The Dickersons have used that range for twenty-odd years; Lute has sunk a hell's smear of money into them fixin's out there and he wants that fella moved pronto. How long," demanded Potter testily, "do you think I can hold down this job if I don't do what Lute Dickerson tells me?"

"The state's a sight bigger than any Lute Dickerson. If Shorty's leased that land the state will protect him. We can't monkey with the state—"

"You don't even know that he's leased that land—"

"He didn't hike up to Phoenix to get him a soda-pop. Now look," Ernie said persuadinglike, "if you'll think for a minute you'll see this like I do. Our best bet's to keep out of it. Old Dame Nature will take care of that feller. We don't even need to lift our hands; the law of averages will move him out for us. You can't build a ranch around here on a shoestring—"

"He don't have to build no ranch," Potter wheezed. "Lute—"

"Yeah, I know. But it ain't the initial outlay that gets you. It's the everlastin' upkeep. His broncs ain't worth two whoops to a carload, but it costs just as much t' keep a plug as a *good* horse. He's got eighteen hungry critters to feed and not enough grass t' feed *one* proper. His pump's broke down and Lute has fenced off the Springs—"

"How do you know?" Potter stared astonished.

"I got my ways," Ernie chuckled. "He's got no water an' practically no grass. You know well as I do what baled hay costs—$45. a ton at the feed lots. I doubt if he's got the price of one bale. I know he ain't bought any from ol' George Kerley."

He lowered one hip to a corner of the desk. "All we've got to do is sit back and keep out of it."

"Okay," Potter said. "I don't think you'd lie to me. But here's somethin' else—somethin' we better be watchin' for. Notice I got through the mail last evenin'. There's a nut got loose from that Phoenix asylum—some goofy bird that thinks he's a preacher; spends all his time writin' half-baked sermons that he never delivers. This notice says you can easy spot him by his 'Moses beard' and a kind of glassy stare he gets when he's thinkin'. It's a all-sheriffs warning; better be keepin' your eyes skinned."

"I'm goin' t' need to wear glasses," Ernie sighed, "if you give me any more stuff t' watch out for. I can't see why s' much riffraff congregates round here—how'm I ever goin' to get that new book of mine finished? Vanderhoof come in here last night mad enough t' chaw the sights off a six-gun. Claims the beef-haulers has been getting into him again—says they've got away with two carloads of critters since February. That's a lot of cattle.".

Sheriff Potter scowled. "Damn right it is! That's bad, Ernie—bad. It's that Whetstone Mountain bunch pickin' up guts again. You better ride out an' put the fear of God in 'em—"

"What about that murder out on Dutch Woman Creek? Thought—"

"That fella's dead—he can wait awhile, can't he? Vanderhoof's a big gun around here; we ought to oblige him if it ain't too much trouble. You ought to *anyways* go over an' poke around a little bit. You can go after lunch—"

"An' miss that dance?"

"That schoolhouse dance ain't till next Saturday, Ernie. You could easy make it back by Friday if you struck up a canter."

Deputy Ernenwein's face took on a look of reproach. "You know how canterin' upsets my bladder— Damn! The's somebody out in the store again! Why don't that counterduster stick around sometime—"

"Here we are!" Potter called— "back here. Jest help yourself if you're in a hurry."

The floorboards creaked beneath a heavy-set stranger. He was a smooth shaved man with round cheeks and sunglasses. Though he was dressed in store clothes, without the Hollywood glasses he might have been taken for a retired rancher, except the sun had not tanned him any great deal and he did not show a stockman's wrinkles.

"I seem," he smiled, "to have gotten myself lost. Could either of you gentlemen tell me where I am?"

"Collossal Mercantile—Geo. Provencher, prop.," Ernie said sarcastically. "Hub of the universe—Horsehead Crossing. You *must* of got lost t' land out *here*."

"Thank you; I expect I did. I . . . ah—have a car outside.

Would one of you put some gas in my tank while I'm getting my bearings? You said Horsehead Crossing—that's in Arizona, isn't it? Ah . . . my name is Lee Forest."

"Mine's Ernenwein—the 'Great Ernenwein'—perhaps you've read some of my stuff? I write novels—books—when I ain't busy lawin' some widder woman out of her homestead for Sheriff Potter here."

"Choke off the blat an' go squirt him his gas," Potter said. "Glad to know you, Forest. Come a long piece, have you?"

"Long enough to know better," Forest smiled. He said wryly: "Is Tucson hid out in this county somewhere?"

"Twenty-odd mile northwest of us," Potter told him. "County seat—a dang political cesspool," he declaimed indignantly. "Had t' move my office clean outa there—only way I could keep my shirts clean. You just passin' through, or are you lookin' to locate? Now if it's property—"

"I merely asked about Tucson to get my bearings. I'm looking for the WHS Ranch," Forest said.

Potter looked puzzled. "I don't believe—"

"He means the old Dickerson horse camp; Wild Horse Shorty's place," Ernie said, hanging the nozzle back up in its sprocket. "About eighteen mile southeast of us," he added; and Potter frowned.

"What're you huntin' *that* place for?"

"Why, you see— Here!" the stranger took a folded newspaper from his side coat pocket and called a marked item to the sheriff's attention. The item said:

Horse ranch in historic Southwest to entertain a limited number cash-in hand guests for balance of season. Excellent opportunity for people with means to see big horse breeding establishment in actual operation; also chance to use guns on really Big Game—participation optional. Not responsible for accidents. Hot and cold water, mild climate; permission to hunt, fish and shoot at no extra cost. Forty minutes from Tucson. RATES: $50. per day, $120. per week, or $300. per month—payable in advance. Address all enquiries: WILD HORSE SHORTY, WHS Ranch, Horsehead Crossing, Arizona.

The sheriff's stony look included not only the item and Forest himself, but Chief Deputy Ernenwein, also—in fact, Chief Deputy Ernenwein in particular. "I thought you said—"

"Mr. Forest isn't interested in your thoughts," declaimed Ernie. "All he wants is the directions for getting there; an I'm jest the fella to give 'em to him. You see that 'dobe road—" he pointed, "that one cuttin' in just beyond the *ho*-tel? That's it; stay right with it an' you'll finally get there. Figuring to put up with Shorty, are you?"

"Haven't made up my mind yet. I thought I'd run out and have a look at the place; I might if I like it. The doctors have ordered me to take a good rest—"

"You won't get much rest out there," Potter grunted. "What part are you from?" he said, handing back Mr. Forest's Phoenix paper.

"Tyrone— New Mexico."

Ernie said, "Whereabouts in New Mexico? Never heard of the place."

"Burro Mountains. Grant County. Old Phelps-Dodge camp," Mr. Forest informed them, and stared out over the desert.

"Which way did you come?" Ernie asked, kind of odd-like. "Silver?"

"I came in by way of Apache Junction."

Ernie looked disappointed. "Guess you wouldn't have seen any then."

"Beg pardon?" Mr. Forest took off his Hollywood glasses and his mild eyes looked Ernie over enquiringly. "Any what?"

"Strangers. There's a—"

The sheriff kicked Ernie's shin without subterfuge.

"Here!—what the hell are you up to?" Ernie cried, bending over and hoisting his pantsleg. "Lookit that what you did! You tryin' t' put me into a horspital?" The stare he gave Potter was extremely jaundiced. Then he spit on the place and rubbed it and, with a scowl, finally adjusted his clothing.

"There's a nut got loose from the Phoenix bughouse," he told Mr. Forest, still glowering. "Thinks he's a cousin to Mahommet, or somethin'. Got a big Moses beard an' a fishy eye. We got orders t' pick him up—thought mebbe you mighta seen him."

Mr. Forest stared into the distance. He put on his dark glasses again before speaking and got out his wallet and paid for the gas. "I haven't lost any nuts," he said, "or seen anybody that looked like Moses. Much obliged for the gas and directions," he waved; and got into his big yellow car and drove off.

Potter said: "You ain't got a lick of sense! What did you want to go telling him that for? You wanta start a panic? Why, dang it!—if folks get wise there's a nut turned loose the whole population's apt t' up an' fly outa here!"

"Don't be a ninny," Ernie said with his lips curled. "Who'll he tell? He's aimin' to go out an' live with Wild Horse, ain't he?"

"How do *I* know? Claims he come from Tyrone, which is two hundred and fifty-five mile northeast; but that paper he shoved me was printed in Phoenix—*Now* what?" he muttered as boot sound again pounded through the store front. "Oh, Lord," he mumbled, and slumped back in his chair as Phil Cinch came in grimly followed by Logan.

Cinch's handsome face showed tight with anger. Rimfire's eyes looked hot and ugly.

Dickerson's range boss wasted no time. "What have you done about that squatter?—Ahr! don't interrupt me with any of your bullspit! Like always you've set right here on your fanny!"

Cinch banged his fist down hard on the desk top. "Dickerson told you to get him out of there. All you had to do was fix up a handful of papers and serve 'em— You're about as much use to the Roman Four as a .22 cartridge in a eightgauge shotgun!"

Logan put his hands on the desk and, bracing them, thrust his jaw within an inch of Potter's. "I ort t' push yore face in!"

"Shut up," Cinch said, "till I get done talking."

He bent beside Logan and tapped Potter's shirt front.

"You got any idear what's been doing on out there? No; I didn't think so! Well, that Wild Horse ape has repaired the place—got it to looking like a going outfit. He's hired two hands and that Happy Harp hasher. Rimfire jimmied the pump and we fenced off the waterhole; but the hound-lucky pup is stil there and still runnin'. Got a big dug tank out back of the barn—must've tapped a gusher by the look of the thing!—got a big capped pipe sticking out of the middle. He's plowed a great swath an' sewed it to radish seed. Got dudes out there and he's rolling in coin—got enough, anyway, to give that horse doc a holdin' fee."

He tapped Potter's chest a great deal more emphatically.

"You got one last chance to wipe the slate off. Keep settin'—that's all we're asking you to do: *just keep settin'.* Never mind what goes on in the foothills. Just set right here and keep your face shut—savvy?"

The sheriff went still. "You—you mean that . . . ?"

"All you got to do is keep settin'."

9.

MATTERS DIVERS AND SUNDRY

The next day was Sunday; and Mrs. Fergie took her two dogs, the two-legged one and the Boston terrier, and drove off in the Dodge to see what the ladies wore to church in Tucson.

It looked to be a busy day all around. Hellbound, shouting hymns and cusswords, choused Shorty's mares hellbent round the pasture, this being his notion of giving them exercise. McGee rode up on Figure 8 and cut Columbine's sister—the sway-backed one—out of the bunch and led her off somewhere for reasons not mentioned. A Mexican kid loped out from town with a gallon jug of the wire-cut medicine; and Rose O'Grady, the ex Happy Harp hasher, held another of her housecleaning orgies— the fourth hand-running in the space of five days.

At the Roman Four Phil Cinch and Logan held a two-sided conference while Dickerson, being a thorough-going Christian, drove off in a surrey behind four matched palominos to learn what the Tucson preachers had up their sleeves and, incidentally, to collect the rents from his Meyer Street properties.

He took Baisy with him, much to Shorty's disgust. Shorty had come out to go riding with Baisy, but the girl's old man, saloonkeeper Fritchet, did not use much tact in explaining her absence. "She's gone off drivin' with Dickerson someplace."

Business that day was not confined to the country. At the Crossing the townsfolk were busy, likewise. Doc Wallace was hoeing the weeds in his garden. Jack Williams was building a shed for his new Jersey milch cow and Provencher, having borrowed the tools from the Double N Ranch, was busily trimming the hoofs of his pinto. In the Sheriff's Office Ernie, hemmed by masses of paper, was deep in the tortures of producing a love story, and his boss, the fat sheriff, was embarked on a bender in Fritchet's saloon.

This had ever been Potter's custom when the woes of his office got too heavy for packing. It was Fritchet's custom to enjoy not at all having drunks on the premises— official or otherwise; so, about mid-morning, the barkeep clamped down. "That's your last," he said, mopping off the bar. "You know Fritchet's rules, Obe. No drinks for the sponges."

"So I'm a sponge, am I?" Potter snarled, cocking a bleary eye at him.

"No offense—but you know the rules."

"Rules be damned! You know *me*, don'tcha? Sher'ff thish county! Sher'ff b' God; an' I drink w'en I feel like it! Knock the neck off that bottle!"

The barkeep looked scared. This was no new story between him and Potter, but that did not make things any less difficult. The sheriff could be downright obstreperous when under the influence of liquor—even such liquor as Fritcher dispensed; and especially when Mrs. Potter wasn't round, which the barkeep knew mighty well she wasn't.

Mrs. Sheriff Potter was a *somebody*. Very superior and cultured. She was Number One reader at the Friday evening gatherings of the Literary Lantern, president of the local chapter of the Ladies' Aid, the Methodist Sewing Circle and the Crossing Uplift Club, and as such she was the final arbiter of social destiny — or what passed for that at the Horsehead Crossing.

Unfortunately, as the Fritchet barkeep was well aware, she was not, right now, available, being off to Tucson to play the organ for the service at the Methodist Sunday School.

The bartender sweated profusely.

But he had his orders, and very explicit. He said, "I'm too good a friend of yours to let anything come between us like likker, but—"

"Don't call that hogwash 'likker'," Potter roared; "an' don't gimme none of your dadburned lip! I know what I want an' I'm goin' to hev it!"

"Sure, but—" The barkeep stopped, staring wide at the doorway. The sheriff wheeled round and saw an unknown face.

It was the physiognomy of Mr. F. E. Farrar, the hardboiled dude from Oneco, who had slipped away from the Sabbath services while his wife was engrossed in the preacher's sermon.

Mr. Farrar advanced and propped a foot on the bar rail. He gingerly removed his ten gallon hat and dabbed at the moisture beading his forehead. "Does it get any hotter here?"

"Who're you?" Potter growled with his red eyes slitted.

Mr. Farrar struck a pose, loosed a stream at the cuspidor. "Flip'n-Shoot Fred, if yo're cravin' t' know, seh."

"I ain't cravin'—I'm *knowin'!*" scowled Potter. "Case you don't know it, I'm Sher'ff thish county! You look like one of that Whetstone Mountain gang—"

"Now, Obe," the barkeep said, "take it easy. For all you know he may be the Governor's uncle—"

But Potter wasn't listening. He had just recollected the primary purpose for which he had come here.

He fumbled a .45 slug from his shell belt and solemnly stood it on end on the bar. Then his red rimmed eyes found the dude from Oneco. "Can you whittle!"

Mr. Farrar said, "Shore!" and looked like he meant it.

"Then whittle me out a wood ca'tridge like that 'un."

"You mean *now?*"

"Sooner," Potter said, "if you know what's good fer you."

The dude unfolded a ten-inch blade and looked around for the wherewithal while the sweating barkeep watched with his mouth open. The sheriff wasn't one to fuss over details; he grabbed up a chair and snapped a leg off. This he tossed at Farrar; and the dude started whittling.

He gave the appearance of having whittled before, and five minutes later he stood a reasonable facsimile alongside the cartridge.

"Good enough," Potter growled. "Now git out of the way."

There was a barrel in a cradle on the bar's far end. Potter whipped out his pistol. There was a loud report and the barrel sort of shuddered. A quarter-inch stream spouted out of its side. Potter took up a glass and went over and filled it. When it brimmed he stopped up the hole with Farrar's wooden cartridge; after which he truculently eyed the barkeep.

"This is a lesson for you, Albert. Never argue with the law."

When Farrar had handed Wild Horse that six hundred dollars it had been Shorty's voiced intention to run up to Phoenix, but one thing and another had conspired to prevent him. Doc Wallace, for one thing, had been close to hand and the money Shorty had passed him had nicked the roll a mite more than he'd figured. He had aimed to give Doc a fifty dollar bill, but later examination of the roll showed he had parted with two of them. And then, next morning, just a bit before noon, two of his mares came down with the scours—Columbine and her sway-backed sister.

"That sway-back's the limit," McGee told Shorty. "Just a hard-luck outfit. As if them scours wa'n't enough, she's gone into that fence again—slit one ear and laid open a shoulder."

So Wild Horse stayed home and applied the Doc's medicine. He had a full jug so he used it liberally. He was no man to stint when it came to his horses.

Ernie dropped by on his way to the Whetstones. They asked him to supper and he was glad to get some. "Them rustlers," he said, "is so dang bold it's pitiful. Made off with two carloads of cattle since February. You better watch your bangtails."

Shorty showed his teeth. "They better not mess around *me*, by grab! Wasn't some fella killed over on Dutch Woman Creek?"

"Yeah—deserved it, prob'ly. Ain't nothin' to get all worked up about. The fella that killed him likely had a good reason." Ernie always found reason in the crimes he looked into. He was famed all over the great Southwest as the 'Sheriff who never got his man'. Mostly this was on account of his conscience; a gent with more conscience had never pinned on the tin. He could see good in everyone; and the tougher the hombre the more good Ernie could find in him. "There ain't no sense jailin' that poor lug—*any*one's apt t' lose their head *some*time. Think of his mother—his gray-haired mother! What would she do if we jailed her boy? Starve t' death, prob'ly; be ostracized anyhow. It's a wicked world," Ernie declared morosely.

Shorty said: "Them rustlers will think so if they light on *me*!"

Ernie clucked with his mouth full. When, finally, he got his windpipe clear he said: "That's a helluva crack for a Christian, Wild Horse. You wanta think what's be*hind* it—how can you tell what's in a long-looper's noggin? Hell, he's prob'ly been *drove* to it. Mebbe his sister—"

"Rustlers ain't got no busines with sisters! They ort t' be circum—circumvented some way," Shorty growled heatedly. "I'll see the Gov'nor about it, by grab! Bad as the gawd-awful price on this hay!—Forty-five dollars a ton! Why, them dang profiteers ort t' be shot down like dawgs! I tell you, us ranchers ain't like t' stand it much longer; they'll freeze the last one of us outa the business!"

He got up, angrily shoving his chair back. "An a nother thing! That gol-rammed Dickerson has fenced off the Springs an' put that tarantula, Logan, t' watchin' 'em. They've give him a rifle and a beltload of ca'tridges—There ort t' be a law ag'in' guys like him!"

"Amen," said Ernie absently. "Say! you got any new dudes on the register?"

"We got two," Shorty said. "Man an' wife from Oneco—why?"

"That's funny. Didn't a guy from Tyrone come out in a tourin' car?"

"I ain't seen no tourin' car," Shorty said, and Rose and the boys gave him confirmation. "No fella from Tyrone stopped by here. What'd he look like?"

"Big guy," Ernie said with his forehead all rippled like a washboard. "Smooth faced—dark glasses. Dyked out in store togs. Damned funny. Said he was comin' out here—had a Phoenix paper with your ad in it an'—Say! that reminds me; you wanta keep your eyes peeled. There's a loose nut floatin' round the country—got outa the 'sylum an' killed his keeper. We got a all-sheriffs warning. This bird thinks he's a preacher. Always writin' up sermons. Got a Moses beard and a glass-eyed stare. You better stick handy to a rifle till they get him."

Having finished his dinner Ernie mounted his horse and went circulating around with his eyes cocked for rustlers; and the dust had not hardly settled in his tracks when a big yellow car roared up and stopped just beyond the bunkhouse doorway.

It was Mr. Forest in his Hollywood glasses and he said straight off he would take a cabin for a month or longer. Shorty showed him the renovated harness shed and the heavy-set stranger pronounced it quite adequate. He allowed he had eaten. "What I'm wanting right now," he said, "is some sleep." He took off his dark-colored glasses then and a faraway look got into his eyes as he dug out his wallet and handed Wild Horse a sheaf of crisp bills.

"Hold on—" Shorty said. "You've give me ten bucks too much."

"Eh? Oh, that's quite all right. Treat yourself to a stogy."

He was wheeling to enter his makeshift cabin when the sound of a car jerked him round as though startled. "Who's that?" he said, clapping on his dark glasses.

"Just a couple of the guests. Been to town for the day. Mr. Farrar and Mrs. Fergie. The two dudes from Oneco; Wait a sec an' I'll give you a knockdown—"

Mr. Forest said queerly: "Some other time, thank you," and, diving into his cabin, he shut the door.

Wild Horse eyed the closed door. Then he snorted and turned. "Hev a good time?" he called to the others, and saw right away they evidently had not. Mrs. Fergie's look would have blighted a cactus. Mr. Farrar said nothing and he was not chewing. It looked, Shorty thought, like they would slam right past him. But they didn't. Not even the demands of decorum, it appeared, could bottle the wrath in the good lady's bosom.

She took a deep breath and said, clearly acidulous:

"We have been to church; and we sha'n't go there again, I can tell you!"

"Now, Mary . . ." Mr. Farrar said nervously, but the look of his wife stopped the flow at its fountain.

"People should be told these things," she declared. "Just as the sermon got under way, Red had to go to the toilet—there isn't anything wrong with that, is there? Of *course* not! The call of Nature is the common lot. But while he was in there somebody locked the door on him and we've been all this time trying to get him out! I never *heard* of such a thing! It is utterly disgraceful!"

Mr. Farrar looked as though he thought so, too; and Mitzy—the other dog—barked in agreement.

Wild Horse put up his head and sniffed.

Mrs. Fergie nodded in bitterest disgust. "That's the whisky you smell—I haven't told you the worst of it yet.

WILD HORSE

When Mr. Farrar stepped into the lavatory, two men—Fred thinks they were Elders, forced him to drink an entire quart of the vile stuff; then they went out and left him locked in there!"

Still bristling with indignation the good lady helped her unsteady spouse off toward their quarters and Wild Horse, left alone at loose ends, decided to hunt up Hellbound. But he aimed, at the first likely chance, to find out from Farrar which church that had been—not that he was hunting any liquor, but a little religion, he thought, might come handy. Even out here in the cactus.

He found Hellbound busy with the Pyketyne Blue, doctoring a brand new abrasion on the gray mare's hide. "Thet ornery stud of yore'n," Hellbound said, "jest won't leave the pore forlorn critter alone. Jest lookit thet bite!"

But Shorty had something else on his mind. "I'm goin' up t' Phoenix tomorrow—figger t' ketch me a ride on that afternoon freight. I would like to ask yore advice about somethin'."

Hellbound, carefully setting down the jug, drove the stopper in and looked up and grunted. "I done told you onct about ad-vice, son—"

"But this here is different," declared Wild Horse. "Baisy's hevin' a birthday. She wants a silver-mounted saddle to put on that palomino Lute give her. Way I look at it, Dickerson give her the horse, so it's up t' me t' git her the saddle. Thought mebbe you would know of some place I could git one without hevin' t' pay the guy's rent fer a year."

"Why'n't you give her yores?" Hellbound said. "It's pretty near good—"

"I was goin' to, but I'm a little mite scared she may recognize it."

"How much dinero do you wanta put into it?"

"Right now I got eight hundred an' ten bucks; but I don't wanta pay any more'n I hev to."

Hellbound mentioned an Hebraic gentleman who had once sold his great-aunt's cousin a saddle. "He's a pretty good sort an'll treat you right, but you better hold back enough t' git some hay fer these critters. They're gittin' all-fired gaunt on this pig-weed stuff."

But the morning brought a kid from the Crossing to put Shorty's Phoenix jaunt off indefinitely. The kid's name was Dodo and he was some relation to one of Hellbound's flames who had once burnt bright on Meyer Street. They talked quite a spell in the lingo, well garnished with grins and quick gestures. Then Hellbound said: "The express company hez telephoned from Tucson they got a horse fer you an' you sh'd come in an' git it right pronto."

"But I'm goin' up t' Phoenix—"

"Boy, you git down t' thet office," growled Hellbound. "You can't play tag with the railway express—they'll ship thet studhorse back where he come from an' double their profits without turnin' a hair."

"I'll drive you in if you'll wait till I get into my town clothes," Farrar said.

"But how'll I git him out here—"

Mrs. Fergie said, "I don't think there would be room in the Dodge."

"Of course there wouldn't," Farrar said testily, "but there's a trailer company in town— Don't you remember? We passed it. Shorty could rent a—"

"Sure," Hellbound said; "an' as fer thet saddle you don't hev t' go clean t' Phoenix t' git one. They got plenty of saddles right yere in Tucson. Try Porter's or the Tucson Tradin' Post."

So, half an hour later, with Mr. Farrar at the wheel with a big chunk of chewing and his ten-gallon hat, they set off for the county seat; and when they got back, quite a while after supper, the car had a heap of new brush scratches on it and Shorty's billfold was flat as a stove lid.

But they had the horse. It was the stud McGee had ordered from the Lanteen Ranch down near Hereford. He was yellow as gold, with shiny black hoofs and mane and tail like a flame of silver.

"It's a palomino—half Arab," McGee said. "Take a good look, folks. That's a real *cayuse.*"

"But isn't he awfully *little?*" Mrs. Fergie asked.

"He'll grow," McGee grunted. "What do you expect of a weanling? That feller ain't hardly six months old—he's as fine a little horse as you'll find in the state. His pappy's a World's Champ—Antez, a pure-blood Arab."

He patted the colt on the rump and chuckled. "This feller's pappy ain't never been beat at the half mile—not in all the hist'ry of Arabs, he ain't. An' that's goin' some!"

Mrs. Fergie said, "But I thought Man-O-War—"

"Man-O-War!" McGee snorted. "Beggin' your pardon, ma'am, but I'm speakin' of Arabs. This here Antez is about the most traveled horse this side of Syracuse—or any other side, either. Bred by Lewis on a honest-t'-God cow ranch. Lewis," he said, warming up to his subject, "sold him, young, to Carl Raswan—one of your biggest guns on them kinda horses. Raswan taught him a lot of tricks an' turned him over to Kellogg—I guess you've heard of who *Kellogg* is? He cranks out the stuff you eat before eggs. Mister Kellogg sold him to the Travelers Rest, a big Arab outfit near Nashville, which raced him an' made him a champion.

then the Poles heard about him—y' know they're nuts about Arabs: race 'em just like we race Quarters an' Thoroughbreds. These Poles took him away off t' Poland to improve their breed. Then this Lantcen outfit, down here t' Hereford, got t' huntin' a stud they could cross on palominos an' still have a horse to get first-class pure-breds; an' they bought him from the Poles an' brought him back here to Arizona; and now Mister Kellogg has him again. He's over on the Reese ranch in California. An' this little feller right here is his son!"

Mrs. Fergie said: "My gracious! Why don't you buy that Antez, Fred?"

Mr. Farrar took out his chaw and regarded it. "Mary," he said, "do you have any idea what that horse must be worth?"

"Why . . . ah—Well! I suppose he's worth quite a bit—"

"Now you're cookin' with gas," Mr. Farrar said, and spat. "Shorty paid five hundred dollars just for this weanling."

"For that little colt? Why, he's only—"

"Be six months old tomorrow, ma'am."

The good lady looked from McGee to Farrar and back again. "Why, I didn't suppose—"

"Yeah; an' that ain't all," Shorty grumbled. "That durn express outfit nicked me twelve dollars jest fer givin' him standin' room from Hereford—"

"An' the Tucson Tradin' Post," Farrar tucked in, "dented Shorty's pocketbook another couple hundred for a saddle with Mexican dollars all over it."

"I would think he was too young to ride yet—" Mrs. Fergie began; but Wild Horse's cheeks showed a darker color and he made haste to shift the talk elsewhere. "How's that mare doin'?" he questioned Hellbound.

"Bad as ever," Hellbound said, disgusted. "Runs off jest like one of them sprinklers—eats the same dang stuff as the rest of 'em, too, which ain't noways enough t' put a gnat's eye out. I've tried rubbin' bacon grease on 'er, but even thet don't seem t' be helpin' much. Thet pore critter jest lets go somethin' frantic."

"Got 'em bad," McGee nodded. "Must be some kinda weed she's eatin'. But I dunno—she may of got into that paint the Doc sent you. Jug's gone down better'n half already."

"That stuff ain't t' drink," Wild Horse told Hellbound, and the old man snorted and glowered around madlike and finally shoved off toward the stable without answering.

Lee Forest came up in his Hollywood glasses. "Where are you putting the colt?" he asked.

"In that 'dobe corral," McGee said, pointing. "Scratch him all up in them pole ones. 'Dobe's the only thing for a hot-blood around this place. Build 'em round an' of mud an' with plenty of foot room. Never make the walls less'n five foot high. Take a pole corral an' it keeps 'em excited—always watchin' the mares. Makes 'em ranicky. But you take a five-foot solid wall like that one, your stud's got t' stretch if he wants t' see *anything*. An' that's what you want; you want to learn him to get his head up. Same way with a feed rack; don't make a feed box where he can eat from it comfortable. Build it high so's he'll have t' keep his head up to use it."

Forest said: "Suppose you've got a horse that's *too* high-headed?"

"Put a martingale on 'im and you won't have no trouble."

Forest looked at Shorty. "Do you have a trainer?"

"Sure—Wild Horse McGee. Right there," Shorty said.

"Wild Horse" McGee said "Humph!" and grunted. Then Forest asked him: "Do you believe in using weights on their feet to secure correct posture? Special shoes or anything?"

McGee said, "Most horses, if sound, will stand right nacherally; if they're built right, I mean, and if you keep at their feet regular. Trouble with most guys, they don't take enough time to their horses' feet—"

"Nor to their tails, dadburn 'em," muttered Hellbound dourly.

"That's a right neat saddle," he said to Wild Horse later. "Set you back two hundred, did it? Watch out or you'll rub all thet silver off'n it. Don't look like you'd be hevin' t' shine a new saddle—"

"They had it packed in grease."

"In grease? My soul! Thet what turned all them silver things green?"

"If you come out t' find fault with that saddle—Anyways," Shorty said, "they won't *be* green when I git done with 'em."

"When you figgerin' t' give it to 'er?"

"Soon's I git it shined up proper."

Hellbound peered toward the adobe corral. "You reckon it's smart t' keep thet stud in there? Don't look like he'd git much exercise."

"That's McGee's worry. He aims t' git in there an' run him."

"Ever' day? Reg'lar?"

"That's what he says."

"He's sure pilin' up a real job fer hisse'f. Ef thet critter was mine I'd turn 'im out in the pasture."

"I reckon you would. But that there stud cost me *five*

hundred dollars. I ain't turnin' that much money out in no durn pasture—"

"Well, I'd shore hate t' be yore pocketbook. You save out enough t' buy them mares some hay?"

"Expect I kin manage t' buy a ton, anyhow."

Hellbound stared. "When it comes you better be round t' give it to 'em. When them seventeen critters sees thet one ton of hay ther' ain't goin' t' be no room fer by-standers."

Wild Horse frowned above his saddle polishing. "There's a couple hundred pounds of grass seed out in the back of that dude's green Dodge. You better get busy an' start scatterin' it 'round. By the look of the sky we'll git some rain before mornin'. Kick it into them hoof tracks an' smooch some dirt on it."

Hellbound said, scowling, "I never noticed it before, but I guess you must've come from Oneco, same as thet Fryar guy; you an' thet pilgrim's got a heap in common—special when you stick out yore jaw like thet an' git yore eyes squinched up like the light was too bright fer you. I call t' mind Bill Hart when he was—"

Wild Horse snatched up his saddle and got out of there. If he was going to be likened to a dangfool dude what hadn't no better sense than to get locked in a toilet, it was high time him and Bill Hart parted company.

10.

THE MAN ON THE BUNK

Though he had not mentioned it to anyone and the dude, so far, had kept his lip buttoned, Wild Horse was feeling pretty glum and nervous; and it wasn't on account of he had gone through his money.

It was the Dickerson didos that were getting him rattled—the undreamed-of lengths to which the rancher would go to get himself shed of an unwanted neighbor. Why, only just this evening they had dang nigh killed him! And it wasn't their fault they had not succeeded— naught but Farrar's quick thinking had saved him.

Those scratches lacing the Dodge's green paint had not been put there by wind or weather; they were tangible evidence of the Dickerson hatred. Coming home this evening with the stud from Tucson the Dickerson hay truck, with Rimfire driving, had mighty near run them off into a gully. It had come tearing around the wrong side of a bend, hugging the road and honking like fury; and Wild Horse's hair still rose at the thought of it.

He thought of it all the way home from taking Baisy

the saddle—and this, despite Baisy's rapturous gushings. She had even promised to attend the schoolhouse dance with him, and had let him hold her hand a few moments. But these recollected pleasures proved impotent to disperse the gloom of his worried forebodings. He watched every patch of deep shadow he passed, and passed without pausing, his spine all a-tremble with the fingerings of fear. Because if Dickerson's mind were made up to get rid of him he would hardly stop with engineering "accidents"—he would knock off the brakes and give his hard case the go-sign. It would be an all-out engagement with hell for the hindermost and no holds barred.

It was a logical thought, but a trifle previous. No untoward incident marred his trip from the Fritchets'. He got home about ten to find Hellbound still grumpily scattering grass seed.

With an eye on the sky Shorty said, "There's a rain comin' sure!"

But Hellbound was not to be cheered by such optimism. "Then it won't be nawthin' but a piddlin' dew—not enough t' wet down the hair of a jackrabbit." He sent a sour look at the sky himself. "You're jest th'owin' this seed away—jest th'owin' it away. The sun'll come out an' bake it t'morrer. An', even ef it don't, it won't make no diff'rence t' us or them horses because the ants'll git busy an' lug it all off anyhow."

Old Hank was no tonic for a man with frayed nerves and Shorty made haste to take himself elsewere. He found McGee on the porch. McGee knocked out his pipe. "You had any word from that Montana crowd yet?"

"About that Apaloosa stud, y' mean? Yeah, I done heard from 'em. Already sold to a guy near Joplin. Just as well," Shorty added, "fer I'm about shed of cash. How's Wire-Cut doin'? I see you been workin' on her."

"She's shapin' up," McGee said cautiously. "Biggest trouble is her feet, but I guess I'm lickin' 'em."

The night proved Hellbound a first-class prophet. No rain drummed down on the roofs—none whatever, and the morning's sun got up bright and early, with a face copper red and hot as hell's hinges.

Wild Horse, with the Farrars and Hellbound, went out to look over the stock after breakfast. Several were pot-gutted even yet but most of them—to quote old Hell-bound—showed "ribby and ga'nt as a flea skun fer tallow."

Mrs. Fergie, who Farrar had told Shorty had got her nickname on account of she had used to keep a boarding house and that was what the hungry guests had called her, was in her most faultfinding mood it seemed like. She said, pointing to the nearest animals, "What in the world is the matter with their hoofs?" and then her spouse got in his two-bits' worth. He offered the suggestion it might be termites.

"Termites!" Wild Horse glared. "That's my *brand*, you ignoramous!"

"Why, I thought," declared Mrs. Fergie, "brands had to go on the hip or—"

"Brands," Shorty scowled, "kin go anyplace the Board'll let 'em. Plenty of horses is branded on the hoof—on the leg, too. I've even seen 'em branded in the crotch. This here is valu'ble livestock—y' don't ketch *me* scarrin' up their hides. I brand on the hoof an' the next guy gits 'em kin brand any place he damn' well feels like."

"Good stock," Hellbound declared pontifically, "ain't worth much with their coats all marked up like a barn door. Fer one thing, worms—"

"Goodness!" Mrs. Fergie exclaimed. "Must we talk about worms? I—I think I will go and lie down for a while—"

"Now, Mary," Farrar said, "what's wrong with worms? Worms is the common—Say! What's McGee fixing to do with that mare?"

"God on'y knows," grunted Hellbound. "I've tol' the dang fool time an' ag'in there's on'y one cure fer scours— fresh bacon grease. But d'you think he'd listen? Not much! 'It's their *feet* you got t' work on,' he says. I sometimes think he's got feet on the brain!"

But they all trooped over to where McGee squatted with one of old Wire-Cut's feet in his hand. There was a little flat-topped scale on the ground and a hoof knife lay by his knee with some parings. There was a rasp by him also; and he did not bother to look up at them—not even when Hellbound glared and snorted.

Hellbound said: "Don't you reckon she knows the difference between hay an' them there hoof filin's? No wonder she's allus comin' down with the scours!"

But McGee paid little heed to him, going soberly on with his work without comment.

Farrar said, "Maybe he thinks that will straighten her back."

And Mrs. Fergie said, eyeing the medicine-splotched hide of old Wire-Cut: "Is that what you call a 'strawberry' roan?"

"No, ma'am," Wild Horse answered politely. "She's a Palamoosa—a rare breed, ma'am. Worth every pound of her weight in doxfees."

Farrar wrinkled up his brow and said, "What in the

devil's a 'doxfee', Shorty?"

"It's what that vet charges ever' time he comes out here."

After which the Oneco dude said he reckoned he would take a pasear if nobody had any objecitons. Shorty said, "Go ahead," and told Hellbound to saddle up Columbine for him; and at McGee's sour grin he said resentfully: "She's the gent'lest horse I got on the place. What's more, she'll take you from hell t' breakfast—or from breakfast t' hell, if you got a itch t' go that way."

"I ain't," McGee said; and Mrs. Fergie looked nervous. "Fred, do you think you ought to? The doctor. . ."

Mr. Farrar scowled across at her fierce-like and crammed his mouth full of Redman. After he had masticated awhile he said, "Go saddle 'er up an' leave me at 'er," and he gave them all a real tough-hombre look with his jaw thrust out and his eyes squinched up like he knew danged well he could ride anything that had hair on it.

So Hellbound shrugged and went off to saddle Shorty's "sweet" up for him.

It was getting right hot and breathless, kind of, with the air laying yonder like a blue haze of smoke; and Mrs. Fergie, setting off to write letters, declared she did not know if she could stand Arizona.

"Don't run that horse," Farrar was told when he left; "you kin kill that mare in this kinda heat." And, after he had gone, Wild Horse said to McGee: "That old rat-tailed mare is too danged good t' be ruint jest so's a fool dude kin play cowboy."

"We're gettin' powerful low on feed," McGee reminded him as Hellbound tramped over to the adobe corral to see how the Lanteen stud was doing. "I just give the last of the hay to His Nibs—"

"Is *that* what his name is? I thought them papers—"

"Sure—*Free Wheeling!* That's a helluva name to wish on a horse!"

"No accountin' fer tastes. Notice the outfit that dude rode off in?"

"I seen the hair pants," McGee nodded. "Where you reckon he got hold of that shell belt an' pistol?"

"He bought the belt yesterday at the Tucson Tradin' Post. They told him it was the outfit Curly Bill wore when he killed Fred White down t' Tombstone. He a'ready had the pistol." Wild Horse scowled around kind of nervous-like. "You notice where he's ridin'? You don't reckon he's a spy Lute's planted on us, do you?"

"He ain't got brain enough t' spy down a rat hole. But—" McGee said, lowering his voice, " 'twouldn't surprise me none t' know we got a spy hid out here. I been watchin that guy Forest. Somethin' almighty queer about *that* duck. Lets out he has t' have lots of sleep, never crawls outa his cabin till noon. I took a look through his winder awhile ago."

"Sleepin', was he?"

"He was in bed, right enough, but he wasn't sleepin'. Had a pad of paper an' a pencil; *an'* "— McGee said ominously—"he was all stretched out on that bunk, jest a-layin' there, starin' blank as hell at them cobwebbed rafters!"

"No!" Wild Horse licked at his lips uneasily. "Starin', did you say?"

"Starin'! Glass-eyed as a mantel ornyment! Why, you'd a swore—"

McGee broke off with an oath himself. "What in Tuesday has got up *his* pants?"

He was referring to Hellbound Hank who had just come out of the new stud's corral and was plowing full-tilt across the dusty yard.

"Hey! What's the idear?" Wild Horse hailed him.

"Huh?" said Hellbound, stopping and staring. He cupped a hand to his ear. "What'd you say?"

"I said what's the tearin' rush about?"

"Oh, my soul!—it's thet palomino! Got somethin' stuck in his throat—I can't budge it! I'm goin' after the bacon grease—"

McGee grabbed a rope and made for the corral with some muttered remark about Hank's mentality. "Git a bar acrost that pole-corral gateway—knee high," he panted. "Boot him over it when I lug 'im past."

By the time Shorty had the bar in place, McGee hove in sight with the end of his rope about the young stud's neck. Both were running and not wasting much time at it. "Got some of that dang hay stuck in his windpipe—fetch him a good slap so's he'll jump now!"

McGee, with scarce enough slack in his rope, went over the hurdle clean as a whistle; but the colt dodged aside and stopped, head down, wheezing.

"We gotta make him jump or he's a gone goose sure!"

"Mebbe if we took off the rope—"

"If we took off the rope he'd duck every time. Wait—let's get him back a ways—there! Git that stick—now whop him with it!"

And away they went like a witch on a broomstick.

The colt cleared the hurdle like he'd been born to it. McGee tossed the free end of the rope to Shorty. "Run with 'Im now! I'll make him jump it!"

The clout of his hand was like the sound of a pistol. The Lanteen colt went over the bar with twenty-four inches of air showing under him.

Shorty pulled him up and McGee came running to feel of his throat.

"Whew!" he sighed. "Well, he's all right now." He massaged the young stud's throat for awhile, all the time passing on advice to Shorty. "Any time you see a horse start frothin', or hangin' his head an' wheezin' that way, grab hold of his windpipe and, if there' a hard place in it, you get him to jumping—and make him jump pronto. A horse'll die right quick if he gets somethin' hung up in his throat for long. Only one thing t' do if you can't get him jumpin'—git you a stick an' poke it down his gullet."

McGee put the colt back inside the corral, put up the gate and brought water in a bucket till he'd filled the concrete tank. Then he rounded up the Palamoosa and took up his work where the stud had stopped it.

After lunch—the dude had not yet come back for his—Rose reckoned she was going to have to go to the Crossing for groceries. "Trouble is," she mentioned, "I might not be back in time to fix supper."

Mrs. Fergie said, "We could take the Dodge if you think you can drive it." Rose guessed she could and off they went.

McGee returned to his work with the horses.

It got hotter than sin.

The sun beamed balefully, turned murkily pale and, as the noonhour passed, a host of clouds piled up in the east, towering and black and billowing wildly around the upthrust peaks of the Santa Ritas. A wind sprang up and howled through the greasewood, rolling loose brush and dust before it.

Shorty, high-strung and restless, tramped the bunkhouse floor with the quick, cagey step of a cougar. Any moment now, Lute might try some further devilment, and God only knew how far he'd go *this* time. It bathed Shorty's back with sweat just to think of it, and to think how impotent he was to prevent it.

He was right there in his thinking when Hellbound came in and, without any ceremony, took off his shirt. He wrung it out and pulled it back on. "Hotter than love at the crossroads," he growled; and tramped over to the water pail and dippered a drink. "The's a big blow over in the Santa Ritas—rain comin' down like hell a-horseback."

"Mebbe we'll get a little," Wild Horse said absently.

"Not a chanct," Hellbound grumbled. "Not a chanct. It'll foller the mountains round like it allus does—take a act of Gawd t' make it rain yere. Where you reckon thet dude hez got to?"

"No wear an' tear on *me*," Wild Horse said. "I ain't responsible fer dudes or accidents. Damn! What do you figger I ort t' wear to the dance? I'm takin' Basiy, y' know," he added important-like.

Before Hank could answer, Lee Forest came in. He looked down in the mouth, his gestures resentful.

"I can't think out there," he grumbled. "Too blamed hot; and your man, McGee, has been rasping the hoofs of that Palamoosa ever since lunch right outside my window. Don't that fellow ever rest?"

"Mostly he does it standin' up," Hellbound said quietly. "What's the weather doin'?"

"No one but a fool or a tenderfoot would try to predict that in Arizona!" Forest flung himself into a bunk disgustedly. "If it *should* happen to rain, I hope one of you will think to go shut my window. I wouldn't want that bunk to get rained on."

That sounded like sarcasm, Hellbound thought; but

WILD HORSE

Wild Horse said, "We better go out an' give Nels a hand."

But there wasn't any sign of McGee around anyplace, nor did they see the purple-splotched Palamoosa. The Lanteen stud stretched his neck and nickered and off in the pasture a mare whickered back at him.

It was quiet in the yard as the night before Christmas. The sky, to the east, was blue-black as a bruise. Lightning flashed in the Santa Ritas and the Rincon rim could not be seen at all. In the middle distance, against that murk, dust boiled up in a swift advancement, dun and swirling and filled with mutterings. There were stringers of rain all around through the mountains but, off to the west, beyond the mission belfry, the Tucson peaks lay bright with sunlight.

Then a wind jumped roaring out of the east. The bending cottonwoods swayed and creaked and the tamarisks shrilled with its buffering fury and the air turned cold and smelled damply of rain; and Hellbound, pointing, suddenly shouted.

But his words were lost and the dust swept over the yard in great clouds, enveloping them in its stinging grit, choking and blinding, almost bowling them over. A rush of hoof sound rocketed through it as the mares in the pasture took off round the fenceline. Rain struck down in battering sheets and lightning daggered the murk with its flashes like something lugged out of Dante's Inferno. The shriek of the wind was like the roar of a freight train; thunder banged like bursts from a cannon.

"Whew!" gasped Shorty, yanking open the door. Old Hellbound lurched in and slammed it after him. "Gawd a'mighty! I'm plumb drowned as a rat!" he wheezed, trying to knuckle an excess of water form his eyes. He shook his head and his plastered hair clung tight to his temples, and water dripped off him in spreading pools that hastened to join the pools around Wild Horse. "Dang if this roof ain't leakin'!" Shorty growled as he squeezed some of the wetness out of his pantslegs.

"Nev' mind the roof!" panted Hellbound. "Where's the trap t' thet cellar door?"

It was so dark in the bunkhouse they could scarcely see: but the old man found the ring in the floor and gave it a tug and jerked the trap up. "Ain't much better'n a hole," he muttered, "but a hole's what I'm huntin'—you comin' or ain't you?"

" 'Course I'm comin'!" blared Wild Horse. "Do I look like a idjit?"

He clambered down the steps and Hellbound pulled the trap back in place and let out his breath in a long, relieved sigh. "I shore don't envy thet Fryar dude none, trapsin' aroun' through them mountains. In a way I kinder feel sorry fer him—"

"Don't waste no tears on *him*," Shorty snorted. "He's prob'ly hevin' the time of his life—ain't rained like this since Noah, hardly. Lookit the yarns he kin tell the home folks."

But Hellbound had something else to worry him.

"D'you feel any wind?"

" 'Course I feel it! 'F you think it's funny t' blow down my neck—"

"I ain't blowin' down yore neck! It's thet gol-rammed wind—even gittin' down yere! An' rain! Wet as I am I could swear the's more water hittin' me ever' minute!"

"Me, too! There sure *is*!" Wild Horse shivered. "Dang! Don't it seem t' you like this place looks lighter? Don't seem like it could, but—Hey! Open yore eyes, dang it! Wh—"

"Do' bother me, son; I'm commutin' with Nature—"

"But lookit that trap!" Shorty bleated. "It's *movin'!*"

"Movin' where?"

"Up an' down! My Gawd!—lookit it! jest like somebody was stompin' on it—"

"It's thet Forest dude," old Hellbound said. "Ther' ain't no room f'r 'im—tell 'im it ain't no drier down yere—m' clo's is floatin' off me right now, practic'ly."

"Mine, too!" Shorty's teeth chattered. "Water's over m' boot tops a'ready—her'm slosh? We gotta git outa this place or—"

"Wher' kin you go? Be worse out there—Here! Hold on—don't leave me yere!"

"I'm jest goin' up them steps a piece—"

"The' ain't but three. You'll bump yer head."

But Shorty went anyway. A few moments later he said, kind of hopeful, "I believe it's quittin'; gittin' lighter, anyway—I kin make you out plain."

Hellbound nervously opened his eyes.

"Lookit thet water! Plumb up t' m' knees!"

"Git up here with me on the steps why don'tcha? Say—that reminds me. What happened t' that feed rack we had by the gate in the no'theast pasture?"

"Them mares et it up—"

"Et it up! Are you *crazy?*"

"Ef I am it's no wonder—but they et it a'right. I seen ol' Wire-Cut chawin' the last of it. Heck—they gotta eat *some-* thin'! Thet Oneco dude—thet Fryar guy—says he's knowed horses thet et 'em reg'lar—*feed racks,* mind you! Says some of 'em prefers 'em *cooked!* The durned fool! . . . Whew!" Hellbound said, and mopped his face off. "Retch up an' h'ist thet trap a little. Gittin' orful clost yere—how's thet storm look?"

Wild Horse heaved and got the trap up.

Hellbound said: "Lord God!" and goggled.

They were staring straight up at the naked sky.

They clambered out and Hellbound muttered "Lord God!" again and Wild Horse Shorty looked past speech entirely.

"But where the hell is it?" Wild Horse wanted to know; and Hellbound pointed a shaking hand.

There it sat, more than forty feet yonder—the bunkhouse they had so recently dashed into; calm and snug over against the fenceline as if that had been where its makers had built it. Not a board out of line. Not a window glass fractured. Forty feet off from its erstwhile foundation.

Shorty shook his head.

Hellbound said, "The' ain't no perdictin'. Why, I've seen winds—"

"Hell's fire!" Wild Horse cried—"that dude! That Forest feller! He was in the bunkhouse—don't you recollect? Come in an' stretched out an'—"

With a sweat breaking out clear down to his tailbone, Shorty broke into a floundering run, slipping and sloshing through the lakes of water, as he dashed for the still-closed bunkhouse door.

He yanked it open and both of them goggled.

Mr. Forest, still clad in his Hollywood glasses, sat propped on a bunk quite composedly scribbling.

11.

A WET TRACK IN THE OFFING

It was almost dark when McGee showed up. He looked bedraggled and weary and there was a disgruntled twist to the set of his lips; but he had all the mares rounded up and enclosed again. "Run dang nigh over t' the Roman Four ranch house. I've throwed up some bars t' keep 'em penned in, but we'll have to be riggin' a new gate for that pasture, wind blowed the other 'un all t' kindlin'."

"That gate ain't what's eatin' you," Wild Horse guessed. "C'mon—spill it! Lute ain't made off with my new colt, has he?"

"Better if he had," McGee said drearily. "That colt's plumb dead. I guess the lightnin' got him."

"Told you we couldn't never beat 'im," Hellbound growled. "When you pick on a Dickerson y' might jest as well go an' order yer coffin! He's got ever-thin' sidin' him—even the elements."

But Shorty wasn't listening. It looked like he had got smoke in his eyes.

Old Nels put a comforting hand on his shoulder. "He

was a swell little guy."

Hellbound looked pretty daunsy himself. "We know how you feel, son. It's jest like one of the fambly had went. The Lord giveth and He taketh away. Alls we kin do is t' git us another one—"

"With what?"

McGee scowled. He dragged off his hat and, glower-ingly, squeezed the water from it. "This outfit's bogged to the hubs, by godfries. We're out of feed again or so close there's no difference; we ain't got a stud for them mares, an' no prospect—we won't even have *water*, onct, the sun, comes out, an' that Dickerson polecat happens to get wise about that pipeline we planted on him. Alls we've got is a bunch o' blamed dudes—"

"We got hay," Hellbound told them; "which is more'n we had before thet twister. Thet wind moved four of Lute's biggest stacks right off'n his range an' inter our pasture."

"Hallelujah!" McGee said sourly. "He'll prob'ly come over an' burn us out for it. An' while we're speakin' of skunks. I might's well tell you that Oneco squirt—Farrar or Fryar or whatever his name is—had been over to Lute's place ever sinct he left here. Him an' Lute an' that flame of yours—Baisy, has been settin' out there on Lute's big veranda, dunkin' their wattles in whiskies an' sodas. Sure goes ag'in' the grain to admit it, but I guess your hunch was a good one, Shorty. If that dude ain't takin' spy money from Dickerson—"

"Why—" Hellbound came raring up like a scorpion, "I'll kick his gol dang galluses off!"

"You leave him alone," Wild Horse grunted. "Ain't a thing he kin tell that's worth half what he's payin' fer it. Anyways, I can take care—Humph! There he comes now."

WILD HORSE

The dude looked startled when he saw the bunkhouse;
but he made no remarks save to say he had been over to
Dickerson's and had sat on Lute's porch while he waited
the storm out. "Now there's a fella that has got some
horses!" he said enthusiastically. "Every one of them
PHBA registered— Boy, howdy! Just wait till you see
those nags hit the Sweepstakes—be a regular walkover!
And that San Felice—what a horse! Nothing in this
county can touch him—"

"Says Lute!" McGee snorted. "What else is he enterin'?"

"Couple more of his palominos. San Salvator and San
Luis de la Paz."

After Farrar had limped off toward the cook shack,
McGee said sourly: "It sure beats all what a mixed-up
bunch of bangtails gits called 'palominos' round here any
more—anyone can dig up a dun-colored skate claims he's
got one! Ain't that Club got *no* rules, Shorty?"

"Sure," Shorty said. He was a great admirer of palominos
and read everything he could get on the subject, including
all the literature of the Palomino Horse breeders. "They
got plenty of rules, but they're still young, yet—ain't got
down to the fine points—"

"You don't have to tell me! I hear they even take draft
horses in!"

"Well, that ain't so," Shorty said indignantly. "The's
jest three types of horses they'll take; the parade, utility
an' stock-horse types. And then, only if the color's right."

"And what color's that?"

"New minted gold coin is the standard. But it kin go
five shades either darker or lighter—"

"Might's well make it fifty," McGee said derisively.

"You're like all the rest that orate on the subject. You
ain't took the time," Shorty said, "to look into the facts.

115

Some dimwitted nump pops off half cocked an' you an' the rest of 'em takes it fer Gospel. Why, they've only been registerin' stuff fer *two years*—they got t' start *some*place! Give 'em time. They'll make a breed yet an' it'll be a dang *good* one—"

"With all kinds of breeds wrapped up in gold coats!"

"All right," Shorty said. "But you called Free Wheeling a palomino—you acted right proud of him. I didn't hear you kickin' about the *A*rab blood—"

"That's diffeent. Palominos," growled McGee, "have always had *A*rab and Quarter blood back of 'em. Now they're takin' in Saddlebreds an' Standardbreds an' American Trotters an' Tennessee Walkers an' Gawd only knows what they ain't takin' in! Jest so's they're danged hides is yeller—that's all they care about. Even crossin' Albinos on bay and chestnut mares of no breed at all so as t' get the right shade of color into 'em!"

Shorty looked kind of dark in the face. Palominos were a kind of hobby with him; for years he had longed to get right into the business and try breeding the golden horses himself; and it sure rubbed him wrong to hear them talked down that way.

He said, kind of strangled like: "You don't know what you're talkin' about. *Some* guys may be gettin' the color that way, but a honest-to-God palomino breeder would rather cut off his right arm than get within gunshot of a dang Albino! You won't catch no PHBA member doin' it! You demand *their* registration when you buy a palomino an' you kin dang well know you're gettin' the genu-wine article. 'Cause why? Because no horse with a drop of Albino blood kin ever git papers from the Palomino Horse Breeders of America! They're dang particular what they register. Your horse has got t' hev a *black skin, black or brown eyes; white, silver or ivory mane an' tail an' good conformation.* Palominos is the fastest sellin' horses today an' you can't work fer me, by grab, an' go around knockin' 'em—"

"You haven't even got one on the place—"

"I will hev! Before I git done I'll hev a lot of 'em!"

"All right," McGee grinned. "You must like Dickerson's horses—"

"I like *any* good horse. No matter what breed it is. An' I don't like to hear any breed run down. I hate that side-windin' Dickerson's guts, but I don't pack my grudge to his horses."

"What do you call these critters *you've* got? Aside from that Palamoosa, I mean."

"I do the best that I kin," Shorty scowled; and McGee suddenly chuckled.

"Mebbe you've done better than you know. How'd you like to walk off with—"

But Shorty was walking off already. He was sick at heart with the luck that had struck him and he craved to get off by himself someplace.

They buried the Lanteen colt next morning. Shorty rigged up a cross and carved the little fellow's name on it; but he wasn't around when the boys threw the dirt in. Nor he didn't show up at the table for dinner. They found him, hours aferwards, glum and gone silent, in the adobe corral that was to have been the colt's home. No one had expected he would take it so hard. He hadn't ever bragged on the colt or praised it—had not done one thing but rail at the cost; but they could all see now how much Shorty had loved him.

The mail was heavy that evening; the Mex kid, Dodo, fetched it over from the Crossing. Twenty-seven letters, and every last one of them from folks hunting lodging with Wild Horse Shorty.

"It don't make sense," Hellbound muttered. "What in the world do they wanta come *yere* fer? Looks like haff Colorada's packin' up t' move!"

McGee said, "Them Phoenix papers must sure get around! Here's a guy claims he's chief of police up t' Colorado Springs—wants t' come down here for his whole vacation."

"Did y' see this one from the widder woman what says her husban' allus swore there was horses like thet? What d' you reckon she's talkin' about?"

"I dunno," Wild Horse said; "but we can't take 'em in. We ain't got no room for 'em."

"We might fix up them extry stalls in the stable!"

"Even a *dude*," McGee snorted, "wouldn't pay three hundred to get put in a stable. However," he said, slowly rasping his chin, "looks like we *could* crowd in *one* more. That chicken house—"

"Who's that?" Shorty growled, angling his head toward the window. "Wasn't that a wagon jest drove into the yard?"

"Yeah," said McGee, putting his head out. "Some fat old dame with a pair of thick glasses on the end of a stick."

Hellbound looked and said: "Lord deliver us!"

It was Mrs. Sheriff Potter and she had come to stay a month, she told them. She had her bags in Kerley's wagon and the money in her hand. "This *is* the place, isn't it?" she said to her driver.

"Yes, ma'am," said Kerley. "This is the WHS ranch, all right."

Mrs. Potter addressed Shorty: "You've still got them,

haven't you? I'd feel *so* put out if we'd come way out here—"

"I ain't got a idear what you're talkin' about—"

"Why, those *horses*—those—what-do-you-call them?" She flapped open the paper she'd had under her arm and hoisted her lorgnette to speed up her memory. "Those . . . There! Those '*Palamoosas*'! I'd like to see them first thing after dinner; and tomorrow—right after breakfast—you must let me ride one—they're still here, aren't they? Oh! I'm so *glad*! Just think—*purple horses*! Why, I'd never have believed it if I hadn't read it right here in the *Denver Post*!"

Shorty said: "Mind lettin' me hev a squint at that paper?"

Mrs. Potter passed it over; and there, sure enough, in great black letters running tall and proud across three columns it said: REMARKABLE DISCOVERY— ARIZONA RANCH DEVELOPS NEW BREED OF HORSES. Beneath this heading the article went on to say that Wild Horse Shorty, well known rancher in the Santa Cruz Valley, by the most rigid control and strenuous precautions in the selection and handling of foundation stock, had evolved a new breed which was known as the "Palamoosa." This was mainly, at present, a "color" breed, being gray generously splattered with brilliant purple splotches. But it had, the article stated, a quite distinctive conformation which, once seen, could easily be remembered. Much attention was devoted to the alleged origin, habits, behavior, home life, love life, etc. of these "truly amazing animals," and a bright future was predicted for them and for their discoverer whose work had so "profoundly revolutionized" all previous concepts of pigmentation.

Shorty, swelling his chest with pride, returned the

paper and explained with tact they had only one genuine Palamoosa left on the place. "You may notice one or two grades around and about, but the truth is, ma'am, folks has plain gone dotty about 'em—come out here in droves t' buy the breed off'n me an' won't take no fer a answer. Had twenty-seven letters jest this afternoon from people thet wants t' git put up out here; an' we jest can't take 'em—"

"But—"

"We ain't got the room, ma'am, an' that's all there is to it. However," Shorty said, seeing her agitation, "seein' as how you're the wife of my friend, Sheriff Potter, an' all, if you think it'll be worth five hundred a month to you, I'll try an' make out t' find room fer you someplace."

Mrs. Potter blinked like she could hardly swallow. She glared through her lorgnette indignantly, but in the end she agreed to put up with the increase in tariff, and Shorty put Hellbound to work on the henhouse.

That night, after supper, there was considerable talk about the Whetstone Mountain bunch and the outbreak of rustling that was being laid to them. Farrar had been in to the Crossing and had come back bulging with the latest rumors. The Dutch Woman Creek murderer had got clean away and Ernie, coming back from the chase, dropped by long enough to pay Wild Horse the money he owed him and to mention, in passing, he had better watch out for the Roman Four. One other bit of news he gave Shorty, also. The Tucson track, Moltaqua, had been recently sold to some Eastern dude who was against its continued use as a racetrack; and so, this year, the Southern Arizona Breeders were going to hold the Sweepstakes on the Dickerson track at the Roman Four. "You better figure to get in on it," Potter's deputy said. "Pays twenty-five hundred bucks to the winner—you could use a pile like that in your own business."

Then, just as he was aobut to ride off, Ernie turned in the saddle and eyed Shorty soberly. "It ain't none of my business," he said, "but Lute is right peeved about those haystacks of his that blew over on your place. Fact, he's threatenin' to go to law about 'em."

The night of the Schoolhouse Dance came around and McGee had Rose press his "Deacon" suit and Hellbound took his frayed shirt off and shook it and Farrar combed the cactus out of his hair pants while Shorty loped over to the Fritchets' for Baisy. He came back pretty quick. He was alone and scowling.

"Won't go with you, eh?" Hell bound shook his head sagely. "They're all alike, son—ever' last one of 'em; all alike when you git down t' cases. Contrary as fish-hooks and meaner than gar soup sprinkled with tadpoles. It was a gal thet blighted my life, I recollect; one of them sparkly-eyed kind with taffy hair an' a helluva temper—some of the sweetest lookers is jest like ginger. Did she give you any reason—"

"It's that blasted Lute Dickerson!" Wild Horse snarled. "An' that dang saddle! Everything was fine as peach fuzz till she rode over t' the Roman Four yesterday. That toothpaste mug went an' told her that saddle was one he had give away t' the Tucson Tradin' Post account of it was gittin' so shabby.".

Old Hellbound's face remained strictly sober. "Made 'er mad, did it?"

"I didn't see her," Shorty said with a growl—"she wouldn't even come near the door. Her ol' man tol' me; said she'd gone with Dickerson an' hoped she would never see me again— But *I*'ll show her! I'll—"

"Why'n't you take Rose? Thet ort t' fix 'er."

"By grab," Shorty said. "I'll do it!"

12.

COMPOUND INTEREST

The crossing schoolhouse was below the Happy Harp on the road that led up to Greaterville. It stood by itself in a wire-footed yard; and the sagebrush band was just tuning its fiddles when Shorty and Rose climbed down from their horses and pushed through the clutter of wagons toward a doorway made noisy by the loud talk and laughter of the boisterous men round the barrel. Several of these clapped Shorty's shoulder and one of the Roman Four hands, wiping the froth off his mouth, passed some muttered remark about "purple" horses.

But Wild Horse ignored the whole push of them. He was a Somebody now, with his name in the paper, and hadn't any need to take wind off nobody. He put his nose in the air—a la Dickerson—and swept Rose in through the entrance just like he'd brought her from choice and didn't care who knew it; and she looked a heap better than he'd thought she would with her best dress on and her face all flushed up and sparkle-like. The inside confusion avalanched against them, heated, hilarious—a bit rank with the smell of body sweat, horses and fumes from the barrel. The orchestra struck up a fine burst of music and Shorty grinned like it had been for him special, and all across the floor filled sets commenced gyrating and stamping and twisting as the red-faced man on the platform yelled: *"Throw yo' loop an' jerk yo' slack—Go meet yo' honey an' turn right back!"*

Shorty, looking across the floor, saw Baisy being swung by Lute. Baisy saw *him*, too, and stared right through him. Lute grinned derisively.

Wild Horse scowled.

Then McGee came up and Wild Horse asked him to do the polite with Rose over to a bench by the wall. While he fought his way over and got some refreshments. McGee said "Sure," and steered Rose over to a bench by the wall.

Heading for the cloakroom where the punch was being ladled, Wild Horse observed Farrar in his hair pants swinging a girl more accustomed to moccasins; she had the straight black hair of the Papago tribe, but her face was rouged and plenty lively. Shorty wondered where Mrs. Fergie had got to. Mrs. Potter was peering around through her lorgnette; and the Forest dude was on hand with his glasses; and, talking with Mose, the Tucson banker, stood tall Cramp Fritchet with his face round a stogy. Everyone and his uncle, it seemed, had managed to turn out for the schoolhouse dance. Jack Williams was swinging his good-looking Missus, Doc Wallace was crow for Mrs. Geo. Kerley, and George, the storekeeper, was conspicuous in a pink silk shirt and his wife had one of those flowered skirts on.

Coming back with his hands full of brimming glasses, Wild Horse found McGee by himself. "Where's Rose?" Shorty said; and Nels jerked his head toward where some sets were forming for the Texas Star. There stood Rose with the perspiring Potter, and the opposite couple was Basiy and Lute.

WILD HORSE

Wild Horse scowled and his fingers clamped tight round the still brimming glasses.

McGee nudged him nervously. Shorty, turning, saw Cinch in a set with Farrar and his Papago. "That Cinch," McGee said, "ain't no guy to give sass to; that fella's about as reliable as a case of thawed dynamite. You mark my words. We're goin' to hear from him before this jamboree's done with."

But Wild Horse sniffed. He said he hoped them fiddlers wasn't going to go on playing forever.

They didn't; and when the set ended he saw with amazement that Sheriff Obe Potter was leading Rose off to a bench clean across the room. His face got dark as a thundercloud as he watched Potter seat her between him and Ernie.

"Hold this hogwash," he told McGee, glaring. "I'm gonna—"

McGee wrapped both hands around him. "Take it easy. Don't grab at the bit. If it's a hound you're huntin', better start on me. I'm the one done got her mad up—don't go hoppin' the Sheriff about it. I'm the one— I s'posed she knowed you'd been aimin' t' take Baisy—"

"You tol' her *that?*"

"I know," McGee said. "You ort to fry me in oil. But there it is; I dumped the pot four ways from the ace. I'm the world's prize fool. She didn't give me no chanct t' back-track; went prancin' off madder'n a centipede with chilblains."

Wild Horse gave him a bitter look; clapped on his hat and went out to the barrel. His eyes said he hoped somebody would start something and the swing of his shoulders dared them to try it. He would have liked nothing better than a halfway excuse for poking some smart guy square on the kisser.

It was a dangerous mood for a man in his boots, but the Dickerson hands had all packed themselves elsewhere. There was no one in sight Wild Horse knew but George Kerley.

Kerley looked at him shrewdly. "Well, I swear," he said. "How's the horse business, Shorty?"

Wild Horse put down a drink and went back again.

Baisy was still in a swirl with Lute Dickerson. Rose was in a set with the long-legged Ernie, and was looking dang cute in that new flowered print—not noways, of course, in a class with Baisy, but a whole heap better than you'd expect of a hasher. Ernie was grinning like he was all-fired proud of her; and that did not help Shorty's temper any.

The fiddle screech stopped and the couples sought benches. Quite a crowd got to building by the side door some way, and Wild Horse shoved over to see what the row was. When he saw, he snorted.

It was only Hellbound, busied as usual being the Bad Example. He had one leg flopped over the other and into that tight-clamped uppermost knee, while the crowd watched bug-eyed, he was driving a pin, tapping it in, bit by bit, with the handle of his pocket knife. He had it almost in to the head right now. "Naw," he was saying to the goggle-eyed watchers—"Naw, it don't hurt none t' speak of."

Wild Horse, feeling more ornery with each trip to the barrel, was ripe for anything when Dickerson, passing him and McGee said: "How did you like what we did to that colt for you?"

Both men stared. McGee's jaw dropped. A hard-held

pressure whitened Shorty's cheeks. "So it wasn't the lightnin', eh?" he said slowly, and the horse breeder laughed.

"What do *you* think? You better take my advice and get out while you're able."

Something snapped in Shorty. Tried beyond caution, he hooked out a fist and lifted Dickerson's face for him. The rancher staggered. Shorty popped him again — a genuine post-splitter brought from his bootstraps. Dickerson groaned and went down in a huddle.

The next time they saw him there was quite a crowd gathered. Someone was helping Lute up on his feet. "He's been slugged," Fritchet said. "Lookit that jaw, would you?" Kerley obligingly held up the lantern. "Oh!" Baisy cried. "The unspeakable brutes!" and stood wringing her hands in a paroxysm of anguish till Ernie came up and, like the law would fix it, said: "Lute, who done it? Did they get your wallet?"

Lute glowered. He was coming back fast. He shrugged himself free and adjusted the fit of his rumpled clothing. "Get that damned light out of my dial!" He brushed past Ernie like he wasn't even standing there. Potter, pushing up, caught hold of him nervously. "What's happened? What's the trouble here? Isn't that you, Mister Dickerson? — Lord a'mighty! What's happened to your face?"

Dickerson flung him off with a snarl of intolerance. "Keep your hands off me, you fat old fool! If you'd been tending your job this wouldn't have happened! — Get out of my way!" With a growl in his throat he stamped into the schoolhouse.

The next time they saw him he had his face patched up with a strip of Doc Wallace's stout horse plaster. There was a glint in his eye as it fell on Wild Horse; and McGee, leading Shorty toward calmer surroundings, showed a sober face darkly graven with worry.

Shorty, feeling much better now, was well in the midst of extolling the virtues of the Palamoosa to Mose, the banker, when Phil Cinch steped up and tapped his shoulder. The fiddlers were out freshening up at the barrel, and all across the room knots of people were gossiping, but they all choked off when the handsome Phil said:

"It takes a lot of practice to ever think of that Petrified Creature as belonging to the horse family, mister. Why, that purple-splotched fright ain't even got a *tail.* A tail is supposed to have *hair* on it and, usually, a man thinks of a horse as something that *runs.* Don't waste people's time with any more wind about *that* plug. You haven't got a horse in your whole dang outfit. San Felice could leave that bunch so hung up behind they wouldn't ever get within the smell of his dust!"

Shorty looked at Cinch and then back at the banker. "Was that a draft I felt?" Then he felt McGee's elbow, and looked up to find Lute Dickerson eyeing him like he was something the pigeons had left on the doorstep.

Dickerson said, strolling over coolly, "I could take San Felice and beat any one of them wrecks you call 'horses'— any or *all* of them," he added derisively.

The way Lute said it got Shorty stirred all over.

"Just talkin' t' hear yore head rattle?"

Dickerson stuck out his jaw, winced and said like it choked him: "I'll back that brag any day that you name!"

"With what?" Shorty scoffed. "Wind or frijoles?"

"With hard cash!" Dickerson snapped, and grabbed out his wallet.

He thumbed out a thick sheaf of banknotes. "There's a

thousand greenbacks says San Felice will come off better in the Sweepstakes next month than any one of your plugs you want to put in it. *One thousand dollars* — now put up or shut up!"

It looked like Dickerson had him; and in more ways than once. In the first place Shorty did not have that much money; he didn't have anywhere near that much money, because most of the cash he had got until yesterday had gone to buy badly needed grain for his horse herd. Also, a bet with Lute on any such issue looked just the same as throwing it away.

But he couldn't back down with half the country looking on. He sent a glance at Fritchet, but Fritchet looked away. So did everyone else who had money. They either looked away or grinned at him wryly.

"Who you figurin' t' hev hold the stakes?"

"I'll hold 'em," Frichet said.

"All right," Shorty growled, wheeling round on Dickerson. "I'll jest call yore bluff, Mister Wise Guy! I ain't got that much on me right now, but I'll see Fritchet gets it by tomorrow night sure — by tomorrow midnight. Any—"

He stopped in mid-sentence with his stare on the door. Everyone else was staring that way already. A swaying man stood, spent, in the opening; a wild-eyed, hatless, dust harried figure. There was a gash in his head. Blood blackened a cheekbone.

"*Store!*" he gasped. "*Collossal — bandits!*"

Sheriff Potter snatched out his gun. "Which way?"

But the man was done, dead beat on his feet. He went down the jamb with his legs buckling under him.

While those nearest sprang to render him aid, Obe Potter rapped out his orders. "Here!" he scowled, thrusting his pistol at Wild Horse. "You light out with Ernie while I scare up a posse. Don't try t' come up with 'em—just go out far enough t' make sure where they're headed. There's a couple tied broncs just beyond the side door."

There were—and both bridled. But only one of them had a saddle, and that one Ernie grabbed without pausing. The other was dun with a white mane and tail and, yanking the reins loose, Shorty piled on it. He expected he might have to kick some speed into it, but the big dun took off without any urging.

They caught up with Ernie. "There!" Ernie yelled, and following the point of his hand Shorty saw them—black in the moonlight, five men riding hard!

Ernie yelled more, but the wind made off with it; and Shorty, twisting to ask repetition; discovered the deputy stopped, twelve lengths back.

High time, Wild Horse thought, he was stopping himself.

But the dun did not think so—it had a mind of its own. Shorty hauled on the reins, but he'd nothing for purchase; and the dun grabbed the bit and they went like thunder.

It was then Shorty made his portentous discovery. He was astride of a whirlwind that didn't know "Whoa!"

He was aboard San Felice—the head Dickerson racer!

13.

A WELL TRAINED HORSE

There wasn't any use in kidding himself; after the first
seven bounds of that all-out travel Shorty knew plain as
paint he would never collect on that bet with Lute
Dickerson. Just another few hoofbeats aboard this rocket
and he would be within range of the owlhooter's arsenal.
There was not much doubt what he would collect when
that happened.

It was kind of too bad, too, he thought, reviewing it.
For now he would die with Baisy still hating him; without
any chance to make amends for that saddle. And, come
right down to it, what was wrong with that saddle? Not a
dad-burned thing—except it had happened to belong to
Lute Dickerson. He had bought her the best that his
money could buy, but luck had sure played against him.
She ought to have seen it was not the present but the *spirit*
that counted. Yes sir. She had ought to of seen that.

It was a miserable prospect to pass out from a bullet—
specially now that the papers had finally woke up to him.
Why, he'd been right on the road to being made famous!

The thought of it roused him to further effort, but nothing he tried slowed the dun by a fraction. The horse had been trained for running—trained plenty!—and just laid back his ears and ran all the harder.

Some minds, in a crisis, are prone to work overtime and Shorty, it seemed, had one of those kind. All manner of queer notions popped into his head as the dun settled down to overhauling the robbers. For instance, why, Wild Horse wondered, weren't they firing to drop him?

They were, in a way, but not very whole-hearted. In their place, Shorty thought, he could have done a heap better. The way to get shed of him was to drop the horse under him; and old San Felice with his bright, dappled hide streaking through the moonlight couldn't hardly be missed. They were mising him, though. Right consistent like.

Might be they knew this was Dickerson's race horse.

But what if they did? What would *they* care for Lute Dickerson's property? Unless— Yes! that must be it! Hoping to get their dang hands on it, probably, once some lucky shot settled his hash for him! Yep, that was it. They didn't care about him; they were a heap more anxious to get hold of this horse . . .

Or were they?

With a cold rash breaking his neck into gooseflesh, Wild Horse noticed the change in their tactics. They were firing low now—slugs shrilling all round him. They had got tired of his following and they were bent on stopping him.

Like a bolt from the blue then it burst on Wild Horse that here was another of Dickerson's traps for him! Sure it was crazy—fantastic, incredible; yet the more he considered it the less he doubted. Every step of the way tendered proof that was damning! The Dickerson hands, so suddenly quitting that barrel! The conspicuous absence of Rimfire Logan! The spectacular way of the robbery's announcement—that guy falling down in a faint so handy and Potter, like he couldn't hardly wait for it, thrusting Shorty his pistol and sending him after them!

Cute—slick as slobbers! You just had to hand it to them. When it came to skullduggery that Luther K. was a corker! The mealy-mouthed way they'd palmed off those tried horses—and just one with a saddle to make sure Ernie took it and left this danged whirlwind for Wild Horse to straddle!

But Hellbound had warned him! "The Dickersons *is* the law," Hank had told him, and here was the proof—here was proof in plenty! Sheriff Potter conniving to get him killed off for them!

It was Potter had told him about the tied horses, being plain to remark they shouldn't try to catch no one but just go and see where the robbers were heading.

Oh, it fit all right. Like a cup and a saucer. This San Felice racer made sure of everything. Could safely be counted on to bring Shorty up within range of their shooting irons; and there was Ernie to prove he'd gone on against orders. And Potter, who later would draw a long face and say; "I *told* the fool not to!"

And these store-robbing owlhooters!—all Dickerson hands sure as frost makes the apples bounce down off the branches! He was close enough now to see the neckerchiefs pulled up across their noses—the glint of their eyes as their cheeks cuddled rifles.

And that pistol Potter had given him—a fine touch of irony! Might as well be a pea-shooter against those rifles. But that was all part of the arrangements of course, just as using Lute's race horse was part of them. For who would believe Lute mixed in a thing that could hold any peril for his stakes-snatching racer? But, come right down to it, what did Lute care for San Felice—or *any* horse, as against the chance to be rid of Shorty! Why, he'd all but admitted having done for Free Wheeling! *That* showed the stripe of him—there was nothing so low but what Lute would try it if it looked like a chance to get him shed of Wild Horse.

Scowling—fierce—muttering—lying low as he could on his bounding perch, Shorty peered ahead, bleakly scanning his chances; and, try as he would, Shorty could not like them. San Felice was the result of long years of schooling. He had been *trained* to run, and to keep right on running so long as there was anything running before him. No matter how contrary the man on his back might be, San Felice knew his business and he sure aimed to do it.

There was a dip in the rolling ground ahead, a long shallow wash where, during the rains, a creek crossed the desert. From this, in the moon's blue silver, a mesquite thicket lifted dark ferny-fringed branches and dappled the sand with their black, twisted shadows. And, even as he looked, Shorty saw the owlhooters swerve and ride into it.

He could leave the silver-maned dun—could easy jump and quit it, but he could not see how that would help him any. If he had gauged the play right, those yonder lobos were out to kill him and quitting his horse would not keep them from it. This range was desert—plain sand and wide open; there wasn't even a cactus he could drop down and hide by.

Yet if he stuck with the horse it would bring up to them.

Damned if he didn't and damned if he did—a pretty kettle of fish, by godfries! Those slugs they were throwing could not miss him forever!

His next look put the icicles on him. Lute was going to have the last laugh all right. He could see the owlhooters' horses again. Just beyond that mesquite brush. With their saddles empty. Didn't make much guessing to savvy what that meant.

This was it.

With a sigh Wild Horse fetched out the gun Potter had given him.

With considerable amazement Chief Deputy Ernenwein sat in the saddle and stared after Shorty. What in heck ailed the guy? Was he *loco?* Potter had distinctly ordered them not to follow the robbers, yet there went Wild Horse hellity-larrup—not only following them but intent, by the look, on overhauling them!

"That gol dang fool should be bored for the simples!"

Ernie glowered, whirled his horse, and set off at a gallop.

He was back at the schoolhouse inside of two minutes and threading the crowd without care or courtesy. "I'm huntin' for Potter!" he growled. "Where is he?"

"Down to the store, I guess, gettin' rifles," McGee, who was talking to Williams, told him. "See 'em? Where's Shorty?"

"Dang fool's chasin' 'em," Ernie muttered; and pulled up cold at the look they gave him. "Hell! Don't blame *me!* You heard Potter's orders. I'm a deputy sheriff; I got t' do what I'm told to do!"

"That star you're packin' ain't froze to you, is it?"

Ernie's stare locked tight with McGee's. Neither eye wavered.

135

"C'mon!" Ernie grated; "by Gawd, we'll go after 'em!"

"Wait!" Williams said. "Ain't that shootin' off yonder?"

"What'd you reckon they'd be doin'—playin' leap frog out there?"

Before they could answer that choice bit of irony, Ernie spied two rifles. That they happened to be held by Doc Wallace and Provencher mattered not in the least to the law's chief deputy; he tramped right over and clamped his hands on them. "Sorry!" he said. "But the law needs these things a heap worse than you do." He tossed the artillery to McGee and Williams. "Let's go!" he snapped, and they ran for their horses.

They ran into Lute Dickerson out on the steps. Phil Cinch was with Lute and they both looked riled. "Somebody's stole my horse!" Lute shouted; but Ernie snorted and jumped right past him.

"We ain't got no time t' fuss with horsethiefs—see the Sheriff," Ernie bade him, and sprang into his saddle. "You—McGee! Take that roan over there. Williams—" he eyed old Jack a bit dubious. "You reckon you can make out t' sit a saddle?"

"Boy," Williams said, "I was *raised* in a saddle!"

"Well, all right," Ernie grumbled, "but don't come apart on me. Take that—"

"Hold on!" wheezed a voice. "What you up to, Ernie?"

It was the sheriff come back with his arms full of rifles. "What—"

"We're goin' after them robbers!"

" 'Course we are—we'll be goin' just as quick's I git ready. Don't jerk on the cheek strap. I got to swear in a posse first, ain't I?"

"We ain't waitin'—"

"Ain't waitin'!" Potter dropped his wheeze and the rifles,

likewise. "What you doin'?—tryin' t' start a mutiny? Get off that horse. We'll go when I'm ready—"

"Wild Horse is out there!"

"What about it?"

"He's chasin' 'em!"

"Oh, chasin' 'em, is he? Well," Potter said, "it's too bad about him! I told him plain—"

"What of it? You ain't goin' t' let them varmints—"

"He should of thought about that when he went tearin' after them. You heard me—"

"C'mon," Williams growled. "We goin' to gab here all night?"

Potter snarled: "We'll gab if I say so!"

Old Jack Williams raised up his eyebrows and a wintry smile briefly tugged at his lips. "Look here, mister. Mebbe you better think that over."

Before hostilities could be carried further, Dickerson spied them and came storming over, still ranting about his stolen palomino.

"Your horse," Ernie told him, "ain't stolen. It's confiscated—one of a pair commandeered by the Sheriff. I've got the other'n—wanta make somethin' of it?"

"I want that silver-maned dun!" Lute shouted. "I want it right now before something happens to it!"

"You'll pay hell gettin' it! Wild Horse has got it an'—"

"That wart! What's *he* doin' with it?"

"Last I seen he was chasin' them store-robbers."

"On my *palomino*!" Lute looked aghast. He whirled on Potter like he'd bash the face off him. "You pot-bellied fool! D'you know what you've done? You've give that addle-pated brain the best damn horse I ever had in my stables!— I say the *best*! Hand-raised an' trained by the sweat of my —Three times a stakes winner! An' you let that dimwit go

137

chasin' robbers on him!"

While Lute was ranting, Mr. Farrar came up and stood calmly stroking his jaw with Redman. When he'd used up the biggest part of the package he said to McGee: "Reckon you kin use another hand, can'tcha?" and coolly picked up one of Potter's dropped rifles. He opened it up and took a look down the barrel. Then he nudged L. Ernenwein. "How about it?"

"You ain't got no horse."

"I kin git one," Farrar said, and untied Phil Cinch's from the back of a tailgate.

McGee looked at Williams. "Back in Dakota we'd of had them guys now."

Old Jack nodded.

Ernie said, "You fellas acquainted?"

"Well, I guess," Williams said, and McGee declared: "I've et at his place enough times t' know him. Why, me an' Jack's kids—"

"Didn't know he had any."

"Lot of things you don't know, boy. He's got three—an' all girls—by the las' count, anyway. Why, me an' Vera, about the time Jack Scully—"

"That outlaw! Did you know him, too?"

"Sure we knowed him," Williams said. "An' a squarer gent never stepped from the saddle. Except for the way he dabbled in livestock, there wasn't a man I'd trust farther in the whole Northwest. *There* was a lad with an eye for good horseflesh! Remember that time, Nels—"

"I recollect," McGee said, "quite a long spell back we was fixin' t' go out an' salvage Wild Horse—"

"Hell!" Ernie said, and looked around for Potter. Potter was off down the road humping after Lute Dickerson; and Ernie said brashly, "I don't have t' take no lip off that guy

138

WILD HORSE

—C'mon! Let's get out there!"

And, without more ado, they put spurs to their horses and went shacking off at a high, fast lope; but though they hunted well—even perseveringly, they did not turn up any sign of Shorty. They saw plenty of cartridge-case shines in the moonlight; a good many tracks and a coyote or two. But no sign of Shorty or the San Felice race horse.

Finally, even the tracks petered out, dusted over and filled by the wind off the Rincons. "It looks," Ernie said, "like them robbers is lighting a shuck for the Tumacacoris—prob'ly figure to hole up round Tubac a spell."

"Like enough," Farrar said, like he knew all about it.

Old Jack shook his head. "I expect they got him. Too bad. Crazy dang coot, but you couldn't help likin' him. Borry the shirt right off your back. But a real horse lover."

"Broncs liked him, too," McGee said, shaking his head. "But I guess you're right; they've killed him, I reckon. Prob'ly packin' him with 'em so's we can't find his body. Takin' Lute's palomino, too, it looks like."

They stared out into the night and listened but all they could hear was the wind in the greasewood.

McGee cleared his throat. "I guess we might's well go back. This is goin' t' be hard on that freckle-faced hasher— Rose set a heap of store by that boy. I'm goin' t' let you break the news, Fryar— I ain't got the heart to."

Farrar said nothing.

It was a moody foursome that rode back into town.

The dance was over, broken up by the robbery. The schoolhouse was locked, its yard dark and empty. But off up town, near the front of Cramp Fritchet's there was quite a bunch gathered and their tones sounded angry. Even down here you could hear their raised voices.

"*Now* what's up?" Ernie grumbled; and they all felt the same way about it, seemed like, because they all kicked their horses and broke into a lope.

There must have been ten or twelve men in that growling group. The stillborn posse, it looked like. For they all packed rifles and two or three gents were sporting six-shooters, also. Sheriff Potter was there, big and loud—no mistaking him.

There was no mistaking Lute Dickerson, either.

"An' *I* say," Lute was yelling, "you took that palomino *deliberate*!"

"My Gawd!" Ernie said. "It's Wild Horse!"

And sure enough! There he was, hale and hearty and right in the thick of things same as always, with Potter on one hand and Lute on the other. Horrific glances were being chucked round and, when the others came up, Shorty was shaking a pistol under Lute's nose. "I'm a genial soul," he was orating loudly, "not the kind t' go outa my way t' fetch trouble—but there's a limit, by grab, t' even *my* endurance! You open that sassy jaw again an' I'll smack them teeth of yore'n hell west an' crooked!—an' that goes fer you, too!" he told the sheriff; and Potter tucked tail in a hurry.

Lute Dickerson gave him a long black stare. Then he smiled with his teeth and stamped off with his racer.

"How'd you get back here?" Ernenwein grinned, pummeling Shorty like he couldn't get over it.

Shorty jerked a nod after the Dickerson race horse. "Lute's palomino brung me back—an' lucky I had him. Been a goner sure if it wasn't they'd give that horse s' much trainin'. Tell you the truth, I reckoned I *was* a goner; an' I yanked out this pistol, figgerin' t' make it expensive s' I could fer 'em. Y' see, the trouble was I couldn't *stop* that San Felice horse. He'd been trained t' run an' this looked t' him jest like any other race. I couldn't stop him an' I couldn't turn him, an' the more I tried it the harder he pounded."

"What'd you do?" Ernie asked him, breathless.

Wild Horse said, "I never done nothin'. It was all San Felice an' the trainin' they give him. But he sure didn't love that lead buzzin' round, an' I don't reckon he much cottoned to the course we was takin', all his runnin' havin' been done on tracks.

"Pretty soon we come to a place where a wash cut the desert. Off to the right, there was a lot of mesquite brush an', all of a suddent, them robbers all dove fer it. They was washed up with foolin'—they was goin' t' pile off an' nail me proper—an' they'd of done it, too! I tell you, boys, I was lookin' death right spang in the eye!"

"Did they git you?"

"No," Wild Horse said, "they didn't git me. When San Felice seen them other broncs swervin' I reckon he knowed dang well they was loco; an' you can't noways blame him. They'd went *right*, an' all the racin' old San ever done had been pounded on tracks that went *left* in a circle. He knowed what t' do an', boy, he sure done it. He let out a snort an' went streakin' *left* an' straight down the home stretch hellity-larrup!"

14.

"WE'LL PEEL THE SHIRT—"

Wild Horse, taking stock of the situation after making
sure Rose had gone home with Hellbound, guessed it was
high time he set about getting hold of some money if he
aimed to make good on his bet with Lute Dickerson. And
he reckoned he would have to go through with it, even
though he knew San Felice was a whirlwind. If there was
one thing the West had small use for, it was the man of big
words who did nothing.

Unfortunately, the most likely prospect for advancing
the money was the man who, already, had told him
"No!"—had, in fact, stated plainly he would not lend a
nickel. Baisy's father, the saloonkeeper, Fritchet. And the
most logical person to talk *him* over was Baisy, who was
still mad as hops about that second-hand saddle. Didn't
look like much use going to *her* with his troubles.

Women was a headache, take them any way you cared
to. Just look how that Happy Harp hasher had used him
after he'd taken her in and paid her fare at the dance! *There*
was gratitude for you!

He scowled at the backs of the departing posse and tried to think how he might bring Fritchet round. But he could see how Fritchet, being suspicious by nature, was like to be a hard nut to crack. Though he scratched his head, and even lit up one of those tailormade things he had given the barkeep, Wild Horse could not think of any approach that looked like getting him past Fritchet's prejudice.

The truth might be best after all, he mused. So he mounted the steps and pushed through the batwings.

The barkeep's sleepy look held no pleasure.

"Fritchet around, Johnny?"

"Gone out to the ranch."

"Mebbe *you*'d be interested—"

"Not me, pal. Not a chance. I've watched too many of 'em drown their sorrers."

Wild Horse stared. "You don't even know what—"

"The whole country knows. You better pack up your duds an' start hikin'. You won't get no money in *this* town."

It was late—awful late, when Shorty rode up to Fritchet's ranch headquarters. There wasn't a light showing anywhere and even the stars were beginning to turn dim. But it was Hobson's choice, he though bitterly; and got wearily out of the saddle.

He tied Figure 8 to the porch rail and clanked his spurs up the steps and knocked. Wasn't no use trying to shush things; he would have to get Fritchet up anyway—but it was Baisy who slippered her way to the door.

There was anger in the way she clutched at her wrapper, and the look in her eyes struck Wild Horse cold as she held up the lamp and saw him.

"I should think you'd be ashamed," she said; and Wild

Horse recollected the ring he'd picked up in Tucson that day he had brought her the saddle. He had been packing it around ever since, plumb forgotten; but now he fished it out, all snuglike and cozy in its plush-lined box, and put out his hand to give it to her; but the look of her eyes was disdainful.

"More presents?" she said with a twist of her lips. "No thank you—really, I'd be afraid to touch it. I'm afraid it might give me gan*grene* of the finger. Any man that would give a girl a second-hand saddle . . . No, really, I wouldn't care for it. Give it to Rose—she'd never know the difference."

Wild Horse, glowering, thrust it back in his pocket. "All right," he said, though the words nearly choked him. "Will you call yore father? I've got some bus—"

"I don't think my father would talk business with you. If it is money you've come for you're wasting your time." Then she stamped her foot. "It's ri*diculous*! The whole country is laughing at your silly wager! The Dickerson horses are *pure*breds! You haven't any more chance of winning that wager than a June frost would have in Brownsville!"

Shorty looked at her somberly as he stood with his black hat gripped in his hands. She was probably right; but she would never hear him say so—not for all the race horses in Dickerson's stable. "Just the same," he told her, choking down his pride, "I would like t' talk to him anyhow."

"Very well—but it will do you no good," she said peevishly, and went off to get the old man out of bed.

Fritchet was not in the best of his tempers when he came to the door with his shanks sticking out of his nightshirt.

144

There was a red flannel cap on his grizzled head and he said, scowling blackly: "What's eating you *now*? If you come for a loan—"

"Save yore wind," Shorty growled; "I got all that from yore daughter. Matter of fack, I come over t' do you a favor. How much interest you gittin' from the bank?"

"Not enough to paint the front door, but—"

"You're a sportin' gent, ain't you? I mean, you'd back a good thing if there was plenty of profit—"

"If you're building up to those mares you can stop right now; there ain't an ounce of profit to a carload of 'em."

"I expect you're right," Shorty nodded dismally. "But it ain't them mares I came to see you about—"

"It ain't?" Fritchet eyed him suspiciously.

"No. I wanted t' see you about that bet I made with Lute Dickerson— Hey! Hold yore pants fer a second, will you? I don't want no loan. I'm spreadin' my cards right out on the table. What I got in mind won't cost you a cent."

"It's a cinch you don't look for it to cost *you* nothing!" Fritchet scowled at him, like if he scowled hard enough he might discover the catch to this. "Well," he said finally, grudgingly, "get on with it. Don't bother me with any gold paint or nothing. Just give me the guts of it."

Wild Horse said: "I expect you know I've rode San Felice. He's the best Lute's got, ain't he?"

"Anyway," Shorty said, rushing on with it, "I know how *he* runs; an' I tell you, Fritchet, I got a horse that kin beat him—"

"Beat *San Felice*!" Fritchet laughed. "Boy, you're crazy!"

"All right," Shorty said. "They laughed at Columbus, too, don't forget." And he turned straight around like he was quitting the premises.

"Here! Wait—hold on!" Fritchet grumbled. "I never said

I wouldn't listen. But you've got to admit—"

"I ain't admittin' nothin'. You want t' see this horse run, or don't you?"

"No strings?"

"You be over t' Hague's pasture at sun-up tomorrer. I'm goin' t' show you somethin'— I'm goin' t' show you a horse that'll run Sand Fleas ragged!"

And again Shorty turned to climb back in the saddle.

But Fritchet wouldn't have it that way. He left go of his lip and caught Shorty's shoulder.

"Here—wait a bit, will you? What's the damn hurry? Man would think you come after a chunk of fire instead of—But, about this horse: what horse is it? Has he got a track record? What's his bloodlines—breeding? Can I put a clock on him?"

"You kin bring a wash tub full if you wanta. Bring anything you want; but come alone an' keep yore mouth shut. There's a kind of path worn around Hague's fence—on the inside, I mean. A little rough. Ain't much like a track, but it'll do, I reckon."

"That's a pretty small pasture," Fritchet said dubiously.

"It's more'n a half mile around the inside though—What do you think I'm stagin'—a marathon?"

"This bronc'll have to be *good*. You know what the stud's time was last year, don't you? Forty-nine and a half! That's a tough time t' beat without you're running a Thoroughbred."

Shorty said: "I kin worry about that for both of us. You be there an' bring your check book."

"Damn it all! *Wait* a minute!" Fritchet growled, grabbing a hold again. "You haven't told me this critter's name even—"

"He'll run jest as fast without any name. By the way,"

Shorty said, as though carelessly, "what kinda breedin' has San Felice got? Who's he by and what out of?"

"Seems like I heard he was by Nadir by Mesaoud by Aziz—anyhow, it was a bunch of Arabs," Fritchet said. "His dam was a PHBA palomino Dickerson leased from the Double N—"

"That accounts fer it—f' the speed, I mean. That Arab background. Arabs is fast—*dang*fast; but it takes quite a stretch, McGee says, t' warm 'em up to it. Time we got back t' town tonight Lute's stud was really layin' 'em down. But on a half-mile track—"

"Forty-nine an' a half," Fritchet said like he didn't aim to have anyone forgetting it. "He's won that race three years hand-running—"

"That hand'll need a whip *this* year," Shorty told him.

"Talk's cheap," Fritchet said, "but it takes hard cash—"

"That's where you come into the deal. You back my bet and, when we git Lute's money, you take two-thirds. That's fair enough, ain't it?"

"I'll watch him," Fritchet said, "but I make no promises. Just remember that—I ain't promisin' nothing."

But he was right there and waiting when Shorty arrived at Hague's pasture next morning. The sun hadn't yet got over the mountains and the brush to the north of Hague's fenceline was still plenty dark with Night's leftover shadows.

Fritchet's greeting was dour. He had had to get up before breakfast and he felt pretty sure this was all a wild goose chase. "Where's your horse?" he said, scowling round suspiciously.

"Right here," Shorty grinned, and slapped Figure 8's shoulder. "Bring your clock?"

"You goin' to run *that* thing? Hell! I thought you was serious—"

"Never mind passin' any toadstool boo-kays. This lad's got some dang good ancestors. He kin trace straight back t' old Figure 2, an' I guess you know what a runnin' fool *he* was! Most advertized horse owned in the West, an' this shaggy boy's goin' t' be jest like him."

Fritchet made a noise with his tongue sticking out; but he fetched out his stop-watch anyway. It was an antique affair made some place in Switzerland with great fancy hands and a painted face. But he guessed it would work and keep time good enough.

"Okay," Wild Horse said. "I'll let the old boy at it. Y' want t' remember though, no bronc does his best till you git him warmed up; jest keep that in mind because we're tryin' him cold."

This was not quite the truth. It was a good ten miles from Shorty's ranch to this pasture, and Figure 8 had not walked all that distance, either. But a lot of the appearances here this morning were not strictly as represented. Unbeknownst to Fritchet and Shorty, Lute Dickerson and Cinch, stop-watches in hand, swapped a grin with each other off yonder in the brush; and Baisy, agile-minded hussy, likewise had *her* eyes glued to the fenceline.

"Another thing," Shorty mentioned as though the idea had just come to him; "when we race Figure 8 in the Sweepstakes we'll have someone else up—someone lighter, an' he won't be carryin' no stock saddle."

"Okay—okay," Fritchet grumbled. "Quit wastin' breath an' get at it. Ready?—then *go!*

"Wait a sec," Shorty said, and climbed out of the saddle. "I better wind 'im—it's the Model T in his bloodlines, I reckon." He grabbed the stud's tail and gave a couple quick twists, ducking barely in time to escape the slammed hoofs. Figure 8 put his ears back and swung his head like an outraged snake; but Shorty was ready for that one, too. "Here we go!" he cried and made a grab for the horn; and the snorting bronc took off like a twister.

They were halfway around the fenceline before Wild Horse got his pants in the saddle, and ere he had gotten his breath, they were back.

"What's that timepiece tell you?"

Fritchet stood chewing the ends of his mustache. "It ain't possible!" he growled in a stunned kind of voice. "There's somethin' gone wrong with this confounded watch—" He broke off and shook the thing savagely. "Ain't *no* horse could do it!" he muttered—"not no grass-fed crowbait like you got!"

"Musta been pretty good," Wild Horse chuckled.

"Fifty seconds! Why, the thing's *impossible*!"

"Suit yoreself," Shorty said. "I expect I kin interest somebody else in this crowbait—"

"Here—hold on!" Fritchet grunted. "What'll you take for that plug?"

"You ain't achin' t' *buy* him?" Wild Horse looked down his nose; raised his eyebrows.

"Cash money," Fritchet said. "Paid right in your hand. How much?"

"I wasn't figurin'—"

"I'll give you two hundred." Fritchet tugged out his wallet.

"For a horse that kin cover such a track in *that* time? Uh-uh. No soap."

"Now," Fritchet said, "let's be reasonable. I'll admit fifty seconds is pretty good— I'll own it *surprised* me, even. But San Felice's time is forty-nine and a half—"

149

"Not on no ground like this, it ain't! What's more, his time was took on a half-mile flat. This here's better'n a half mile, an' dang mean goin'. Keep yore money— I'll git someone in Tucson t' back me. Walker Hyde or—"

"*I*'ll back you," Fritchet scowled, "if you'll sell me the horse. Look here—I'll give you three hundred."

"Ain't you scared that wallet'll squeal?"

Fritchet glared. "I'll give you four hundred dollars—an' not one damn cent more!"

"So long," Shorty said, and climbed back in the saddle. "I kin do better in Tucson without liftin' my voice."

The saloonkeeper glowered. He slammed down his hat and stamped on it. But he spoke quick enough when he saw Shorty leaving. "Here—*wait*! Hang hold, you halfwit; I was only kiddin'. Four fifty's an awful price, but I'll do it, dang you—"

"You'll give me four fifty—an' put up the cash fer my bet with Dickerson?"

Fritchet nodded, still glowering. "An' you keep your trap shut till after the Sweepstakes. If it ever gets out I've bought this horse we'll never be able to clear a nickel on him—Here's your money. Just write me a receipt on this envelope . . . . Now run him around that fence again."

"Might not make it so good this time."

"Never mind. You run him. Start whenever you're ready."

So Figure 8 raised the dust once more; and when they got back Fritchet's eyes were gleaming.

"How bad was it?" Shorty asked, poking a tailormade into his face and lighting it up with a flick of his thumbnail. "Fifty-seven? Fifty-eight?"

Fritchet closed the case of his watch with a snap. "Just a shade less than fifty. Why—*we'll peel the shirt right off Lute's back*!"

150

WILD HORSE

15.

ON DUDES AND BANGTAILS

All the way home Shorty seriously debated if, now that he had all this money in his pockets, it might not be smart to run up to Phoenix and get that loose end tucked in pronto. On the other hand, as things stood right now it was Fritchet who stood to be lining his pockets if Figure 8 galloped off with the Sweepstakes. Not content with two-thirds of the wager money, Fritchet claimed as his additional right—by virtue of being Figure 8's new owner, the twenty-five hundred dollar Sweepstakes purse. This little item had escaped Shorty's notice and the saloonman had slyly refrained from mentioning it until after the deal was completed. Therefor Shorty, if he were to get anything at all for his trouble, would certainly have to get it by betting; and the bookmakers' policy was for strictly cash business, so it looked like Phoenix would better wait awhile.

It was still fairly early in the morning, and he was angling to bypass the Crossing, when he noticed a dust cutting in from the south. It was McGee on the Palamoosa, alias old Wire-Cut, alias whatever came handiest when you wanted to call her. They seemed to be headed for the hoof-shaper's shop and Wild Horse, curious, decided to follow them.

Harold Cochrane, the blacksmith's mother had named him, but because he was big he was called "Little Harold"; and as Shorty rode up he was squatted by the anvil, hunkered back on his brogans, astonishedly giving McGee's mount the once over. "So this is the famous 'purple horse', is it? Boy, she's a daisy. Betcha she goes right back to the Stone Age—where'd you uncover her, Shorty?"

"Never mind wise-cracking," Wild Horse muttered. "She's got a heart of gold, no matter if she does look a little mite queer. She's got bottom, too—which is more'n you kin say fer a lot of them fancy ones." He turned to scowl at McGee. "What's the big idear," he said huffily, "ridin' her when you had the whole cavvoy t' pick from?"

"When you got somethin' special," McGee winked at Harold, "you might's well get a little advertizin'."

"She don't need no advertizin'," Wild Horse growled. "Why, dang it, you mighta killed the ol' goat, ridin' her all that ways with the scours—"

"I got her practically cured of the scours," McGee said; and right then Wire-Cut lifted her tail.

Shorty glared. "If that mare kicks off," he said dustily, "you won't git no pay till hell freezes—"

But McGee just grinned in the sour way he had. "Don't look like I'll get any anyway," he said; and Shorty was making to ride off mad when he pulled up short and snarled:

"Lookit that setfast!"

McGee looked and said, "What about it? She's got

another one on the other side twice as bad—"

"An *you*, what's supposed to know horses, ridin' her!"

"Shucks. What ridin' I'm doin' ain't hurtin' 'em. A setfast," McGee's was the tone used to lecture the young, "ain't nothin' but a agg'avated saddle gall. It was Hellbound brung them out on her. The skirts of that saddle he favors is curled from the way he throws it down when he's done with it. This round-skirted saddle don't even touch 'em."

"What else's she got wrong with her?" Little Harold asked, grinning.

"She's all right," McGee said. "Get busy on them shoes—I got a heap of chores t' get done before dinner. Y' ought've been round for breakfast," he told Shorty who was looking mean enough to be taken for a tax collector. "You ought've seen that Oneco dude eatin' cooked radishes. Thought they was rudabakers. Like to of throwed the whole works up when I said how good them radishes was. 'Minded me of the one he played on Hellbound. Hank was always borryin' his Redman, so Farrar took t' cachin' it out places, but the ol' man kept right on gettin' into it. So the dude, he fixed up a sack of secondhands, an' next time he seen Hellbound chawin' he says, 'Hope you ain't got into that sack I had in the box stall—them was old ones I was savin' for Wire-Cut.' Gentlemen, howdy! You never see a guy look so plum reproachful."

"Must've turned him pretty near inside out," Harold said.

But McGee shook his head. "Nope. He's still chewin' from the same ol' sack."

Shorty figured Hellbound had monopolized enough talk. "How come you're hevin' ol' Wire-Cut plated?"

"Little idea I'm workin' on. There's a pile of ailments can

153

be traced right back to a horse's feet. Take lampers now—there's a lot of folks figures greasin' their tails is the quickest way to rid 'em of it. Some has an idea cuttin' off the last joint of the tail will help 'em—splittin's pretty good if it's a fistula you're workin' on; but me, I always get the best results just workin' on their feet. Reckon I've spent more time with horses' hoofs than most guys spends with the gals they get hitched to. I studied the blacksmithin' business once—Maw always said I cut my teeth on an anvil; but the more I see of 'em the more I figure the most of your e-quine troubles comes right up outa their feet. Now you take that setfast—take both of 'em, even. I'll have them things off inside of a week."

Shorty said nothing, but the hoof-shaper grinned. "Not by whittling on her feet, you won't."

Back in the brush to the north of Hague's pasture, Dickerson was giving Phil Cinch a look no man would ordinarily take unless it came from his wife. "Why, damn it!" he burst out bitterly, "that lop-eared critter might actually *beat* us! Fifty seconds—an' on *that* kind of going! It gives me a cramp in my gut just to think of it."

"Don't then," Baisy smiled cutely. "No real need to, is there?"

Dickerson's eyes came round narrowly. "How's that?"

"Well . . . perhaps Figure 8 won't run," Baisy said. "There's almost a fortnight between now and the Sweepstakes. Shorty might even change his mind—"

"Won't make any difference if he *does* change his mind. That stud belongs to your father now."

"Perhaps he won't . . . very long," Baisy said. She gave a quick hitch to her garters and giggled. "I'll take care of Father for you."

Cinch showed his teeth in a wolfish grin. "And I'm just

the lad to take care of that horse for you—"

"You'll have to be careful," Baisy warned; and Lute said crossly:

"We don't want no rough stuff—no more bungling. This has got to be smooth. You keep Rimfire out of it."

Cinch winked at Baisy.

Dickerson said: "Has he got anything else in that bunch he could enter with?"

"I might give him two," Cinch murmured reflectively —"and that's being generous. I'd give him entries, but they're last-chance hopes, either one of them. Pair of fillies. Ringboned dun he calls 'Dust Churner' that'll go lame before she's took ten hops, and a grulla named 'Trymore' that'll roar like a freight crossing the Cienega trestle. Cheer up; you good as got that money in your pocket."

"But it's a three-horse entry—"

"So what? He'll enter Trymore, Dust Churner and Figure 8. Let him. We'll collect that bet just like guttin' a slut."

But Dickerson flipped up his eyebrows. "You aimin' to let that cussed stud *run?*"

"Why not? Look better, won't it? I thought you wanted this smooth."

"That's cuttin' it pretty damn fine!"

"Okay. Get it out of your hair. Closest competition we'll have for that purse will be that Double N Morgan and the Diamond Bell mare. Let's get home. You worry too much."

Back at the ranch Shorty found Mrs. Fergie helping Rose in the cookshack. Both her dogs were outside watching Hellbound who was vigorously scrubbing Dust Churner's tail with a grease-soaked corncob. He had the dun tied up to a snubbing post and every few seconds the mare would open her mouth like she figured to gobble every last thing in sight; then she'd drop down her head and take a look at her stomach.

Wild Horse ran up and grabbed Hellbound's shoulder. "What in hell's furnace do you reckon you're doin'?"

"This mare's got colic," Hellbound scowled. "Leave loose of me—"

"Take that bacon grease back to the cookshack. There's times, by grab, I don't think you got 'em all! Farrar—run over to the barn an' git me that bottle of paregoric an' the one that says 'appapectin' off the medicine shelf; we got to drench this horse an' drench her pronto!"

He untied the mare and she hit the ground and stretched out flat. Wild Horse looked at her dubiously. Hellbound came back from the cookshack and said: "Them mares—"

"Get away," Shorty growled, "you make her nervous."

"But them mares—"

"Never mind. Way you been slappin' that bacon grease on 'em it's a wonder they ain't *all* down with somethin'. Get a pick and a shovel—Go on! *Scram!*" he shouted at Mitzy who was dashing back and forth and hectoring the mare. "Go tie up that dog so the mare kin roll; then get busy and lower that pipe at the spring end. Water's gone down s' much there ain't but a trickle of it comin' through, and that tank out back's as empty as yore head is!"

"But them mares—"

"Will you do like I *told* you? Tie up that dog—"

"But the rest of them mares is out!"

"Out?"

"Well, look fer yoreself!" Hellbound grunted. "See 'em?

—there they go! Peltin' fer Dickerson's!"

Shorty swore and felt plumb like screaming.

Farrar came up with the bottles he'd gone for. "You'll hev t' do it," Shorty told him hurriedly. "Two parts paregoric, six parts appapectin an' the rest plain water—get a bucket or a bottle an' shake it up good."

"What do I do then?" Farrar said.

"*Drench her!*" Shorty snarled, and made off after Hellbound. He swung the old man around. "Git yore rope!"

He hurried to catch up Figure 8 where he'd turned him out in the pole corral. Luckily he had not put his saddle away but had hung it, with the bridle, on the top corral rail. He grabbed for the bridle and ducked under the bars.

But Figure 8 had other ideas. He very likely figured he had worked a-plenty for *one* day, what with all that racing and that ride back and forth. He was craving some grain or some hay—not that bridle. He kept edging around with a nice eye for distance, warily keeping his head just beyond Shorty's reach.

Wild Horse scowled and made a dive for him.

Figure 8, with a snort, swapped ends like lightning. His head ducked down and his heels went up; and he came mighty close to taking Shorty's hat off.

Shorty slammed down the bridle and went for his rope.

He was getting it off the saddle when his glance fell athwart Mr. Farrar and his doings.

"Ahr—" Shorty growled, "t' hell with it!" and he let go the rope and climbed from the pen. "If there's one damn thing more useless as a dude, I'd admire t' know what it is, by godfries!"

Hellbound came lugging his rope from the bunkhouse where he always slept with it under his pillow. "Go ahead," Shorty said. "You'll hev t' git 'em; that dude over there's got a priority on me. Take Figure 8 an' if you run into Lute don't swap no back talk."

Striding off, he dug up a whisky bottle from the dump Lute had built alongside the cookshack. Then he crossed to a pail on the wash bench and dippered him out some of the sun-warmed water. Carrying bottle and dipper he tramped over to where Mr. Farrar had tied Dust Churner. The dude had got her up onto her feet again and there she stood, a most dreary picture.

"Any of that left?" Shorty asked in a tone that was closely bordering sarcasm.

Mr. Farrar looked perplexed. "What's wrong?" he asked, holding out the bucket. "Ain't I drenched her enough? She looks pretty wet—"

"That stuff," Shorty said, "was s'posed to go *inside* of her."

16.

"NEVER MIND ABOUT ME!"

That afternoon, while Shorty was baking himself on the porch so the dudes could feel like they were getting their money's worth, Mrs. Fergie rose up and suddenly sprang from her chair.

"Fred—quick!" she cried, pointing. "There's Indians up in those mountains—don't you *see* it? Away up there near the farthest peaks?" She whirled to Shorty. "That's smoke talk, isn't it?"

Wild Horse squinted and let go of an oath. "That's a forest fire, ma'am, an' it looks like a bad one!"

"But there isn't any forest up there— Why, that rock looks as naked as a jelly bean!"

"It may look that way t' you," Shorty said, "but there's thousands of acres of timber up there and—"

"Well," Mrs. Fergie said sharply, "don't stand there! *Do* something!"

Shorty said patiently, "Them mountains is the Rincons. By trail that fire's eighty mile from here, an' it ain't no trail you kin use a car on. Anyway," he added to comfort her, "the Rangers'll hev seen it by now an' they'll be doin' whatever they think kin be done fer it. Jest keep yore seat, ma'am. They'll take care of it."

After a considerable discussion of forest fires the talk bogged down in other subjects till the Tyrone man, wiping off his glasses, asked if Shorty thought it likely the sheriff would catch those store robbers. Shorty opined it was not likely and furnished free a description of Potter that would have got him in jail had the sheriff heard him. He had just got through when Mrs. Potter appeared.

She was twirling her lorgnette around on its string and there was a suggestion of scowl between her sharp, roving eyes. "I think there must be something ailing that McGee; he's acting mighty peculiar. I think he must be sub-normal—you don't suppose the man's dangerous, do you?"

"What's the matter with him?" asked Wild Horse, shaking out a smoke from his packet of tailor mades.

"A-ah—*please!*" Mrs. Potter said, shying away from him. "I've hay fever, you know. Smoke—it's bad for me. I—I'm afraid I can't stand it."

Shorty scowled and put his cigarettes away. Times, he thought, was getting dang bad when a man couldn't smoke on his own porch, even.

Mrs. Potter said: "You've no idea what I found the man doing—he was inside that adobe patio. With the Palamoosa. Down in the dirt on his hands and knees and saying—you'll never believe it!—the craziest things. 'C'mon now, girl; pick it up, pick it up. For'ard a little—no! Not like that! Back up! A little more on the side—now this back one; step, now, step.' And then he'd pick up a foot and file it a little. Then he'd make her move again and file some other place. I think he's whacky—"

"He's getting her rid of the scours," Wild Horse said.

And Forest said: "He puts a lot of store in the care of the feet."

"He thinks feet is everything—"

"But what good could it do to file on those horse shoes?"

"I got no idear, ma'am. Mebbe it's them setfasts he's workin' on. Told me he could cure 'em inside of a week."

"He thinks feet is everything," Farrar said again. "Was telling me yesterday I needed mine worked on—said if I'd have my shoes built up a mite it would get me rid of—"

"Fred!" Mrs. Fergie said. "It is not very nice to go airing your ailments."

"Aw right," Farrar said grumpily. "Can I recite a little poetry?"

"Well, don't try to do it till you've spit that tobacco out."

"Goodness!" Mrs. Potter cried, clasping her hands. "Do you recite, Mr. Farrar? Do you write it yoreself?—Oh, how marvelous! How simply *divine*! It must be heavenly," she said to Mary, "to have a real live poet in the family. Obediah used to try his hand at it sometimes—before we were married. But just to think! Here we've had a poet in our very midst— You *must* come to our Literary Lantern next week, Mr. Farrar—it *is* Farrar, isn't it?—and read us some of your writings. Now, *really;* you simply *must*. Do you have anything you could do impromptu?"

"I could roll up my sleeves," Mr. Farrar said hopefully.

"Fred—quit acting up and recite something for us."

Mr. Farrar spat out his wad of Redman, adjusted his tie and said:

"I stood on the bridge at midnight
    And took out—"

"*Fred!*" Mary said.
"Well—what is it, Mary?"
"Mrs. Potter wouldn't care for that one—"
"How do you know she wouldn't? She hasn't heard—"
"*I* have," Mrs. Fergie said; "and *I* don't like it. It's vulgar—"
"Now what in the world is vulgar about a man taking out his watch?"
"Hey—wait a second," Shorty said. "Ain't that Hellbound?"
They all turned to look but he wasn't in sight yet. There was a dust coming through—and you could see its dun cloud spreading up through the greasewood that sat like a crown on the yonder hogback; and they could hear old Hellbound roaring:

"—Sweetest carol ever sung,
    Jesis, blessed Jesis."

" 'Sweetest story ever told' is the way we do it at the Tucson Methodist," Mrs. Potter informed them. "But a body couldn't hardly expect *him* to get the straight of anything. That wretched old man would distort the Lord's Prayer—if he knew it."
"Not that it's anything to do with the Lord's Prayer," said Farrar, "but I'd sure like to get in some of that shootin' you adve'tized. I was speaking to Brother Dickerson about it and he said he reckoned I could look for a season to start almost anytime now."
"Oh he did, did he!" Wild Horse muttered; and it almost seemed he might have turned a shade paler. Though it may have been just the way he got up—some trick of the

light as he stepped off the porch. "Excuse me, folks," he said gruffly; "I'll hev t' give Hellbound a hand with them mares."

Hellbound, peeling the saddle off Figure 8 later, said: "Might turn out t' be a mighty good thing them mares got away like they did—you know?"

"This ain't the time for hallelujahs. That pick an' that shovel is still sittin' there waitin'."

"Ef you ain't the dangdest guy," Hellbound sighed. "Allus twistin' an' squirmin'—a fella'd think y' had *worms*. As a matter of fack, I wasn't even thinkin' about thet pipe. What I meant, them mares got in with Lutes Arab stud—with thet *Galab* critter." He jabbed Shorty's ribs a jaunty dig with his elbow. "Ef haff them mares ain't stuck I'll eat 'em!"

An increasing unrest had got its hooks into Wild Horse. His appetite was poor and his sleep didn't give him any comfort. Mostly, his thoughts were like a horse on a treadmill and, like the horse, they did not get much of anyplace either. Just kept juning around like a fly in a bottle; and he layed the whole business onto Luther K. Dickerson.

Just about all of his troubles could be traced to Lute's doorstep. It would almost seem a relief, he thought, if the guy would brash up and fetch his gang over; that way they would get the thing done with. It was this all-the-time waiting that whipped a man down so—this never-know-what-to-expect-next part of it. Why, for two measly cents—way he felt right now—he would roll up his cotton and hit for the high spots.

Instead, he clapped on his hat and stamped out to the pasture. Looked like the whole place was asleep but himself; no lights showing and not so much as the tiniest mutter to break up the night's monotony. Only thing you could catch was such lonesome sounds as were stirred by the wind; those and the occasional grunt of a horse. The mares looked better since he had started graining them. Lespedeza, especially. But they were all picking up except Wire-Cut; feed did not make much difference with her.

Shorty hooked a boot on the fence wire. Sure got under his skin to think of Baisy turning down that ring so uppity; and after he'd argued almost half a day getting it. Giving him the high and mighty like he wasn't no more than dirt under her feet!

He let fly a couple of stored-up cusswords and, sudden-like then, found he wasn't alone. Off yonder, again the moon-laved tracery of the trembling cottonwoods, he saw Rose O'Grady. Alone. Like him.

She must have seen him, he guessed. But a fellow wouldn't know it. So he grunted kind of testy and went stomping over there.

"Well," she said, heaving up a sigh. "Be kinda sad to leave, won't it?"

"Leave what? Leave where?"

"Why, this ranch," she said. "There's only nine days more—"

"What are you talkin' about?" Wild Horse peered at her anxiously. "You got a fever?"

"You're not looking to be here after that race, are you?"

"Huh! Mebbe we won't lose that race—"

"Mebbe," she mimicked, "ducks won't swim. Be yore-self. Some ways you're a great guy, Wild Horse; I expect if you had a brain, there wouldn't be any stopping you. But—" she smiled wryly, "if you had any brain you wouldn't

164

have come here; so that doesn't get us much of anyplace, does it?"

"Don't none of it git us much of anyplace that *I* kin see. If you savvy what you're talkin' about, why not wrap a little English round it? That way, mebbe I could git yore drift."

"All right," she said; and the look of her someway got soft and got sad like. "It must have seemed a real bright idea, moving in like you did on Lute Dickerson; falling heir to this place. But you're not the first that's hankered to beat Lute; there's been a few others kind of figured they could do it. But where are they now? No, I'll tell you—they're planted."

"You . . . you mean—*dead*?"

"Plenty dead," said Rose dryly.

"But the law—"

"What law? Ain't you learned by now," she said pityingly, "that laws are made to keep the little man in line? Not that it matters," she said bitterly. "If we had an *honest* sheriff, you'd be no better off. You had a real chance when you started, but you threw it away buying presents for Baisy. When are you going to grow up and quit horsin' around after that—"

"You hesh!" Shorty growled, turning scarletly angry. "I ain't a-goin' t' stand fer no talk like that. Baisy Fritchet is a mighty sweet girl; she's the belle of Tucson an'—"

"Anyone that's got enough cash to afford her!" Rose stamped her foot, lips curling derisively. Then her chin came down and all the fire went out of her. "Go ahead; I can't help you. You've got to live and learn, my father used to say. But if you want to wind up like Gentleman Mac did—"

"Mac? Who's he?"

"Mac Jones—the last man that tried your stunt on a shoestring. *He* tried bucking Lute and, real sudden, he vanished. They say he pulled out—got discouraged and quit; but I knew Mac Jones. He wasn't that kind.

"Now look—" she said. "You've got just one chance. Get the goods on Lute before Lute gets them on you."

"Hoo hoo!" Wild Horse jeered. But it had a bad sound; and Rose nodded.

"You know what I mean. Like everybody else, Lute is sold on the notion you have leased this place. But if he ever thinks to go to Phoenix and check . . . ."

Rose had said quite enough. She'd said more than plenty.

Just as slick as a whistle—just by thinking things out, she had dropped her loop taut and true round the nubbin. She had got right down inside of him and uncovered the source of his worries.

Be a good idea, Shorty thought the next morning, to take all his mares over to Hague's for a workout. The Tucson Sweepstakes was a three-horse entry and, while he was pinning his hopes on the stud, he might just as well get a couple mares into it. Lespedeza, now, or Columbine, maybe.

He was just tramping over to breakfast when Hellbound loose-shackled up from the pasture. There was woe all over his herringbone features. "We're cooked!" he growled—"licked 'fore we started! Thet daggone stud's gone s' lame it's pitiful; he's out there hobblin' aroun' like a jackrabbit—won't touch his front foot down on the ground!"

McGee, coming back with the feed bags, nodded. "No use your glowerin'—he'll never run a step. You'll have to get that vet out again. He's got a thorn druv clean up into the fleshy part of his hoof—his off front one. Can't think how he done it. Horses're always foolin' round mesquites, but it's the first time I ever saw one druv in like that. You better send Hank in after that doc."

So Hellbound, on Columbine, took off for Doc Wallace; and just as the rest were finishing breakfast Cramp Fritchet rode over on his bay Morgan gelding. "What's this I hear about that stud I bought?" He got out of his saddle stiffly. "Baisy tells me—"

"And how would Baisy come to hear about it?" McGee asked, frowning; but Fritchet was not in a mood to be bothered with details.

"She says he's gone lame. Where is he? What're you doing about it? Is he going to be able to race?"

This was the first time that most of them had heard about Cramp Fritchet being the owner of Shorty's stud, Figure 8; but they all trooped down to the pasture where Nels had left the horse hitched to a fencepost. Even Rose and the dudes went along; and that Lee Forest man in his Hollywood glasses. They all clucked sympathetically and said soothing things to him when they saw what a misery old Figure 8 had. All but Fritchet. Fritchet said: "Tough. The deal's off—dig up my money."

"Well, you dadburned Injun! Why, fer—"

"None o' your back-chat! All I want is my money—an' be quick about it!" Fritchet snarled while the rest looked on in blank-eyed amazement. "You knew all the time that old skate couldn't win! You—"

"So I guess you ain't backin' my bet any more, eh?"

" 'Course I ain't backin' it! Do I look like a nizzy?"

Wild Horse shut his mouth real tight. He counted out the four hundred and fifty and bitterly flung it down into the dust; but that was all right with saloonman Fritchet. He scurried round nimbly and gathered it up. And when he was back in the saddle, and had picked up his reins and was ready to go, he said:

"Keep out of my place hereafter, and don't let me catch you moonin' round my Baisy! She ain't for no damn saddle tramp!"

"Ahr—no saddle tramp would hev her! There's a name fer her kind in the Bible, but I wouldn't embarrass these ladies by speakin' it. Jest tell her fer me she kin keep that saddle, an' I hope it wears holes in her underwear!"

Doc Wallace came out in the middle of the morning. "Lovely day," he said, passing out the blessing. He beamed around brightly, then he got out his gadgets and got down to cases. He took out all of the thorn he could get and showed no sign of any undue alarm; but as he doused the affected place with iodine he said, "McGee's right. You can't use this horse in any race for a while. Put him right in the barn and feed him lightly."

After the Doc had left and they had made the stud as comfortable as might be, McGee said grimly: "I ain't had no chance t' mention it sooner but that Tyrone drip had better be got out of here."

"It wasn't *him* done it—"

"I sure wouldn't bet on that," McGee said. "He was out there last night, in the dark, feelin' him over. I never *see* him do nothin'—you can bet if I had he'd be takin' a rest *permanent*. But if you want to play safe, git rid of him. There's somethin' wrong with that fella—always starin' or scribblin', scribblin' or starin'—it's enough, by cripes, t' give a fishworm the willies! An' now he's taken t' shavin'—shaved three times yesterday by my own personal count!"

McGee wiped his face with a handkerchief. "You know what I think? I think, by the gods, he's that nut from Phoenix!"

"No!"

"Yes, by godfries!"

Hellbound gulped "Lord God!" and departed.

But no one spoke of this to Mr. Forest. Shorty allowed he would keep an eye out for him, but he was a heap more worried about Luther K. Dickerson. For he did not doubt for one holy second who it was had spiked Figure 8's gun for him.

He had aimed, after that talk with Rose, to make sure of his lease right away, and no fooling. But that was out now. Fritchet reneging on the deal they had made had cut too vasty a hole in his bankroll. If he failed to back up that bet with Lute folks would laugh him clean out of the country. It would take every cent he could scrape up to do it; but he would rather go broke than be laughed at.

And he wouldn't admit they were licked—not to anyone.

"But, Shorty—" Rose said: "you can't *possibly* win."

"That's all right. I made the bet an' I'll stick to it."

"But what will you *run?*"

"Never mind about *me!* I'll run *somethin',*" Shorty blared, "if I hev t' git behind all the way an' push it!"

17.

A JUDGE NEVER BETS

And that was the way of things the eve of the running.

Piecing out what he had with a loan from McGee, who still had the bulk of his ranch sale money, Shorty had put up his thousand dollars and the entrance fees on his horses; but no one knew yet which hags he would run—not even the folks at the ranch had a notion. He was keeping his mouth tight shut this time. Speculation, however, was rampant. The whole country was nodding and winking about it and Dickerson had some good belly laughs. "Why, the damn fool might as well run himself as to pull anything out of *that* bunch!"

But the roundabout papers were whooping things up with a picture of Wild Horse on every front page. The *Tucson Citizen* called him "The Grassroots King of the Santa Cruz Valley" and the *Arizona Daily Star* poked uproarious fun at the "broomtail breeder" and his "band of scrub mares." But the *Denver Post* had the inside track, featuring daily exclusives replete with pictures and WHS datelines. They even broadly hinted he stood a good chance

170

of walking off with the money. But the only evidence to support this opinion was that their writer claimed to have seen a few tryouts and appeared quite impressed with what he—or she—had witnessed.

But the public just laughed all the harder. Regular Charlie McCarthy, that *Post* writer. Better than a circus, so long as you took him with plenty of salt. And that was the way they all took him; for they had not forgotten his great full-page spread on the medicine-splotched "Palamoosa". When it came to hot tips on the races, they would pick theirs up somewhere else, thank you kindly.

But they kept right on reading the papers and the *Denver Post* more than doubled its output. Wild Horse made good copy and the newspapers made the most of him.

Shorty and Hellbound rode off every day to chouse the old mares round Hague's pasture. Along toward the last they had large crowds of watchers—a few even coming from Tucson and Phoenix; and one fellow drove up from Ajo. They were a noisy bunch and passed plenty of comment but Wild Horse guffawed and winked with the best of them. He slapped people's backs and put on a show of trick riding and roping and passed out cigars till you'd have thought him a factory; but his head was not turned by a long shot. He knew all these folks had come out for a show, and he made sure each batch had a good one.

Dickerson had announced his entries and, like everyone had figured, they were all palominos, PHBA registered: San Felice, San Salvator and San Luis de la Paz, the three best runners in the Dickerson stud and—to quote again the *Tucson Citizen*—"every last one of them fit for a king."

Doc Wallace told Shorty, "Outside of Figure 8, which

you can't run noway, you ain't got a horse in the bunch which can ever get near enough to smell Lute's dust! You better kiss that thousand dollars goodbye."

"Worries you, does it?"

"No skin off my fingers, but I hate to see you made a fool of that way. You might have known—"

"Of *course* I knew," Shorty scowled. "It's jest one of Lute's stunts t' bust me—but what else *could* I do when he come right out with it public that way?"

"You didn't have to oblige him—"

"An hev the whole blame push gimme the horse laff, eh?"

"They're laughing now," Wallace pointed out, and Shorty stamped off in a fury.

"What's the Big Shot running?" Dickerson asked with a laugh when the Doc came over to check on his entries.

Doc Wallace frowned and rubbed his ankle. He said, at last, testily: "Does it make any difference? I suppose he'll enter Dust Churner, certainly. Very possibly Trymore. But neither of them will much more than get started—that Trymore groans like a busted accordion; it's a shame to take the fellow's money away from him."

"He should have thought of that," Lute said, "before he moved in on me. I try to treat everyone fairly and squarely and I'd go out of my way to do the right thing; but I let *no* man wipe his boots on me. When I find myself with a Philistine . . ."

And Rose said to Wild Horse: "You ought to let folks know which horses you're running. People have lost all kinds of good money—"

"Ain't that too bad?" Shorty said without sympathy.

"It isn't right and you know it isn't. Mr. Farrar says the racing people are furious with you—you knew he'd been made one of the judges, didn't you?"

"That wart! What's *he* know about racin'? I guess that's another one of Lute's slick tricks—that guy don't aim t' take *no* dang chances!"

"I'm surprised at you, Wild Horse. You know Mr. Farrar would never stoop—"

"Oh, he wouldn't, eh? Lemme tell you somethin'. Lute an' that guy has got thicker than clabber—spends s' much of his time over at Dickerson's lately a fella would think the dang dude was *livin'* there! All he shows up around here for's his grub!"

"You know that's not so! If he goes over to Lute's it's because he likes Lute's horses. Why, he's potty about them; you should—"

But Shorty had heard all he cared to on that line. He clapped on his hat and stamped off toward the stable to see how Figure 8 was getting along. As he was passing the remodeled harness shed he heard the high clack of Hellbound's voice and, sudden like, a hearty, kind of tickled sort of chuckle from Forest.

Shorty ground his teeth with the bitterness of fury.

Even the dudes had taken to laughing!

After lunch—more cooked radishes, he saddled Lespedeza and rode down to the Crossing. There he sent off a wire to the *Denver Post*. Then he bought a few things at Provencher's Mercantile—among them glue and a book he could paste things in. After which he rode over to the saddle shop and made a brief call on Doc Wallace.

The Doc pumped his hand and got out some cigars. "Try one—here, put a couple in your pocket. A new brand I have shipped in from the coast. How do you like them?" he asked as Shorty fired up; and Wild Horse said ungraciously:

"Taste like them three-fers I been givin' away. Look here; jest before that race gits started t'morrer I want you to give Lute's stuff the saliva test—savvy? I don't aim fer him t' put nothin' else over on me."

"He might refuse."

"He won't open his mouth," Shorty said. "He can't afford to—not after all that talk he's stirred up. You give him the works."

"He could insist that yours—"

"You kin test mine any time you git in the notion. You won't find no High Life inside o' *my* horses!"

"But what— I mean, which ones are you figuring on entering, Shorty?"

"Dust Churner, Trymore an' Cannonball—now rush over an' tell Lute *that*, why don't you?"

The Doc looked pained; but just the same, almost before Shorty's dust had settled he was driving his piebald buggy mare, Toothpick, over a little used trail toward Lute's place. He had his living to look after, and the way things looked to him right now old Luther K. was still going to be here a long time after Shorty wasn't anything more than a name out of memory.

" 'Cannonball', eh?" Dickerson said with a sneer, and his dark eyes glittered malevolently. "Which nag is it?"

"I don't know," Wallace said. "He's going to insist your horses be given the saliva test."

Baisy—she was over there, too—threw back her curls and laughed till the tears came. "Oh dear!" she cried. "The poor boob hasn't a gram of sense, has he?"

But Phil Cinch said with a reflective frown. "He might not be quite the damn fool that we take him for. He's been acting all week like he's got some kind of joker up his sleeve—"

"How could he have?" Dickerson rasped irritably. "The terms of the wager are plain enough, surely. He's bound by those terms just as tightly as I am, and I'll make sure they're announced again before the race tomorrow. Why, he hasn't got a chance without outside blood."

And Baisy said: "Of course not—he's just bluffing again."

"Maybe so," Cinch said. "But we'd better have Doc—"

"Nonsense! Utter rot and nonsense! He hasn't got a chance—not with all the High Life in Texas!"

The racing commission and its selected judges was holding a final meeting that night in Ben's Happy Harp at the Horsehead Crossing. As Farrar was about to drive off to attend it Shorty came up and tapped the dude's shoulder. "You kin tell that outfit I'm runnin' Trymore, Dust Churner an' Cannonball. I've already notified the newspapers."

"Okay," Farrar said, and let out the clutch; then he stamped his foot down on it hurriedly. "How're you fixed for money, Wild Horse? If you want to get in on the bettin' I can—"

"Keep yore coin," Wild Horse growled. "I ain't askin' no favors off *no*body. Didn't notice you offerin' t' hold my head when Figure 8 got that thorn in his hoof." He turned to move off, then said over his shoulder, "By the way, Oneco, which one of Lute's nags are you backin'?"

"Oh, a judge never bets," Farrar reminded him virtuously.

"So you ain't gettin' in it—"

175

"My wife is." Farrar winked. "Backin' the same horse Rose and McGee are. Well—keep yore guns oiled."

He waved and drove off; and Wild Horse stood a long while frowning after him.

18.

THE TUCSON SWEEPSTAKES

The day of the race dawned bright and fair.

Shorty was out and around before breakfast, whistling away like a happy young mocker, when McGee came up bleary eyed and said, "They're as ready now as they ever *will* be. Got the burrs combed out of those two skates' tails an' Hellbound's out there keepin' a eye on 'em. Whew!" he growled, "I'm about pegged out—that kid showed up yet?"

"Not yet," Shorty said, " but that race don't start until two o'clock. How's Cannonball?"

McGee grinned sour-like and shifted his chew. "Be all right if she don't come down with them scours again. Just t' play things safe I've cached her out in that shed off yonder. Keep them dudes away an' don't let Hellbound throw any feed in her."

"Jest a sec—" Shorty said. "Which horse are you backin'?"

McGee gave him a saturnine look and grunted. "Joke—ha-ha!" Then he turned and went wearily off toward the bunkhouse.

"Now look!" Shorty growled, overhauling him. "I'm serious. Did you tip—"

"I didn't tip nobody. When I work for a man I keep my mouth shut."

"Well, that dude—"

"Dudes!" McGee said; and went into the bunkhouse and slammed the door.

Shorty looked kind of beat and went over to breakfast. McGee was probably right, he reflected. Dudes was dudes, and there wasn't no sense getting worked up over it. Farrar was just trying to be funny, most likely.

But Farrar wasn't there for his breakfast. And when Shorty asked Rose about it she said: "He rode out of here more than an hour ago. I fixed him a raw egg and some coffee. He saddled up Columbine and rode off toward Dickerson's."

Wild Horse quit chewing and looked plainly uneasy.

Mrs. Fergie said: "He'll be all right. As a boy, in Vermont, he used to ride a great deal; he was practically raised with horses. Of course, since he's been sick—it's his lungs, you know. But this air out here has been fine for him. All this heat and—"

"I wasn't worried 'bout his *health*," grunted Wild Horse; and Lee Forest turned and looked out of the window.

Wild Horse glowered at him huffily. Then he mopped up the egg in his plate with some toast and made up his mind, when the rest had departed, he would question Rose about which horse she was backing.

But it looked like Farrar's wife would dawdle all day, so he finally got up and stamped outside. Lee Forest got up and strolled out after him.

"Lovely day," he said pleasantly after the style of Doc Wallace. "Be a glorious day for the race by the look of it. Have you seen the programs? Unique is the word for them." He brought a throwaway out of his pocket and passed it. "Too bad they didn't get Cannonball's name in; I notice they've got your other two down."

Shorty looked at the program indifferently. "S'prised Jelks ain't entered Old Joe."

"You mean the Quarter horse? Joe Reed II? I thought he belonged to a cowboy—to that fellow, Bert Wood—"

"Did I say he didn't? That don't keep him from standin' at Jelks' does it?"

"But he's got a bad knee," Forest said. "Didn't somebody tell me he got into the wire?"

"Sure—a long time back. He done growed up with his knee like that. Didn't hurt him last week in the Horse Show, did it? He was Grand Champion of the 1942 Tucson Horse Show—an' better'n that last week, by godfries! Grabbed Grand Championship Cowhorse honors an', besides bein' best in show, was first in the heavyweight stallions class, an' top spot in get of all them studhorses! What more do you want in a Quarter horse, dang it! You know what his time on the track was two years ago? 22.3—an' that's *movin'*!"

Forest nodded. He was staring again. Looking kind of vague toward the blue-rimmed line of the Tumacacoris. "The Double N's entering their Morgan, Nan Tucket."

"An' that two-year-old palomino—What's her name?"

"Pola Ne-Ag-Ray," forest said. "Nice little mare. Got a lot of class. Had her picture in *Western Livestock* a while ago."

Wild Horse fingered the program and scowled. "Can't see what they want t' go enterin' all them fancy breeds fer."

"Imagine they're doing it more for the sport than with any real hope of taking the money," Forest said. "Folks with good horses usually like to show them. Take this Standardbred now—"

"Good horse; I've seen him. But he won't hev a chance in this kind of a race—nor them Saddlebreds, neither," Shorty growled, disgusted. "An' whoever told that Walkin' Horse owner—"

"Everyone to their taste—"

"Every time," Shorty nodded. "But from what I hear of it this Tucson Sweepstakes ain't a heap different from a cattle stampede! You wouldn't ketch *me* puttin' no registered horse in it!"

"Perhaps that's why they're not running Joe Reed."

Shorty scowled at him slanchways. "You seem t' know quite a pile about racin'. Got any money up? Which horse you backin'?"

"Expect I better be getting my nap," Forest said, getting up. He peered around vaguely. "Doctor's orders, you know. Well—see you at the race, Shorty."

Wild Horse shoved back his hat and scowled after Forest. Seemed a shame for a man who could talk so bright when the mood was on him, to get himself saddled with a thing like that. Shorty reckoned he had ought to pass on the word and let the sheriff take Forest off his hands.

No, by grab, he'd be danged if he would. The law hadn't never done *him* any favors.

Farrar, of course, had gone off on Columbine; but the rest of them, Mrs. Fergie said, could all go in the Dodge if Rose would drive it. Just an hour or so before they were ready, a horse van from Fletcher's drove up for their entries; and Shorty told McGee to ride along with them and to keep his eye skinned out for trouble from Dickerson.

Then he said to Hellbound: "Dang funny where that kid has got to. You reckon he understands it's *today* we want him?"

"I tol' Rosita an' she said she'd hev him yere—but you know them Mex'cans. Always man-yanner."

"I'll man-yanner *him* if he don't show up. Git the dudes in the car whilst I hustle up Rose."

Rose was putting the finishing touches on her hair before the cracked mirror in the cookshack. She looked right tricky in her lavender-flowered print. "These *freckles!*" she groaned. "I can't do a thing with them!"

"Never mind," Wild Horse said; "I've come t' *like* them freckles. They're common as dirt an' jest as honest—which is more'n you kin say fer *most* things round here."

She whirled, eyes big with surprise and pleasure. "Why, Shorty! That's the nicest thing you've ever said!" Then she said, as though remembering, "But of course you don't mean it—"

"The hell I don't! Take a squint at *this*!" and he flashed the ring he had got for Baisy.

"Try it on," Shorty said; and when he saw the look of her eyes he swept her into his arms and kissed her.

"You—you mean it for *me*? You mean you want me to *wear* it?"

"Sure—why not? Jest fer luck," he said; and all the radiant joy went out of her.

"I don't wear rings just for luck," she said, and she handed it back and left him standing there.

The ranch headquarters of the Roman Four was a blaze

of color that afternoon. Flags and streamers and gay bits of bunting were everywhere fluttering in the desert breeze. The big yard was packed, and mobs of people lined the trackside and gabbed and wagered where the jockeys were fiddling around with the horses; and a clutter of cars, spring wagons and buckboards was parked every which way, just where their drivers had jumped out and left them.

It was so doggoned noisy you couldn't hear your head rattle.

Dickerson had a good track for a training course, loamy and loose from constant harrowing. The rails were of four-by-fours, white painted and sturdy. It was a half-mile course with a judges' stand and modern stall gates. Right up to the minute—you could trust Lute for that. You could always trust him to put in the flourishes. He never sold a horse with anything less than a good leather halter on it, and, if the price were especially attractive, he sometimes even chucked in a new saddle.

At Moltaqua such music as pleasured the customers was dragged up out of records via a public address system. But nothing like that for Luther K. Dickerson.

"Oh—look!" Mrs. Fergie cried, pointing. "Over there—in those cowboy suits! Aren't they the ones who play for the KVOA Barn Dance at the Pioneer Hotel down in Tucson?"

They were, sure enough. Larry and his Sunset Riders, all togged out in rodeo clothes and riding up high and handsome on the choicest of Lute's palominos. Yes sir! There they were, turning loose with *Riding Down the Canyon,* and the whole bunch played like forty monkeys, just like they did at the Pioneer Hotel. Jerry, of course, didn't have his piano, but he more than made up for the lack of it by the way he was swinging that squeak-box around; and Larry a-strumming away on his guitar, and Chick with his tooter and Jack all puffed up around his black clarinet. But the best treat of all was to see little Woody tucked up in the saddle behind his bass viol.

"Lively affair!" Clark called to Buck Fletcher; and it *did* look to shape up pretty dang handsome. All the counts of the country had gathered, and more than a few of the no-accounts also. The Mayor of Tucson was jovially present; and smiling Nick Hall on his big prancing charger; and there was Wiley McCray in his checked shirt and derby and Juan Salinas, the Iowa calf roper—even "Fog Horn" Clancy had flown down for the day. Rodeo talent was well represented and a KTUC man with his bagful of gadgets was rushing in circles like a chicken with its head off.

Shorty, peering ahead as he barged through the talkers, saw that most of the owners were already over by the judges' stand. And over there, too, he saw the *Hoofs & Horns* editor, "Ma" Hopkins, chewing the rag with stocky-built Ben, the Rodeo Tailor; and, just behind, stood cute Polly Mills with her mouth open, laughing.

19.

"OH, IT'S 'ARD TO GO WRONG ON THE RACES"

Just as Wild Horse and his exclaiming dudes quit the
saddling paddock, and Lute was giving his jockeys the
final secrets, Donald Coyle gave over his bickering with a
Yuma grass raiser, climbed into the judges' stand, gently
and firmly set Mr. Farrar to one side and said in his
plump, twinkling way through the microphone:

"Hello, everybody! This is your master of ceremonies,
Donald Coyle, speaking. I want, first of all, to apologize,
folks for any inconvenience those programs have caused
you. Several entries came in so late we simply didn't have
time to wait for them and that is why you find those blank
spaces where the names should be found. I believe the
committee is at work on the drawing for post positions
now. While we are waiting there are one or two announce-
ments I'd like to get in.

"Three of the listed entries are being withdrawn and
will not start; Pola Ne-Ag-Ray, Dust Churner and Trymore.
I would like to mention, also, the thousand-dollar wager
that is up between Mr. Wild Horse Shorty and Mr. Luther

Dickerson. Mr. Dickerson has bet his palomino stud, San Felice, will come off better in this race than any horse Shorty may enter. Since Shorty is withdrawing two of his three entries, this means the sole horses concerned with the wager are San Felice and Shorty's third entry, Cannonball. Now this bet, please remember, is *not* based upon either of the horses having to win; the parties concerned are betting simply that, of the two horses, their own will come in ahead."

Mr. Coyle sent a quick look behind him. "Have you the official post positions, Mrs. Hopkins? . . . Fine! Thank you," he smiled as she passed him the list.

"Now, if you've all got your programs handy, I'll read off the entries and you can jot in their numbers. Here we go, now—here's the line up!"

Shorty dug out a pencil and when he had finished filling in the blank spots, this is what he had:

1. Cannonball — Wild Horse Shorty
2. Taffydip — Diamond Bell Ranch
3. San Salvator — Luther K. Dickerson
4. Nan Tucket — Double N Ranch
5. Caliope — J. R. Jelks
6. San Luis de la Paz — Luther K. Dickerson
7. Harpsichord — Buck Fletcher
8. Bighoof Peavine — Walter Hyde
9. Jinx — Geo. Provencher
10. Cunard King — E. C. Steinheimer
11. Rowdy — L. Ernenwein
12. San Felice — Luther K. Dickerson

The bookies were shouting their opening odds. "Nine to five on the favorite—San Felice, nine to five! Cannonball opening at twenty to one—"

"*And there goes the paddock call!*"

An expectant hush gripped the gathered customers as each and all turned to peer for his choice. The bugler blared forth with *Boots and Saddles*—he even played the call twice, and *still* nothing happened. Then a laugh roared up from those nearest as a purple-splotched nag came reluctantly into the multitude's sight—Cannonball, with the big No. 1 on her side to prove it—propelled by the furious, hard-swearing efforts of McGee, who was angrily yanking her on by the lead-shank, and Hellbound, shoving on the critter's rump, while a diminutive Mexican jockey sat slumped, fiercely scowling, in the sagged-down hollow of her roller coaster back.

"*Cannonball!*" Baisy glared in the way of a woman cheated. "Why, it's nothing but that rat-tailed, swaybacked joke of a Palamoosa!"

And it was, sure enough—old Wire-Cut herself.

And what a noise that crowd did make!

But McGee finally got the old girl moving and, single file, the field moved down past the judges' stand, executed a more or less ragged turn, came around and, milling a bit, was eventually eased by the jockeys into position behind the stall gates.

In that narrow confinement old Wire-Cut sat down.

McGee looked whipped. Hellbound scrabbled to lend him assistance. Wild Horse, looking like dust in the thunder, vaulted the fence and went bitterly out there while the crowd, uproariously, called all manner of facetious advice.

It was the Mex kid, Dodo, who showed the real horse sense. With both hands locked in the old mare's mane he was lustily calling on the Mother of Jesus.

Divine intervention must finally have moved her for she presently got up without visible assistance and stood there, unhappily, blowing through her nose and groaning most dismally.

"The old girl's feeling a little coy today," Coyle told the hooting crowd through the amplifier.

But McGee had his mouth against Dodo's ear. "Don't whip her, son—remember, don't whip her. An' don't set up on her. Keep down along her neck and talk to her."

Shouted odds on the favorite were even now; odds on Cannonball thirty-five to one. Lee Forest clutched at a passing bookie. "Five hundred dollars on the Palamoosa—"

Hellbound, followed by McGee and Wild Horse, ducked back through the rail. The starter raised his flag and—

"*They're off!*" Coyle yelled through the microphone. "*Cannonball getting a step the best of it!*"

The matched team of Percherons hitched to the stall gates were laying into their collars. Wild Horse was trying to get Lee Forest to lend his binoculars and everyone stood stiff in his boots trying to see through the dust swirling round them.

"*Going into the first turn it's San Felice by a head, Cannonball by a nose, and Nan Tucket!*"

The crowd was whooping like a bunch of school kids. "San Felice! San Felice! Come on there, San, feed the golram dust to 'er!"

"How's she doin'?" Shorty shouted at Forest.

Dickerson, standing nearby with Baisy, reached over and poked Shorty's shoulder. "Feel like raising the ante? Lay you another full grand old San there takes it."

"You're talkin'," Shorty said, never quitting his efforts to get Forest's glasses. He didn't have the money, but he couldn't back down with that taunt in Lute's voice. He shook

187

Forest's arm. "How's she doin'?" he grumbled.

"If you'd let go a minute I might be able—"

"It's this goddam dust!" Mrs. Potter snapped bitterly. "You can't make out a precious thing for certain. All you can see—"

"I know it!" said Mrs. Fergie indignantly. "I don't see why they didn't think to sprinkle it!"

"How's she doin'? Shorty muttered, still harrying Forest.

Forest lowered his binoculars and declaimed, darkly menacing: "If you don't stop poking me—"

"*Down the back stretch it's San Felice by half a length, Nan Tucket by a head, and Cannonball!*"

Lute, in his supercilious way, reached over once more and nudged Shorty's shoulder. "Sorry, old boy. Just like stuffing your money right into the furnace. You would bet, though. Don't you feel like raising it?"

"I'll make a bet with you," Rose curled her lips at him. "I haven't got much—about a hundred dollars—but—"

"Taken!" Lute grinned. "I'll even take it at two-to-one . . . Just like owning the Mint," he told Baisy.

"Kin you see anythin'?" old Hellbound asked; and Shorty forgot there were ladies present.

"I could if this yap would just lend me his glasses!"

Forest said, fed up: "For the love of God, take 'em!"

"No use in your looking," Luther Dickerson chuckled. "That purple wreck's slid clean out of the money."

He stood up on the rail and, while Baisy held onto his coat-tail to steady him, refocused his glasses. He shortly said in derision, "Can't even *find* your nag. Provencher's paint has moved up into second. Nan Tucket and Taffydip are—"

Mrs. Fergie said, glowering: "I wish you'd keep still so

we could hear the announcer!"

And then Coyle's voice: "*Rounding the stretch it's San Felice by . . . by almost a length. Jinx by a nose, and the Diamond Bell mare!*"

Hellbound flung out his arms, disgusted; and his right one took Mrs. Potter's hat off and Dickerson, getting down off the rail, made a four-point landing square on the crown of it.

Unaware of this tragedy he slapped Shorty's shoulder with a hearty chortle. "Well, old man, have you found the wreck yet?"

He found himself in the grip of a twister. "I'll 'wreck' *you*," Mrs. Potter declared, "if you don't get those brogans out of my hat!"

"Good sakes!" Lute said, looking down at it, startled. "Gee, I'm sorry! Here—use my binoculars. You'll surely want to be in at the finish—"

The good lady, glaring, snatched the glasses and focused them. Wild Horse, scowling, passed Forest's to McGee.

The handsome Lute was much too pleased with himself to worry long about the Potter bonnet. He had Wild Horse well on the hip and was not of a mind to let him forget it.

"Still figure you've got any chance?" he sneered.

"Ain't heard me hollerin' calf rope, hev you?"

"It looks," said McGee, "like that paint's creeping up on you."

Baisy laughed and, in a superior way, Lute Dickerson guffawed. "That won't help you any," he said. "I don't have to *win* this race; all I have to do is come in ahead of you. I guess I better start figuring what I'll do with your money."

Mrs. Potter, bent across the rail with Lute's powerful glasses, said "That horse—"

But Lute wasn't listening. He knew Shorty's pride and the way to play on it. "I wouldn't let *no*body call *me* a piker; if I was sure of that purple-splotched fossil as *you* are, I'd sure up the bet another good thousand."

"Okay," Shorty blared. "I'll jest do that, Mister!" and Lute, with a saturnine grin, told Baisy:

"Old Shorty'll have to hire him a bodyguard if he expects to get home with all that money. Three thousand's a pretty fair pile these days—there's a heap around here would slit your throat for less."

Mrs. Potter tried again. "I think that horse they were—"

But, at that precise moment, Mr. Coyle's voice shouted:

"*At the three-eighths pole it's San Felice by a shoulder, Jinx—HEY! Wait a sec folks; that horse isn't Jinx! There's the number—Number One!—It's CANNONBALL! Lorrdy—They're coming down the home stretch now and it's San Felice on top by a neck, Cannonball by a good clean length, and the Diamond Bell mare!*"

The uproar was tremendous. Everyone was shouting. The Double N boys were bellowing for Nan Tucket, who was only a head behind the Diamond Bell entry, and the Diamond Bell hands were whooping for Taffydip; there were three or four shouts for Ernenwein's Rowdy. But the most of the crowd was dividing its yelling between San Felice, still leading, and the Palamoosa who, as all could now see, was steadily inching that lead away.

The bared, clenched teeth of the Dickerson jockey were a curled, white gash in his hard-set face and his flogging bat left red welts on the stud; but the Mex kid, Dodo, never lifted his whip.

Coyle was keeping up a running commentary but you could hardly hear his voice for the shouting. San Felice had the inside track but the Palamoosa was overhauling him. Inch by inch the mare's bony nose crept along his neck—reached his head, and kept coming.

And then Coyle yelled:

"*The winner is—Looks like Cannonball by a nose—but just a minute till we get the official from the judges—That's right, folks! It's Cannonball the winner, San Felice second and Rowdy third!*"

20.

DICKERSON DEALS A PAT HAND

"It's a swindle!" Lute yelled; and he was not smiling, either. "*Any*one could see old San— Why, his whole damn' face—"

Hellbound and Rose were dancing a jig when Shorty reached over and tapped Lute's shoulder. "I wouldn't let *no*body call *me* a piker. If I was you I'd pay up or shut up."

Dickerson stared for one thunderous moment. "*I'll be back*!" he gritted, and whirled off toward the paddock. "Don't crow!" Cinch growled, and followed Baisy after him.

"They're bringing up the mare now," said McGee to Shorty. "Better go out there and say a few words. Crowd'll expect it. An' them judges'll be wantin' to give you the purse—"

Wild Horse cuffed back his hat, and then stopped. "It ort t' go t' *you*, Nels. You done all the work—most all of it anyhow. You been workin' her steady ever sinct you come here. Why, I never woulda guessed—Shucks! When it comes t' plain horse savvy—"

"Get out there, you idjit!" McGee said grumpily; but you could see he was tickled to have his skill recognized. There wasn't one horse fancier out of a hundred could have done with old Wire-Cut what McGee had; wasn't one would have had the patience to try. But McGee was no glory hunter. He was just an old man with a keen love of horses.

"She had the speed—I just brought it out of her; there's good blood back of that old girl somewhere. Now you take that yellow cyclone of Lute's—there's a critter I could *do* somethin' with. Alls he needs is proper handlin'— But we're holdin' the show up. Get out there an' grin for 'em."

So Wild Horse did, and the crowd roared and yelled for him. It was nearly five minutes before you could hear him; then he held up both hands and the photographers shot him.

"The fella," he said, "which deserves all that cheerin' is old Nels McGee—Nels McGee from Dakota; that old coot over there what looks like a deacon. He trained the mare an' this Mex kid here rode her. They're the ones—them two an' the mare. Let's give 'em a great big hand—how about it?"

So all those people opened up again and it was just like hell with the clapper off. Then the judges gave Shorty the twenty-five hundred dollar Sweepstakes purse and Mr. Coyle hung a great horseshoe of flowers around old Wire-Cut's neck and everyone cheered and shouted all over—everyone but Dickerson, who stood off to one side with Cinch and Baisy and looked mean enough to bite his nose off. Then the photographers lifted their cameras again, and reporters were squatted around the yard everyplace scribbling like lightning; and Wild Horse had his great inspiration.

He had been a fool traipsing round like a dog after Baisy; and then, when he'd finally gotten her number and realized how it was Rose all the time whom he really had cared for, he had gummed up the works trying to ape Lute Dickerson. Of course she'd got mad—what decent girl wouldn't? No dame cared to sport a man's ring "jest fer luck"!

But Shorty would show them he could live and learn.

He held up both hands and when, again, the crowd quieted he said: "That's fine, folks—fine! Makes a fella feel right good inside him t' know all you people have been wishin' him luck. But there is one other person at this jamboree which has long deserved yore good regard," he said; and Hellbound pricked up his ears and nodded, and retiring-like twisted the ends of his mustache because it was only plain justice that a public acknowledgment should at last crown his efforts.

"This person," said Shorty, "has been too dang modest—always content t' set back an' let other people hev all the glory; people, I might say, what's been a heap less deservin'. I'm talkin' about that first-rate cook an' all-around helper which is goin' t' be Mrs. Wild Horse Shorty!"

And the crowd turned loose with a mighty cheer; but when Shorty stared round to find Rose she was gone.

"If you're huntin' that Happy Harp hasher," Lute jeered, "she's gone home—"

"I'm goin' home myself," Shorty blared, "when you've paid me them honest debts you've contracted. You laffed at my mare—now pony up the money!"

"You'll get your money. Go talk to Fritchet—"

"I'm talkin t' *you*!" Shorty raised his voice to a full-throated bellow. "You know what I'm talkin about!—that extra two thousand you jest got through bettin'!"

"Certainly I know what you're talking about. And I expect you will know what *I*'m talking about when I tell you that Logan just got back from *Phoenix*."

So the axe had fallen.

It took Shorty hard, like a hoof in the midriff. Rose had forewarned him and now it had happened. Dickerson was wise to the bluff Shorty had run on him.

"Better rattle your hocks before I have you arrested—"

"I'll rattle when I'm dang good an' ready!" Shorty yelled. "What kind of cheap skate are you, runnin' up the bets an' then tryin' t' worm out of 'em? Go dig up that money 'fore I work you over!"

Lute's eyes glittered like a stepped-on snake's and his jaws shut so hard it looked like he'd break them. But he said, cool enough, "You don't suppose I carry that much with me? I'll write you a check—"

"I'll take mine in cash—an' I'll take it right now! Go spin the knob on that safe in yore parlor an' let some of them butterflies out fer a airin'! You kin scrape up—"

"You heat-crazy fool!" Dickerson raged through his teeth. He thrust his face within an inch of Shorty's. "I've got you so tight," he said, cat soft, "you can't even wriggle so much as an eyebrow! The Bisbee bank was robbed last night. They've found an old hat of yours alongside the vault, one of your fancy gloves by the window, and the tail-strap off of that third-hand vest was clenched so tight in the dead guard's hand it took half the night to pry it loose of him! An' if that ain't enough, that dude, Farrar, will swear you was away from the ranch until breakfast; and Phil Cinch will swear he saw you last night on the Huachuca road between Hereford an' Bisbee. And that Happy Harp hasher ain't goin' to save you—she headed for home by the sawmill cutoff and Rimfire Logan—"

But Shorty, with his cheeks gone the color of chalk, was listening no longer. One sweep of his hand slapped the horseshoe of flowers off old Wire-Cut's neck. That same split second saw him into the saddle and scattering the crowd like a load of buckshot.

In far less time than the telling takes, they had left the crowd and its shouts in the dust and were pounding full-tilt down the narow dirt road that led from Lute's toward the sawmill cutoff. There was one bare chance, Shorty knew, he might stop it. If he could come up with Logan before Logan reached Rose . . . .

He stretched along the mare's neck like he had heard McGee tell the Mex kid to do; and he growled queer words of encouragement to her while his soul cried out in savage protest at the way Lute had chosen to even things with him. He groaned in a very agony of spirit to think that his feud with the vengeful Lute could ever have led to an end like this; to a fate so dire for a girl so dear.

For himself he cared nothing. His every last thought was of Rose and her danger, his whole store of energy devoted entirely to catching and stopping the Dickerson hard case before that devil should catch up with Rose.

For a fleeting moment he had felt a faint wonder that Lute should have thus laid bare his villainy—should have forewarned his victim of what lay in store for him; but his mind was too dull, Rose's plight too desperate, for him to winnow the truth from Lute's fabric of part-truths.

They were getting close now to the start of the cutoff. Hillside timber was giving way to the unsightly stumps left behind by the sawyers. The sun struck down with a brassy fury—there was no breeze stirring; and the long hard run, so close on the Sweepstakes, was taking grim toll of the game old mare. She was going strong still but she was running on nerve. Shorty hated to use a horse this way, but he had no choice; it was Wire-Cut or Rose.

They came into the cutoff and a frown puckered Shorty's eyes as he keened the trail to be sure Rose had taken it. She had, all right—no doubt about that. For there were the tracks and fresh horse sign to prove it. But what had become of Rimfire Logan? There was only one set of tracks on this trail that looked recent enough to be concerned with him. Where, then, were Logan's? Had Shorty somehow passed him? Or was Logan wise to some faster trail?

Had he been less distracted, less urgently compelled by the need for speed, Shorty must have thought twice before following farther. Vaguely uneasy he turned into the cutoff and went plunging on.

There was a point up ahead—they were almost onto it—a kind of wind cut promontory, from which you could stare out over the desert that, below, stretched clear to the Tucson Mountains or, if you were looking southwest, to the Tumacacoris.

They pulled up on this shelf an, while Shorty sat peering, eyes probing for a movement, the gaunt mare stood head down, sides heaving, her purple-splotched hide turning dark with sweat while she pulled great breaths of air through her nose. Unnaturally bright were her large, soft eyes, and never before had there been a time that she found it necessary to brace herself just to merely stand still and inhale the sweet air. There was no resiliency left in her muscles. They quivered rebelliously and her heart

197

was pounding most strangely inside her with a bumpety-bumpety-bump. But when Shorty reached down and brusquely patted her, she nickered softly and pulled up her head. She heaved out a sigh that was not quite a groan and she forced the lax muscles to do her bidding.

Back they whirled and onto the trail again, flashing along through the blue cedars, waving the edges of scrubby undergrowth, recklessly lunging on—ever on, while the trail dipped and twisted, doubling down to the desert.

The reins were loose and the mare was proud at such patent evidence of Shorty's trust; but she knew he was fretting to get someplace quickly and she seldom slackened except on the turns, and then only barely. She suspected Shorty might be heading for home, because home was off yonder in that sand and catclaw that was spread below, mile on tawny mile of it.

And then they were onto the desert's floor, still running, going into it rocket style, fast and furious, with the brush giving way to a maze of mesquite that threw back the pound and the slash of their travel. And the heat boiled up from the sun baked sand and her hoofs churned the dust to a great plume behind them.

But it was hard to breathe and her lungs felt scalded and, suddenly, something let go inside her and she broke her stride and lurched left and staggered; and she felt Shorty's weight pitch out of the saddle.

It was then, with her legs gone rubbery under her, that she saw the squatting man with the rifle—heard its rapid-fire roar and screamed with the pain of it.

WILD HORSE

21.

MAC JONES' BONES

When Rose came back from inspecting the thirteen-day-old palomino filly Baisy had insisted on showing her, she looked around kind of surprised and said: "McGee—where's Wild Horse?"

"Gawd on'y knows," growled Hellbound gloomily; and McGee said:

"He had a few words with Mr. Dickerson. I didn't catch the talk, but whatever it was it sure riled Shorty plenty. Jumped on old Wire-Cut an' went tearin' off like a bat out of Carlsbad. Beatin'est thing I ever seen."

"Probably rollin' his cotton," Geo. Provencher said. "Skippin' out from his debts now he's got him some money."

Rose gave him a look that would have curled up a juniper. "He's not the quitting kind!" she said fiercely; and Provencher found work that took him elsewhere.

"Looked to me," Fritchet said, coming over, "like he was headed for home. He took the Valley road anyway. What do you want me to do with this money—it's what him and

Lute put up on that wager. It's—"

"I'll take it," Rose said. "I'll see that—"

She broke off, flabbergasted, as Sheriff Potter, bustling up, without so much as a by-your-leave, reached out and took the bills from Fritchet.

"Sorry," he said, "but the law comes first, ma'am."

"Law? What's the law got to do with it?"

"You're goin' to find out it's got a-plenty to do with it. That scamp robbed the Bisbee bank last night!"

"Are you *crazy*?"

"Not so crazy as some, Mr. Forest—if that's your name," Potter said. But his mind was too taken up with Wild Horse to spare many thoughts on a loose nut from Phoenix.

He turned back to the girl. "You'll find it's true enough; I just got the word but the news'll be out before night, like enough. My deputy's saddling—"

"But this is ridiculous!" declared Rose, looking angry. "How *could* he have robbed any banks last night? He was at the ranch—"

"That'll stand some provin'! You can't twist the evidence," Potter said doggedly. "They've found a glove and a hat and a strap off a vest that have all been identified as belonging to Wild Horse. Besides, Cinch saw him on the Bisbee road!"

"I don't care," Rose said; "he was at the ranch. We were out by the pasture looking over the horses—"

Potter lifted his eyebrows. "Very romantic. Maybe you can make the jury believe that, but if you want my notion he's just overplayed his hand. We got a quick way with bank robbers round here. We don't figure t' waste more'n the price of a rope on 'em."

And, with that parting shot, Obe Potter left them.

Before Rose could open her mind on the subject—which, by her look, she had certainly aimed to— Phil Cinch came over from the house to say that Wild Horse was wanted on the telephone. Pronto.

"He's gone home," Rose said. "Couldn't I take the message?"

"For all of me. It's Western Union," Cinch said— "Claim they been calling all over. Gettin' all-fired important, ain't he?" he jeered, and strode off to help Lute get rid of the race crowd.

When Rose came back she eyed Forest oddly. Then, despite herself, she grinned up at him. "I don't feel like grinning at all; but really, you seem to have played this pretty smart, Forest. If the *Denver Post* hadn't said so themselves I wouldn't have believed it."

"What's that?" Forest said, jerking out of his trance. "Did I hear you mention the *Denver Post?*"

"You certainly did. That wire was from them—looks like Shorty was getting just a little suspicious of you. I never supposed writers were as modest as that."

"Shucks," Forest said, looking kind of sheepish. "So you've found me out. I had hoped—"

Mrs. Fergie said crossly: "It's all very well to have secrets—"

"It isn't a secret any longer, Mary. Mr. Forest's a writer. He's the one who's been writing all that stuff for the *Post*—about Shorty and the ranch and his horses and everything. All those 'exclusives', and that story they ran about the Palamoosa. Gee," she said, holding out her hand to him, "that was swell of you, Forest!"

Mrs. Fergie said, "My goodness! Did he *really?*"

And Hellbound said: "I knowed all the time who he was—I used t' read his yarns in that Ranch R— Anyway," he said, kind of flustered, "I like to of busted all my buttons loose when I hear'n McGee tellin' Shorty he was an escaped daffydill fr'm thet Phoenix bughouse!"

Mr. Forest looked kind of flustered himself. Then he laughed and said he guessed "the most of us are a little queer some way or other."

Hellbound didn't get the drift of that; but before he could get any wind up over it Farrar came back from the judges' stand and wanted to know if anyone had seen Shorty. "Since he left, I mean. Do you think he went home?"

"I don't know *what* to think," Rose said uneasily. "The sheriff says—"

"Yes— I heard him spouting. We had better figure something about Dust Churner and Trymore. Fletcher's had a call about some cattle at Ajo and he's got to have the van to go after them—"

"I'll get 'em home," McGee mumbled; but Hellbound wanted to make a project out of it.

"You're coming with us," Rose said. "Don't argue. Wild Horse told you last night that dug tank pipe needed lowering. The springs have gone down and there's no water coming through. You'll have to—"

"But, dang it," grumbled Hellbound. "T' git the end o' thet pipe back into the water I'll hev t' dig up an' lower better'n forty feet—"

"Then you'd better come home and get right at it."

"Mebbe," McGee said, "if you'd rub some bacon grease on it . . ."

Hellbound ignored him. "It ain't thet I mind the work, Rose, but t' git at thet pipe I'll hev t' tear yore radish garten plumb t' flinders—"

"Then tear it to flinders. I've got more seed—"

"But gol dang it!" Hellbound exploded, "where'n tarnashun's the *sense* to it? Lute knows by now we ain't leased thet land. How long d'you s'pose—"

McGee murmured thoughtful like: "If that sheriff could be showed Lute wasn't goin' to be head man much longer—"

"Now don't you fellows get to talkin' like that," Farrar broke in with an unaccustomed vigor. "You leave Lute alone; he's a dang nice feller an' I like him a heap just the way he is—wouldn't want to see him changed a particle. Why—he's that generous you wouldn't hardly believe it! Offered me five hundred dollars just to get up in court and tell how I seen Shorty saddlin' up last night and sneaking off real furtive like—"

"*Did* you see him?" Nels McGee snapped bluntly.

"Ah!" Farrar grinned, and sent a bright look toward the yonder barn doorway where Lute and the sheriff had their heads together. "C'mon. Pile in," he said. "We better get along—it's gettin' chilly round here. An' this here Redman—good as it is—don't take up the lack of hot victuals noway."

Shoving back from the supper table with Shorty still absent, Rose said worriedly, "He *might* have taken that sawmill cutoff—"

But Hellbound growled, "Ef he had, he'd of been yere. It's shorter'n the way we come."

"Something may have happened to him. He might have been hurt."

Old Hellbound snorted. "He's done dragged his picket pin, thet's what's happened to 'im. Not thet I blame him— I'd of drug mine long ergo if I'd been in *his* boots! Crossin' them Dickersons—"

"You mean you think that bank job—" Forest began; but Hellbound yanked him off that line pronto.

"Don't you go t' makin' out *I* said so! I ain't sayin' no sech a thing! Alls I know is the las' guy thought he could buck them Dickersons sure took off in one whale of a hurry—never even stopped t' blow out his lamp. Mac Jones, thet was. Had a real nice place yere; house stood off yonder jest no'th of our stable. We foun' some of the ashes whilst we was diggin' thet pipe line."

"What'd he do—burn out?" Forest asked.

"Thet's what they tell you. Alls *I* know is one night, 'twixt dark an' dawn, ol' Mac took off the same way Shorty's done—jest plain up an' vanished! An' the' ain't nobody set eyes on him sinct."

"So Lute moved in and took over the property?"

"He didn't hev t' move in. He was yere already. Owned them springs an' all the land round except this one little slice right in through yere. After Mac left, these localities got t' be knowed as right onhealthy fer folks t' squat on."

Farrar said, "Lute must've been pretty much of a kid, wasn't he?"

"We-ell . . . thet was a long time back, but he musta been seventeen or eighteen, anyways. An' tough—my soul! Jest as lief spit in a wild-cat's eye an' then turn round an' give 'im first chaw! He may look fancy as a egg on toast, but onderneath he's jest like a anvil."

"Suppose you 'anvil' out and get to work on that pipe," Rose said, getting up. "Those horses have to have water and you can't spend all your time lugging it in buckets. When Nels gets back perhaps he'll give you a hand."

It was 8:53, and McGee had returned, when Hellbound let out that startled yowl. It was such an ungodly screech—

and so scared-like, everyone on the place—including Mrs. Potter in her boudoir toggery—dashed yardward at once to find out what Hellbound had done to himself.

He was not killed, anyway, for they could see him plainly in the light of the lantern. He was kind of crouched over like a got-too-hot candle. He had a tight grip with both hands on his pick and his staring eyes looked big as sauce pans as he peered down into the hole at his feet.

"What is it?" Farrar called, hand reaching hipward.

And Rose cried, anxious: "Have you hurt yourself, Hellbound?"

"If it is a snake"—Mrs. Fergie trembled—"perhaps you had better let Fred take care of it."

"If it's a snake," Farrar scowled, putting on the brakes, "the boys'll know better what to do with it than *I* would."

But McGee, who had not said anything, was the first to reach the old man's side. With his breath coming just a bit jerky and nervous, McGee took a quick squint into the trench. Then he snorted. "Is *that* all you raised such a rumpus about?—that little old wart of a harmless horn-toad?"

"*Horn-toad!*" Hellbound bawled, indignant. "Are you *blind!* Whadda you think thet toad's a-*settin'* on?"

McGee bent down. He said "Oh!" kind of startled. Then waved the women back. "This ain't no sight fer—"

"But whatever *is* it?" Mrs. Fergie cried, frantic.

And old Hellbound yowled: "It's Mac Jones' bones!"

"Are you sure?" Forest said.

" 'Course I'm sure!" Hellbound snapped. "D'ye think I'm an idjit? Look there!—that's Mac's six-gun an'—Yes, by godfries, that's Mac Jones' ring!"

"What's this?" Forest said, stooping over and pointing. "Sort of looks like it might be metal of—"

"Gol dang," Hellbound said. "It's thet silver plate Mac had into his shoulder!"

"If you're right," Forest said, "we ought to get the sheriff—"

"What fer? What in tarnashun—*Shh!* I hear horses!"

They stood stiff with listening, all except the dude from Oneco who was down on his knees at the edge of the hole interestedly exhuming the relics.

"One horse," McGee decided. "It ain't Wire-Cut. I'd know *her* step—"

"Until we learn who it is," Forest suggested, "Mightn't it be a good hunch to keep away from—"

"Be a very good hunch," Mr. Farrar agreed, and got up, dusting the knees of his pants off. "Fetch the lantern, Hellbound."

"It is probably my husband," Mrs. Potter guessed, clutching her gown more firmly about her.

But as the matter turned out it was a corpulent stranger in the garb of a cowpuncher. The butt of a .45 swung at his thigh and his round cheeks were solemn, expressionless. He looked, McGee thought, first of all at the dude, and it almost seemed like he nodded. Then he got out the makings and, across the smoke's manufacture, he said:

"There's a dead horse layin' on the trail, back a piece."

The women gasped. Forest and McGee exchanged swift glances. Hellbound, peering past Forest's shoulder, got suddenly intent and lifted up the lantern.

"*Shorty!*" Rose cried.

The man on the horse jerked around in his saddle, but the man who limped into the light never noticed him. It was Wild Horse, all right, and his look was ugly. There was blood on his face and his shirt hung in tatters. His scarf was bound tight across his left shoulder.

He made straight for Farrar.

Mr. Farrar looked nervous.

"Where's that gun you been packin'—"

Out of the dark Cinch's voice said sharply: "Never mind no gun, Shorty. This is the payoff. I've got a pistol plumb ready to take your picture and all I'm needin' is the barest excuse. Get over by that lantern where we can have a good look at you."

Shorty stood there, caught, flatfooted and chanceless, full in the glare of Hellbound's lantern. You could see the black hate and the strain of it twisting him. You could sense the thoughts so uncaringly urging him as he lifted one foot off the ground and turned; but the click of the drawn-back gun hammer stopped him.

"Okay," he growled. "You got me—git on with it."

"Tame as a house fly," Dickerson gloated, stepping out of the shadows with his cocked pistol gesturing. "Better frisk him, Phil—he may still have that gun he killed Logan with."

Shorty's laugh was a bark that was bitter as wormwood. "I never had no gun. I killed that skunk with a rock."

"You mean," Dickerson sneered, "you hoped that's what folks would *think* you did. What you *did* do was bash in his head to hide the bullet hole—but we found it. We even found the place where you laid in wait for him. *Pfah!* Get his gun, Phil."

Still gripping his pistol, Cinch moved forward.

Farrar said mildly, "The game's up, boys. It won't do you no good, Cinch, to plant that gun on him."

So quiet were they spoken it took several seconds for the dude's words to register. Cinch was reaching a left hand to feel Shorty over when their impact struck. You could see the man stiffen. Across that quiet the strange cowhand drawled, "That Bisbee job misfired a little. I got a witness that saw you leavin' the bank, Cinch. We've also found a herd of stolen cattle you've been holding to butcher till your packin' plant trucks come. We've got the trucks and we've got the cattle. And it just happens, boys, I came across Rimfire's corpse before you did."

"And," Mr. Farrar said gently, "we've just got Lute's bullet out of Mac Jones' skull; and while I'm noways sure, still I'm willing to bet—"

Lute spun with an oath and flame jumped from his pistol. But the dude's spoke first and Dickerson stumbled and sat down heavily while the lead he had loosed droned skyward futilely. Farrar's eyes twinkled while the stranger cowhand, Elmer, assured Cinch gravely he could have some, too, if the lesson weren't plain enough.

Cinch did not argue. He thrust both hands up.

"Smart fella, ain't he?" Farrar said, chuckling. "Shake his left sleeve, Elmer. I've a halfway notion we'll find the 'murder gun' cached there."

And sure enough. Cinch *did* have a six-gun cached up his sleeve.

They examined Lute's wound and Farrar tied it up for him; and then, while Elmer prodded the handcuffed pair onto seats in the Dodge, Mr. Farrar—having shown the others his shiny Pinkerton badge—endeavored to answer a few of their questions.

It was the murders, he said, he'd been sent to look into; Elmer was a range detective come to unravel the cattle end. They had guessed quick enough which were the guilty parties; their hardest job had been getting the goods on them. But Elmer had at last found some of the cattle allegedly stolen by the Whetstone Mountain gang and now, with all the rest they'd uncovered, it looked like they had a fairly airtight case. "Even," Farrar said, "if nobody squeals. Lute was just about set to hold a dispersal sale—owed everybody from hell to breakfast."

"How will Shorty," Forest asked, "ever get his three thousand?"

"He won't," Farrar said, "but—"

Shorty said, kind of wistful, " 'F you could jest make out t' git me that San Felice stud. . . ."

"Reckon I could wangle that much for you—"

"All set," Elmer called. "Are you ready to go, Fred?"

Farrar had aimed to say a few things more to Shorty; but Wild Horse and Rose were kind of sauntering off, so he waved to the others and got into the car. "If it's all right with you," he told the range dick, Elmer, "suppose we stop at the Crossing and pick up Ernenwein, the sheriff's deputy. We don't need any credit for capturing these guys, but Ernie—Hell! can't you see the headlines:

"Noted Author Turned Sheriff Unmasks Desperadoes!"

BLOOD OF KINGS

1

THE GOLDEN HORSE

THE FIRST TIME he laid eyes on the horse, Shorty just stood there, struck dumb. By God, it was like a dream come true! Like a picture out of some fairy book! All his life had been spent with horses, all his life he had loved them and cared for them; and the sight of this one put a lump in his throat for never had he seen a horse half so grand.

Yellow, he was; a living gold-coin yellow, pulsating and rippling like a field of ripe grain—a horse carved from gold with mane and tail of spun platinum. An impatient creature with quivering limbs. A magnificent, muscular, well-groomed stallion whose fiery eyes and proud carriage might well have held King Midas spellbound.

Shorty stared with open-eyed envy at the man who could own such a creature.

He was not a big man, yet he gave that impression. Good living had padded his waist and shoulders and there were folds of flesh underneath his chin. He wore a stovepipe hat and bright eyes peeped out from its brim, sharp and bird-like. A mare's nest of hair hung unkempt to his collar. Mutton-chop whiskers framed his plump cheeks and a diamond flashed from his soiled cravat. A rusty frock coat, a-shine at the seams, shaped snug to his shoulders and a shirt of pressed linen, that had once been white, was a grayish blur beneath his cravat, telling well of the miles he had put behind. Meaty legs bulged the buff great-checked trousers that were carelessly stuffed into ornate-topped boots. The boots had runover heels and Ernie—L. Ernenwein, the sheriff—was looking him over with a jaundiced stare.

He was quite alone, this man with the stallion at the end of his lead rope. He had a fine taste in horses, the one he bestrode being a big bay gelding built after the manner of the Waggoner stock, as good as you'll find through the whole length of Texas.

But it was the *man* Ernie watched, and his eye was not friendly.

Sheriff Ernie himself was a fancy dresser. Nothing loud or blatant, but within the confines of expense and good taste the Ernenwein wardrobe was distinctively progressive. A big-boned gent who had run to lankness, with a steel-gray mustache and twinkling eyes. But those eyes, just now, were doing anything but twinkling as they suspiciously probed the unknown horseman.

He said without preamble: "Come quite a ways, eh?"

The man with the led horse shrugged his shoulders. Then his beak nose twitched and he grinned expansively. "Haw!" he said. "I've come fur enough, I can tell you that! Gawdawfullest country I ever got into—rode half the night an' never seen one house! What burg is this?"

"Hub of the universe—Horsehead Crossing."

"*That* place!" The man scowled disparagingly, pursed his lips and spat. "I like a *horse*-raising country—never could stomach these damfool hoe men. What do you do around here for excitement?"

While Ernie, who had neglected to pin on his badge, was endeavoring to think up some fitting rejoinder, Wild Horse

211

said just a shade on the timid side: "What do you call that stud you got, Mister?"

"Why, the name of this horse, sir, is *Sangre de Cristo*— Blood of Kings," said the stranger sonorously, rolling it over with evident relish. "Blood of Kings—that's a free translation," he added gratuitously. "Royally bred—I mean *royally!* You'll not find his like if you search the world over. Raised by the Aga Khan, he was, and brought out of France at terrible sacrifice . . . But I'll have to get on," he declared, abruptly tugging out a gold watch and taking a squint at it. "I'm headin' for Tucson. Goin' to show those Tucson sports a few things."

"You don't hev to go that far," Shorty said, wistfully eyeing the mincing stallion. "Plenty horses right here you could git a matched race with—"

"Farm horses! Chicken feed!" The man spat contemptuously. "When I match this horse it won't be for no marbles!"

"What'd you say your name was?" asked Ernie.

"Tranch— Call me Tranch."

Shorty said with his glance still patting the stud horse, "If you could hang round a bit, it might be I could mebbe put you next to a good proposition. There's a number of things—"

" 'Fraid not," the man sighed, though his glance said he'd like to. "Got too big a deal on—got to get up to Tucson an' see Melville Haskell."

"That's a awful good horse . . ." Shorty's talk was half groan.

"Ain't another one like him— *Say!*" Tranch said, eyeing Shorty closely. "I can see you're a sport. You've got the real look about you. How'd you like to own this horse?"

Shorty said like a shot: "What'll you take fer him, pardner?"

"Well, I—"

Ernie growled, exasperated: "Don't be a fool!"

The stranger's bright stare rummaged Ernie mildly. He glanced over his shoulder, then he looked at Shorty. "Here's what I'll do," he said, slapping one leg with the slack of his reins. "I hadn't rightly figured on sellin' this horse, but I'll make you a sportin' proposition. I'm in a hurry. Ain't got the time to look after him proper. Got to get up to Tucson and I'm late already. So here's what I'll do: I'll let you have Blood of Kings for five hundred dollars— Sure, I know! It's plain *givin'* him away; but I can see you'll take care of him. You're the kind to appreciate a good ridin' horse. You'll give him the kind of home he's—"

"Bunk!" Ernie snorted. "Do you know what I think?" he said, looking at Shorty. "I think, by God, that stud has been stolen!"

Mr. Tranch looked shocked. "That's a hard word, stranger."

"Never mind," Shorty gulped. "I'll take him anyhow!"

"Don't be a chump!" Ernie snapped at him testily. "Try usin' your head. Nobody'd sell a stud horse like that for five hundred dollars without there was a snake hid out in the woodpile someplace. You start buyin' stolen horses and—"

"Gentlemen!" Tranch said hastily. "The horse ain't been stolen. You have my word for it. He's my own lawful property—bill of sale and everything. But you're right about one thing," he grinned at Ernie. "I've my own good reasons for letting him go cheap. Like I said, I'm in a hurry; and I can't give you any papers—"

"No papers!"

"Well, no. He's got papers all right, but I can't get hold

213

of 'em. Had him over in Mexico— You know how them Mexkins are! Had a mite of trouble over there last evenin'. Nothin' serious; but I had to come away without getting his papers. Fellow got awful excited. It was the judge, you see; claimed *Sangre* had fouled a bay the old fool had slopped all his coin on. He hadn't, of course, but it was a claimin' race—"

"I can savvy the rest of that," Ernie said. "Your stud got beat—"

"Gentlemen! You have my word of honor! The horse *won*. But the judge, as it happens, was the Chief of Police and, rather than get in an unpleasantness with him, I simply packed up and got the hell out of there. But in order to race on their track at all, I was forced to put up *Sangre's* papers with the Presiding Steward and— Well, to cut a long tale short, I just came off without 'em."

Ernie said skeptically, "A likely story."

"It's the truth!" Tranch said. He slammed both hands down hard in his pockets, jerked them out kind of mad like and picked up his reins. "It's no skin off *my* nose," he rasped at Shorty. "You can believe it or not. This horse won't go beggin' at five hundred dollars!"

"Not if *I* know it," Shorty told him heartily. "I'll buy that horse—"

"Not now you won't," Tranch flared with a scowl. "It shall never be said that any Tranch— Hell!" he snorted. "If the sheriff of these parts was some tough old mosshorn always huntin' for trouble, I could maybe understand all this shilly-shallyin'—but your sheriff ain't nothing to worry a rabbit! That Ernenwein dude—that book-writin' lollypop! My Gawd! He don't know his asp from a hole in the ground."

214

Ernie jumped up. "Why, you—"

"Bah!" Tranch said. He jerked on the lead rope and kicked his horse. "I'll be at the Emery Park schoolhouse to-night—at ten, sharp. If you want Blood of Kings, be there with the money."

2

MATTER OF OPINION

"Now YOU done it!" declaimed Wild Horse bitterly. "That's the last we'll see of that—"

"Then you're damn well rid of him! Did you hear what that peckerneck *called* me? I ought to—"

"You're enough t' cramp rats!" Shorty flung at him scathingly. "If you hadn't kept swingin' your jaw so dang free—"

"You ought to thank your stars you had me with you!"

"I ought," Shorty snarled, "to knock your gol durn head off! Hell's fire! I *wanted* that horse!"

"You want to compound a felony? That bastard's a crook if I ever saw one! You can damn well bet he *stole* that stud—"

"So what if he did? He didn't steal it *here!* You seen where he come from—straight up from the Border. What he done over in Mexico ain't no splinters in *our* pants. Dadburn it, I could chaw up a sixgun! All my life I been hankerin' after palominos, wantin' t' git right into the business—*you* know that! An' you know what kinda luck I been hevin'. *No luck at all!* I sorta figgered I was gittin' a break when I got that Free Wheelin' colt from Her'ford, but ol' ory-eyed Lute had t' up an' kill him. Then Farrar sent Lute to the pen an' fixed things so's I could git Lute's race horse

—that San Felice half-*A*rab palomino; but along comes Logan an' feeds him poison. I mighta knowed that guy would do me a meanness! But now comes *this* guy—this Tranch, with as classy a stud as a gent could ask for, an' *you* got to open *your* feed hatch at him!"

"I was tryin' to keep you from losin' your money."

"Whose money *is* it?"

"Now that you mention it I begin to wonder."

"Well, you don't need to strain yourself."

Ernie let that one pass. "I thought you were broke."

"Ahr! That was yesterday. I got a new shipment of dudes las' night. I could of bought—"

"You can *still* buy him, can'tcha?"

"I dunno. If the guy's a crook like you called him, he'll be hittin' the trail fer Home, Sweet Home." Shorty kicked at a stone and growled, disgusted.

"Humph!" Ernie said. *"He* don't know I'm the sheriff around here. You don't reckon he'd of called me what he did if he had, do you? The damn overstuffed sausage! I oughta—"

"Ahr—git away!" Shorty snarled, exasperated. "I don't *never* hev no luck!" he wailed; and he was, sure enough, feeling just about as low as a man could honestly feel, without stretching it. "No luck with the bangtails an' no luck with the women!"

"Why, I thought you and Rose—"

"Rose won't hev me. Says before she ever gits married to me, I got t' show her I kin take care of her. Says I can't take care of her with all them horses— Claims I can't even take care of the horses." Shorty sighed. "It's her or them. She tol' me this mornin'."

"Then get rid of them, damn it—that's plain enough, ain't it?"

Ernie liked Rose and he did *not* like the horses. He had known Rose away back when she had been chief cook and bottle washer at the Happy Harp Hotel, which was before she had ever gone out to the ranch to keep Shorty's house and take care of his dudes for him. Ernie had always admired her capabilities. "She's a damn good woman. She does a lot of work," he said. "Was I you, I'd sell those skates for dog meat."

Shorty glared.

"But why don't you get wise to yourself?" Ernie went on unabashed. "Even a fertilizer factory wouldn't take a second look at the kind of nags *you* got."

"By grab, I've heard about enough—"

"You ain't heard anything!"

Ernie was a great hand for reforming his friends and when the mood was on him could be rightdown insulting; for their own good, of course. "Quit dreaming you're a second Lucky Baldwin an' get down to earth. Why, it was only a fluke you ever won that race—"

"Fluke! A lot you know about horses! Nels McGee worked *months* on that mare—"

"All right, all *right!*" Ernie said. "It was a case of pure merit—but the mare's dead now, and you've got nothing else could even beat a turtle in a forty-mile tail wind. Folks are giving you the laugh all over the country—"

"Oh, they are, are they?"

"You ought to know. What the hell do you think them dudes come out here for? The pleasure of sleepin' on those pine slat bunks? Wake up! It's all right for you to keep a horse or two—"

"What do you think them dudes are t' ride on—broomsticks?"

"I'd as soon ride a broomstick as one of *those* crowbaits.

218

What do you want to waste your time with those dudes for? Clean the whole bunch out—"

"An' where do you reckon my livin's t' come from?"

"Shake loose of them dudes and get you some white-faces. You can make more money off a good grade of cattle—"

"There's more to this life than grubbin' fer money—"

"You must of found it then; you ain't made any money," Ernie said sarcastically.

"If cattle's so good why'n't you git you some 'stead of cartin' that star around?"

"I hope you don't think I can live off the County! I consented to be sheriff because the tax-payers drafted me—not because I wanted to. I make my money off of books—the ones *I* write; an' if there's any better written I want to know what they are! Now look," Ernie said persuasively, "forget that bunch of mismated monkeys—"

"Don't you go throwin' down on my horses! By grab, I've listened to— You *hesh!*" Shorty blared, plumb fed up with the business. "Mebbe some of them critters don't amount to a whole lot, but old Wire-Cut's sister—that Sweet Columbine filly—kin trace straight back to old Steel Dust hisself! An' what's more, by grab, she's in foal to that Ali ben Ghaszi, Pete Hague's top *A*rab!"

"Well, don't count none on it," Ernie told him sourly. "A good stud means a lot, but it can't cure everything. Play this smart for a change and get rid of the whole lot of them. Get yourself three-four *good* horses—"

"With what?"

"I thought you *had* money—"

"I could of bought that stud, but I ain't got enough t' buy no harem fer him. You talk like money comes outa the air! How do you git into that book-writin' business?"

"You keep away from it. There's a lot easier ways to make

219

a livin' than that. Why don't you get in touch with that Lanteen outfit. Get a registered stud and—"

"That Lanteen crowd has gone outa business. Pulled down their horse barns, corrals an' everything. Gone into Herefords—"

"Just what I told you!" Ernie grinned triumphantly. "The money's in cattle. Get you a good grade of white-faced cattle—"

"An' disappoint all them doggone dudes? I don't *want* t' raise cattle. There ain't no fun chousin' cows' tails around. Might's well be a sheep herder an' be done with it."

"What *do* you want to do?"

"I wanta raise HORSES!"

Ernie lifted his eyebrows. "Well, there's other breeders you could buy from; you don't have to keep that bunch of ravenous scrubs. Get in touch—"

"I already done it," Shorty grumbled, scowling. "They want everything but the kitchen sink. I wrote a feller named Selby—lives up in Ohio. Gits two thousan' dollars fer a four-months'-old weanlin'. He don't give a whoop if he sells 'em or not!"

"Sure he don't. He's way out of your class. What you want is some good Quarter Horses— Do you know anything about Quarter Horses?"

"Didn't I cut my teeth on a Quarterhorse saddle?"

"Quarter *type* and *Quarter Horse* is two different things," Ernie said. "Quarter type come a dime a dozen. Quarter type is what you've got. For all-around utility the Quarter Horse can't be beat," he declared enthusiastically. "His physical characteristics have been fixed by generations of purposeful breeding; and it's entirely by virtue of these characteristics that the Quarter Horse has those priceless qualities which have made him supreme in the cow-chasing
220

business. He is a horse, an' the *only* horse, you can work all week and race on Sunday."

"Humph!" Shorty said. "I could do that with Wire-Cut."

Ernie grimaced. "Pay attention. Cow work's *hard* work; and that's where your Quarter Horse really shines. He's got lots of early speed, he's sure footed and he's got *real bottom*. What you want is a Quarter Horse, Shorty."

"How come I never heard none about 'em before?"

"Don't ask *me* to account for your ignorance. There've been Quarter Horses in this country since the earliest days— Paul Revere rode a Quarter Horse. The breed antedates the Revolution; they were originally called American Quarter Running Horses, and were bred to race one-quarter of a mile. The first important sire, and one of the greatest, was Janus, imported from England in 1752. Then there was Diomed, just two jumps removed from King Herod, who goes to the Byerly Turk; and Diomed's son, Sir Archy, and so on down the line. A great breed of horses. And out of it, in 1845, there was foaled a horse that even *you* have heard of—*Steel Dust*, the horse they brought into Texas and made a whole damn town go bankrupt. Then, in 1877, along comes Barney Owens to clean the pockets of the skeptics; he was owned by Sam Watkins of Petersburg, Illinois. Barney Owens sired Dan Tucker, and Dan Tucker was the father of Peter McCue. Pete was homelier than sin—no conformation at all, hardly. But you could breed him to a boxcar and get a perfect Quarter Horse."

Shorty said, "I guess you're pretty well up on your horses. What about Figure Two, the horse that raced a velocipede over near Silver City that time— Was *he* a Quarter Horse?"

"He was a Quarter Horse, too," Ernie said. "And Bob Wade that was raced in Montana and Oregon. They're the

221

fastest thing ever come out of the chute. Then there was Yellow Jacket, that was known as the only dun race horse in the United States; an' Blue Jacket, the most famous race horse at Mexico City— They were by Lock's Rondo. And then there was Little Rondo that was known as the Bunton Horse— Come to think of it, *he* was the father of Yellow Jacket. Anyhow, I could go on for hours an' hardly mention one horse that wasn't a daggone Quarter Horse."

"An' I always thought the real race horses was Thoroughbreds—"

"Lots of them are; and there's lots of good Quarter Horses with Thoroughbred blood—"

"Then they ain't real Quarter Horses, are they?"

"Sure they're real Quarter Horses. Both breeds sprung from the same common ancestors. Take Sir Archy, now. He's in the American Stud Book as a Thoroughbred; but he was a real Quarter Horse. Steel Dust goes to Sir Archy. So does Peter McCue— In fact, Peter McCue is in the American Stud Book, too, though by rights he hadn't ought to be.

"You see," Ernie continued, "lots of folks think the Quarter Horse ain't nothin' but a stock horse; and he *is* a stock horse—been trained to that work for generations. But he's a race horse, too. Back in Sir Archy's time the Thoroughbred breed was just gettin' started. There was lots of top horses turned out in that process that never was listed in the A.S.B.—horses with the identical breedin' of the ones that *were* getting listed. Horses like Old Bacchus an' Peacock an' Babram an' Printer. But they weren't *distance* runners so the Thoroughbred people didn't have no use for them. They were called 'Short Horses.' Now what you ought to do," Ernie finished, "is to go up to Tucson and see Bert Wood—"

222

"He's too hard t' find."

"See Haskell then, or the Double N Ranch. They're raisin' Quarter Horses."

"Them Tucson sports is too rich fer *my* blood," Shorty grimaced. "You'd think Tucson was the Horse Capital of the World, t' hear 'em. I reckon some of them gents'll be pullin' in their horns now the tracks has closed down."

"Ever think of goin' down to Dragoon or Willcox? There's some good stuff down there."

"I wrote that Ben Hur woman a letter, but she ain't got nothin' fer sale," Shorty said. "I wrote that bunch over at Willcox, too. One ol' gal's got three young studs—wants a thousand dollars apiece fer 'em. Most of them birds won't even *give* you a price. Browning's the only one ain't fixin' to retire on his profits. He's got a comin' two-year-old filly, a dappled gray, that he'll sell for three hundred an' fifty dollars. By Johnny Kane's Quarter stud that was by Jo Mc-Kinney's horse, Mack. Her mother was out of Wear's stud, Tony. Me an' Sam Hoard was figgerin' to go down there, but there ain't much sense goin' so far fer one critter."

"One *good* filly would be a hell of an improvement over what you got now."

"That's a matter of opinion," Shorty growled, getting huffed again. "I'm gettin' plumb fed up with people knockin' my horses!"

"I ain't never heard *McGee* praisin' any of them."

"Never you mind about McGee," Shorty said. "When I buy another horse it's goin' to be a palomino."

Ernie stared. Then he shrugged his shoulders.

"I give you up. Rose is right, there just ain't no cure for you."

3

YELLOW SHOES

HAVING GOT SHUT of the soul-blighting Ernie, Wild Horse
had just hitched up his chaps and was bending his steps
toward Fritchet's Saloon, to learn if his credit would stand
hoisting a couple, when he spied a yon rider coming hellity
larrup. This was January, a bright fresh morning, and a
heap too hot to be moving like that without a fellow was
hunting a sawbones or the sheriff.

Shorty pulled up and stared.

There wasn't much to the town of Horsehead Crossing.
It was just a wide place in the road where the Helvetia Trail
had once joined hands with the Greaterville trace to cross
a roaring Santa Cruz River—which stream had not roared
in the memory of the oldest living inhabitant.

Largest and most conspicuous of its buildings was Provencher's Mercantile, a rambling overstuffed barn of a place
that smelled to high heaven of sorghum and soap and the
gunnysacked fertilizer piled by the counter. There was a
blacksmith shop; and a leather-goods store which was owned
by Doc Wallace, the local vet. One hotel, called the Happy
Harp, which was run at a profit by a man known as "Ben."
A combination livery stable and feed corral kept by George
Kerley, a transplanted Texan, who knew a deal about horses

and could rope with his eyes shut. Lastly, there was the Mill where Sam Hoard, an old horse buyer, made cactus lamps which he sold the rich dudes in the Catalina foothills.

These, and a handful of tumbledown houses, were all that was left of the town where once Curly Bill had roared, where Earp and the Clantons had once thrown shots, and red-shirted miners had made the nights wail. The town still clung to its faded glories, but its take these days was largely dependent on what it could get from the roundabout tight-fisted hen raisers, who charged three prices and were loath to pay one.

Shorty's stare at the yonder rider was abruptly distracted by a hail from behind. The impatient scowl he flicked over a shoulder picked up Sam Hoard, who said, "Hello there, Shorty. What's new with the horses? Didn't I see you talkin' with some stranger a while ago?"

"Sounds that way." Dismissing Sam Hoard, Shorty looked once again at the oncoming rider.

"Nice lookin' horse he had—claybank, wasn't it?"

"It was a palomino."

"We called 'em claybanks in *my* day," declared Sam. "There was just two kinds of yellow horses then. Claybanks an' duns. But the duns, or 'buckskins,' was by far the most popular. *There* was a horse! Great hearted an' tougher than mesquite. Proud was the gent who could own one. There was three kinds of buckskins. The golden buckskin had a yellow hide, like your palominos, but with a black mane and tail and a black stripe down his backbone. The red buckskin—he wasn't so common—was a kind of rose-gold color with a red mane and tail. The grulla, or blue buckskin, had a coat that shone like gun steel, but with that same familiar dark stripe down his back. They was a great breed of horses. You don't see many nowadays. They was smart as a whip."

"Oh, I dunno," Shorty said argumentatively. "Palominos is smart enough fer *my* money."

"Have you seen that new filly at the Double N? *She's* a buckskin, and a darn good one, too," Sam said. "A golden buckskin of Quarter Horse breeding. Goes time after time to King Herod himself, and I don't know how many times to Steel Dust . . ."

But Shorty's interest had gone somewhere else.

He was eyeing the nearing rider again and a dark tide of color was deepening his complexion. Both the horse and the rider were plain to make out now, and Shorty made toward them with a face like thunder.

The rider pulled up in a great cloud of dust.

"What the hell you been thinkin' of—pushin' that mare in all this heat! She's a broodmare, you idjit! An' *my* broodmare, at that! What you tryin' t' do—kill her?"

"Why, I . . . er . . . Well—*Shucks!*"

It was Hellbound Hank and he was all of a lather. "I got *news* fer you, son—*real* news, by godfreys! Them Tucson sports is gittin' up a Trail Ride! Like the kind they hev in Vermont— Like thet Merced-t'-Mariposa one what them Californians hev ever' year! On'y this one is diff'rent! Gonna be a Handicap Trail Ride—some kinda claimin' business. One hundred an' fifty miles— Jest think of it! *One hundred an' fifty mile,* by godfreys!"

"What of it?" Shorty snapped at him crossly. "That any reason to git my mare in a uproar?" He peered at her closely; went and felt of her temperature. "If you've foundered—"

"Why, thet mare ain't hurt! She ain't hurt a partical—"

"You got her all over foam! Jest *lookit* her!" Shorty wailed, glaring and cursing. "I've a notion to knock your numskull head in!"

"Well, thet's thanks fer you!" Hellbound said, mad like.

226

"Here I been breakin' my neck t' git you this news in time fer you t' *do* somethin' about it, an' all thet I git fer my trouble is threats an' vile cursin'. Is thet any way t' treat a ol' man's loyalty?"

"That ain't what *I* call it," Wild Horse snarled, "when a locoed old loafer, what I been tryin' to be kind to, grabs up my best broodmare—an' her in foal, at that!—an' goes churnin' her guts up on a day like this! Whoa, girl—Whoa!" This last to the mare; and then, indignantly, to her rider: "You ain't got the sense you was borned with!"

A couple big tears rolled down Hellbound's cheeks; but Wild Horse was not impressed. He was plumb fed up with the old man's antics. Before Shorty had hired him, Hellbound Hank had been the town's Bad Example—had seemed quite proud of the distinction, even; and it looked like Shorty's influence had not much improved him.

He was a tall, cadaverous sort of jigger who was built like a bed slat and had to stand twice to cast one shadow. He had two buck teeth in the front of his face which gave him a kind of rabbity look—or would have if it had not been for the twelve droopy hairs that framed his mouth (seven on the north side and five to the south), which he pridefully cherished and called a "mustache." These, like the scanty locks on his dome which he wasted ten minutes every morning parting, were of a shade most resembling a henna-rinse red. Mrs. Ex-Sheriff Potter could tell you about him; he had caused her husband no end of trouble.

"I hired you to *work,* not to larrup around like a eel in a skillet! This is the last time I'm warnin' you. When you ride my mares don't *larrup* 'em! Mares is got feelin's jest the same as you hev. A horse is a man's best friend. Never sasses you back, never argues nor asks fer things. An' they don't never claim you ain't good enough fer 'em— Mebbe you ain't, but they don't keep harpin' on it, nor spend half their time tellin' you what you *ought* to do. They . . ."

Shorty's talk trailed off. He had whipped his head abruptly around like something had caught his gaze and held it; and old Sam Hoard, peering that way also, took off his glasses. "Holy cow!" he said.

And small wonder!

A big yellow touring car had just pulled up and stopped before the Happy Harp Hotel. A colored chauffeur plopped out and plucked open the door. But it wasn't the chauffeur all the gents were ogling; it was the platinum blonde so regally alighting. A vision of loveliness— Lord, what grace! What pulchritude! What seductive lines that silver gown displayed!

Shorty stared with his eyes bugged out like saucers.

"Must be one of them movie stars," Sam Hoard whispered. "There's a whole tribe of 'em campin' round Tucson now. Makin' a picture called *Duel in the Sun*—"

But Shorty wasn't interested in pictures. He *was* very definitely interested in the girl; and when she dropped her kerchief going up the steps Shorty went for it just like a dog to a bone.

Round the car he dashed, grabbing wildly for it. He would have gotten it, too, only a dadburned wind sprang up just then and whisked it right out from under his fingers.

Off it sailed and Wild Horse after it.

The wind let it go just in front of the car and Shorty dived like a football hero. His hand shot out and clutched it fairly. But he didn't pick it up; he did not get up himself. Something came down hard on his hand with the grinding feel of a circling steam roller.

It was a big yellow shoe. There was a man's foot in it.

Shorty let out a curse. He tried to get the shoe off him.

" 'Ere! Wotcher up ter?" a gruff voice demanded.

Shorty craned his neck and glared up at the fellow. He was a sunburnt, solemn kind of horse-faced chap, not overly tall, but tough looking, wiry. He had big rough hands and thick black brows on a corrugated forehead. He was clad in plus fours and a rough tweed coat. The hat on his head was the largest Stetson that had ever romped into the Horsehead Crossing. But Shorty did not give a dang *what* he looked like just so he got that clodhopper off him.

"You're standin'—"

But the man said, scowling: "Blimey! Cawn't yer leave me bloomin' foot alone?"

"You got your foot on my hand!"

"Wot's yer blinkin' 'and doing dahn there?"

"Never mind that!" Shorty snarled. "Git off it!"

" 'Oo's on it?"

"By grab, you'll know if I ever git loose!"

The man in the plus fours casually looked round. Hellbound was slapping at a passing horsefly. Old Sam Hoard was looking curiously at Shorty. Mr. Ben, all smiles, was obsequiously assuring the platinum blonde that his Happy Harp Hotel was the best in town, was ushering her in with divers bows and scrapings. The yellow-shoed man looked again at Hellbound. "Wot's 'e torkin' abaht? Wot's the matter with 'im any'ow?—crawlin' arahnd on the ground that w'y! Is 'e 'arf dorg or somethink?"

Whatever wild threat Shorty's growl was shaping was lost in the honking of the big yellow touring car. The smart-liveried chauffeur was back in his seat and not at all minded to wait on horseplay. He tooted again with his triple-toned thunder.

"You're standin' on his hand," Hellbound said. "It hurts him."

"Oh! Lumme!" the man in the plus fours said; and stepped back.

Wild Horse snatched up his hand and shook it.

Stepping round him, Yellow Shoes whisked up the kerchief. He blew off the dust and got into motion.

"Hey!" Wild Horse shouted, scrambling up in a fury.

But it was a little too late. The yellow-shoed man was taking the kerchief up the hotel steps.

Muttering curses, Shorty bounded after him, following him into the hotel bar. Sam Hoard and Hellbound hastened, too.

"What'n hell's whiskers d'you think you're up to?" Shorty blared; but it was all too evident.

At the far end of the bar Mr. Ben and Yellow Shoes were in close converse. "Oh, yes—" said Ben, "*very* famous. That was Trillene Tralane, the Oregon Oriole. She has quite a part in that show they're filming."

Neither man looked around at the fuming Wild Horse.

"Tike 'er me compliments," said Yellow Shoes grandly, like his compliments were something you could put in the bank. "S'y that Mister Halbert Crowsnow would be hextremely grateful fer the pleasure of a few words with 'er."

He peeled a thousand-dollar bill from a sheaf of the same and slid it across the mahogany. Mr. Ben, with a knowing grin, pocketed the money and started upstairs.

Yellow Shoes lifted a sandwich off the free lunch platter.

Shorty caught him by the shoulder and yanked him round. "I'll be takin' that handkerchief!"

"Wot 'ankerchief?"

"Never mind all that. Jest hand it here—quick!"

"And 'ose 'ankerchief his it?"

"Well, it sure ain't *yours!*"

" 'Oo said it was?"

Wild Horse glared. He scowled like a gargoyle. By all the signs he looked ready for murder. "Listen here, you—"

"Aw, close yer fice!" Yellow Shoes yawned and started eating his sandwich.

Shorty tried a bluff. He sent one hand reaching inside his shirtfront.

Yellow Shoes roused like a stepped-on rattlesnake. A short-barreled pistol appeared in his hand. He jabbed its snout into Wild Horse's belly.

" 'Op at it! G'wan! W'y don'tcher, guv'nor?" He grinned into Shorty's face malignantly.

But Wild Horse was not feeling warlike—not against a man with a pistol. Heck! this was *today*, right now in the present. Folks didn't go around with their clothes full of firearms—nor stick their tongues out at firearms, either!

He looked at the gun, then he looked at Yellow Shoes. And all his bluster ran away like raindrops. "What's the big idear?" he said kind of meek like. Then he scowled at Hellbound. "You goin' t' let him git away with that?"

Hellbound looked pretty weak the way he slouched there. He managed a sickly grin. But he did not stir from his tracks. Not a muscle.

Wild Horse looked back at Yellow Shoes. He sure didn't like to take water that way. Especially in front of Hoard and Hellbound. But no sensible man was going to argue with a six-shooter.

Wild Horse suddenly remembered he was hungry.

He reached toward the platter. Another paw got there first. Shorty snatched back his hand like a snake had been under it. Yellow Shoes drew his hand back, too.

Shorty scowled at the platter and reached forth again. Once again his hand came down on Yellow Shoes'.

"Blimey!" the man in the plus fours said. "Cawn't yer leave me bloomin' 'and alone?"

Wild Horse wrinkled up his face and swore. "Then get the dang thing outa that dish!"

"Does them sandwitches berlong ter *you?*"

"No, but—"

"Then don't try to keep me from eatin' 'em."

Shorty choked back his anger and counted ten. Then once more he reached.

But it was just the same thing all over again. Only more so. He said: "Now look here, you swivel-eyed polecat! I want some of them sandwiches myself!"

"Why'n't yer tike 'em then?"

"Are you figgerin' to stop me?" Wild Horse bellowed; and, right then, Mr. Ben came down the stairs flying.

"None o' that, now!" he said, mighty riled like. "I've had all the trouble with *you* I aim to! I run a respectable hotel for respectable people and I don't want to have any ructions round here. I ain't askin' for saddle-tramp trade; and keep your hands off those sandwiches. I put them out there for *customers.*"

"Well, I like *that!*" Shorty snarled.

"I don't care if you like it or not."

Mr. Ben gave Wild Horse a dirty look, dusted off his hands and went behind the bar.

Yellow Shoes licked his chops and helped himself to another sandwich. "What'd she s'y?" he asked the hotel-keeper.

"Said she'd be right down." Mr. Ben gave Yellow Shoes the knowing eye. "I can see you know real class when you meet it."

The man in the plus fours finished his eating. He wiped

off his mouth with a grin at Wild Horse. "Yus!" he said. "I mike quite a 'it with the lydies."

"You'll git hit one of these days," Shorty told him.

"Hit will be a far day hif it's left ter you!"

4

TIME FOR A CHANGE

SHORTY was so riled he couldn't see straight. He came out of that place looking meaner than chili powder thickened with tadpoles, and he exploded new cusswords every step he took.

He was still orating when Hellbound caught up with him. Hellbound wasn't keeping very quiet either. "Now you done it, son— Now you done it!" He looked down at Shorty like he was viewing old Nero fiddling the doom of Rome. "Now you done it—"

"I ain't done it yet, but I dang soon will! I'm gonna crawl his hump! I'm goin' to bat down his ears t' where they'll do fer wings! I'm goin' t' whip that guy to a whisper!"

"No you ain't, son—not ef I kin help it! Why, Lord God," declared the old man horrified, "don't you know who thet feller is? He come in jest this mornin'. He's a guest of the ranch—"

"I'll *guest* him!"

"But you *can't!*" wailed Hellbound. "He's *royalty!* A real belted Earl!"

"Humph!" Wild Horse glowered, but he calmed down a little. And he stood there looking kind of thoughtful a
234

minute. Then he snorted. "He don't look like no Earl t' me!"

"How do you know he don't? You ever seen a real live Earl before?"

"If that guy's a Earl I don't wanta see none. If he's a Earl I'm a pop-eyed Eskimo!"

Shorty snorted again and, still muttering, went and untied his horse and got onto him. Then he scowled afresh and got out of the saddle. "Here," he said, tossing Hellbound the reins. "You ride Figure 8. I'll take care of Columbine. She looks plumb frazzled. If she has a miscarriage I'm goin' to pin your ears back."

"Well, so long," Sam Hoard called, coming out of the hotel. "Remember what I told you about them mares."

Shorty waved him a grumpy goodbye and mounted. He felt about as cheerful as a centipede with chilblains.

And he was feeling no better when they got to the ranch.

McGee met them at the gate. "You've got more company. Place is full up now—every shack taken."

"Don't turn nobody away," Shorty said. "That duke's clearin' out—that belted-Earl Crowsnow guy. He's crowed his last around *this* outfit. When I hev to take in the likes of him I'll be hard up indeed!"

"You can't put him out—"

"I'm *puttin'* him out!"

"Well— But he's already paid for a month in advance."

"That's tough," Shorty said. "That's jest too bad! Who's the other new guy?"

"I dunno—some writer feller. Name of Sinclair. He's writin' a book about beans or somethin'. Tall, lanky jasper. Ugly as a Paiute squaw without clothes on. Used t' punch cows, he tells me. He *looks* the part, I'll say that for him."

"Well, you make sure he don't chouse my mares around.

You know them cowpunchers! All the time goin' like hell wouldn't hold 'em—or the other place, either. I ain't in business to supply rodeos. 'F he can't ride right he needn't t' ride a-tall.

"An' by the way," Shorty said, "that reminds me! Sam Hoard was tellin' me that Ed Echols' brother-in-law, or somebody, is figgerin' to sell a stud an' ten mares—good Quarter-type stuff. They're over in Sonora. He only wants a thousan' dollars fer the bunch."

"You don't want 'em."

"Who says I don't?" demanded Wild Horse, scowling.

"They'll cost you another seventy-five apiece jest to get them across the Border," McGee said, with a year of being Shorty's foreman behind him. "Not t' even mention haulin' charges! I don't call that cheap for a bunch of scrub range stock."

McGee spat out his chaw. "Hang hold to your money. Take another couple months an' the price of horses is goin' to go down like a kicked-over tent."

"Yeah? Who says so?"

"*I* say so, dang it! It stands to reason. Now the Gover'-ment has ordered all the race tracks closed—"

"Hoo-hoo!" Shorty jeered. "You don't think no feller what's put his pile into horses is goin' to sell 'em off wholesale jest to keep from hevin' to feed 'em, do you? Cripes! You talk like Hellbound!" Then he said, getting mad, "Dad-burn it! If you don't like the way I do things, you kin go someplace where things suits you better. Don't let *me* put no spokes in yer wheel! *I* ain't standin' on *no*body's shirt-tail!"

McGee gave him a long look, cold and hard like. Then he shut his mouth and headed for the bunkhouse.

He didn't stay long and when he came back out he fetched
236

his bedroll with him. He never asked for his time, for a lift, or anything. He strode past Shorty like he never saw him with his roll on his shoulder and flinty eyes straight front. He let himself out the front gate and closed it after him and struck off down the dusty road.

Wild Horse stared like he couldn't believe it. Then his mad came back and he snorted, scowling. If McGee couldn't take a little joke, then to hell with him!

"SHORTY," Rose said, "this is John Sinclair. He's a regional novelist—"

Shorty scowled at Sinclair. "Don't want any," he muttered, grabbing a handful of matches from the kitchen match box.

The novelist gave him a dour Scots smile. "Stories," he said. "I write—"

"Got you the first time. I don't want any—never read 'em nohow."

Rose looked at him sharp like. "Mister Sinclair is a guest —a cash customer. He came here for a vacation, he's not trying to sell you anything."

"He better not," Shorty said, giving Sinclair a hard eye. "An' he better hev a care how he larrups my horseflesh. I know all about them cowpunchers—git on a horse an' ride the dang hoofs off it! They—"

"Shorty!" Rose said; and Wild Horse closed his mouth. He cuffed back his hat and went out of the house. He heard Rose telling the dude he wasn't always like that; and that did not smooth his temper out any. Making excuses for him!

He was sure enough in a sod pawing mood.

Whose business was it if he wanted to buy horses? It was *his,* by godfreys, and no whiskered this-and-that was going to talk him out of it! And what's more, by grab, he'd buy the kind *he* wanted—palominos!

He had finally gotten this ranch under lease, but if he could not do like he wanted around here, he would dang well go where he *could* do it! No slat-sided foreman was going to tell *him* his business—nor no dadburned housekeeper neither, by gee!

He was feeling hard used, and no mistake.

Nothing went right for him—not a blamed thing! More you did for people the worse they treated you. Every slat-sided time, by godfreys! Look how he'd taken McGee in; given him a home, given him a chance to work with horses — And what did you get for it? Just a lot of cheap slurs and high-toned advice about saving your money!

Hell's fire!

And that freckle-faced Rose was just as bad! All the time snooting down at him—right from the first time he'd ever laid eyes on her! Always hunting up ways to belittle him. Even when she was sweating her sides out for that bald-headed toad of a dang hotel leech she'd had nothing good to say for him. And when she'd lost her job and come whining around for some place to stay, he'd taken her right in just like he'd wanted her; given her a place out of the kindness of his heart. Why, he'd even imagined he was in love with her! And given her a ring— Yes, by godfreys! And none of your Woolworth diamonds, neither!

And when he'd asked her to marry him she'd turned him down. Turned him down cold with a lot of hot air about "good providers." Said she wasn't tying herself down to no feller that couldn't even take care of a bunch of scrub horses!

There was gratitude for you!

And her a snub-nosed hasher!

238

Be a mighty cold day before he asked her again. He wasn't crawling on his belly for no durn woman.

The more Shorty turned things over the madder he got.

He was right in the middle of counting his injuries when Hellbound came caterwauling round the harness shed.

"Fare thee well to
OLD JOE CLARK,
Fare thee well, I say—"

"It'll be farewell t' *you* if you don't shut up that yowlin' an' git to work!" Wild Horse snarled. He sent a glance round the pasture. "Did you rub Sweet Columbine down like I told you?"

Hellbound shuffled his feet uneasy like. He scuffed at a pebble and shifted weight. "I rubbed her tail good with bacon grease—"

"Ain't I told you t' leave that bacon grease alone?"

"Now son, don't yowl at me thataway. I ain't deef. Ef I've tol' you once I've tol' you forty times *all a horse's ailments comes down t' the tail*. Man an' boy I've keered fer horses, an' I ain't never seen no trouble yet thet you couldn't trace smack-dab back t' the tail. Work on the tail— Thet's the on'y thing thet'll git the results. Jest work on the tail an' you kin cure 'em of anythin'."

"I've heard you blowin' that horn before. It's a lot of durn foolishness! No wonder her tail ain't got no hair on it! By grab, there's goin' t' be some changes round here. From right now on, *I'm* givin' the orders— An' they better be carried out! You hear me?"

Hellbound nodded. He licked at his lips and nodded again. He halfway opened his mouth to say something but the look of Shorty was not encouraging.

239

"That's right," Wild Horse told him. "The bigger the mouth the better it looks when it's shut. Now you git back over there an' rub her down right. Rub her *all over*."

Having laid down the law, Wild Horse made for the shade of the bunkhouse. He tilted back on the porch, put his feet on the rail and was just getting settled to retabulate his sufferings when he spied Rose coming across the yard.

She was making straight for him with a glint in her eye.

Shorty thought some of ducking but there wasn't rightly time.

She started right in. "I should think you *would* hang your head. Sometimes you make me downright ashamed of you. Pouting an' squirming like a sulky boy! When are you going to turn that new leaf you've been telling about? I thought you were going to get shut of those horses—"

"Why don't you hev some confidence in me?"

"Do you ever make an effort to *merit* my confidence?" Rose glared, shook her head and bit at her lip. She kind of blinked her eyes like she'd got something in them, then her shoulders drooped. "You're just going to be another Hell-bound, Shorty; every day I see it plainer and plainer . . . Oh, well!" She gave it up, unable to find any words to reach him.

"Go ahead," Shorty growled. "Call me a no-account bum an' be done with it."

"I didn't come out here to argue with you, but there's got to be a few changes round here. You can't go on insulting these dudes and expect them to grin and bring their friends next year. You've got to mend your ways or you'll not have one nickel you can rub on another."

Shorty said nothing. He just twiddled with his fingers.

"Stop that twiddling!" Rose snapped, "and pay attention.
240

I know you don't like to hear me talk this way— I don't like to have to. But *some*body's got to wake you up. It's for your own good. You were going to be a big horse breeder. You were going to make Luther K. Dickerson look like a piker. You were going to raise the best palominos that had ever been foaled. Now just what have you accomplished? Another whole year has rolled around—"

"Rome wasn't built in a day," Shorty scowled.

"There must have been some sign it was started," Rose said. "You're just where you were at this time last year. You haven't got one solitary horse—"

"Now don't you start runnin' down my horses!"

"I don't have to run them down," Rose said tartly. "They were all run down before you ever got hold of them! Why don't you listen to someone—just once! To Ernie, or Kerley, or Nels McGee! They're your friends. When they give you advice—"

"Yeah—advice!" Shorty snarled. "Advice is all I git around here! I got more bosses than a dawg has fleas!"

"We're not trying to boss you," Rose said indignantly. "We're trying to help you; but you're too bull headed to listen to anyone! I don't see why I waste my time on you— you're just a crusty old saddle tramp and you won't never be no different!"

"Well, you don't hev to bawl about it," Shorty said. "How do you s'pose them old mares would feel if I did like you wanted an' turned 'em out? Why, them old mares *depends* on me!" He glared at Rose fiercely. "Look here! If I cut loose of them critters they'll be dawg meat tomorrer— Why, dang it all, Rose, them mares are a-trustin' me! Can't you see it in their eyes? This is all the home they've ever knowed. You wouldn't want me t' turn 'em out, would you? I know they ain't much shucks as *horses* but, dang it, they've had hard lives. This here's about as near to heaven as they'll ever git. I—I can't turn 'em out, Rose. I jest can't do it!"

"Why—Shorty!" Rose said. "I didn't know you felt that way about them. Of course you can't do it. And we won't— We'll keep them."

She took out her handkerchief and blew her nose. "Here I am, blubberin' like a kid," she sniffed. "But you're absolutely right! We'll find *some* way to keep on feeding them."

She came up on the porch, put a hand on his arm. "You've made me feel plumb ashamed of myself."

"Shucks," Shorty said, and slipped an arm around her. "Tomorrow," he said, "we'll hev a real stud out here. Jest as gold as butter—*a real palomino.* Like I've always wanted! We'll show these fellers!"

"You've really *found* one? Oh, Shorty! . . . But can we afford it?"

"We kin afford *this* one," Shorty said. "He's the slickest thing ever peeked through a bridle. Blood of Kings is his name— I'm goin' to buy him tonight."

"Well, that's fine," Rose said. "By the way, where's Mc-Gee?"

Shorty's grin dimmed away. He looked a little uneasy.

"To tell you the truth," he said, "we had words, an' he quit me." He told her the way of it.

"Oh, dear," Rose said. "And he's really gone? Oh, Shorty! You should never have let him gone *afoot!* How *could* you?"

"Never mind," Shorty growled, "I'll make it up to him. When I go for Blood of Kings I'll fetch McGee back with me. He'll be all right when he gits over his mad. McGee's a good guy—"

"I know he is. I just hate it that you had to have words with him that way. You apologize to him, Shorty. He's been hunting all over to find a good mare for you—"

"Never mind," Shorty said. "I'll make it up to him. An' when he finds the right mare for me, we'll use Blood of Kings an' we'll really be into the horse business. Don't you worry; I'll fetch him back."

5

TALL IN THE SADDLE

But he did not bring McGee back that night.

Things at the Crossing looked about as usual. Light puddled the windows of Fritchet's saloon. Other lights sent a glimmer from the Happy Harp Hotel, and Provencher's Mercantile was still doing business.

Shorty swung down in front of Cramp Fritchet's and tied Figure 8 to the snorting post. Then he hitched up his chaps and tramped inside.

It was about 8:30. Business was not lively. A couple of half-asleep townsmen were playing cards at a table. Four other gents had their bellies to the bar and Doc Wallace was bragging about the hogs he was raising. Shorty knew them all and was glad L. Ernenwein was not among them for he'd had all the arguments he wanted, for one day.

"How are you, Shorty!" Doc hailed him, grinning. He came over and slapped Shorty's shoulder. "Been a lovely day, ain't it? What! Haven't you got your guitar with you this time?"

"It's out on the saddle," Shorty explained. "Anybody seen McGee?"

"Nels McGee?" Sam Hoard shook his head. "No, he ain't been seen around here. Somethin' on your mind?"

"Nothin' special," Shorty said. "Only I'm goin' to hev the best palomino stud in the country by this time t'morrer. An' I say the *best,* by grab—bar none!"

Old Jack Williams peered over his spectacles. "Well, now. Buyin' another horse are you, Shorty? Where you gettin' him?"

"I'm *importin'* this stud," Shorty said impressively. "Comes clear up from Mexico City—fastest horse in that country since Blue Jacket beat Little Joe down there. I tell you, boys, he's a daisy."

"That's fine," declared Doc Wallace with a great show of heartiness. "I guess congratulations are in order. What you going to call him, Shorty?"

"Blood of Kings is his name. Royally bred—crack stock. Raised by the Agger Clan, they tell me. They had a lot of trouble gittin' him over the ocean. Oh, he's a daisy! I'm goin' to show that Tucson bunch where to git off at."

Fritchet, coming in just then, said, "Don't you know the Government's stopped racin'? Told all the tracks they better close up; an' now, accordin' to the way I heard it, they're figurin' to stop folks from taking horses any place off their own property."

"If they keep on," Shorty said, "we'll hev to git a ration card t' breathe! I never heard of such knothole barkin'. What good does it do to stop horses racin'?"

"Don't ask *me,*" Fritchet said. "I don't have no hand in the Government."

Sam Hoard said, looking over at Shorty, "I thought you was goin' to buy them Echols mares. You forget about it?"

"*I* never said so." Shorty sniffed. "A fine fool I'd be, puttin' out seventy-five dollars a head jest fer the privilege of crossin' the Line with 'em. An' range stock, at that—not to

245

mention sales cost an' haulin' charges! You must think money grows on cactus!"

"Humph!" Hoard said. "What are you figurin' to *use* this stud on?"

"McGee's got his eye on a couple of mares fer me. Best thing to do, I always claim, is to start out small an' breed to good blood lines. It's quality that counts in the horse business *these* days. Take a guy that's got quality, he kin always unload at a pretty fair profit. You take these Johnny-Come-Latelies; what they can't git through their durn heads is that you got to keep your eye on the kind of stuff's bein' raised an' sold *round* you. There ain't much sense raisin' a bunch of Saddlebreds where everybody wants to own a Quarter Horse."

Fritchet said drily, "Gettin' kind of twisted in your rope, ain't you?"

"If I am, I don't need *your* help t' git me out! This new stud of mine is a palomino—but I never said what kind of blood lines he's got. An' I *ain't* sayin', neither. You're goin' to hev t' wait till you see him. But let me tell you, feller, there's a HORSE!"

"Well, I hope so," Fritchet said. "If it is it'll be the first one *you* ever owned."

"Oh, is that so!" Shorty blared. "I recollect you once thought enough of ol' Figure 8 to give me four hundred an' fifty bucks fer him!"

"Why, damn your impudence," Fritchet said angrily, "that was supposed to be kept secret!"

"I reckon it was supposed to be kept secret you backed out of the deal when Dickerson's bunch durn near ruined the horse. You an' your secrets! You're enough to cramp rats!"

Fritchet shut his face like a wolf trap, but Wild Horse grinned. "How's your daughter Baisy passin' the time while Lute's shut up in the pen?" he asked; and Fritchet stamped out and slammed the door after him.

Shorty had got him on the hip *that* time.

"Hear about Provencher's mare?" Hoard asked; and Williams cut in to say Ernie, the sheriff, had bought a coming-two filly—a pretty little thing that looked like a race horse.

But Shorty had caught something odd in Sam's voice. "What about Provencher's mare?" he asked. "Has she had her foal yet?"

"Yep!" Sam nodded. "Horse colt—dropped him yesterday. By one of them high-priced studs, you remember, Lute Dickerson was always spendin' his money on—one of them *palominos*. It don't take none after its Daddy. Goat-faced, pink-skinned, glass-eyed an' white as the riven snow," Sam said, with a smug little smile in Shorty's direction.

Shorty said, scandalized, "A dang albino!"

"Yep," Sam said; and they all looked disgusted, for if there was any one thing a palomino man could not abide it was a horse in whose veins ran the least taint of albinism. It was the curse of the yellow-horse breeders.

They all shook their heads, and Ed Nagel said, "Man's the only animal can be skun more than once."

Wild Horse said, "If George don't hit that foal on the head he ought to hev his *own* head looked at!"

Doc Wallace nodded. "Be a crime, in a way, to raise a critter like that."

"They raise 'em up in Nebraska," Hoard said. "Even gone an' got up a registry for 'em."

Jack Williams said, "I never saw a Nebraskan yet that had sense enough to pound sand down a rat hole," and that took care of Nebraska nicely.

247

"Goin' to take in the Horse Show, Shorty?" Doc asked. "Haskell says they're goin' to have a big turn-out; lots of outside blood being brought in this year. New Mexico, California, Texas—all over."

"Where they holdin' it— *When,* I mean?"

"Rodeo grounds. February second."

One of the card-players said, "Why'n't you enter Sweet Columbine, Shorty?"

But Wild Horse took the quip seriously. "Don't guess she'd stand much chance. I wouldn't hev no time to git her groomed up. Anyhow, she's in foal."

"You c'ld enter her in a circus," Fritchet's barkeep guffawed, "if she has five foals in her *next* litter, Shorty!"

"Well, you needn't t' sneer," Wild Horse told him. "I don't notice *your* get pullin' down no prizes!"

IT WAS ABOUT six miles to the Emery Park schoolhouse, six miles through the greasewood and prickly pear tangles. But the miles were as nothing to Wild Horse that night. He had perked up considerable with the prospect of taking that golden horse home with him. Laugh at him, would they? Well, let the fools laugh! He guessed they'd be singing a different tune when he turned up with Blood of Kings under his saddle!

The stars blinked down like sleepy mockers and all that vast country lay hushed and quiet beneath the pale sickle of a silvery moon. There was not much light, but Shorty didn't need any; he could have found his way around this country blindfolded. He knew it and loved it—loved every spike-weeded, dusty inch of it.

He took up his battered tin-plated guitar and lifted his nasal voice in song:

> " 'Twas onct in the saddle
> I used t' go dashin',
> 'Twas onct in the saddle
> I used to feel gay—
> I first took to drinkin'
> An' then t' card-playin',
> Got shot through the belly—
> I'm dyin' to-day."

If his voice was any criterion, he surely was.

All the gophers jumped for their holes and the coyotes yapped derisively.

But Shorty didn't give a hoot. In a time now measured by mighty short minutes he would be the proud owner of as fine a gold stallion as ever raised dust at the Horsehead Crossing! So entranced was Shorty at this glowing prospect, he must needs raise his voice in another stanza:

> "Oh, go write a letter
> To my gray-haired Mother,
> And break the news gently
> To sister so dear—
> But still there's another
> Even dearer than Mother,
> Who will weep bitter tears
> When she knows I am here."

Even the wolves lamented, it seemed like.

Getting warmed up, Shorty next tried a song for the folks at the Crossing, a song about Friends and Relations. But he laughed at the finish just to show he held no rancor. "That's the one I ought've sung at Fritchet's when the Doc piped up about my guit-tar," he chuckled.

Oh, he was in a merry mood all right.

Then a sobering thought kind of clouded his brow. "I

hope, Figger 8," he said to his horse, "that that bustard of a Tranch don't fergit t' show up."

That would be a blow indeed!

Somewhat uneasy, now the possibility had occurred to him, Shorty stepped up the black stud's pace a little. Probably Tranch had not forgot about it, but he might be so mad account of Ernie's deviling, that he had plain packed up and quit the country.

Shorty sure hoped not.

He began to peer ahead anxiously, straining his eyes against the desert gloom. But he could not make out any great deal, just the low murky huddle of the school's rambling buildings, with here and there the occasional upthrust blotch of some foliaged tree limb.

He crossed the S.P. tracks and then the highway, that narrow tar ribbon that curled down into Mexico, and still without seeing one solitary soul. He was opening his mouth to let out a yowl when he happened to think that maybe Tranch wouldn't like it. Tranch might not care to have their meeting noticed. In fact, Shorty thought, there was a very good chance Sheriff Ernie had been right when he'd suggested Tranch's title to the stud was somewhat foggy.

Not that such notions were bothering Shorty. Possession, he had found, was pretty nearly always worth as much as the law; and, if it wasn't in this case, he reckoned he could handle any difference.

"That you, Mister?"

Until that moment, Wild Horse had not guessed how anxious he had been.

The sound of Tranch's voice was just like a blessing.

He drew a great breath of relief and said: "It ain't nobody else. Hev you got that horse?"

"Yeah," Tranch said, and came forward. "You brought
250

cash, I hope— I don't want no checks. This is strictly a cash proposition."

"I *always* deal in cash," Shorty said; and suddenly wished he had kept his mouth shut. There was another guy watching back there in the shadows; and it came over Wild Horse he was face to face with a mighty good chance for a stick-up. He didn't even have a pea-shooter with him! And there were tramps aplenty roving through this country, who would do a guy in for less than five hundred.

He backed Figure 8 kind of nervous like.

"Here! Where you off to?" Tranch demanded.

"Who's that feller back under them trees?"

"Oh, him?" Tranch laughed. "Just a friend—Mule Ear Swenson. He's holdin' the horses. No need to worry about *him*," Tranch said.

He dug out his wallet. "Ain't you goin' to get down off that horse?"

"I don't never feel nacheral when I ain't on a horse," Shorty hedged, still watching that guy in the shadows. "Where's the stud?"

"Where's your cash?" Tranch countered.

Wild Horse sighed. He guessed it was going to be neck meat or nothing. If they aimed to rob him there wasn't very much he could do about it. So he dug out his roll and waited for the pistol.

But nobody pulled any on him. Nothing happened at all.

Tranch said, "That moon could stand a little touchin' up. But I guess I can see enough to sign my name. Here's your bill of sale— What name do you want me to put for buyer?"

"Wild Horse Shorty is the name I go by."

"Kind of a nom de guerre, eh?" Tranch chuckled. Then he called to the other man: "Bring 'im over."

The fellow came out of the deep gloom by the buildings and bow-legged toward them with a led horse in tow. Even in this murky light Shorty could make out the stud's bright coloring; and he drew in a tickled, proudly satisfied breath as he visioned what the home folks would say when they saw him.

Mule Ear was champing a cud. When he came up he looked at Tranch and spat. "You're a dang fool, Tranch, to let 'im go so cheap. You could get four times that money—"

"We ain't goin' over that again," Tranch said. "I know what I'm doin'. I'm damn well sure I ain't goin' to Texas."

He turned back to Shorty. The bill of sale crackled. "Here you are, Mister. Let me see that money."

Shorty passed it over. Tranch thrust it in his pocket.

"Ain't you goin' to count it?" Shorty said.

"I guess I know an honest man when I see one."

"Well . . . But I sure aim t' look this bill o' sale over."

"Sure," Tranch nodded. "You go right ahead, young feller. I *want* you to. Always like to have everything shipshape an' regular. Strictly business—that's me every time."

Shorty struck a match and took a look at the document.

There was his name, all right, and the name of the animal, BLOOD OF KINGS, bold and clear. Then Wild Horse scowled. "Here—what's this?" he said suspicious like. " 'Fer the sum of one dollar an' other val'uble considerations—' "

"Just a form," Tranch said. "That's just to protect you in case you should decide to sell the horse later. If we was to put it down in writin' that you'd paid five hundred dollars, you might find it kind of hard to get the price up any. Just a handy form—used every day in legal transactions. Anybody'd know you paid more than a dollar. This way you
252

ain't tied to any stipulated amount. Of course," he said, "if you'd rather—"

"Well, no," Shorty frowned, "I guess we'll leave it that way. There's some as might think I'd paid more than I did fer him. Yeah," he said with an admiring grin, "that's a pretty slick stunt. I could even say I'd paid a *thousand dollars* fer him—"

"D'you think anyone would *doubt* it?" demanded Mule Ear sourly. He handed the rope to him. And Tranch kind of tittered like he couldn't imagine anybody being such a fool.

Shorty chuckled, too.

"Well," he said, waving goodbye to them airily, "I'll be seein' you, gents," and he tugged on the lead rope and started for home.

6

"MAN'S THE ONLY ANIMAL—"

SHORTY rode home with his head in the clouds. To him, that ride was in the nature of a triumphal procession. It made no difference that he rode alone. By his rapt expression he might have been leading the scarlet-robed hosts of Pharaoh with all the concomitant crash of cymbals. He was in the seventh heaven of the horse fancier's delight; he had found THE HORSE and had acquired him.

He rode without hurry, savoring to the full each anticipated pleasure, each look and exclamation bound to mark his prancing passing when, on the morrow, he should ride his high-stepping stallion before the awestruck, staring multitude. He knew dang well they would be impressed— why, their dadburned eyes would bug out with envy when this satin-sleek Blood of Kings came a-mincing along with Wild Horse bowing right and left and, maybe, throwing a few coins to the rabble.

Oh, it was a splendid vision!

Even as a kid he had been wacky about yellow horses. There hadn't been a time he had not wanted one. And it wasn't just their scarcity which had made him fall in love with them; even now, when they had become more common, he still wanted nothing half so much as to own a palomino. And now, at last, he *did* own one—the grandest one of them all!

Yes sir! The King of all Palominos!

To be sure, there were a number of quite excellent others —horses like Pirate Gold and Colonel Sappho, Oro Intringo and Hugh Dorado, El Tovar, Condado King, Dr. Clays and such like. But there was only one Blood of Kings and he stood head and shoulders above all of them.

Shorty wondered briefly where Nels McGee had gone, and if he had quit the country. He felt kind of mean about old Nels McGee; but he was much too enchanted to dwell on him long. McGee would come back when he got over his mad. He was too square a guy to nurse grudges.

Time and again Shorty turned in the saddle for a quick, backward glance at his dandy. It was really too dark to observe a great deal but Wild Horse, viewing that spirited head, would murmur encouraging words to him, croon to him, praise him and admire the glory of that shimmering mane and the sleek bright glowing hide of him.

It was a pity Lute Dickerson was locked in the Pen and so could not witness this triumph; handsome Lute who had looked down his nose and so often made Shorty the butt of cruel laughter.

But it would be worth something to see Fritchet's face when he cast his eye over Shorty's treasure—and Baisy's, the girl who had jilted him.

It was close on to midnight when he reached his own gate and let himself in with his horses. The ranch looked darker than a stack of stove lids—even the dudes must have turned out their lamps and gone to their beds like Christians.

Thinking of dudes brought Shorty's mind back to Crowsnow; and he turned to see if the bustard's trunk was still out in the road where he'd heaved it. But it wasn't. The beetle-browed blighter must have come out and got it; and Shorty was glad to be rid of him.

Wild Horse wished McGee had not quit him so soon; he would like to have had him look over Blood of Kings, to have seen the old man's eyes light up, for McGee sure knew his horseflesh.

He decided to get Hellbound Hank up. Old Hellbound didn't know doodle de squat, but even an old ignoramus like him was better than no one to show off his horse to.

So he went out to the barn and kicked over a bucket, and Hellhound's E-string voice rose quavering: "What in Hannah be you up to?"

Shorty said, "Dang if you don't put in more sleep than a tarnal grizzly. Eat an' sleep. Them's the best things you do— Sometimes I think you're half St. Bernard. Come out of that loft an' fetch a lantern. Got a little surprise fer you down here."

"Can't it wait till mornin'?"

"You come right now!"

So, with a deal of grumbling snorts and muttering, Hellbound Hank came down the ladder. He said peevish like, "I can't figger what's so durn important. Where in tarnashun are you?"

"I'm over by the door. Git a lantern, can't you? I want you to see this horse I got— Has McGee come back?"

"No, he ain't come back; an' he prob'ly never will come back. An' I don't know as I blame 'im," Hellbound growled, pawing round for the lantern. "Don't see why thet horse can't wait till daylight—"

"The horse kin wait till hell's froze over, but *I* don't aim to. Can't you light that lantern?"
256

"I could ef you'd give me time!" Hellbound snarled.

He finally got the lantern lighted and, holding it up, came shuffling over. "You can't see nothin' by lantern light nohow—"

"You kin see enough," Shorty said impatiently. "Fetch it over here. Now then, what do you think of him?"

He watched Hellbound's look. He wouldn't have missed seeing the old man's face for all the dudes this side of 'Frisco.

But the old man's face didn't look like it ought to. Instead of the delighted surprise expected, Hellbound's look was a study in puzzlement.

"What the hell!" Shorty growled. "Are you struck plumb speechless?" And he turned around to look at Blood of Kings himself.

He looked, and stared. And looked again.

"What's the matter with that lantern? You better clean that chimley! Durn light almost makes him look—"

"Lord God!" exclaimed Hellbound, finding his voice. "Ef you ain't gone an' lugged home a durn Al*beaner!*"

"Albino!" yowled Shorty. "Why, you ignorant dimwit—"

His voice kind of broke in the middle. He stared at the horse like he couldn't believe it. And the more he stared the more certain it seemed he had someway got mixed and brought home the wrong horse.

"Them *eyes!*" Hellbound screaked; and Shorty swore in a fury.

But there was one way to make sure—one final proof.

He jumped toward the horse, bent and peered underneath. *Sangre de Cristo* had had a black whatzit and . . .

But Hellbound was right.

He'd brought home an albino. And far worse than that, this thing he'd brought home was an albino *mare!*

7

THE SCOOTER ENTHUSIAST

THERE ARE TIMES in this life when a man feels like murder; and Wild Horse Shorty felt like murder then. It was not just the money, or the lost dreams even, that got into him so much as did the swindling way Tranch had pulled it on him. It was the *affront* which cut—the blow to his dignity and self-respect.

A durned albino mare, by godfreys!

Why, it was enough to make a man hone up his razor!

Like taking candy from a kid!

But the problem was, What could he *do* about it? It was not a heap likely Tranch would do any lingering. He had pulled off his swindle and now he would go. Him and that mule-eared compadre of his would be off to green pastures to find them another fool.

Five hundred dollars for an albino mare!

Why, Jesse James in all his glory had never dreamed up anything like that!

Shorty had never figured to be yowling for help. He had always aimed to take care of his own chores. But he didn't much think he could take care of Tranch—not without going to jail for it.

But Ernie, as sheriff, had means at his disposal which

were not open to Tom, Dick and Harry; and he had not cared for Tranch in the first place. Ernie was the one to do Tranch's business. It sure went against the grain to do it, but it looked like Shorty had best eat humble pie if he wanted to get any change from *this* deal.

"You see to this critter," he told Hellbound, scowling. "She can't help it if she's a dadburned albino. Get her some feed an' see she's made comfortable. But keep her tied up where nobody'll see her, an' *don't* let her loose whatever you do!"

Having said which, Shorty clapped on his hat and departed.

It was 3:15 when he got to the Crossing and Figure 8's hide was wet with sweat. It was no proper time to be rousing folks out, but Shorty was a man in search of action. Anyhow, to judge by the looks, Ernie was already up. There was a shaded light in the office window.

In Potter's time the Sheriff's Office had been in the back of Provencher's Mercantile; but Ernie had moved everything to his house. Renegade's Roost, he called it; and there were those who said the place was well named.

Shorty pounded the door. "Lemme in— It's Wild Horse!"

"Well, come ahead in. You ain't crippled, are you?"

"Humph!" Shorty snorted, and stormed inside.

Ernie was busily pounding a typewriter.

"What the hell?" Shorty growled. "Do you work all night?"

Ernie said, "Shh! Just a minute— I'm right in the middle of a story for *Ranch Romances*—about a girl on a stagecoach. I'm right at the spot where a couple tough citizens are fixing to stick up the stage an' make off with her."

259

"Well, criminy jispus— Look here!" Shorty growled. "I got law business fer you."

"Okey. Just a minute. This is a life-an'-death matter—"

"So's this!" Shorty bellered. "My life an' his death if I ever ketch up with him! You do' wanta see me jailed fer *murder*, do you?"

"Oh, hell!" Ernie sighed; and with a scowl he swung round. "What's the matter now?"

"Matter enough," spluttered Wild Horse. "I been swindled!"

Ernie looked at him sharply. "You haven't bought that yellow stud, have you?"

"Well . . . Yes an' no," Shorty mumbled, kind of red about the gills. "I *thought* I was buyin' him, but when I got him home he was a albino mare."

He spun off the story and Ernie whistled.

"I *told* you to keep away from that feller. Let me look at that bill of sale."

Shorty fished it from his pocket. "Bill o' sale's all right—"

"You wouldn't know whether it is or not. Why didn't you *look* at the horse?"

"I *did* look at him. It was *dark*. He looked all right in the dark. At night that mare's a dead ringer fer him."

"And this animal you've got— Are you sure it's a mare?"

"Am I sure! Don't you reckon I know a mare when I see one?"

Ernie said, "It seems kind of doubtful"; and Shorty shut up because there wasn't much of anything he could say about that.

"Well," Ernie said, handing back Tranch's paper, "I guess you've got yourself a mare this time, Shorty. I don't see anything that *I* can do about it. You wanted Blood of Kings and you've got her."

"I never wanted no albino mare! He said—"

"Yeah. I heard him. He said the stud's name was *Sangre de Cristo*. You've been around the Border long enough to know Mexican. *Sangre de Cristo* means Blood of God— Tranch told you that 'Blood of Kings' business was a *free* translation. It sure was. Kind of expensive for you, though."

"He can't do me like that!" Shorty shouted. "I ain't a-goin' t' *stand* fer it! Why, I'll curl him up like a wore out rope! I'll—"

"Have to catch him first," Ernie grinned.

"I'll ketch him! I'll wring his dodblasted neck!" Wild Horse bellowed.

Ernie picked up his pipe. "You better take my advice an' forget about him. That fellow's too slick for you to mess with, Shorty. Touch him and he's got you hogtied. He could even put you away for *threatening* him; and I don't much doubt but he'd do it. You better stay clear away from him."

Shorty looked wild enough to bite a centipede.

"I'll git him fer frogulant—"

"The burden of proof would be entirely up to you. If you couldn't make it stick you'd be in a hell of a fix." Ernie sat back and puffed at his pipe.

"Hell's fire!" Shorty shouted. "Would any guy in his right mind pay *five hundred dollars* fer a albino mare?"

"Who's paid five hundred dollars? Not *you*. You gave him 'one dollar and other valuable considerations.' It says so right on this bill of sale. You haven't got a leg to stand on."

"Is that so!" Shorty howled. "We'll see about that!" And he slammed outside and onto his horse and lit out through town at a gallop.

ONE OF the hardest things to find in this world is a man who enjoys losing. There are many who put on a guise of enjoyment and are loudly acclaimed and held in highest esteem for it; but scrape away that frozen face and you will find underneath the selfsame tumult which now had hold of Wild Horse Shorty as he tore through the night, telling the winds of his troubles.

He was plenty sore, and no kidding.

Had he happened onto Tranch in his present mood he might easily have killed him without compunction. Deeply ingrained into every palomino man worthy of the name is the fearful hatred of albinism; one would as soon cut off his good right hand as to be found with an animal tainted by it.

Like a good many other fellows raised in horse country, Shorty had been brought up on the idea that albinism was ever and always the direct outgrowth of albino blood. There was no other way for a horse to get it; for blood was thicker than water, and blood, folks said, would always tell. Which was the reason most breeders wanting yellow colts were up against a pretty stiff proposition. They would rather breed chestnut studs to palomino mares, and vice versa, than chance the result of mating two palominos. For palomino on palomino appeared very unlikely to get palomino. There was too much chance some unscrupulous breeder was hiding albino blood behind his palomino's coat. And albino blood was mightily prepotent. Just a trace of it was more than enough to mark the colt, even unto the third and fourth generations.

There was, in some remote sections of the country, a story extant to account for albinos. This legend held that albinos were a breed descended from the Arab-crossed wild mustangs of the plains. Bands of these wild horses, endeavoring to escape the encroachments of civilization, had fled to the badlands and to the mountain fastnesses and there, hidden away from the sight of man, had flourished in a natural state until inbreeding had turned them all snow white. These were fierce wild creatures, given to recurrent forays from which they returned with their numbers swelled by domesticated mares they had lured from outflung pastures. These mares, sometimes with a colt or two, occasionally came home; and it was by such colts, or so folks said, that albino blood was being infused into so many good palominos.

Still another school of thought maintained that albinism, being the result of inbreeding, would eventually do away with itself. Albino, this school declared, was not a basic color. It was no color at all, but an utter lack of color. A minus, the result of unwise and improper breeding. The albino would not reproduce itself. When mated with its kind it would, in a few short generations, bear foals that could not live to be more than seventy-two hours old.

And so, with such thoughts pounding through his head, what wonder Shorty writhed and cursed. Why, he would sooner breed to a jackass!

He said so, too. Very bitterly.

He labeled Tranch with every hard name he could think of, and then started in all over. He even called Ernie a couple of names for refusing to help him out of this mess, and old Hellbound for having made the discovery.

But there was no sign of Tranch at the Emery Park schoolhouse. It was just like Shorty had figured. They had gotten their money and pulled for the tules—gone off to find them another durn fool.

Muttering profanely, Shorty headed for home.

He felt just like a wrung-out dishrag.

But his fury was spent, burned away in its own savage breath. He had spit out the most of his venom and had gotten his tongue unsnarled from its flapping, but he could not forget that great rascal Tranch, nor the manner in which the rogue had flouted and robbed him.

Some day there should be an accounting, and lo and behold if that day ever came!

SHORTY was awakened next morning by exclaiming voices. Seemed like the voices were all around him. He suffered their babble for quite a spell, tossing and pitching and turning until at last, in great wrath, he jerked the blanket up over his head. But that did not hush up the racket much. The blanket was really a "general store quilt" of the kind commonly sold to cowpunchers; the cotton had all gone down to one end and the thin stuff left did not shut out anything. With angry growl Shorty finally got up.

He went out and doused his head in the bucket and slicked back his hair with his fingers. Then he clapped on his hat and fared scowlingly forth to see what the devil was cooking.

The racket was coming from in front of the barn with Hellbound, naturally, right in the midst of it, gesturing and spluttering and running his E-string voice up and down. He had brought the white mare out to water her and all the dudes had tromped over to help him. You could still hear their upraised arguing voices, and for two cents Shorty would have fired old Hellbound. Only then he would have had to do *all* the work.

So, biting off a cuss word, he started for the house.

Hellbound's quavery voice came after him. "Hey— Shorty! They's a new dude out yere lookin' fer lodgin's."

So, perforce, Shorty dragged up a smile and went over.

It was no trouble at all to pick out the new dude. Dude stuck out all over him. He was a wrinkled up, wizened, kind of skinny old codger almost hidden under a huge sombrero. He wore a floppy old coat over his bald-faced shirt and had buff-colored saddle pants stuffed into boots with ornate tops. He wore gold-rimmed glasses to help out his sight and sat awkwardly perched on the top scraped pole of the nearby corral.

The bean writer, Sinclair, spoke up to say, "This is Bee Bee Dunne from Santa Fe— Used to be a big time writer for the papers back East till he took to drink and chousin' the women. But he's swore off now—getting too old I guess. Come out here for a rest, he says. Can you make room for him?"

"I dunno," Shorty said, "I've got about enough arty guys round here now. Writers an' artists! It sure beats me what brings 'em all out here. Last year we had Lee Forest. Now you're here an' the Hammocks an' that Tobacco Road feller's bought a place north of Tucson, an' Walt Coburn's shacked up in the Catalina foothills, an'— Cripes! a common gent can't hardly move without bumpin' into some Big Shot or other."

Hellbound said, "You c'ld put him in the hen house now you've kicked that Earl out. Mister Dunne thinks this mare is the las' word in horses."

"A remarkable mare," Mr. Dunne said. "Remarkable."

Shorty looked at him sharply. But Mr. Dunne seemed in earnest. His ascetic-looking face expressed distinct approval.

"Humph!" Shorty said. "You know anything about horses?"

"Well, yes—a little," the man in the big sombrero said. "Ah . . . Did I understand this gentleman to say you've had an Earl staying here? Which Earl, if I might ask?"

"The Earl of Clank," said Hellbound. "But Shorty—"

"You know him?" Wild Horse asked; but Mr. Dunne shook his head.

"I'm afraid I don't. I know the Earl of Windsor—"

"What do you know about horses?"

"Well, a lot of my friends have *raised* horses. The late Lucky Baldwin, Mr. Frank M. King, Jack Culley, Carl Raswan, Colonel John Wall and George Fitzpatrick, to name just a few."

"This Fitzpatrick," Shorty said. "What kind of horses does he raise?"

"Well, hobby horses, mostly," Mr. Dunne admitted apologetically. "But he would raise *real* horses if his wife would let him put the money into them. He has a lot of good theories—good judge of liquor, too. But, going back to horses, I've spent quite a lot of money on the bangtails myself. And I know Mrs. Emily Underwood—great friend of mine. She raises Arabians; and—"

"I know the King of Siam," Shorty said, "but it ain't never put no money in my pocket. Now I'll tell you, Mr. Dunne, this here establishment is run accordin' to Hoyle. It's a pretty flossy outfit— You can ask Carl Hayden; *he* stayed here once. My friend, the Governor, has rode some of these horses. We don't take in everybody that comes down the pike. Only people of means—"

"I assure you—" began the Santa Fe man; but Shorty waved him quiet.

"I'll put you up, as a favor to Mister Singkler here, but it'll cost you five hundred a month," Shorty said.

"That's quite all right. I'm sure it's cheap at the price. I've read quite a bit about your place in the papers—and in that book Nye wrote * about you—"

* "Wild Horse Shorty" by Nelson C. Nye (1944, Macmillan).

"A bunch of dang lies!" Shorty muttered cross like.

"Well, but do you still have any of those 'Palamoosas'?"

"No. Lute Dickerson killed off the last one I had—but I reckon I could git you one if you really got your heart set on it."

"Oh, I didn't wish to *buy* one," Mr. Dunne declaimed hastily. "I was just sort of curious to see what they looked like, having read so much about them in the Denver papers."

"I guess you know what curiosity did. By the way"— Shorty added, taking a quick squint around—"didn't Mister Singkler—"

"Sinclair," Sinclair said.

Shorty frowned, the way a man will if he gets a little irritated. "Didn't Mister *Singkler* tell me you was from Santa Fe? How'd you git down here? Come in on the train?"

Sinclair said: "He scootered down."

"Scootered?"

"You know—those little contrapshuns kids have—stand on one foot and push with the other? Bee Bee's got one with a little motor on it. He can ride with both feet—don't have to push it. Just grab hold of the handlebar; motor does all the work. Bee Bee's nuts about them. Gets up scooter clubs—"

"Hell! it must be pretty nigh seven hundred mile!" exclaimed Hellbound.

"That's nothing," Sinclair said. "Bee Bee don't think anything of a little jaunt like that. Next year he's figuring to make a coast-to-coast trip on one of those gadgets—"

"And what's strange about that?" Mr. Dunne inquired. "Scootering is one of the most healthful recreations a man can have. Ten miles every day will keep the doctor away."

"Humph! So will a shotgun," Wild Horse said, "an' it don't take so much time. You keep that thing away from my mares. I don't wanta come out here an' find 'em piled up in no fence."

8

GULLIVER'S TRAVELS

SOON AS BREAKFAST was over and the dudes were congregated on the porch where Hellbound had promised to show them how to build smokes out of Durham and rice papers, Shorty headed for the barn to saddle up. The problem now was to get rid of that mare.

He felt pretty dang certain he would not get his money back, but even a part of it was better than none. He was in a mood to take any reasonable offer. He was positive of one thing. He was *not* going to keep her any longer than necessary.

He sat down on a feed bin to do some figuring.

If he was ever to sell her he would have to show her. The best place to show her was obviously in town. But to be seen with her in town would get him marked for life. He didn't hanker to be known as "the man with the albino."

But the question was, Who would *want* her? Who would have any use for a danged albino?

Nobody *he* knew! Try as he would he could not think of anybody who would so much as be willing to be caught dead with one. All the breeders around Tucson felt they'd rather have the Plague than have a horse even *tainted* with albinism.

Shorty was about there in his thinking when Sinclair,

the bean wrangler, sauntered over. He said: "You sure do have a fine climate here, don't you?"

"Hadn't noticed," Shorty scowled. "Say! how would you like to own that white mare?"

"Not me," Sinclair grinned.

"Why not? What's the matter with her? She's sound as a dollar."

"I wouldn't buy the soundest horse going."

"Humph. I thought Rose said you used to be a cow-puncher—"

"You can say that again. I *used* to be; an' I got all the ridin' I need for a lifetime. Used to work for the Blocks—Bell Ranch, too, an' the Diamond A's. I was a young squirt then and it looked pretty good, readin' stories about it. Take my advice—don't ever be a cowpuncher."

"Gettin' back to the mare," Shorty said. "You could probably double your money on her."

Mr. Sinclair showed a canny Scots grin. "I'd rather watch you double yours," he said. "What do you do for a pastime around here?"

"Shoot. Fish. Hunt."

"What do you hunt for?"

"Anything you want."

"Quite a ways from town, ain't you? How do you get there?"

"There ain't no way, unless you fork a bronc or bum a ride off of Hammock. That picture artist," Shorty explained, "in No. 2 cabin."

"Maybe I can borrow Bee Bee's scooter," said Sinclair, strolling off.

He must have had luck because pretty soon Shorty heard the gadget getting tuned up; and with a loud phut-phut Sinclair sailed off down the dusty road.

270

It was then Shorty got the real inspiration.

Buck Fletcher!

There was just the man to buy Shorty's mare. Buck was a dealer in cattle and horses. *He* could get rid of her—he could unload her easy. Didn't his ad read "One Horse or a Carload"?

Shorty figured he'd better ride over and see Buck.

He guessed he'd go right away. When Fletcher was in town he could generally be found somewhere in the vicinity of the El Conquistador Stables which, across country, was not above ten miles away.

Shorty stared once again at the mis-named mare, trying to heft up his nerve to ride her. It was not the mare he was scared of, but what folks might say if they saw him on her.

She wasn't bad looking, except she was white all over and had pink skin, and eyes that were blue instead of brown like most horses. She was pretty well slung together. Small, alert ears, well developed neck, good sloping shoulders, long belly, short back, considerable heart girth and a heavily muscled thigh and forearm. Her legs were short but firmly jointed and well let down, with the knee and pastern desirably close. She would stand about fourteen three.

She looked, Shorty thought, like a Quarter Horse.

He guessed he would ride her. Ought to find out what she felt like, anyhow. Case they chanced to meet up with anybody on the way, he could always say he was moving a horse for Buck Fletcher. He would take Figure 8 on a lead rope, just to make sure he'd have a way to get back.

IT WAS coming on to noon and the sun was hot when they hove in sight of the Conquistador stables. The place was set well back from the environs of the El Conquistador Hotel, one of the swankier family outfits some three or four miles from the heart of Tucson. Galab, the fine Arab stud that had once been the pride of the Double N Ranch, nickered from one of the corrals as they passed, and went dancing around like he was built on coiled springs. Probably, boy fashion, he was hooting at the mare; but Blood of Kings never opened her mouth. Never batted an eye or slowed her step, even; so Shorty nickered back just to save the stud's feelings. And then Mose, Fletcher's pardner, came out from the hay pile leading a trappy looking Saddlebred gelding.

"Hi there, Shorty!"

"Hi, Mose— Buck around any place?"

"In the office," Mose said. "Thinkin' of selling Figure 8 to him, are you?"

"I was thinkin' of sellin' this mare," Shorty said.

"Umm. Where'd you get her?"

"Bought her off some feller driftin' through. Be all right if I tie her here while—"

"You won't have to," Mose said. "Here comes the Boss now."

And sure enough, there was Buck Fletcher just come out of the tack room, his twinkling blue eyes looking Figure 8 over. He said, "How're you doin', Shorty?"

Wild Horse said, "I ain't doin' so good. I rode over to see what you'd give me for this mare. . . ."

"I'll buy that stud," Buck said, poking around at Figure 8's anatomy. "What'll you take for him?"

"I'm hankerin' to sell this mare," Shorty said.

"What's the matter with her?"

"If you can't see it, she ain't got it."

"Must be somethin' wrong with her. Never knew you to want to sell—"

272

"Well, hell's bells! I got more mares now than I got money t' feed 'em!"

"Ain't we all!" Buck said, tipping his hat to a lady dude passing.

"Well—good luck," Mose said, and went off to tend to his chores with the horses.

"I'll tell you about these mares," Buck said. "Sometimes a feller just can't get enough of them. Other times—like now—he can't get shut of the ones he's got—"

"But them's *range mares* you're talkin' about! This ain't no range mare! This mare's got *quality*—you don't see one like her every day. Lookit that white coat! Why, she's even got a *name* an' she's royally—"

"What book's she registered with?"

"Well, I dunno about that. But she's got a walk like nobody's business; walked over here in one hour flat!"

"That's right good," Buck said. "But you can't even *give* a Walkin' Horse away. Trade just won't go for 'em. They don't want nothin' but Quarter Horses. You see that *A*rab stud over there? He's as nice a little horse as a feller could ask for. Style an' class to throw away. Fire an' bloom—run like a deer. But does anybody want him? He's by Kellogg's Antez—holds the World's Record for the half mile. Ain't never been beat. An' there he stands, day in an' day out. If a horse ain't a Quarter Horse this ain't no place for him."

Buck looked at the mare and shook his head again. "She's a nice lookin' filly; I'd like to oblige you, Shorty—"

"She'd make jest the thing fer some of them movie people. Smarter'n heck. You could learn her anythin'—"

"Yeah. But they want stock horses, Shorty."

"Mister Fletcher," Shorty said, "if a cow comes within ten mile of my place that mare lets out a snort an' goes hellity

273

larrup around the fence line. She jest *cries* t' work cattle!"

"Yeah—but the trouble is," Buck pointed out, "these cow wallopers is set ag'in' a mare by nature. Jest won't have 'em. Claim they're always squattin'—"

"You don't see *this* mare squattin', do you?"

"Sorry. I jest can't use her, Shorty. If I took her off your hands I'd probably never get rid of her. Folks around here don't go for white horses." He said, "All foolishness, of course, but there it is. You can't *give* 'em away."

"Some of the most famous horses in hist'ry was white—"

"Mebbe so," Fletcher said, "but they was not albinos."

WILD HORSE rode with his chin on his chest.

He sure felt low.

Seemed like he just didn't have no luck at all.

What in the devil was he going to do? Five hundred dollars sunk in that mare and no dang way to get it out of her. She'd not bring fifty dollars at the dog meat factory; and, anyway, he wouldn't wish *that* kind of fate even on an albino. But something had got to be done, and pronto. Why, you might as well keep a yard full of skunks as to have any truck with a durn albino!

Maybe he had better sift around to the Crossing. He could do with a drink. And maybe if he kept his ears skinned he might pick up something that would give him an idea.

So he bent his course a bit more to the east. He rode with his scowl on the white mare's ears. They were nice ears, really; alert and sensitive. She was always waggling them around and listening. He thought it downright odd she didn't ever nicker—not even when Galab had run up and whinnied at her. She hadn't ever opened her mouth since he'd got her. She was the most close-mouthed female he had ever bumped into.

274

Maybe she was mad account of him trying to get shed of her.

Let her stay mad then. He wasn't shouting with joy himself.

There was considerable greasewood just beyond where the road passed Fritchet's saloon; there was a low place there where water from the infrequent rains collected and had grown the brush twelve to fourteen feet high. It offered ideal cover to Shorty's purpose and so, before he reached town, he swung a big circle that would bring him up through it.

When he got in the thickest tallest part of it Wild Horse dismounted, pulled his gear off the mare and strapped it on Figure 8. Then he tied Blood of Kings with Figure 8's lead rope, swung onto the stud and, with a quick look around to make sure he wasn't seen, swung into the open and approached the saloon.

Three or four townsmen had their chairs tilted comfortably, enjoying the coolness of the porch roof's shadows. Just as Shorty rode up, Fritchet came through the batwings, and Doc Wallace after him.

"Hi, Shorty!" called Doc. "Did you get that stud?"

Wild Horse, mentally consigning Doc and all his works to a much hotter region than Arizona, said "No!" real gruff like, and got out of the saddle. "McGee been around yet?"

Kerley shook his head, and Fritchet, standing squarely in front of his doorway, said: "If you're fixin' to loaf you can loaf right out there."

"Well!" Shorty said, reading the hate in his stare. "What are *you* so puffed out about? Wipe off that scowl an' I'll buy you a drink."

He chucked fifty cents into the dust by the steps and Fritchet leaped down to scrabble after it. Shorty, watching

275

him, grinned fleeringly until Fritchet said, "Takin' off this four bits leaves you still on the cuff for thirty-two dollars and twenty-nine cents; and you don't get inside that door till you pay it!"

"Why, you pot-lickin' walloper!" Wild Horse glowered. "How many times do you collect your bills? Sam Bass himself never had *your* gall! Here—" he spluttered, counting it out and slamming it where he had chucked the two quarters, "take it while I got people around what kin prove I paid it if you try that again! And don't go round tellin' I don't pay my bills!"

A diversion came when Doc Wallace, looking up, said suddenly: "Hey! What's that?" and they all followed his glance out into the road, and then George Provencher began to snicker.

Wild Horse peered around. There, nonchalantly ambling toward him and dragging her picket rope, came the albino mare with her ears cocked, watching him.

Irresolutely she stopped and nickered loudly.

"Well, I swear!" Kerley said. "She seems to know you, Shorty!"

Shorty, just then, could have cheerfully shot her.

"Humph!" he scowled. "She ain't talkin' at *me!*" and would have made out like he had nothing to do with her, but Blood of Kings wasn't to be disowned that way. She came right on up to him, pushed against his shoulder and whinnied softly.

The bunch on the porch front guffawed loudly.

Provencher chuckled. "That your new stud, Shorty?"

And Fritchet roared. "Boys, he's a *daisy!*"

Shorty shoved the mare off and looked at Fritchet like he was minded to do him a bodily injury. "You keep chawin' my mane an', by grab, I'll—"

276

"Ho, ho, ho!" guffawed Fritchet, bent double. "Ho, ho, ho! By Gawd, he's a daisy!"

And the barkeep, poking his head through the batwings, said: "Imported from Mexico an' royally bred—"

Shorty swore in a fury. Snatching hold of the lead rope he slammed into his saddle and whirled Figure 8, with his face black as thunder. He told the dang bunch what he thought of them, and he didn't have to hunt round for no decorated language to make his meaning understood by them, either. Then he fed Figure 8 a taste of the spurs and was building a dust cloud when Ernie, dashing out of the Mercantile, yelled:

"Hey! you crazy galoot! Hold on a minute—I got somethin' to tell you!"

But Shorty had heard all he wanted to for one day.

9

A PRETTY KETTLE OF FISH

THERE WAS no doubt about it. This was the dangdest country he had ever got into! A guy naturally expected a few ups and downs, but around here Shorty just didn't have *any* luck. Life was just a procession of downs. Every least thing he did went haywire, and he was just about fed up with it.

The only way to get ahead in this world was to be a writer or a artist, it looked like. Take these dudes for instance. Sinclair was writing a book about beans. Dunne was a newspaper writer—or *had* been; anyway that was how he'd gotten his pile. The Hammocks were artists; they went around painting pictures, and every place they showed them it was just like a one-cent sale at Woolworth's!

But it wasn't only these daggone dudes! There was that Coburn feller in the Catalina foothills, living in a castle, just wallering in dough! And that Tobacco Road feller—he was wallering, too! And Sheriff Ernie, and O'Connor, and Westbrook Pegler. And that Rosemerry gal that was always writing that stuff about her family. And Burl Tuttle, and that school-teaching dame that had someway managed to get fruit out of rock. Why, the woods was full of them and a common gent couldn't hardly grab a living!

It was just plain hell any way you took it; and Shorty was not feeling any better about it when Hellbound met him at the gate with more grief.

"A couple of them mares got into the wire ag'in, an' we're about outa hay. An' thet Columbine critter ain't in foal— she sure ain't. I been out an' measured her an' she ain't swole a bit—not a daggone bit!"

"Don't come t' *me* with your troubles," Shorty growled.

"She's your mare, ain't she?"

"Not no more, she ain't. I'm givin' her to you— I got all the worries I kin tackle right now." Shorty slid from the saddle and was making ready to tow his horses to the stable when Hellbound reached out and grabbed his arm.

"Hey—wait!" he quavered. He peered down at Shorty like he could not believe it. "Y' mean yo're ackshully *givin'* her to me? Givin' me thet mare fer my *very own?* What in the world hez come over you? Y' mean Sweet Columbine? Ol' *Wire-Cut's* sister?"

"Yeah. Sweet Columbine. Ol' Wire-Cut's sister," Wild Horse said impatiently. "An' you feed her *with your own money*—hear me?"

" 'Course I hear you. I ain't *deef!* Gosh—jest think of it," he muttered, marveling. "Ol' Hellbound Hank with a mare of his own!" And he tramped away, still mumbling, to take a look at his new possession.

Shorty sighed. Maybe he had better give them *all* away. It would probably come to that before he got done.

SHORTY was sunk so deep in his woes he couldn't enjoy his grub any more; and Rose had a whopping big supper, like usual. Steak and onions and plenty of gravy, and good hot biscuits fresh from the oven with Oleo on them that

279

looked like butter. Ernie always liked to eat with them because he thought it *was* butter; and just then Ernie's horse,
Rowdy, was heard outside; and Ernie himself came dragging
his spurs in, and Rose said "Pull up a chair," like she was
tickled to have him, and went hurrying off to fetch a clean
plate while Shorty, ungraciously, made him known to the
guests.

"L. Ernenwein?" Hammock frowned. "Didn't you write
Kincaid of Red Butte?"

"You bet!" Ernie said. "An' the *Boss of Panamint,* an' a
whole slew of others too numerous to mention."

"He's a writin' fool," Shorty said; and Ernie shook hands
all around and passed out a fistful of White Owl cigars, like
maybe he was having a baby, or something. Or it might just
have been he was keeping his hand in for next year's election. "Ever read my—"

"I'm partial to Nye's stuff, myself," Mr. Dunne said.

Ernie said, "Humph!" and took a look at Dunne sharp
like. "You the guy they call 'Beau Dunne' up to Santa Fe?"

Mr. Dunne shrugged it off like he was used to such pleas-
antries. "Oh," he said modestly, "I get around a little. I
write the Village Gossip column for the *Santa Fe New Mexican*—great paper."

Ernie sniffed. "That's nothing. I used to manage the
Schenectady Sun. There was a fightin' sheet—crusaded the
islands out of Erie Boulevard an' the floozies off Front
Street. By the way," he added, "that was quite a book you
did for Winston."

Before Mr. Dunne could get his mouth empty, Hammock
asked where Shorty had been with the new white mare.

"Been givin' her a workout," Shorty said, glad to get hold
of the talk again. "Walked her over to the El Con stables—

Buck Fletcher's place. Ten miles, an' she made it in one hour flat. That's *walkin'!*"

"Um-*hmm!*" agreed Hammock's wife, Ethel.

"See Buck?" Ernie asked, carving off some more Oleo.

"Yeah," Shorty said, and scowled like it hurt him.

"How's that Joe Reed filly he's raising?"

"Didn't see her," Shorty said. "Anyhow, I don't think Buck goes much for mares. He wanted to buy Figure 8."

"He did!" Rose said, looking up with interest. "How much did he give—"

"I didn't sell him," Shorty growled. "Anyhow—"

"You'd of been well rid of him," Ernie said. "Figure 8 ain't no good to you. He won't ever find your mares any foals, and he can't race any more. What the hell good is he? You could have taken that money—"

"Never mind," Shorty said. "I'm still roddin' this spread an' I wasn't born yesterday. If Buck really wanted him it was for somebody else."

"What of that?"

"Don't you reckon he'd git more'n he paid me fer him? I could sell Figure 8 t' this guy myself—"

"If you knew who he was."

"It ain't worryin' me," Shorty answered.

John Sinclair asked if he was going to put anything in the Horse Show. He said: "Why don't you put that white mare in?"

Shorty made out like he didn't hear that. But Ernie said, pushing back his chair, "Where is that mare? I'd like to see what she looks like."

"She looks like a mare," Shorty said belligerently.

"She's a *nice* looking mare," Ethel Hammock said; and they all trooped out to have another look at her and see if she'd changed any since that morning. All but Rose, that is. Rose stayed behind to take care of the dishes.

Blood of Kings had not quite finished her supper but she made no objection to following Shorty.

Ernie looked her over from various angles and then bent nearer to poke her with his finger. Blood of Kings, like a flash, nearly chopped it off for him.

"Hell!" Ernie swore, backing out of reach hurriedly. "You want to break her of that before she hurts somebody —slap her good every time she tries it!"

"She don't do that t' me," Wild Horse said. "I don't hev no trouble with her. She's a one-man horse. She don't want nobody else pokin' round her."

Ernie snorted. "I've heard all about these one-man nags— That's a lot of hooey! That's the best damn way to get a man-killer started. You bat her good every time she does it or you're going to wake up with real trouble on your hands. What'll you do if you have to get a vet to her?"

Shorty shrugged. He wasn't figuring to have her that long.

Ernie stepped around her, bending and looking like he was thinking perhaps to find a gold mine on her. "She's got a skin like a baby's bottom. But that wouldn't matter so much if it wasn't for those glass eyes. . . . You know," he said, straightening up and nodding, "that's not a bad looking mare you got, Shorty. She's a damn albino, but she's built like a Quarter Horse. Got nice legs—got damn nice legs. Well let down. She might have a little speed. Plenty of muscle. Why don't you enter her in the Speed Trials this year? You probably wouldn't *win* anything, but it would be good advertising—good experience for both of you."

Shorty looked at him slanchways, but Ernie's face was

serious. Just the same, advertising was the last thing Shorty wanted in connection with that mare. "I'm figgerin' to sell her," he said, kind of huffy like.

"You won't ever sell her around *here*," Ernie snorted. "You know what this Tucson crowd thinks of white horses. Anyway, Fritchet's spreading word of her from hell to breakfast. He's tellin' everyone that comes in for a drink how you paid five hundred for what you thought was a stud and when you got him home he was an albino mare."

"It's too dang bad about Fritchet," Shorty said. "He's had it in fer me ever sinst that girl of his played up to Lute an' got stuck with a jailbird. That Fritchet's so sour he'd pickle a pig's mouth!"

They all laughed at that; and then John Sinclair said, "Not to change the subject, but do you know, I just can't get over this climate—why, it's *marvelous!* Never saw anything like it. If I could get me a place, and it wasn't too expensive, I think I'd like to settle here."

"You could git Farrar's place pretty reas'nable," said Shorty. "He's got a five-acre place down the road near Ben's. Got a well an' a pump an' a couple acres of fence around a little tile shanty he was figgerin' to use for a garage after he got his house built. Never built the house. His wife's from Vermont an' she had to go back there. Couldn't stand the desert."

"Do you think he'd sell?"

"You could write him an' see. He's over at Oneco, Florida, right now. Expect he'd want around fifteen hundred fer it —probably take it on time."

"Guess I'll write him," the bean wrangler said. "This country—"

"You couldn't stand it here for more than two weeks," Dunne said testily. "Save your money. Too monotonous for you around here. You'd miss all the excitement you're used to. You won't find any cocktail bars or any Santa Fe senoritas around here."

Shorty said, "There's some pretty cute Sonora dames down at Nogales."

"An' plenty of Papagoes," Hellbound said, "acrosst the river."

"I'll write him tonight," Sinclair said decisively.

The dudes started back toward the house, having stood about as long as their legs were good for. Ernie gave Wild Horse a significant look and, with a jerk of the head, casually went behind the barn.

Shorty followed him.

"That was a damn good supper," Ernie said, "but I can get good meals at home. Why didn't you stop when I called you this noon?"

"Never mind the lectures—I kin git them from Rose."

"How much money can you scrape up right quick?"

"You mean you've found a palomino?"

Ernie said testily: "I'm surprised you ain't turned into a palomino! Palominos an' blondes!" he snorted. "I asked how much *dinero* you could get hold of right quick."

"I dunno—not much. What's bitin' you?"

"Somethin's going to bite *you*," Ernie said, "if you don't get your hands on five hundred dollars! Mr. Halbert Crowsnow has been in to see me—"

"*That* guy!"

"That guy," Ernie said, "has gone to court about you. I got a summons here for you"; and he passed it over.

Shorty tore the thing up without even looking at it.

"Why, you addlebrained nitwit!" Ernie said, halfway angry. "You can't tear up the law like that! What the hell good do you figure that did you? You can't brush off the law

284

like it was dust on your coatsleeve. Sometimes you act like you ain't got 'em all! What did you want to throw that guy out for, anyway? You took his money—"

"I never took a dime off him!" Shorty bellowed.

"Well, McGee did—it's all the same. McGee's your foreman. He was actin' for you—"

"McGee quit me cold. I ain't responsible fer what he does!"

"You can be held responsible for what he did as your foreman. He was your foreman when Crowsnow paid him five hundred dollars for a month's board and lodging. You better scrape up that money and get him paid off if you don't want to find yourself feedin' off the county."

"He can't git away with it—"

"He's *getting* away with it! And tearing up that summons ain't going to make your case any easier. If the thing goes to court it'll cost you a heap more than five hundred dollars. Now you better work fast," Ernie said, "because the hearing's set for February 4th—that's only twelve days off."

"I can't help it," Shorty scowled. "You can't git blood out of a turnip."

Ernie looked at him and sighed. "I'd sure hate to bet on it. . . . Well," he said, and shook his head sadly, "it's little enough I can do for you, Shorty, but I'll give you the best cell I've got."

10

"HORSE! HORSE! HORSE!"

It was getting along toward dusk as Ernie rode off, but Sinclair, never a man to put off till later what could be done right now, told Shorty he'd like to have a look at Farrar's place.

"In the mornin'," Shorty said.

"Let's go now. Let's go in the gloaming."

"I ain't in no mood t' go house huntin' now—"

"*I* am," Sinclair said. "I'm fidgeting to go right away. I'll go borrow Bee Bee's scooter—"

"You ain't goin' with me if you take that contrapshun! If you got to go, we'll go a-horseback, like a couple of Orthodox Christians," Shorty scowled. "Pers'nally, *I* don't care if we *never* go."

"Well . . . if you've a nice gentle horse—"

Shorty looked at him. "You've sure got the coldest pair of feet ever struck Arizona. I thought you used t' be a cow-puncher—"

"I got stove up a few years ago," Sinclair said. "On a horse. Stove up bad— It's why I had to give up cow punchin'. I got piled up on a saddle horn, an' that ain't any joke I can tell you!"

"Well, I'll git Sweet Columbine fer you," Shorty said.

"She's s' gosh blamed gentle you could stake her to a hairpin."

He yowled for Hellbound. When the old man finally came shuffling up, Shorty said, "Throw a hull on that mare of yours. Singkler wants to go for a ride."

Hellbound looked at Sinclair kind of dubious. "Can't he ride none of them other critters? I dunno's I want no cowpunchin' outfit hellity-larrupin' *my* mare around!"

"He ain't goin' t' hurt her. Go do like I tell you an' button your lip."

Hellbound still hesitated. He looked as though he were minded to say more, but Shorty said, "An' saddle up Figger 8 for me while you're at it."

The old man came back with the horses and said to Shorty: "Don't stay out all night—an' don't run 'er. She runs off easy. She ain't used t' excitement. It's bad fer her blood pressure. Gits 'er all worked up an' she's liable t' git strangles—"

"They don't get strangles from running," Sinclair informed him.

"Oh, don't they? That's all *you* know about it! I calculate you never heard o' workin' on the tail, either, did yer? How would you go about curin' a fistula?"

"Haven't any idea. But strangles are usually the result of a cold—"

"Is thet so! I've knowed plenty of broncs thet got the strangles an' never had so much as a sniffle till some dang fool took an' run their pants off! You keep Sweet Columbine down to a walk. Don't run 'er, don't hit 'er, an' don't use no durn spurs on 'er."

He looked at Sinclair without much charity. "You'll be the first gent I ever let ride her, an' ef you don't ride easy you'll shore be the last."

"QUEER OLD COOT," Sinclair said, chuckling, when they had put the ranch a couple miles behind them. "Quite a character."

"Who—Hellbound?" Wild Horse snorted. "He's a dang ol' loafer! Never lifts a durn hand unless you're standin' right over him. I don't know what that place would come to if I wasn't around t' tell 'em what to do. Depend on me like a bunch of babies— It's a wonder I don't hev t' spoon their food to 'em!"

Mr. Sinclair laughed. "You've got quite an outfit. Must have cost—"

"It didn't cost me so much. I kind of inherited it from Luther K. Dickerson. All's I had to do was fix it up a little. It's my payroll that keeps me broke all the time. Would you happen t' hev any extry cash on you?"

Sinclair took a covert squint at Shorty. This sounded like a touch, and it went against his Scotch raising to be touched. "If I like Farrar's place I might be able to scrape up enough to buy it—on time," he said cautiously.

"Humph," Shorty said. "Don't look like I ought t' be showin' you this place. If you git it I reckon you'll be movin' right over."

"But you'll still be seeing me," Sinclair reminded him.

Shorty didn't much care if he saw Sinclair or not; it was the prospective drain on his income that bothered him. He didn't like to think of that money departing. Especially now when that yellow-shoed Halbert was figuring to take him on a legal sleigh ride.

He did not see how he was to get that money. Of course, McGee might not have taken Crowsnow's rent money off with him; there was a faint possibility he'd turned it over to Rose.

Shorty felt somewhat better after thinking of that. It was

a pity he had not thought of it sooner. He had been supposing all the time McGee had had it in his pocket when he went high heeling it down the road.

It was kind of odd, Shorty thought, how McGee had vanished. Just like the earth had opened and swallowed him. He must have been so plumb riled he had clean quit the country.

It was too danged bad. Shorty had not meant to rile McGee that way. It was just that he had been so worked up himself, thinking about that dang Crowsnow, and all, that he had not stopped to count ten before talking. He had really liked old Nels McGee, and knew for certain that without McGee's help he never could have won that race with Wire-Cut.

But there was nothing he could do about it now, he reckoned. It was a case of spilled milk, that was all there was to it; but if Nels came back he would treat him different.

"Know anything about these here Trail Rides?" he asked Sinclair. "That Tucson bunch is figgerin' to hev one."

"All I know," Sinclair said, "is what I've heard. There's three or four trail rides held every year. The biggest one is up in Vermont. The idea is to help stimulate interest in the use and raising of better saddle stock. Takes a pretty good horse to make one of those things, and he's got to be in the pink of condition. He's got to be sound an' have a lot of real courage. After all's said and done, it's courage that counts in a horse, you know."

"What kinda courage?"

"Guts," Sinclair said.

"The do or die kind, is that your idear?"

Mr. Sinclair nodded.

"How about breedin' an' conformation?"

"He'd ought to have good blood, I should think. To tell

you the truth, I don't know much about these trail rides. I'm no expert on horses by a long shot. Like most fellers that have worked cattle I've rode a lot of horses. But I ain't never made any study of 'em. I've noticed them and seen they had what they needed—always kind of cottoned to them, but not to any one horse in particular. I've sat so many damn broncs in my time I've always been pretty well suited to forget 'em, what time I wasn't on one. Conformation is a thing you can't put too much trust in—I mean, it's tricky. I've known some right good horses that would never get a glance in a judging contest."

"You think a horse ought t' be *built up* fer one of these trail rides?"

"You wouldn't expect to take a long hike without breaking into it—"

"I wouldn't figger t' hike," Shorty grunted, and Sinclair laughed.

After a while Shorty said: "You reckon Blood of Kings could make a ride like that?"

"I don't know how far they're goin' to ride, but I should think so, with training. She *looks* strong enough. Like I said, a whole lot depends upon courage and willingness. It was the work a bronc did, and his way of doing it, that always shaped *my* judgment of him. There's a lot of folks in town that's been knocking your mare, on account of she's white and got glass eyes; but in my experience, and I've worked with livestock better than eighteen years, the looks of a horse is a poor way to judge what his capabilities are. Color don't count if the colt won't trot— Not that a cowhand," he added, grinning, "would give two cents for a trotting horse."

They rode a way without talking. Then Shorty said, kind of thoughtful and nodding, "I expect you're right. Guts means a lot in a horse. You should of seen ol' Wire-Cut winnin' the Sweepstakes. She wouldn't never of taken no beauty prize, but she was the guttiest horse I've ever knowed. She would go till hell froze an' then take you skatin' acrosst the ice."

"Got killed, didn't she? Seems like I read something about it in the papers."

"Yeah," Shorty said, mighty curt and grim like. "Here's your place."

Sinclair got down and they looked it over. There were several small trees, a drilled well with Delco plunger pump, and a small oblong building of unpainted tile.

"This is just what I need," Sinclair said approvingly. "I could pull out that wallboard partition, put a couple more wings on, give it a plaster job inside and out, and make a pretty snug place of it. Good view, too."

"Might leak a little around them winders," Shorty said; but Sinclair passed that over with a wave of the hand.

"I wouldn't have *those* windows anyway. I want big, paned windows like they have up to Santa Fe with bright wee pictures painted on the glass— Maybe I could get Earl Hammock to do that. Yes, sir! I *like* this country, and I like this place. It's marvelous! Who lives over there?" he said, pointing next door.

"That's Mr. Ben's place. The Happy Harp *Ho*tel. On the other side of you is Mister Pipesley; he'll make you a good neighbor. Always minds his own business."

"How far back does my land go?"

"Back to Kerley's fence— That's Kerley's place back of you. He runs the livery. Them's his chicken houses you see off there."

"I'll put a good hog-tight fence around it," Sinclair decided. "And a 'dobe wall round the house after I get it fixed

291

up. I've got a little model of the way I want it to look. Can I get somebody to grub off the greasewood?"

"Kerley might do it fer you. Or Scott Dyer, mebbe. Whyn't you do it yourself?"

"You forget my accident," the ex-cowpuncher said. "I can't do much in the manual work line. Anyway, I can't spare the time. My publishers are after me all the time as it is. Every two-three days I get a telegram from them wanting to know where my new book is. I haven't even got the thing done, yet. But I could work here *fine*," he said, warming up again. "It's so quiet and restful. And the people— You've no idea what a relief it is to get away from that artificial Santa Fe crowd. All those terrible cocktail parties and— Why, it makes me feel like a different person!"

Shorty said, "I wisht *I* could feel like a diff'rent person."

WHEN HE SAW old Hellbound waiting at the gate, Shorty screwed up his wincing nerves for more trouble. *"Now what?"* he said, scowling fiercely at Hellbound.

"It's thet dang mare—"

"He ain't hurt your mare."

"I ain't torkin' about Sweet Columbine. I'm torkin' about thet Blood of Kings hussy— She's been runnin' me ragged ever sinst you left yere!"

Wild Horse looked startled. "Mean to say she's been *chasin'* you?"

"Chasin'! My soul an' body— I been chasin' *her!* I ain't had one minute's peace sinst you an' thet dude took outen yere. All the time I was saddlin' Figger 8 I seen her keep watchin' me, starin' an' starin'— I knowed dang well she was thinkin' up devilment. She musta been on the watch t' see was you ridin' him, because the minute you left yere

she started right in. Lord *God!* I never seen sech tantrims! Kicked her water buckit off the wall! Stamped it flatter'n Billy-be-damn! I had her in thet big box stall, an' time I got out there she had kicked her feed box plumb t' glory an' was gittin' all set t' start in on the door!"

The old man mopped his face with a sleeve. "She aimed t' git outen there an' I didn't argy with 'er!"

"You let her *go?* Where is she?"

"I don't know—an' keer less! I don't keer ef she's gone fer good! I'm a sick man, Wild Horse; I been ailin' fer weeks an' all this stompedin' hez brought it down on me. I can't *stand* these tarnal excitements! I'm a ol' man, you know—I don't travel like a colt no more. You got t' git me some help or let me go to a sawbones."

"You better ride right in an' see Doc Wallace—"

"He's a *horse doc!*" Hellbound said indignantly. "I don't want no horse doc messin' with *me!*"

"What's the matter with a horse doc?" Shorty said. "If he kin cure dumb critters what can't even talk, he ought t' be able to fix *you* up."

"It's my *bones,*" Hellbound quavered. "It's all in my bones. A kinda achin' misery till I can't hardly lift one foot beyond the other'n. What do you reckon c'ld be wrong with me, Wild Horse?"

"Well, it ain't too much work—I kin tell you that! You won't never drownd in your own sweat, that's sure."

Hellbound looked at him with stricken eyes. "How you kin tork thet way after all I've did fer you! Worked my pore fingers to the bone, I hev— Why, I ain't hardly nawthin' more'n a livin' shadder! Stayin' up all hours with sick horses, scrubbin' their tails fer 'em— I tell you, a man's true worth ain't *ree*lized till he's gone."

"You ain't gone yet," Shorty said unfeelingly; and Hellbound shuddered. He clucked his tongue and shook his head sad like. "I'm jest like a pore ol' horse—"

"What you want me t' do? Turn you out on pasture?"

Hellbound gave a pitiful sniff. "You'll be sorry when the ol' man's gone," he said, like only sheer pride was keeping the tears back. "I won't live fer*ever*."

"Well, that's the truth—there won't none of us," Shorty said.

The old man tottered, mighty feeble, to his mare, took hold of the reins and weakly reached up to catch at the horn. "You'll remember all I've done fer you someday; you'll be missin' pore ol' Hellbound who never shirked a chore."

"My God!" Sinclair said. "Maybe the old man *is* sick."

Wild Horse snorted.

Hellbound said, "Kind words is wasted, Mister Saint Clair. Thet man's got a axle washer where most people packs a heart. But he'll regret it. I been jest like a ol' horse around this place, never noticed till he drops."

"Yeah— Speakin' of horses," Shorty said, "where's my mare?"

The old man looked blank.

"What'd you do with her?" Wild Horse growled.

"Do! I never done nothin' with 'er—Gawd A'mighty couldn't of done nothin' with her! Las' time I seen her she was trompin' up the front porch steps an' lookin' in the winders. She's prob'ly in the parlor now readin' the Denver papers!"

And in the parlor was where Shorty found her.

She gave a joyous little nicker and came prancing right over to sniff at him and, pleased like, rubbed her head against his shoulder. Rose said, white faced, "You've got to get rid of that animal! Just *look* at this room—and after all my work! Look at that *lamp!* and that *chair!* I've stood
294

all I could—either *she* stays out of this house or *I* do!" And she flopped herself down in the only chair left and covered her face with her apron.

Wild Horse looked at Rose uncomfortably. "I'll do the best I kin," he said meekly. "What was she doin' in here anyhow?"

"She didn't take me into her confidence," Rose said, snatching down the apron and glaring at him. "You get her out of here and *keep* her out. I don't know what Earl Hammock's going to say. Ethel had just brought in one of his pictures to show me—a new one that he painted just this very afternoon. It was still wet—a cactus picture. And that brazen horse came right through the screen door and poor Ethel let out a screech and dropped it *right face down on the floor!* And that durn horse came across the room and she barely got out of the house in time—Ethel, I mean!" Rose's eyes snapped: "You get rid of that horse before she *kills* somebody!"

Shorty looked at the mare. "She wouldn't hurt anybody—"

"She hurt that picture! You better pay Earl for it."

"All right, I'll *pay* him fer it! You don't hev t' git up in the air about it—you can't expect a horse to know nothin' about pictures."

"Well, you get rid of her."

"I been *tryin'* to git rid of her— You ain't seen nobody bustin' t' buy her, hev you?"

"Then *give* her to somebody—"

"An' lose all that money I got tied up in her? That's a likely notion! I'll git ahead *fast* pullin' stunts like that!"

"Well, you don't have to keep her up all the time. You could put her out with the other mares—"

"Them other mares don't like her. Anyhow, she'd rather

295

be up here in the yard; she likes t' be around humans."

"Well, you mark my words. If you keep that horse you're going to lose all your friends and all your paying dudes, likewise. They're not going to put up with that stuff. Mr. Hammock told me how she tried to bite Ernie—"

"Ernie was pokin' her," Wild Horse said. "She's a spirited animal. Would *you* like t' hev somebody pokin' you? Dad-burn it, you kin *make* a horse mean! Them kind with courage an' a bold free spirit makes the worst kind of outlaws if they ain't treated right. A plucky, sensitive mare like her—"

"Horse! Horse! Horse!" Rose flared, disgusted. "That's all you think about! Do you ever stop to think about *me?*"

" 'Course I think about you," Shorty said—"an' say! That reminds me! A guy named Crowsnow come by here a couple or three days ago. He figgered to stay here; I guess McGee put him up. Anyway, *I* put him out an' he's gone t' law about it; claims he paid a month's rent in advance. He never paid *me* no money. Ernie says he paid McGee. McGee say anything to you about it?"

"He gave me the money," Rose nodded.

"Well!" Shorty said, "that's sure a relief! Hope you've got it where we kin find it when—"

"You've already got it," Rose said bitterly. "That was the five hundred dollars you paid for that mare."

11

"IF BRAINS WAS SALT—"

THE WAY SHORTY stood there you'd have thought lightning had struck him. His sun-burned face was awry. He looked dazed. But Rose didn't soften. She said, "I'm all fed up! If it isn't one thing, it's twenty-three others—and every durn time it has to do with your horses! It may be like you say about those mares; but that doesn't excuse the antics of *this* horse! I've a mind to pack and get out of here!"

She flung up her head and swirled off mighty peeved like, and Wild Horse couldn't think of anything to say.

He finally pulled himself together but it was not easy.

He felt just like Jonah when he'd got in the lion's cage.

Something had got to be done, and done quick.

He shook his head, muttering, and called to the mare. Blood of Kings blew a loud blast through her nose and came gingerly picking her way round the furniture—*very* gingerly stepping across the wreck she had made of the best maple chair; and docilely followed him down the steps.

Bee Bee Dunne stood waiting in the light from a window. He looked kind of startled when he saw the mare come walking out of the house with Shorty. But Mr. Dunne was a gentleman and whatever he thought he did not say it. He said: "About those horses—"

"Mister Dunne," Shorty said like it was painful to speak, even, "I hev jest had a bereavement. I'm not in no mood to talk about horses."

And he would have gone tramping past except that, just at that moment, he spied the bean guy, Sinclair, coming out of his cabin. He was scared he'd be stuck for the balance of the evening if Sinclair ever started unwinding some yarn of the time he'd punched cattle for the Diamond A outfit. And there was always the chance he might want to go and see Farrar's place again—dark or no dark.

So Shorty turned back to Dunne. "What horses? What about 'em?"

"Ah?—Oh! The horses. Yes, indeed. I was about to say," Mr. Dunne remarked, "that I have frequently persuaded myself that a wager on the bangtails was not a half bad investment. I have occasionally found it a very good investment. You know—back East. Thoroughbreds. Churchill Downs—Latonia—Belmont Park—such places. I understand there are to be some . . . ah—Speed Trials here at Tucson very shortly. I should like to attend them— In fact I'd like to make a few wagers, but I don't know the horses."

"Well, I don't know who's figgerin' to run stuff this year," Shorty said, "but if they run you won't go far wrong backin' Shue Fly, Clabber, Joe Reed II, or Squaw H. They're all crack stuff. The sixth race will be the big one, the Open Championship; that's where you see those nags *if* they run. Shue Fly's been World's Champ fer several years. But she may not defend her title this year. Somebody was tellin' me she's got a bad cold."

"A local mare, is she?"

"Nope. She's from Carlsbad, New Mexico. Owned by the Hepler Brothers. *You* oughta know her! You're from Santa Fe, ain't you?"

298

"We don't have a race track there—"

"Well, they've got one at Albuquerque. That's where Shue Fly got beat last year—first time in her life, I guess. At the State Fair," Shorty said.

Beau Dunne asked, "Isn't there a horse named *Queeny?*"

"You mean the Club Footed Queen of the Quarter? Heck, yes! That's the mare that beat Shue Fly at Albuquerque!"

"Did you say she was club footed?"

"She's so club footed they can't hardly train her before a race for fear she'll go lame an' not be able to run when the time comes. She's by Flyin' Bob, an' owned locally— She's one of Jelks' horses. If she didn't hev that bad foot," Shorty said, "there wouldn't be no ketchin' her short of the Jordan."

"I think I shall bet on her," Dunne said, jotting her name down in a little book he carried. "Haven't I heard of that Joe Reed before?"

"Be surprised if you ain't. He was up in the money a couple years back. Tops in the racin' an' tops in the stud show—at Tucson, I mean. His name's Joe Reed II. The original Joe Reed, this stud's daddy an' No. 3 in the stud book, is up at Elk City, Oklahoma; he's a pretty old gent. But this horse was seven years old before he ever saw a track. Took his first start with hardly no trainin'. Had trouble with a quarter crack every time they worked him. But he won his first start. Made a rep on his second; carried a hundred an' seventy-five pounds an' won by a length and a half of daylight. I wisht t' hell *I* had him!"

"Why not breed that new mare to him, Shorty?"

Wild Horse said, "The less said about that mare, the better."

Mr. Dunne kind of stared and changed the subject. "What

are some of the other good ones? No use going just to bet on one race."

"Well, I don't know what outside stuff'll be runnin'," Shorty said, "but if they hev any race with Lilly Belle in it, bet on her. She was into the wire two-three months ago, but I don't guess it's anything t' worry about— Seems like somethin' or other happens to all the good horses. The Double N's buckskin, War Bonnet, got into the wire the other night, too—pretty bad, Doc says. But about this Lilly Belle. She's a comin' three an' plain greased lightnin' on a straight-away; she's by Red Man, another good Quarter Horse. Then there's Bessie Girl an' Nettie Hill. An' Wayward Girl an' Ready. Texas Boy ain't nothin' to be sneezed at, nor 803 Babe, nor Buster. I guess them'll do you for the moment," Shorty said hurriedly, having noticed the bean authority making tracks in their direction. "I'll be workin' half the night t' git my chores done up; but if you want any more dope see me t'morrer."

"THESE RICH DUDES an' their money!" Shorty muttered as he stood in the box stall surveying the wreckage. "It sure beats all what a time they hev spendin' it— I never hev no trouble gittin' rid of *mine!*"

He scowled around once more. "Well," he said to the mare, "you sure played hell all over, didn't you!"

He glared at her, sour like, and scratched his elbow. "Guess I'll put you in that corral outside. Wisht I could think up some way t' git shed of you—some way, I mean, that would build up my pocketbook."

Blood of Kings rubbed his shoulder with her velvety muzzle.

"Humph!" Shorty grunted, "I don't fall fer that stuff,"

but he patted her anyhow and didn't look mad about it. "Come on, dadburn you," he finally muttered, picking up the lantern. "Guess you're feelin' kinda empty. You keep on the way you're goin' now an' you'll be daggone lucky if you eat a-tall."

He put a halter on her and led her outside. He put her in the pole corral that abutted the barn. There was a feed rack built below a slot in the wall.

Shorty, gone back inside, looked around for some hay. About a bale and a half was all he had, and there were fifteen hungry mares out on pasture which ought to be entitled to hay once a day anyhow. They wouldn't be getting very much tonight. "That's fer certain," Shorty said, still scowling. "Be as much as a feller's life is worth t' set that bale an' a half in front of 'em. Sixteen mares could *inhale* that much!"

He tore off an armful and thrust it through the slot. He could hear Blood of Kings tearing into it with relish. He swore when he went to get her some grain. He had considerably less than twenty-five pounds. "What does that dang fool do all day? Don't he ever keep tabs on nothin'?"

He scooped up a couple quarts and poured them after the hay. Then he tramped outside to see how the mare was doing.

When he fed them himself, Shorty usually spread the hay out for his mares. If you just set out a big hunk from a bale they usually wasted as much as they ate. So he stepped up beside Blood of Kings to shake out the hay he had given her. It was alfalfa hay and tightly pressed and he decided, after spreading it out, that he'd given her more than she needed. He scooped up an armful and started back to the barn with it. But just as he reached the gate Blood of Kings let out a snort and loped after him. She shot out in front of him and blocked his way.

Shorty said, "What's the big idear?"

Blood of Kings showed him. She shouldered him round till he faced the feed rack, then gave him a determined push with her muzzle and kept right with him till he put the hay back, after which she ignored him and resumed her eating.

"Well, I'm a son of a gun!" Shorty said, and chuckled.

EARL HAMMOCK was the very first person Wild Horse saw the next morning and, if he had seen him in time, he would have ducked him. But he didn't. As a matter of fact, Mr. Hammock saw him first.

Shorty was washing his face in the bucket that was kept for that purpose on a bench out back of the cook shack. The first he knew of Mr. Hammock's presence was when the painter said, "Tell me! Did you get rid of that mare yet?"

Shorty was almost scared to look round. "Not yet. But soon's I eat—"

He took a quick slanchways glance and was considerably surprised to see that Hammock was grinning. He looked again.

Hammock said, "You don't have to sell her to please *me*, Shorty. It wasn't the mare's fault Ethel dropped that painting; and you can just forget all about paying for it. I wouldn't think of letting you."

Wild Horse rubbed at his eyes, dumbfounded. "You mean . . . You ain't kiddin', are you?"

"Not a bit," Hammock laughed. "We'll just count that as practise and forget all about it."

Shorty grabbed Hammock's hand and pumped it vigorously. "I reckon you measure a full sixteen hands. I been figgerin' you was probably packin' your warbag—"

"Not me," Hammock smiled. "How's the mare feel this morning?"

302

"She's still takin' nourishment," Wild Horse said. "How's Missus Hammock?"

"She's all right. Feeling kind of foolish to have caused such an uproar, I suspect. I hope you're not in the doghouse for good?"

"Well, I got one leg out, anyway." But Shorty did not look too sanguine about it. "What do you reckon she went in the house fer? I never had no horse t' do that before."

"I expect she wanted to know if you'd got back. She was pretty upset about you going off and leaving her."

"Humph!" Shorty said; and they went in to breakfast.

"I've got it all settled," John Sinclair announced as they pushed back their chairs and prepared to roll smokes. "I've been in to town and had a talk with Farrar—"

"Farrar!" Shorty said. "Has *he* come back?"

"Oh, I called him on the telephone—Long Distance, you know. I've bought his place. On time, of course." He looked uneasily at Shorty. "Mr. Hammock is going to run me in to Tucson. I am going back to Lincoln and give up my curator's job at the Museum. Do you think I could get someone to stay on the place and take care of it for me till I'm ready to come back?"

"Ain't nobody goin' to make off with it," Shorty said.

"I'd feel better about it if I had a man staying there. All I want is for someone to live there and keep my trees watered. It won't cost them a cent and they can use it like their own."

"Joe Pipesley would probably keep a eye on it fer you."

"I think I'll go over to the Double N this morning," Mr. Dunne declared importantly. "One of the main reasons I came to Arizona was to make the acquaintance of that fellow who runs it—"

"Get him to show you his horses," said Shorty. "He ain't got much now, but what he's got are good ones."

They all got up and went their various ways. Shorty went out and saddled Blood of Kings. Struck by a notion, he tied the white mare to one of the corral poles and hastened over to where Mr. Dunne was warming up his scooter.

It made quite a racket. While he was waiting for Dunne to throttle it down, Hammock backed out his car and drove off with Sinclair. Sinclair waved to them gaily. "Hurry back," Shorty called.

Then Dunne got his racket maker under control and Shorty said, "I don't like t' mention it, but this place is run on a strictly cash basis—as advertised. It takes a pile of jack to keep this spread humpin'. So if you don't figger it would put you out too much . . ."

"Oh! Not at all," Dunne said, shutting off his motor. He got out his wallet and fished Shorty out a hundred and twenty dollars in currency.

Shorty's face looked blank.

"That's right, isn't it?" Mr. Dunne said.

"You jest figgerin' t' stay here a *week?*"

"Oh, I might stay a month—"

"By the month it would cost you less," Shorty mentioned.

"That's all right. I'd rather pay by the week," said Mr. Dunne agreeably. "That way I can pull up and leave any time the urge hits me. Well— I'll be seeing you." And he started up his scooter and boiled off in a cloud of dust.

Shorty looked after him and scowled impotently. "Wouldn't that burn you? All that money an' he's got t' pay by the week!"

He put the hundred and twenty dollars in his pocket. Then he remembered he was about out of hay and grain.

An accounting of the cash on hand showed him down to two hundred and ten dollars, including what Dunne had just paid him.

He put his billfold away with a bitter grimace. And just then Ernie and Sam Hoard, the ex-horse buyer, rode up. "How's tricks?" Ernie called. "Have you unloaded that mare yet?"

Shorty jerked a thumb at the corral off yonder. "Git down," he said, "an' rest your saddles. What's on your mind?"

Ernie, slouched back with a knee round the saddle horn, was building a smoke from his favorite mixture. When he lit it it smelled like a hayfield burning. Sam Hoard got off his apron faced roan and stretched his old legs with a weary sigh. "I been hearin' about that mare of yours, Shorty. Where have you got her?"

"That's her over there," Shorty pointed; and Sam Hoard tramped off.

"I don't see how I'm goin' t' git that money," Shorty said to Ernie.

"Why don't you get some more of that purple medicine an' paint those mares of yours up and sell 'em?"

"You mean sell 'em for Palamoosas?"

"Why not? Look at all that free advertisin' you got last year. Bet you could sell every one of them, Shorty. Paint 'em up an' run a few ads in the stock journals. 'Purple horses'— All the dudes in the country will be bustin' to buy 'em."

"Well, but that wouldn't be honest. Rose would hev duck fits," Shorty said regretful like.

"Well," Ernie said, "you better get that money—"

"Hey!" Sam Hoard broke in just then. "Come over here, will you?"

"What's the matter?" Ernie asked as they came up to the horse buyer.

"Why, there ain't nothin' wrong with this white mare. I supposed by Fritchet's tell of it you had gone and got stuck with some old plug! This mare's no plug. I knew her mammy and pappy, an' they was real fine stock—mostly Quarter Horse."

Ernie said: "The hell they was!"

And Shorty asked, "Do you know what her pappy's name was, Sam?"

"Will Gammill called him Rainy Day. He was by Gammill's Whitey, who were by Waggoner's old yellow Rainy Day," Hoard said. "Her mammy were a sorrel Waggoner mare by Midnight, by Badger, by Peter McCue."

Shorty's face was a study.

Ernie's showed considerable surprise. Ernie said, "Where the hell did she get those eyes then?"

"I don't know," Sam said, twisting up a smoke. "I don't know unless she got 'em from her father—*he* were a blue-eyed horse. Fine lookin' stud, though; big, upstandin', prouder'n a peacock. Waggoner's Rainy Day were a mighty fine horse, too—still is. He were bred to a palomino mare to get Whitey. Whitey were a showy, cream-colored horse— *Creamolines* is what they call them up North, it seems like. Anyway, Gammill bred his blue-eyed Rainy Day to this sorrel mare by Midnight and got Blood of Kings."

Shorty said, "What did Gammill call her?"

"Why, Blood of Kings—same name she's got now. That's howcome I got curious when I heard what you was callin' her. Near as I can recollect, Gammill—he lives over to Randlett, Oklahoma—sold her as a yearlin' to a feller named Coyle, down here to Hereford, Arizona. Is that who you got her from?"

306

"I got her," Shorty said, "from a ingrate named Tranch —an' lo an' behold if I ever ketch up with him!"

Ernie said, "She's an inbred palomino, I reckon. Look— Tell you what you do, Shorty. There's a horse buyer over at the Crossing right now—come in just this morning from the coast—Santa Barbara. Name of Al Manuel—an Irisher, I reckon. Now here's what we'll do. You brush up this mare and bring her in and I'll let on like I'm bustin' to buy her; I'll have this guy Manuel stuck around someplace. We'll haggle over the price a few minutes an' kind of whet up his appetite. Then I'll say, 'Nope—that's every cent I can give you. That price you're talking is way out of my class. There's a feller over at L. A. might give you that much, but not me.' From there on we can leave all the rest up to old Human Nature— What do you say?"

Shorty stared at the mare. "I dunno," he said.

"You don't *know!*" Ernie looked exasperated. "What do you mean, you don't know? You want to feed that hide all the rest of your natural? Use your head, goddam it! Here's a chance to get shut of her an' get your money back."

"Yeah. But—"

"But what?" Ernie said. "You got buts in the belfry!"

"Well . . . But mebbe this mare could really *do* somethin'—"

"She could nicker!" Ernie snarled, "if that's any help to you! If you're wanting to sample county grub for a spell, you're in a first-rate way to be getting your wants, feller."

Shorty stood scowling. He chewed on his lip awhile. "If she was any other color—"

"If she was any other color you wouldn't ever have gotten her."

"I think I'll write Coyle," Shorty said reflectively. "Mebbe I could git her registered."

"Registered?" Ernie stared at him. "As what—an Albino?"

"As a Quarter Horse. With all that good background—"

"Goda'mighty—I give you up!" Ernie said, and climbed back in his saddle. "If brains was salt, yours wouldn't tan a shrunk squirrel hide!"

12

MORE IRON

SHORTY GOT his feed, and a couple days later he got two letters. The first was from Sinclair. It said:

Dear Shorty—

I managed to get someone to live in my house until I can get back out there. I got that Mr. Ben; he was very nice about it. He has sold his hotel and says he will be glad to oblige me by living on the place. I'm to charge him no rent and have told him to use it like his own. He will pay the light bill. I am sending him a hoe, a rake and two shovels—a long and short handled one. He is going to start a garden for me. I don't know how long it will take me to wind up my affairs here; but the sooner the better. Say hello for me to all those swell folks out there, and all the best to you in your work with the horses.

> *Your friend,*
>
> *John L. Sinclair.*

Shorty's other letter was from the Lanteen Ranch, and postmarked Hereford. Shorty tore it open with nervous fingers and read the entire epistle three times.

My dear Mr. Shorty—

I take pleasure in answering your letter of the 25th.

You requested any information I might have as to the back-

ground of a white mare known as Blood of Kings. She was born at an early age of poor but virtuous parents in a big pole corral that she helped her father build. Her early life was carefree and gay, and those who knew her say she was a pretty little thing with big blue eyes and long blonde curls. She attended an exclusive finishing school in Texas and was the brightest one in her class. During her sub-deb years she helped her mother with the work to be done around the stables. She was the apple of her father's eye and he showed her off at the slightest provocation. In her third year she was entered in a beauty contest and won both first and second prizes. (I might add her father was the one and only judge.)

If you should wish further genealogy we have it clear back to the spermatozoon.

Hoping you can find some reason or other to write me again.

> Sincerely yours,
> Donald Coyle.

Shorty cuffed back his hat and scratched his head. He went over Coyle's letter again. "If that guy ain't drunk, he's plumb loco! Or hoorawin' me—one! What the devil's a sper —sperma—spermatozoon? I betcha that ape thinks he's bein' funny!"

Shorty's scowl grew black. "There ain't nothin' funny about *horses!*" he flared. "I don't see why everybody's always tryin' t' make jokes about them— Dadburn it! A horse is a man's BEST FRIEND!"

He scrunched Coyle's letter into a ball and heaved it angrily into the manure pile. He had left Blood of Kings with George Kerley hoping to hold comment down to a minimum; but the idea, he saw, was not working so good. There was quite a bunch grouped around the barn door.

Shorty decided to get the mare later.

He headed for the hotel to wet his whistle and see what he could learn in the way of news.

There was an outside door to the bar. It was padlocked.

Shorty clanked up the steps and went into the lobby. It still needed paint but the dust and the cobwebs were all swept out of it. A smartly dressed lady of about Mrs. Potter's age looked up from the desk and eyed him brightly. A pleasant looking lady in horn rimmed glasses.

"How do you do?" she said. "I'm the new owner—Anna White. May I help you?"

"I dunno," Shorty said. "But I'm pleased t' meetcha. I—uh—I was huntin' a drink . . ."

"The hotel doesn't serve hard liquor any more. There's some pop in the ice box— I don't guess you cowboys care for plain pop, do you?"

"Well, no, I guess not. I'm Wild Horse Shorty—run the WHS Ranch. Dudes an' horses—"

He let the rest trail off. There was a platinum blonde coming down the stairs, and— Yessir! It was the Oregon Oriole, Trillene Tralane! What eyes! What hair! What conformation!

As her glance met his, Trillene paused on the stair and her red lips curved in a somewhat shy and wholly devastating smile. Then she lowered her black lashes demurely and resumed her regal descent. Shorty couldn't help but notice the enticing way the light laid satiny shimmers across the hips her skirt hugged so tightly.

It was a fascinating sight.

Then, just as she stepped off the stairs, a whispy white something seemed to float away from her person and settled with a little flutter on the carpet.

Shorty stared.

Yes sir! By grab, it was another kerchief! She just couldn't seem to keep hold of them—didn't even know she had

311

dropped it! She had gone right along over to the desk and was asking Mrs. White for her mail. Looked to be getting quite a fistful, too; so Shorty went over and picked up her kerchief.

He was turning around to go back and give it to her when he fetched up short with an involuntary gasp.

" 'Ere— Wocher up ter!"

It was Halbert Crowsnow, the beetle-browed Earl of Clank! The man who was suing him for five hundred dollars!

He had been buried in a newspaper over in the corner and Shorty had missed him completely. But now the Earl threw his paper aside. He came out of his chair and advanced belligerently.

"I'll tike that!" He reached forth a hand.

"Go ahead," Shorty said. "Just try it!"

"Do yer think I carn't?"

"Oh— My kerchief!" exclaimed Trillene, coming over. "Thank you—thank you *very* much," and she smiled as Shorty gave it to her right under the nose of the glaring Earl. "Did I hear you say you ran the WHS Ranch. Then you must be *Wild Horse Shorty!*" she declared delightedly; and Wild Horse stuck out his chest importantly.

"Yours truly," he said with a fatuous smile.

She said, "You don't look bad," and Shorty came right back at her.

"You look pretty good yourself," he said.

She gave a gay little laugh; laid a hand on his arm quite intimately. "I'm awfully glad to know you," she said. "You're so *real*, so genuine! Don't you know, I've heard the most *incredible* tales—"

"All a bunch of dang lies!"

"And do you really keep all those funny horses— I mean
312

that ancient stallion and all those mares? Do you still have those wonderful Palamoosas?"

"Well, no," Shorty said regretfully. "I got the mares an' the stud, but the Palamoosas is all sold out."

"Really? You must have had awfully good luck with them— I just *love* horses," she said with a flash of her pearly teeth. "Just crazy about them. I had a little pinto once—he was the cutest thing! But he got his foot in a dog hole and we had to shoot him. It almost broke my heart—I just cried and cried. I couldn't touch food for two whole days! I kept seeing his dear little face, the way he looked up at me just before they shot him."

Shorty understood, and his heart went out to her. "Tell you what I'll do," he said impulsively. "I'm goin' to *give* you a horse—"

"For my *very own*? Oh, Shorty! Not *really?*"

"Yep!" Shorty said. "I'm goin' t' git you a Palamoosa, by godfreys!"

"Oh— But I thought you said you had sold them all—"

"All but one," Shorty said, thinking fast. "I kept back the best one; was figgerin' to hang onto it. She's a fine lookin' mare—jest what you need in the movies."

"I'm so *thrilled!*" Trillene said, and she squeezed Shorty's arm deliciously. "I can hardly wait!"

The Earl looked mad enough to bite his toenails. He said, glowering: "We'll 'ave ter 'urry or you'll be lyte fer yer part—"

"Yes," Trillene said, "I suppose so. Being an actress," she explained to Shorty, "doesn't leave a person much time of her own. But we must get together some time, *real soon*. I want you to tell me all about your horses; and about that funny little Hellbound man— Maybe I could get you a part in the picture."

313

"No kiddin'?" Shorty said, swelling out his chest.

"I'll try. Look—" She leaned toward him, scarlet lips brushing Shorty's cheek as she said, "Why don't you make a little ceremony of it? When you give me my horse, bring it out to the lot—out on location. We're up in the Santa Ritas, you know. You bring it out there and I'll introduce you to the right people—to Mr. Selznick, and you'd be sure to get on. Bring Hellbound, too. We'll make a spot for you both—"

"Blimey!" the Earl snapped impatiently. "Hif you don't 'urry—"

"Yes, yes," Trillene cried. "Well, goodbye now," she smiled. "I'll be looking for you out on location tomorrow— You know where to come?"

"I'll find it," grinned Wild Horse; and with a malignant scowl the Earl whisked her away.

Shorty moved toward the stable as one in a dream.

He could hardly believe it. Wild Horse Shorty— ACTOR!

Such were the roseate visions before him that he quite failed to see Mrs. Ex-Sheriff Potter until he had run right into her. Making a hasty apology he gathered up her flowered bonnet and gave her a hurried brushing off with it till Mrs. Potter recovered her wits and indignantly snatched the bonnet away from him. She eyed it like she was about to pop, and while she was doing it Shorty departed.

But he took to the middle of the road after that. He wasn't taking any more chances.

Wild Horse Shorty— ACTOR!

Daggone!

It just went to show that, sooner or later, if a man had the talents the gods in their time were bound to discover him.

But you had to hand it to Trillene, by godfreys! *There* was a girl with *eyes* in her head. Didn't need no spectacles to know the real thing when she saw it; and she approved of his horses—was wild to have one.

And she should have one, too!

Shorty grinned, plumb tickled to think how this news would hit Fritchet and the rest of the Crossing scoffers.

Wild Horse Shorty— ACTOR!

Hot dog! *He'd* show 'em!

They would have his name in white lights at the show houses.

DUEL IN THE SUN, with Wild Horse Shorty and the Oregon Oriole!

It could *be,* by grab! Yep—it sure as heck could!

WHEN HE GOT within sight of George Kerley's Livery the crowd was still there—it had even grown some. Half the town was there like a bunch of buzzards, trying to see past where Kerley stood in the doorway.

Shorty called: "What's the matter with 'em? Ain't the ignorant jiggers ever cast their peepers on a horse before?"

"Is that a HORSE?"

Through the guffaws and cat calls Fritchet said fleeringly: "Still feedin' them nags of yours post hay, are you?"

Wild Horse scowled. "Post hay" was a term of contempt describing a horse tied up with nothing better to feed on than the post he was tied to.

Then Provencher added his five cents' worth. "When you're ready to breed her I'll bring my new colt around, Shorty. He's shapin' up good and they're both the same color—"

"When I breed that mare it won't be to nothin' I could find around *this* burg!"

315

"To Clabber, mebbe?"

"To King?"

"To Chip Rock?"

"No," Fritchet sneered. "He won't breed *her* t' nothing less than old Man O' War—"

"It sure won't be to anything *you* own!"

"You can say that again!"

The whole crowd haw-hawed, and then Potter said, "Town don't seem like the same place no more since Shorty quit chousin' his nightmares around—"

"You swivel-eyed polecats better dig your ears out an' wake up t' what's goin' on in this country!" Shorty flared, scowling angrily. "When you see me playin' with that Oregon Oriole—"

Fritchet doubled clear over and slapped his thigh. "Haw! Haw! Haw!" he bellowed. "You an' the Oregon Oriole! If that ain't a laugh—"

"You better not let Crowsnow catch you playin' around with that dame," Potter said. And they all laughed again.

"Well, I swear!" Kerley said. "Goin' to act in the movies, are you?"

Shorty strode through the bunch, elbowing them aside without care or apology. Let them laugh, the dimwits! Let them hawhaw their brains out! When they saw his face on the screen with Trillene's—when they saw his name in Big Letters on the billboards, they'd be singing a different tune, by godfreys!

SHORTY got home to find Dunne and Hammock listening to some long-winded yarn old Hellbound was telling.

"—an' the two of 'em stood around glarin' an' glowerin' whiles they waited fer one of them cussed hens t' git up on thet box an' drop 'em a aig. Bill allowed he was so dang starved by thet time he reckoned ef one of 'em finally *did* lay, an' the dang hen made a grab at the aig, he'd kill her with his own two hands b'fore he would stan' there ag'in an' watch her eat it!"

Shorty said, scowling, "Did you go see the Doc like I told you?"

"Yep," Hellbound said. "He sure tol' me what my trouble was. I need more—"

"Never mind what you need! If you don't git busy an' clean out that stable, you're goin' to be needin' a new *job*— savvy?"

"By the way," Hammock said. "You got another letter. Came Special Delivery. A kid just rode out with it."

Shorty took the letter and tore it open.

Dear Shorty:

Well, I guess before long I'll be seeing you. I have given the Museum my resignation. So far, my plans are to leave here on Wednesday—the day after the election (I have to serve as poll clerk) and will arrive in Tucson by the Golden State Limited on the 28th at 6:oo a.m. With me I will bring the following:

Trunk full of clothing and effects.

Typewriter.

Bedroll.

Crate containing "Smoky" the cat.

Unless I change my mind I will also have a cardboard box of writing equipment; also a gunny sack containing saddle and cowboy outfit.

I want to be free of the Bohemians of Santa Fe and live near Tucson where life is saner.

Am now getting my things packed for storage. Will have them sent on to me, piece by piece, after I get settled.

Hasta la vista,
Sinclair

"From Sinclair," Shorty said, thrusting the letter in his pocket.

"Coming back?" Hammock asked.

"So he says. Day after tomorrow."

Shorty was starting toward the house when Beau Dunne asked, "Where's all that hunting your ads tell about?"

Shorty waved an arm. "You kin hunt any time or place you've a mind to."

"Yes—but don't you have anything *special* for us? Any pack trips or hunting parties! That horse buyer, Hoard, claims there's lots of wild pigs—"

"How about getting up a fox hunt?" said Hammock. "Like they have in Virginia, with hounds and horses. Very picturesque, you know, and loads of fun. You've got plenty of horses. You could even make it a kind of neighborhood affair—"

"Too complicated," Shorty frowned. "Anyhow, I reckon to be pretty busy fer the next few days. Got a job in the movies—with Trillene Tralane."

"No kidding?" Hammock said. "Why, that's wonderful, Shorty! When—"

"What's that?" Rose said, coming up somewhat hurriedly with Ethel Hammock. "You've got a job in the movies? What doing, for heaven's sake—watering the horses?"

"Waterin' the horses!" Shorty said indignantly. "I'll hev you know I'm goin' t' *act* in that picture! Trillene says—"

"Oh, Trillene!" Rose sniffed. "Where'd you meet *her*?"

"She's stayin' at the *ho*tel. She wants me to start tomorrow. She says—"

"Well, don't spend the money till you get it," Rose advised. "I think you'll find she's just stringing you along. She probably thinks you're a 'character' or something."

Shorty eyed her with something like pity.

318

She just wouldn't believe he could ever amount to anything.

But this was his chance. By grab, he'd show them! And when they put his name in Big Letters on the billboards, Rose and the rest of them would be glad to know him.

Shorty sighed. But that was life for you. No man was a hero where he paid his taxes.

With a tolerant shrug he picked up the reins and set off toward the stable. Then an idea struck him and he pulled up short to turn it over. Trillene wanted one of his horses, but it was the Palamoosas that had taken her fancy; that rarest of breeds he had hatched last summer with the aid of Doc Wallace and that writer guy, Forest.

It was Mrs. Fergie who had really started it. Mrs. Fergie with her everlasting questions. Shorty had had some wire cut mares the Doc had been treating with Pykotine Blue, a purple medicine sometimes used for that purpose. Mrs. Fergie, happening to notice one of the purple splotched grays, had asked if it were a strawberry roan. Shorty, fed up, said it was a palamoosa, and the Denver papers, through the pen of Lee Forest, had taken it up and made a great stir about it. All over the country and even in England people had heard about Wild Horse Shorty and his "purple" horses. More than a few had taken it seriously, believing he had actually founded a new breed on the pinto order.

And now Trillene, thinking to have for her very own one of these much discussed animals, had told him she'd get him in the movies with her. Not just because of the horse, of course, but because she could see that he really had talent. Naturally, deep in his heart, Shorty always had known he could be a great actor. But no one, before, had ever offered him the chance.

Being in the movies he could forget about Crowsnow—

To an actor five hundred dollars was nothing but chicken feed. Shucks, he might even give the Earl a whole thousand just to show folks, by grab, that he wasn't no piker!

But best of all, here at last was the chance of a lifetime to get himself shed of that danged Albino! He would turn her into a Palamoosa and give her with his blessings to the Oregon Oriole.

It was sheer inspiration— Even *Rose* would be satisfied!

Shorty chuckled to himself and went on to the barn. He put Blood of Kings in the pole corral and got her a heaping armful of hay—even gave her some grain to show he held no hard feelings.

Let him be rid of her and Crowsnow's lawsuit and things would settle back to their accustomed calm and he could proceed with his horse breeding without all this devilment.

And he would be in the movies. Why, he might even get to be more famous than *Sonatra!*

With bucket and brush he curried the white mare till she fairly shone. He even polished her hoofs though she didn't show very great enthusiasm for it. Then he combed out her tail and braided some waves to handsome it up.

She looked pretty good. "Fer a danged albino!" Shorty couldn't help muttering.

The mare turned her head and softly nickered and, for a second, Shorty felt kind of mean about what he was up to. Then he hardened his heart and went hunting the medicine.

He looked all over the stable without finding it. Nor did he see any sign of Hellbound. The more he hunted the more riled he got.

"That danged galoot don't do one blasted lick of work! Not a lick! Lookit that manure!" he growled. "Lookit them grain sacks—an' that pitchfork where he left it! If one of them horses come along an' stepped on it— Dadburn him!

He's about as worthless as a four-card flush! All he does is eat an' sleep—like the rest of 'em!"

He stuck his head out the door and yowled for all hands and the cook to come running.

But nobody came.

Temper was threatening to have its way with him, and he cursed in a passion. "All I do is work an' pay bills! Lookit the payroll I hev to keep up— An' what do I git fer it? Pay! Pay! Pay! Not one durn hand'll lift a finger! If you want somethin' done you got t' do it yourself!"

He stormed out of the stable in a fine sweat and went stomping across to the cook shack. Not even Rose was there. It was empty of humans as the palm of your hand.

Shorty slammed outside and bellowed for Dunne—for anybody that would answer his call and help him find that Pykotine Blue so that he could get on with his work of disguising Blood of Kings so that he would be enabled finally to get shed of her and palm her off on Trillene Tralane.

But nobody answered and nobody came.

With his face in a scowl Shorty hotfooted over to the fixed-up tool shed which had been remodeled with kitchen privileges.

And there they were! All laughing and joking with Hellbound Hank who was bent over a frying pan he had set on the oil heater.

Wild Horse scowled blacker than ever as they all fell silent. He went over to Hellbound and looked in the pan. It contained one stove lid steeped in lard.

"What in seven hells d'you think you're doin'?"

"Fryin' thet stove lid," Hellbound said. "You *told* me t' go see thet horse doc, didn't you? Then git thet gunbarrel look off yer face— He said what I'm needin's *more iron* in m' system!"

321

13

A FEW WORDS ABOUT BANGTAILS

SHORTY said no more about getting into the pictures; but he finally tracked down the purple medicine and took Blood of Kings to the adobe corral that he had used to keep the Lanteen colt in. He got a big cotton swab and started to work.

Hellbound must have told Rose about it. She came hurrying over and stared, arms akimbo. "What in the world are you up to now?"

"I'm fixin' to git rid of her," Shorty scowled; and the look of his face forbade further questions.

"Well, that's a mercy," Rose sniffed, "but I don't see why you're wasting all that medicine. I don't see no cuts where you're putting that stuff—"

"What you don't see won't hurt you," Shorty growled; and Rose went flouncing back to her cooking.

Shorty did a good job with the Pykotine Blue, and when he finally quit he had a sure enough ringer for a Palamoosa. Blood of Kings didn't look like herself any more. All the fire had gone out of her, seemed like, and she hung her head dispiritedly and did not seem to care whether school kept or not. When Shorty finally noticed and spoke her name she gave no sign of hearing him, but stood there dejected with her tail forlornly tucked between her legs.

It was just like he had taken a stick and beaten her.

Shorty eyed her, puzzled, unable to account for this listless attitude.

Then he went to the barn and got her some hay. But she would not eat; she would not even move to go smell the hay. She just stood there, kind of huddled-up like, with no more spirit than an old plough horse.

Just a little uneasy, Wild Horse finally left her.

After supper he saddled Figure 8 and rode off to town.

Seemed like things had been happening. Provencher had sold his COLLOSSAL MERCANTILE to old Sam Hoard and had moved his family off to Tucson; and Ernie, the Sheriff, so the newsmongers said, had sold his new chestnut Quarter Horse filly to the Double N Ranch. "They're talkin' of racing her next year," Hoard said. "Their famous buckskin, War Bonnet, rolled into the wire the other night and Doc McQuown says it's pretty much doubtful if she'll ever set foot on a track again. He reckons to pull her through, but that leg won't ever be in shape for runnin'."

"That's sure tough," Shorty said. "There's a awful lot of good blood in that mare. What in Tophet did you wanta go buyin' this store fer?"

"Always kind of hankered to run a store. Gettin' tired of makin' lamps for them dodrotted dudes, an' I'm gettin' too old to chase round buyin' horses. Take a look at this handbill I'm puttin' out."

SAMUEL HOARD, Esq., one door West of Fritchet's Saloon, has got in this day one hundred boxes and packages of desirable and fancy staple dry goods, selected with care and special regard to style and durability from the manufacturers in Distant States, part purchased at extensive auction sales in the East and Abroad, as follows: Super French and West of England broadcloths, blue, black and Invisible Green, also other fancy colors; London ribbed, Queen's Own, mullgrave and buckskin cassimers, Super Blue (and other colored) satinetts; several cases of French marinoes, all colors and qualities; plain and white figured Kentucky jeans; super scarlet and white Welsh flannels, domestic ditto; cloth rose and Whitney blankets; Edinborough shawls; 4 cases Super undressed grass; bleached Dublin Hall premium Irish Linens; satin, damask, white and brown tablecloths; birds eye diapers; tabinets and poplins; 30 cases fine imported Mohair; worsted angola; lambs wool and cotton drawers; bleached and unbleached muslins; several cartoons French and British silk thread laces— some as high cost as $5. per yard; shantila, semi and Brussels black lace veils; embroidered hemstitch handkerchiefs; childrens caps, new style; very rich new style satins—some as high cost as $30. per yard while they last; blonde and muslin de Cassimere scarfs; richly embroidered Marmot cravats—mostly black; black lace mantillas; silver stripe challeys; printed lawns, etc. Ladies twisted pic nic lile wire thread gloves, super red ditto; sewing silk in thirteen colors; Spittlefield & India Bandanna handkerchiefs for the well dressed cowhand; one case heavy rich super de luxe hosiery, all colors; rich plaid and shaded ribbons, glassia and velvet edges.

BONNETS—Several cases. Super fine French and Florench; English straw and Stetson hats; other Fashionable Bonnets, entirely new shape, by the case, dozen or single; English split straw, Dunstable; Armenian split hairs; Oriental rattan and tissue. COME ONE, COME ALL TO THE COLLOSSAL MERCANTILE—Samuel Hoard, Esq., Prop.

324

"I reckon it's all right," Shorty said dubiously. "Where'd you git all that junk?"

"That'll get 'em into the store now, won't it?" Sam chuckled.

"But hev you got it?"

"Well, no— But what difference do that make?" Sam said testily. "You got to be always pryin', dang it? This here's the same kinda gag all them merchants put up, ain't it? If they ask for some of that stuff, can I help it if I'm outa that partic'lar item? It's first come, first served—like it is in Tucson."

"That where you got the idear?" Shorty asked.

"No. I was rummagin' through some of the junk in the back room an' I come acrosst an old copy of the Cincinnati Gazette—September 16, 1839. Alls I had to do was copy out one of them ads I read in it— Oh! Excuse me whiles I wait on this customer."

Sam hurried off to attend to Mrs. Potter. A tall, bony, red-faced stranger in brush-clawed chaps came into the store, took a quick squint around, spied Shorty and beckoned. "You the feller that's been wantin' to buy a good palomino?"

"What about it?" Shorty said, looking him over suspicious like.

"Step outside an' take a look at these."

Shorty followed him out.

The man had a cavvy of six palominos, two studs, a gelding, and three young mares. One of the studs had a bell round his neck, a smart looking horse with large brown eyes and one white stocking; he seemed to have no trouble keeping the rest in line. The man had his saddle on a big grulla mare. A lead rope anchored the younger stud to the saddle.

"That big stud with the bell on," Shorty said. "What do you want for him?"

The stranger smiled. "You wouldn't want *him*—he's a heavey."

"A what?" Shorty said, peering closely at the animal.

"Broken winded—he's got the heaves. I just use him to keep this bunch in line. He can't go fast an' the rest won't pass him."

Shorty looked at the younger stud. This stallion was not as big as the bell stud, not as smart looking either, but he was a well built horse with good coat color, dark eyes and black skin.

"What kinda breedin's he got?" Shorty said.

"Damned if I know," answered the man. "I got the whole bunch at a auction up-state. Seein' as how I had t' pass through here I thought I'd ask if you wanted any of 'em. Some guy was tellin' me you liked yeller horses."

Shorty thought it was pretty decent of the man to warn him about that stud with the bell on. Not many horse traders would have.

He walked around the other stud. There was still plenty of light to judge him by. There wasn't any doubt he was a palomino. So there was no catch there.

Just the same, Wild Horse was just a shade uneasy about doing further business with strangers—particularly after supper.

"Where you from?" he said, still eyeing the horse.

"Duncan," the man said. "Heatherford's my name. Run the Bar H iron."

Shorty had never heard of it, but that was no good reason for doubting the man; there were quite a few outfits he had never heard of.

The horse didn't have near the class of *Sangre de Cristo*,

but he was a good-looking number just the same; and the more Shorty looked the better he liked him.

So he stepped up closer and reached for a hoof.

"Look out," warned the man. "I don't know much about these horses. Might be they'd kick. They're only green broke."

Shorty nodded and picked up a foot. Looked all right and the horse didn't mind. His feet looked quite normal. No swellings or cuts or anything of that kind. No sprains, no splints. Shorty said, "What'll you take fer him?"

"I'll take a hundred an' twenty-five—right here."

"Well . . ." Shorty said, and began going over the horse in earnest. Once stung, twice shy. He wasn't aiming to get hooked again. He went over that stallion inch by inch, and the longer he looked the more firmly convinced he became that this stud was a mighty good buy at that figure. A bargain, at last!

And he could really afford it, too, he reckoned. Now that he was going to act in the movies he didn't have to worry about that danged Earl's lawsuit. One day's work would take care of Crowsnow. There was no reason why he shouldn't buy this horse.

So he said, before Sam Hoard or Ernie should come around to restrain him, "I reckon I'll take that stud, Mister Featherstone. Write me out a bill of sale an' jest put the price where it kin be seen, right on it."

AFTER WAVING goodbye to the gentleman from Duncan, Shorty dallied the lead shank round his horn, climbed aboard Figure 8 and headed for Renegade's Roost to see Ernie. He was feeling pretty chipper by this time because it seemed like, at last, his luck had changed. And the more he looked over his palomino the more reason he found to congratulate himself. *Now* he could get down to business, by godfreys, and start raising palominos like he'd always wanted to. The way that yellow horse stepped along was a joy to behold. Probably Ernie would throw cold water on him, but Shorty did not see how he honestly could.

He pulled up outside and hollered for Ernie.

Ernie came out.

There was still light enough for him to see the horse. He eyed it a moment and then looked at Shorty. But he didn't say anything. Not a word.

"Well!" Shorty growled. "What do you think of him?"

"If it's color you want why don't you go in for Navajo blankets? You don't have to *feed* a blanket," Ernie said.

"Is that all you kin find t' say about that horse?"

"I could say a whole heap of things, but I reckon Rose said it all—you're incurable."

"You jest can't see palominos. That's all's the matter with *you*," Shorty growled. "If ol' Man O' War had a yeller hide you wouldn't give a plugged nickel fer him."

"Well, there's something in that," admitted Ernie. "Why don't you go in for chestnuts? Now a good chestnut—"

"You kin hev the chestnuts. There ain't no faster sellin' color today than palomino when it comes t' horses. An' it suits me right on down to the ground."

"But as a *breed?*" Ernie said. "No conformation— Well! all kinds of conformation, if you got to be strictly accurate. All kinds of bloodlines. All shades of yellow from skim milk to molasses. How can you ever make a breed out of anything if you keep throwin' in everything that comes along from soup to nuts?"

"You jest don't keep read up," Shorty said. "We're improvin' the breed every day. Gettin' more strict in our standards—"

328

"*What* standards?" Ernie snorted. "If they've got any standards I've yet to discover 'em. On their own figures, taken right out of their latest stud book, they've only got thirty-three horses, out of four thousand registered, with palomino parents on both sides! *One per cent!*"

"But—"

"But hell!" Ernie said. "That club's a farce! They'll never get a breed while they keep throwing in forty per cent of off colors every time they stir up a new batch of material. All that crowd's doing is ridin' a circle."

"That shows how much *you* know about it! Why, only this month they've made some new changes. They're goin' to start a Registry of Merit; nothin's goin' to git into it that ain't out of registered palomino parents—an' besides all that they got to have registered get an' produce. Five get for studs out of registered mares, and three or more registered produce from registered mares by PHBA studs."

"That's just so much hot air," Ernie said. "It'll take a couple centuries to solve anything that way. Unless your palomino breeders, *as a whole,* are willing to quit using off-colored mares, they'll never even get in sight of first base. Your new ruling sets too low a standard. One of its worst drawbacks is in not requiring any definite *percentage of acceptable get.* They'll pass out the prizes to the studs having the greatest number of stands. And there should be much higher standards for the studs than the mares. A mare can only bring in one colt per year; a stud can bring in thirty times that number! And there ain't anything said about bloodlines, nothing definite required in regard to the mothers and fathers of the horses involved. You can't wait six or eight generations to do something about problems that confront you *now*—that's what's ailin' the whole world," Ernie said.

"Well, anyhow," Shorty said, "this here stud'll git me a dang good start."

"With that there stud," Ernie mimicked him, "you're just going to do what the rest of them are doing—crank out as many yellow foals as you can and unload all you can just as fast as you can, regardless of what happens to 'em after you're shut of 'em. Regardless of whether they'll even transmit their color! It's the same kind of stunt the guy you bought him from was playin', an' if you want my opinion you're going to be disappointed in that horse."

"Why?" Shorty scowled.

"Because if the guy had any reason to think the horse was half as good as *you* think he is, you wouldn't have got him at any price."

"So you think I got stung ag'in, do you?"

"Let's talk about somethin' sane for a change. Did you know we got counterfeiters workin' this country? Well, we have—an' dang smart ones, too, by the looks. Got a warnin' from Phoenix just this afternoon. Where the hell would you look for a counterfeiter?"

"Under the bed?" suggested Wild Horse helpful like.

Ernie snorted. "Damn lucky I ain't got *you* for a deputy —Potter's bad enough!"

"You got Potter workin' for you now?" Shorty asked. "Thought he was sore about you gettin' the election—"

"He didn't like it much—doesn't yet. But we fixed up a deal. Whichever one of us gets in next election, he'll keep the other feller on for his deputy. That's a pretty practical working arrangement, and that way there ain't no hard feelings."

"Well," Shorty said, getting back in the saddle. "Guess I'll be siftin' along."

"I hear Tranch is back," Ernie said, eying Shorty.

"He better keep outa *my* way if he is!"

Ernie scowled. "Why don't you learn how to *ride* that horse? Why, damn it, you don't even *sit* right! You sit like a sack of meal in the saddle— Ride around there a second. Get your elbows in! Quit flappin' em! What do you think you are—a bird? Sit *forward*— Get your mouth closed! It's his *back* you're supposed t' be riding on, not his *kidney!* Christ!" Ernie scowled. "You're a disgrace to the Sheriff's Office!"

"I ain't connected with the sher—"

"But *I* am! You ride like a goddam cowpuncher! Why don't you take a few ridin' lessons?"

"Off *you?*"

"No— I ain't got the time. But I'll tell you what I *will* do! I'll lend you a book—just the thing for a beginner. *Heads Up, Heels Down*—by a feller named Anderson. Take it home an' read it. Read it *careful.* Wait a sec an' I'll—"

"I ain't got no time fer book readin'. I'm goin' to act in a picture with Trillene Tralane."

Ernie's eyes jumped open. "You're— Did I hear you right? You're going to *act* in the *pictures?* With the *Oregon Oriole?*"

"All's I know," Shorty said, "is she said fer me t' be sure an' be out there. She's got a part fer me—"

"Well, you son of a gun!" Ernie said, looking tickled. "Congratulations. Say— That'll be all right, won't it!"

"I figger it'll take care of Crowsnow, anyhow. An' mebbe leave me enough t' buy a few good horses—"

"*Horses!*" Ernie eyed him a moment and then shrugged his shoulders. "Well, good luck," he said; and, with a wave of the hand, he went back in his office.

14

A CHANGE OF HEART

As WILD HORSE passed the hotel with his led horse he saw Mr. Ben outside the Farrar place chopping down weeds with the hoe Sinclair had sent him. There were turkeys gobbling around some shacks in the back, so Shorty guessed Brother Ben was making himself at home.

As Wild Horse turned into the trail through the greasewood someone let out a shout from the hotel veranda. Shorty turned his head, and promptly wished he hadn't. It was Halbert Crowsnow, the Earl of Clank. He was hustling his yellow shoes across the road.

Shorty scowled and waited.

" 'Ave yer got that money?"

"What money?" Shorty stalled.

"Yer know wot money! That money yer took under false pretenshuns! I want it back—right aw'y!"

"You kin keep on wantin'. It'll be good exercise."

"Wot's that?" growled the Earl, his face darkening. His sun-burnt forehead puckered up like a washboard; and he came a step closer, doubling hairy fists. "Wot's that yer s'y?"

"You heard me! If you'd of done the right thing, you'd of got your money— But no, you had t' go drag it t' court. You kin wait, by grab, till the court says pay it!"

"Yer'll pay it, orl right! Yer'll find it's no laffink matter w'en I tike that two-bit ranch aw'y from yer! W'y, fer tuppence I'd pull yer orf that 'orse an' bash yer bloody fice in!"

"Hoo, hoo!" Wild Horse jeered. "You an' who else?"

"Jest *me!* That's 'oo!"

Shorty lifted a hand and waggled his fingers. "That fer you!"

The Earl was beside himself, fairly shaking with rage. "Close yer fice!" he snarled fiercely. " 'Ere's a tip, pal— *See?* Keep aw'y from that little wren of mine or I'll put yer dahn w'ere the sun won't find yer!"

"Wren— *What* wren?"

"Yer know 'oo I mean—that *pitcher actress!* You keep aw'y from 'er!"

"I kin see myself," Shorty said derisively.

"Orl right," the Earl muttered, scrinching up his eyes. "Yer been warned!" And he suddenly grinned with the edge of his teeth, swung around his plus fours and went back to sit on the hotel porch.

"Huh! Too bad about *you!*" Shorty scoffed. But just the same he felt a little bit worried and he led the stud home in a scowling silence.

HAMMOCK met him at the gate. "Have you still got your job in that picture?"

Shorty looked at him. "Why?"

"They're raising blue hell about that picture on the radio. That Texas bunch," Hammock chuckled, "claim the story is laid in Texas, and by that token had ought to be filmed there. Some Big Gun or other in the Texas Legislature's going to introduce a bill to get the picture banned there."

"Them Texicans!" Wild Horse snorted. "Them fellers ain't happy if they ain't raisin' hell! How do you like my new stud— Let's git over by the window where you kin git a good look at him."

"Say! He's a dilly! Where'd you get him, Shorty?"

"Bought him off some feller from Duncan. Where's Dunne?"

"Better not go bothering Dunne right now. He's got Troubles," Hammock grinned. "He's madder than a sidewinder at skin-shedding time."

"What's the matter? Bust his scooter?"

"No, nothing like that. It seems he's got quite a bit of real estate at Santa Fe—houses and such-like. Just got a letter from one of his tenants. Been belching around ever since he got it—from some girl named Alexander," Hammock grinned. "She says the roof's been leaking ever since she moved in and if Dunne had fixed it like he promised to do, she would never have gotten pneumonia. Now she's got down with pleurisy, two of the windows won't stay shut, the drain's stopped up and the fireplace won't draw. She says she's turned off the water and closed the place up, and she won't pay any more rent till he fixes it."

"Good enough fer him if he does folks that way! What's he kickin' about?"

"He's afraid," Hammock chuckled, "that his house will blow up. She said she turned off the water, but she didn't say anything about the hot water heater. Beau Dunne is fit to be tied—says he'll have her in court. He's scootering to town quick as he gets his supper—"

"The dang fool's already et," Shorty growled. "How many suppers does he figger to git?"

"I expect he's forgotten about eating," Hammock said; and just then Rose and Hammock's wife, Ethel, came strolling over from the adobe corral where Shorty had left the white mare with her new purple splotching.

"Oh!" Ethel cried, as she saw the new stud. "Isn't he a *beauty!* Such a *gorgeous* color! Can I pat him? Gee, Shorty, what do you call him?"

"*Thunder,* probably," said Rose, smiling sweetly. "Shorty's always been threatening to raise horses by thunder—"

"Jest fer that," Shorty blared, "I'll *call* him Thunder! I don't see why you got to raise such a rumpus every time I come home with a horse."

"Why, I'm not raising any rumpus," Rose said. "Have you got hold of the money for that lawsuit with Crows-now?"

"I'll *hev* it!" Shorty growled. "Don't you worry about that! This here's a first-class horse, an' a *palomino*—what I've always been wantin'. *You* know that! This horse is goin' to raise me some palomino colts what'll make these smart guys' eyes bug out. Lookit them muscles! Lookit them legs, by grab—an' that head! He's a real horse, *he* is!"

"Um-*hmm!*" said Hammock's wife, Ethel. But Rose shrugged her shoulders.

"If you're going to get rid of that mare, you'd better hurry. She looks sick to me. She won't even turn her head or look at you. You can poke her, even, and she won't bat an eye. You'd better send for Doc Wallace—"

"There ain't nothin' the matter with her," Shorty said. "Anyway, I'll be rid of her tomorrow. Where's Hellbound? *He* ain't been messin' around with her, has he?"

Hammock said, "He doesn't have time to mess with anything but Columbine"; and Rose said, "Did you give that mare to him, Wild Horse?"

"Yeah," Shorty said, and led Figure 8 off toward the stable. He took the stud with him, too.

After he'd attended to their needs, he took the lantern and went over to see how Blood of Kings was doing. She stood just like she had been when he left her, all humped over and droopy like, with her head hanging listlessly and looking half dead.

She looked just the same when he went out there next morning. He could not see that she had even done so much as lift one foot. She seemed in a daze, in a kind of stupor, Shorty called her name, but he might as well have talked to a cigar store Indian.

Suddenly alarmed, Shorty opened the corral gate and hurried inside. He walked all around her, looking to see if she'd got hurt or something. He picked up her feet, even lifted her tail, but Blood of Kings showed no interest in him or in anything.

It was uncanny the way she looked.

Shorty patted her, talked to her. She wouldn't even lift her head; wouldn't look at him. Her eyes had a kind of glazed look.

Shorty dashed outside and yowled for Hellbound.

"Saddle your mare right away an' git Doc Wallace!"

"Huh? What's—"

"Never mind talkin'," Shorty snarled. "Git goin'!"

IT WAS the dangdest thing he had ever heard of.

The Doc thought so, too, when he finally got there. He said, "It beats me. She ain't got no more zip than a dishrag. I've been all over her and I can't find anything ruptured or slashed. Of course, this lassitude *could* be a symptom—I mean of sleeping sickness—"

"You don't think she's got *that*, do you?"

"I don't know. They sometimes act kind of like that," the Doc said dubious like. "I could give her a shot—"

"Would it hurt her— I mean if that ain't what she's got?"

"I don't know. We don't usually like to give it unless we know that's what ails them. What did you swab all that medicine on her for?"

"Oh—that," Shorty said. "Just a little experiment."

"I don't notice any cuts," Doc said, running a hand through one of the purple patches.

"No. She ain't got no cuts— I didn't put it on her for cuts," Shorty said. "There ain't nothin' about it that would *poison* her, is there?"

"Not unless she swallowed a lot of it. You didn't put any of it in her mouth, did you?"

"Do I look like a idjit?" Shorty said indignantly.

"Well, it's got *me* beat," the Doc said again. "She hasn't any fever. Worms wouldn't make her act like that. An' there ain't nothing wrong with her feet." He sighed. Shook his head. "It's sure got *me* beat!"

It was a cruel thing to see a horse in such shape and not know what you could do to help her.

"Do you reckon it could be because I've kept her cooped up here?"

Doc shrugged. "Damned if *I* know. I don't see why that would do it. If it was being cooped up I should expect to see her dashing around like she was figuring to jump over; maybe trying to, even. Snorting, pawing, showin' extreme restlessness. You could lead her out and see if it makes any difference."

Shorty did and it didn't.

She hardly had enough gumption to lift her feet up. When

337

he brought her back in she stood entirely indifferent, head down, uncaring.

Wallace said, "It's the damndest thing I ever saw!"

He again approached the mare, peering this way and that, prodding and thumping, patting and slapping her. She could as well have been dead for all the notice she took of it.

"Well—" the Doc said, "there doesn't seem to be anything *I* can do." He glanced at his watch. "Keep her warm and dry—"

"I was figgerin'," Shorty told him, "to git rid of her tomorrow."

"Might be a good idea, at that. Meantime, you better keep her away from your other horses. If she happens to have something contagious, you don't want the rest of them coming down with it."

"She was actin' all right till I put that medicine on her."

Doc Wallace looked startled. He stared again at the mare. Then he looked at Shorty. And he kind of nodded, the way doctors will, as though to something he had had in his mind. "You know," he said, "I believe I've got it! It's that Pykotine Blue you've smeared all over her— I'll bet a thermometer that's all that ails her. She's *ashamed!* So ashamed she'd just as lief die— It's the only thing that will explain that look, that hangdog posture. Get a brush and a bucket—"

"But I *can't!*—I can't do that!" Shorty said. "I had a reason fer puttin' that purple stuff on her—a danged *important* reason!"

"I expect you know your own business best; but if she don't snap out of it you'll have a dead mare on your hands."

The Doc sounded put out; he looked it, too. Then, with a shrug, he picked up his bag. Shorty paid him. "You don't really reckon she'd kick off, do you?"

338

"How long do you think *you* could live without eating?"

"Well, but— Heck! She'll eat all right when she gits hungry enough."

"She's your mare," Doc Wallace said tartly. "You can do as you please about it. Good night," he said, and went out to his buggy and drove away.

SHORTY LOOKED at the mare.

He scowled and muttered. Then he finally swore. But it was easy to see his resolution was wavering. Blood of Kings paid him no attention at all. The miserable, dejected, reproachful look of her became finally too much for Wild Horse Shorty.

He got soap and a bucket and with a good stout brush he fell to work trying to get the stuff off of her. It did not come easy. But he kept right at it, scrubbing doggedly, not even pausing when Rose called him for supper. He scrubbed till it was plain he could do no better. When he gave it up a few of the splotches were still discernible, a kind of faded lavender, but they lacked a whole lot of being as conspicuous.

Blood of Kings came awake and suddenly shook herself. She lay down and rolled. Then she rose and shook again and came up to him, tossing her head, acting like she had used to. She reached toward him, burying her nostrils against his shoulder, and Shorty choked up.

He kicked the bucket and cursed.

He threw an arm round her neck and she nickered softly. With eyes gone blurry like he'd got wood smoke in them Shorty stroked the mare's mane, stroked her neck and broad shoulders.

"To hell with the movie job!" he blurted suddenly. "You're goin' to stay right here—*right here always!*"

339

15

THE CUT DIRECT

MORE AND MORE Shorty wished he knew where McGee had gone. He missed the old man's advice and competent management and, if he'd known where to find him, he'd have gone straightaway and tried to hire McGee back. The ranch hardly seemed the same place without him.

Rose, coming out of the cook shack next morning, intercepted Shorty on his way to the stable. "Isn't this the day Mister Sinclair comes back?"

"I dunno. Anyway, he won't be comin' here. What about it?"

"I thought you might go in and fetch him. It's a long walk from Tucson."

Shorty kicked at a horse apple. "He don't like t' ride horses, and anyway," he said, not looking at her, "I got a lot of work t' do today— Let Dunne go fetch him. Dunne kin bring him out on his scooter."

Mr. Hammock stepped out of his cabin just then and Shorty hailed him. Taking the artist aside after Rose had gone in, Shorty said: "About that fox huntin' stunt you was mentionin'— Jest what do you do at a fox hunt, anyway?"

"You get a bunch of dogs," Hammock said, "and when

they raise the fox you chase him on horseback— It gets exciting as heck. You'd like it, really. Are you thinking of having one?"

"Well, I dunno," Wild Horse sighed. "I reckon I've got t' hev somethin' durn quick. I'm gittin' low on cash— You ain't got any, hev you?"

"Will ten dollars help you?" Hammock reached for his wallet.

"Never mind," Shorty said. "A ten spot wouldn't make a ripple in the tank. If I put on this fox hunt I'll prob'ly hev to charge you dudes extry. Be a lot of wear an' tear on the horses, won't there? Well, I'll think it over, anyhow. I reckon you could sorta coach me a little—"

"Sure. Anytime. Let's invite some of your neighbors. You know the more the merrier. Do you have a lot of foxes around here?"

"I dunno," Shorty said. "I ain't never met none. We got plenty of wild hogs an' lions, though. How you goin' t' know when you get a fox runnin'?"

"The dogs will tell you. Sweetest music in the world to hear them baying a fox," Hammock said. "And a great sight, too, with their sterns up, noses to the line and the field strung out all over behind. I remember one time—"

"I dunno about the dogs," Shorty said, interrupting. "Fritchet's got a beagle or two an' Provencher's got a coach dog. There's a couple of Danes, a police dog, an' a couple housefuls of curbstone cutters. An' the Double N has got a Saint Bernard, but I don't know anyone that's got no hounds."

"Well, the beagles ought to work, I should think. Then we've got to have a horn—"

"Horn? What kind of a horn?"

"A huntsman's horn."

"That's a new one on me. Lute Dickerson used t' play a cornet. I expect that's still around someplace."

"That'll do," Hammock smiled. "It's not strictly orthodox but it will probably serve the purpose. Let's get up a hunt, shall we?"

"I kin tell you better," Shorty said, "this evenin'."

He went off to the stable and let Blood of Kings out. She came to him, nickering, and followed him round while he did the chores, often getting in his way with her curiosity. But he hadn't the heart to chase her away; he was too well pleased by the return of her interest. She was so alive, so eager, so excited to be with him that Shorty couldn't help but feel a secret pride in her.

But, though he had renounced it, Shorty still held hopes of getting that movie job. He would keep Blood of Kings—that was settled now, definitely; but if Trillene had found in him the talent she had seemed to, she would be wanting him to be with her in the pictures anyway. Horse or no horse. And anyway, she didn't know which mare he'd figured on giving her. He could easy enough paint up one of those other mares he had out on pasture. And with that in mind he hollered for Hellbound.

"REDEEMED—how I love t' proclaim it," roared Hellbound, coming up. "Redeemed by the blood of the Lamb—"

"Never mind all that," Shorty said. "How'd you like t' hev *two* mares?"

"Two?" Hellbound said. "Whatever in the world would I be doin' with *two*?"

"You could always sell one of them."

"No. One's enough," Hellbound said, shaking his head determinedly. "One's all I need. One's fust rate; ef I had two there'd be trouble. Me an' thet Columbine is jest like two little flowers a-growin' on the same stem. She wouldn't like it ef I was t' hev another horse. Thank you kindly," he smiled, patting Shorty's shoulder, "but we're doin' fine jest the way we be."

"Yeah, but—"

"I'm a-tellin' you, son. We're satisfied. Plumb content. Jest the two of us."

"But I *need* Columbine," Wild Horse explained. "I told the Oregon Oriole I'd fetch in a horse fer her—told her I'd git her a Palamoosa; an' you know dang well there ain't a mare on the place looks as much like old Wire-Cut as Columbine does. They was sisters—"

"What! Give my mare away?" Hellbound shouted. He looked aghast. *"No sir-ree-bob!* I ain't a-givin' my Columbine t' *no*body! Why, the very idear! I'd as soon give my gran'maw away as ol' Columbine! I thort—"

"I ain't askin' you t' *give* her away. I was figgerin' to swap you—"

"No sir! You give me Sweet Columbine an' I'm hangin' holt of her. You kin give thet warbler some other mare— Give her Lespedeza. She ain't no good to nobody no-how—"

"She's in foal," Wild Horse said. "She's in foal to that good *A*rab stud of Buck Fletcher's. I should think you'd rather hev a mare in foal—"

"I'm goin' t' git Sweet Columbine in foal. I'm goin' t' breed her to Mister Haskell's stud, Pay Streak, when he gits old enough."

Hellbound glared indignantly.

"For the last time," Shorty said, "you goin' to swap or ain't you?"

"No!" Hellbound snarled, slamming his foot down; and

343

Wild Horse, muttering about ingrates, tramped off in a passion to find Lespedeza.

He discovered her in the southeast pasture—in what, at any rate, had *been* the pasture. The land was pretty much gone to rock and the only growth in sight was dead weeds. The termites were busily at work on them.

Shorty looked the mare over and shook his head. There wasn't much use painting up Lespedeza. Not even a Hollywood actress could find much use for a critter in *her* shape. She was lank as a soup bone and with about as much flesh. Her mane and tail were bundled with burrs. She looked to be at least twenty-five and with all the hoof she had grown still in place.

She was a sight, and no kidding. Even Shorty thought so, bad as he needed her.

He headed back to the barn. Ethel Hammock hailed him as he turned into the yard. "Oh, Shorty—" she said, "don't they have any barn dances here we could go to?"

"Sure. The Pioneer Hotel has 'em every week—good ones, too. Larry an' his Sunset Riders do the fiddlin'."

"Oh, really?"

"They're pretty good if you go in fer that stuff."

"Um-*hmm!* We used to hear them in Denver," declared Hammock's wife, Ethel. "I always say there's nothing so invigorating as a good square dance."

Shorty went on to look his new stud over. Thunder looked pretty good as he came prancing up to see what Shorty had for him. Blood of Kings, over in the adjoining corral, nickered jealously. She laid back her ears when she saw Shorty patting him. Her head went down and wove around snakily. She pawed at the ground and blew through her nose as though she'd like nothing better than to take a piece out of him.

344

"That ain't no way t' act," reproved Shorty. "You'll prob'ly like this feller when you git acquainted with him."

He put a halter on Thunder and led him over to the bars near the mare. "Come over here an' see him now an' say hello nice like."

But the mare shook her head. She wouldn't have anything to do with him.

Shorty hitched Thunder to a pole with the lead shank and went into the barn after blanket and gear. When Shorty returned he found the stud backed to the end of his tie rope and Blood of Kings stretching, trying to get her teeth into him.

"None o' that!" Shorty growled. "Git back! Behave yourself! What you tryin' t' do—git him all scarred up fer me?"

He saddled the stud without any trouble though Heatherford and said he was only green-broke. This was what Shorty had in mind to find out, just exactly how broke green-broke might be. The stud seemed calm enough. He made no objection when Shorty swung up.

Shorty had replaced the halter with a hackamore. As he settled in the saddle he reined Thunder to the left. The horse turned easily, willingly and smoothly. Shorty reined him to the right and again he responded.

"Heck!" Shorty grinned. "I'd call you plumb gentle."

But it was better to be certain than to sometime wish you had. Shorty took him out and rode him around the yard. At a walk. At a trot. At a canter. Then he put him into a full run and, at that spanking pace, stopped him easily.

"Shucks," he said, and headed for town.

He often wondered, as he did right now, where Beau Dunne went so much on his scooter. He was gone half the time and was not around now.

Back at the corral Blood of Kings nickered frantically,

circling around and around as though half minded to jump it. Suddenly she rose and *did* jump it, cleanly. She came tearing after them, nostrils wide and mane flying. She made a pretty sight lining out that way, and she was really moving, really burning the ground up.

Shorty reined in and waited.

When she slithered to a stop he said, "You can't go. Go on back now; I'll take you out later."

Blood of Kings shook her head. She went up on her hind legs and pawed and snorted. Coming down like a flash she bucked and shook herself. Then she paused, stood poised, eyed him artfully and nickered.

"Go on!" Shorty said, and made his voice right stern. "You go on back to the ranch and wait for me."

But she didn't want to wait. She put her head down, still watching him, and pawed at the ground. She leaped away of a sudden and cut a great circle, going full tilt, tail streaming out like a white plume behind her. She came larruping back and pulled up, snorting, to eye him again.

"Very nice," Shorty said. "But you *can't go*—savvy? Go on home now," he said; and she did, with heels flying.

Shorty watched till she turned into the yard. And he was filled with a secret pride, tingling with it, grinning, when he finally picked up the reins and rode on.

It was amazing, he thought, that he should feel so about her when all his life he had wanted yellow horses. She was only a cold blood—a despised albino; yet he could not feel that way about *this* horse, and this was of the golden breed that all his life had so entranced him. It was strange, he thought. It was almighty odd.

He put the stud through his paces and felt quite satisfied he had made a good bargain; but his heart wasn't in it. Without at all intending to, without hardly being conscious of it, he was all the time comparing the stud's responses to those of the mare; and Blood of Kings had all the best of it. She was a gay and lively *rollicking* creature; the stud was phlegmatic. She had fire and spirit. The stud had only beauty.

Shorty hitched him before the saloon and went in.

A sleepy-eyed barman was yawning on the glasses to give them a polish. There were no other customers. The place looked dead.

Shorty said: "Where's Fritchet?"

"Out to the ranch. What's your preference?"

"Oh, give me a shot o' bourbon—an' a chaser," Shorty said. "Where's all your customers?"

"Off to the Horse Show— Didn't you know they was having one?"

Shorty scowled. He had plumb forgotten it.

He looked at the clock. He put a coin on the bar and slogged down his whisky. "Where's the place they're shootin' that picture?"

"Damfino," said the bartender indifferently.

Shorty wiped his mouth and clanked out of the place. The sun was like a guy with a hammer. Shorty bent his steps toward George Kerley's livery.

"Well, I swear!" Kerley said. "Walkin', are you? Have you sold off your mares?"

"I need the exercise," Shorty told him. "That's my palomino in front of Fritchet's."

"Well, say! He's a dandy! Where'd you get him?"

"Off some feller passin' through. He's fair," pronounced Shorty. "What hev you got in the way of good feed—somethin' fer mares. Somethin' extry good."

"I've got that *Choice of Champions* I been sellin' you; there's a lot of folks swear it can't be beat. Then I've got

347

some special prepared stuff for young ones—pellets. All ground up an' scientifically balanced to give them all the concentrates, lots of mineral and protein; only three per cent fats," Kerley said. "Capper's Mare an' Foal Feed. Oughta grow muscles on a billiard ball."

"Guess I'll try that. Send me out a few hundred pounds right away, will you?"

"You want to pay for it now?"

"Well, no," Shorty scowled, suddenly remembering his pocketbook. "Put it on the cuff, George; an' look—git it out there this afternoon if you kin."

"Kin do," Kerley said; and Shorty went meandering off, still debating with himself if he should go on out to where they were making that picture and hit Trillene up for that job she had promised.

He sure hated like sin to be passing it up. It was the chance of a lifetime.

After all, it was his *talent* they wanted. It wasn't the gift horse; them moving picture people weren't doing no worrying about horses. Buck Fletcher was supplying all the stock they could use. But you couldn't pick talent off of the bushes. Maybe he'd better go out there. If he could find where it was.

There was that threat of Crowsnow and his two-by-four lawsuit still hanging over Shorty's head like a mallet. And, remembering the Earl's vindictive look, Shorty had no doubt but what the guy would insist on the law's full penalty. Why, they might even take his *ranch* away from him!

They might, sure enough!

Shorty scowled at the thought and, at that precise moment, Trillene's colored chauffeur brought around her big touring car and parked it neatly before the hotel. Then he hopped from his seat and stood holding the door open.

"Hey, Shorty!"

It was Sam Hoard yelling from the door of the Mercantile.

"Got a letter for Rose. It come Special Delivery. You want to take it out to her?" Sam asked hopefully.

"Okey," Shorty grumbled, stuffing it into his pocket and wondering who could be writing a letter to Rose. But he forgot that completely when he saw the door of the hotel open and Trillene coming out with the Earl on her elbow. Crowsnow was smirking disgustingly and had a fresh gardenia in his coat lapel.

"See you later," Shorty growled, and made a dash to intercept them.

Trillene must have seen him but she gave no sign. She smiled prettily at the Earl as he helped her in the car. He climbed in after her and the chauffeur closed the door.

"Hey!" Shorty yelled. "Wait a minute!"

He lengthened his strides and reached the car just as the chauffeur was letting the clutch in. "Whereabouts did you say they was makin' that picture?"

Trillene's glance came around. There was a look in her eye that struck Wild Horse cold. Her red lips parted in a disdainful smile. "Just let's forget about that picture, shall we? Mr. Crowsnow has been telling me all about your horses, and I'm afraid I don't care for any after all. Albinos are out of my line."

16

MR. DUNNE PLAYS TAPS

AND THAT was that!

Shorty was gnashing his teeth when Ernie came up and clapped his shoulder. "Why'n't you forget about that damn palomino! Rose is three times the gal that fah-de-lah dame is, an' you ought to know it! Why waste your time traipsing round after *her*—"

"It ain't *her*," Shorty growled. "It's that goddam *job*! How'm I t' pay off that bustard now? The swivel-jawed polecat— Her, too, by godfreys' D'you hear what—"

"I heard her," Ernie said. "Just forget all about her. Somethin' will turn up—somethin' always does. Keep a stiff upper lip—"

"Yeah," Shorty scowled. "But what if he gits my ranch away from me? Where'll I be then?"

"No sense burning your bridges until you come to 'em." Ernie's mind was off on another track. "You know . . . that guy Tranch! The more I think of it, the more it seems like I've seen him before. Didn't it seem like to you—"

Shorty said, "I never paid no attention to him. I was lookin' at the horse."

"I'd swear him an' me has met up before. If I could only think . . ."

"If you could think how I was t' git that *five hundred dollars* it would be more helpful," Shorty hinted.

"If you'd taken my advice—"

"I know, I know. You don't hev t' sing the chorus of *that* one ag'in."

"What kind of yarn is that Sinclair feller writin'?"

"I dunno—somethin' about beans. He's supposed t' git back here today."

"I don't know what I'm going to do about Potter," Ernie scowled. "Sometimes I think I ought to lock him up—"

"Lock him up!" Shorty said. "What fer? He's your deppity, ain't he?"

"That's what I mean," Ernie grumbled. "It's goin' to look bad for the Office if he goes off his bat—an' I don't know, by God, but what he's off it already! Sits by the hour with that big knife in his hand, never openin' his mouth; just sittin' there starin'. Honin' that knife an' slicin' up hairs with it—an' that *scowl!* By God, he gives me the creeps!"

"What's got into him?"

"It's that pale-faced dude you got out to your place—that damn Beau Dunne! Mrs. Potter—accordin' to *Potter,* anyway—spends all her time with him. Potter says his home's a busted cantalope since his wife took to scooterin' around with Dunne—"

"Scooterin'?"

"Sure—ain't you heard about it? The whole town's talking. That's where she is now—gone off on that scooter with Dunne to the Horse Show."

"He prob'ly means all right—"

"The road to hell is paved with good meanings," Ernie snorted. "He ought to have better sense. Potter's danger-

351

ous! You better give Dunne a hint before he gets himself killed. Way Potter's feelin' he's apt to stick that knife in him."

"Well, I'll tell him," Shorty said; but he had worries that were a lot nearer home. "I'd sure like t' know where I could git that money."

"They're going to put up a five hundred dollar purse for the winner of that Trail Ride—but that'll come too late to help *you*," Ernie said. "You ain't got but six more days now. Maybe," Ernie said, "you'd better take to the brush."

"That won't keep 'em from grabbin' my ranch. The bustard's told me already he's goin' t' do it! I gotta git that money!"

"If I had it," Ernie said, "I'd sure lend it to you. How about Dunne? Maybe you could get it from him."

"I could *ask* him," Shorty nodded. He brightened up a little.

"I'll tell you what *I* wish," Ernie growled. "I wish, by God, I could catch that counterfeiter! Those Treasury Agents are sure raisin' hell—"

"I thought they went after them guys theirselfs?"

"They're after him. They ain't having any more luck than I am. Be a feather in my hat if I could beat 'em to him. The publicity I'd get—"

"Is there a reward out fer him?"

"If there is I ain't heard of it."

"If Farrar was here *he*'d git the guy fer you! When'd you say them Speed Trials was?"

"On the 5th—same day your case comes up. That won't do you any good; they'll make up the purses out of the gate receipts. Twelve races. I doubt if even the Open Championship will pay off as high as five hundred dollars. Of course it *might*. You could *try* if you wanted to. But what would you race?"

"Well, I got t' do *somethin'*," Shorty said, rightdown worried. "I wouldn't want t' rob no bank, but I sure as heck gotta git that money! That reminds me! We're hevin' a fox hunt out to the ranch tomorrer. Better come out; it'll be good exercise. You might pass the word around. Never mind askin' Fritchet, but everyone else will be plumb welcome; an' we could use a few dogs."

ON THE RIDE home Shorty thought the palomino acted kind of odd like. He did not show much spirit. He did not carry his head like a stud, and after awhile Shorty commenced to watch him, kind of puzzled, kind of worried. It did not seem like that ride should have tired him. Yet the closer they got to home, the more Thunder acted like he'd got something wrong with him. As Donald Coyle had once remarked, "The things that can happen to a fellow's horses are enough to give a man gray hair." Shorty was about ready to believe it.

Shorty had spent a lot of time with horses. But the only one he had ever seen act like this was old Trymore. When he thought of Trymore, Shorty's eyes went narrow and his cheeks got dark.

Gradually at first, and then ever more rapidly, the yellow stud's breathing grew harder and harsher. He showed deepening distress and began to cough. Shorty cursed in a passion. It was plain enough now why he'd gotten him so cheap! The stud was broken winded and had the heaves—what that Featherstone crook had claimed the *other* stud had! That rascal of a Duncanite had found out about Shorty's passion for palominos and had played him for a sucker! Probably

353

fed the horse wet food and Fowler's Solution, and that had temporarily hid his unsoundness.

If Shorty hadn't been so dadburned broke he would have gone and hunted that guy up pronto!

When he got the horse home Shorty put him on pasture. He was more than half minded to shoot him and be done with it. The horse was no good and never would be.

Blood of Kings trotted out from behind the barn and threw up her head with a welcoming nicker; and Sinclair came out of the tool shed with Hammock. "Hi, Shorty!" he grinned. "About eatin' time, isn't it?"

"Nobody ever fergits *that!*" Shorty growled, and went into the barn and got some hay for the mare. Hellbound was in the corral feeding Columbine with a hatful of little brown pellets.

"What's that you're givin' her?" Shorty asked, curious.

"Some of that new stuff you got from George Kerley—"

"Well, you lay offa that!" Shorty blared. "That's too rich fer that ol' skate's system! I got that stuff fer Blood of Kings, by godfreys! You leave it alone."

"Where's Dunne?" Sinclair called.

"Off to the Horse Show with Missus Potter—an' you better tell him about that. He better steer clear of her if he wants t' keep breathin'. Potter's honin' up a knife an' he looks like business."

"Wouldn't do no good to tell him," Sinclair said sad like. "Women is like air to him—women an' scooters. You just can't keep him off them—off the scooters, I mean."

"Well, it's his funeral, not mine," Shorty said. "I got troubles of my own. We're goin' to hev that fox hunt tomorrer, Mister Hammock. Everyone's invited—you, too, Singkler."

"Will I be able to ride that Columbine creature?"

354

"You'll hev to ask Hellbound. I'll go over this thing with you this evenin', Mister Hammock, an' you kin put me wise to the best way of doin' it. When you movin' into your new house, Singkler?"

"I'm in it now," Sinclair said. "Ben will be leaving tomorrow or the next day. I don't want to hurry him. I think I'll rip that partition out and have the walls plastered. And I think I'll take those garage doors off and put in a big window—like they have up to Santa Fe. One of those 'picture' windows. How you getting along with your horses? Hammock says you've got a new stud, a good looking palomino. Got rid of the white mare yet?"

"No," Shorty said, "an' I ain't *goin'* t' git rid of her!" And he tramped off to get himself washed for supper.

DUNNE GOT BACK just in time to sit down with them. He said the Tucson Horse Show had been a great success. They'd had some awfully good horses at that show, he said, but he was none too keen about some of the decisions. "That judge hardly looked at Joe Reed II, and he was the best lookin' stud of the lot," Dunne said. "And there were a couple mighty nice looking palominos there that I thought he ought to have given more attention."

"How did the Fulton horses do?" Shorty asked.

"Took five of the prizes. Bombardier got first in the working cowhorse class, and second in the lightweight stallion class."

"Didn't Bert Wood pull down anything?"

"His Joe Reed II got second in the sire-of-get class," Bee Bee said. "And a filly owned by him and a man named Mercer took first in the cowhorse filly class; and Feather, a chestnut, got third in the same. That judge sure went for sorrels. Haskell's Starlight placed second in the broodmare class, and Mrs. Haskell's Ready got third in the cowhorse mare group. You've certainly got a lot of fine horses in this country."

"Yes we have," Rose said; and Hammock's wife, Ethel, said "Um-*hmm!*"

Shorty eyed Dunne slanchways. "How'd Miz Potter like the show?"

"She was kept pretty busy taking care of her bonnet. She's a fine woman, isn't she?"

Shorty said drily, "Obe Potter thinks so."

When they woke up next morning the ground was covered with frost. "Just right for the hunt," Hammock said exultantly. "The dogs will pick up the scent right away. Nothing like a frost to keep them to the line."

"Do we go before eatin', or when?" Shorty asked.

"We'd better go just as soon as enough of them get here —enough to make up a party. Did you find that cornet?"

"Yeah. Hellbound wanted t' do the tootin', but Dunne said he knew all about it so I'm lettin' him fetch the horn," Shorty said. "I sure hope them guys don't fergit their dogs. The Double N sent us word they can't lend us their Saint; she's got somethin' wrong with one of her hocks."

"How about that fellow with the beagles?"

"Fritchet? I didn't ask *him*," Shorty scowled.

Hammock glanced at his watch. It was seven-fifteen. "There comes some of them now," he said, nodding. And sure enough. Mrs. Potter and Ernie, and John Sinclair on a livery stable horse, were just pulling up outside the gate.

Mrs. Potter wore pants and a red roll-neck sweater. She had a purple-colored snood pulled over her hair and was
356

on her own horse, christened Hopalong, but which she sometimes called by names less genteel. Ernie, of course, was up on Rowdy, his spooky gelding that would jump at a paper. The bean wrangler's mount was a benign old gentleman who looked to have discarded every gait but the walk.

"Come in, come in!" Shorty called out jovially. "We'll be startin' pretty quick like— Couldn't you scare up a dog?"

"Fritchet," Ernie said, "is bringing his beagles— Here he comes, now."

Shorty looked kind of mad but he kept his mouth shut and counted ten. Fritchet rode up with his dogs and nodded.

Hammock said, "What's the gun for? We're not going to shoot—"

"*I'm* goin' to shoot if I see anything to shoot at," Mr. Fritchet declared, examining his shotgun to make sure it was loaded.

George Provencher rode up with his coach dog, Pepper. He was riding Jinx, his big paint gelding. Pepper went off to see what Fritchet's beagles had watered; and just then Hellbound came up from the barn with a couple saddled broomtails and his own mare, Columbine, who took all eyes from the moment she was sighted. He had primped and groomed her with loving care. She was shaved and curried like a horse at the show ring, with a little pink ribbon tied around her bare tail. Hank was proud of his work and didn't care who knew it.

"Well," Fritchet scowled, "what the hell are we waitin' for?" He looked at Shorty and said, "Won't find no game in the middle of the day. When that sun gets up it's goin' to be hot."

"I'll be right with you," Shorty said, dashing off.

He came out of the stable with Blood of Kings.

"Ridin' the little white daisy, eh?" Fritchet sneered.

Dunne came up in a frock coat and stovepipe. He had the cornet tucked under his arm and was wearing black riding boots and whipcord pants.

Fritchet eyed the cornet suspiciously.

"What's that thing for?"

"Had you done any hunting, my good man, you would know. It's an old English custom to fetch a horn with the hounds—dates back to the time of William the Conqueror. Why, I once knew a man—"

"You kin save that fer later," Shorty said, interrupting. "We better git started— Ain't your wife goin', Hammock?"

"No. She's going to help Rose with the breakfast. They're fixing up a special hunt breakfast for us. It will be all ready by the time we get back."

"Well, let's git goin'. Give us a toot on that cornet, Bee Bee."

Mr. Dunne played *Boots and Saddles*. They all swung up and lined out after Shorty. He led south into the desert at an easy walk, Blood of Kings looking around her with interest and waggling her ears at each stray sound.

It was a fine, fresh morning. There was a greasewood tang to the westerly breeze, and the sky was blue as only such a sky can be. Everyone seemed to be enjoying himself, and it was a holiday picture they made with their horses. Sinclair was discussing beans with Mrs. Potter. Mr. Dunne was telling Fritchet of the man he once knew, and Shorty was worrying about his lawsuit with Crowsnow.

Of a sudden Mr. Hammock spurred up alongside him. "The dogs have picked up a line!"

And sure enough; it did kind of look like they had picked up something. Pepper, in the lead, was yelping frantically and the beagles, right after him, were giving enough tongue to have done a whole pack. Every face showed interest, and then the quarry flashed in view.

It was a big buck jackrabbit, and he was not stopping to pick any posies.

Mr. Dunne sounded TÁPS and *"Gone away!"* Shorty shouted, and they all took off in wild pursuit.

On they went, and on, with the poorer horses gradually dropping behind. Shorty, Dunne and Fritchet were well in the lead, racing neck and neck, with Ernie next and Sinclair right back of him in spite of any personal disinclination Sinclair might have felt about such headlong progress. The benign old stable horse had grabbed the bit and, with a rashness unbecoming his years, was patently determined to be in at the finish.

Again the rabbit flashed into view. Fritchet let go with both barrels of his shotgun. The rabbit disappeared. Ernie almost did. And the coach dog, Pepper, made a dash for the brush with his tail to his belly, ki-yi-ing madly. Ernie's horse came down with his head bent under him and both hind legs flung straight to the sky. Sheriff Ernie left the saddle and went through the air with the greatest of ease. And Provencher, furious, spurred alongside Fritchet, snatched the gun from his hands and slammed it on a rock. Then he whirled his big paint and went off after Pepper who was still ki-yi-ing somewhere off in the distance.

Fairly frothing with rage Fritchet snatched up the pieces that were left of his shotgun and went scouting through the brush to try and locate his rabbit. Ernie, mortified, got shakily up and brushed himself off, swearing and glaring in the direction of Fritchet. He hunted round, found his pistol, and went after his horse.

The others, meanwhile, had stayed with the beagles who

were again giving tongue, tearing off on a new line. Dunne, Mrs. Potter and Hammock were in the lead now, but Blood of Kings gradually was closing the distance. She was hardly six lengths behind when they reached the first fence.

Dunne, there first, put his horse straight at it—five strands of barbed wire.

Shorty closed his eyes and listened for the crash.

But Dunne must have made it for, when next Shorty looked, there he was beyond the fence and still going after the yelping beagles. Mrs. Potter and Hammock had brought their mounts to a stop, were peering this way and that, trying to find some way around.

"Foller it east a couple miles to the gate," Shorty shouted, and pulled on the reins. But Blood of Kings wasn't stopping. There was a lot of sporting blood in her veins and she was not minded to be swerved by a fence.

With Shorty gritting his teeth she went straight at it.

Over they went and came down like a feather, continuing on at a rising larrup. Shorty drew a long breath and relaxed a little.

It was plain the dogs were not after a rabbit.

With their short legs flying and their noses to the line they were making a mighty racket. There was a noticeable difference in its timbre now. An odd, puzzled note had crept into their music, and every little while one would look up uneasily.

With her head well up and her white mane flying, Blood of Kings was having the time of her life. She was impatient to be up where Dunne was crowding the hounds. She could show clean heels to Dunne's mare any day and could not understand why Shorty would not let her.

But Shorty, for once, was trying to be polite. When Hammock had explained this hunt game to him, to be up with the hounds, he had said, was an honor; so Shorty wanted to let Beau Dunne get his money's worth.

They were only four lengths behind when the beagles went roaring down a draw with Dunne right after them.

Just as Shorty reached the draw the dogs' music broke. They set up a wild barking and quit the line. Almost up to them, Mr. Dunne was spurring madly when Blood of Kings swerved with both ears laid flat. Trembling with excitement she shook her head and snorted. And, right at that most crucial moment, Mr. Dunne's shaggy mare squatted back on her haunches and stopped stone still.

Not so Mr. Dunne.

Perhaps he would have liked to stop, but he was not able. Momentum had him, and application of the brakes had caught him wholly unaware.

In frock coat and stovepipe he left the saddle like an Olympic diver and flew head first toward a black and white animal which was alarmedly lifting its beautiful tail.

Shorty took one look and guessed he'd go home.

It was, after all, about time for breakfast.

17

SOME WILL AND SOME WON'T

IT WAS just about noon on the day immediately following the catastrophic fox hunt when John Sinclair, the bean authority, rode into the yard on a nag from the Livery—*not* the benign old gentleman of yesterday's gallop, but an ancient steed guaranteed to be past all possible hope of rejuvenation. He tied this docile animal to one of the rails of the pole corral and bowlegged over to where Shorty was combing out Blood of Kings' mane.

"I don't know what I'm going to do," Sinclair said irritably, "but I've got to do *some*thing!—I just can't write a blessed word over there."

Shorty leaned an elbow on the white mare's rump. "Over at your place, you mean? Why not? What's the matter?"

"It isn't the place. It's that fellow, Ben!" Sinclair's dour face became more dour than ever. "He says he *likes* it there. He's decided not to move."

"He's *what?*" Shorty said.

"He's decided not to move."

"Whose place is it—his or yours?"

"It's mine, of course. I'm the one that's paying for it. But what can I *do?* I can't just put him out into the *street.*"

"I'd like t' know why not! He ain't payin' you no rent, is he?"

"Of course he isn't. But he's put in quite a bit of work around the place—"

"In that length of time he ain't done ten dollars' worth!"

"He's built two shacks for his turkeys. He's planted a little grass and alfalfa, trimmed up the trees and repaired the fence a little. And he's paid the electric bill—about a dollar, that was. He declares he'll not get out until I make him an adjustment—"

"I'd adjust *him* with a sock on the kisser!"

"There's no use my antagonizing the fellow. He's obstreperous enough as it is," Sinclair said. "I've got to get him out of there. Why, it doesn't hardly seem like my own place, even! That *atmosphere!* The way he clatters round and bangs all the pans—he's broke more than half of my dishes already. And never a word about paying for them! He sleeps in the bed—"

"Where do *you* sleep?"

"I spread my bedroll out on the floor—"

"Well, I'm a son of a gun!" Shorty said, and looked at Sinclair with his eyes wide open. "Why, I'd put that louse out so dadburned quick he'd come down with pneumonia on account of the draft! What's the matter with you? You ain't goin' t' let him git away with it, are you?"

"But what can I *do?*" Sinclair asked desperately. "He's got a shotgun he fiddles with half the night, and last night he took a shot at Kerley's cat when it came over to visit with Smoky. He says if I don't keep Smoky outside he'll step on his neck one of these fine mornings—and he'd do it, too. He's a beast—that's what he is! A plain beast!"

"If you don't wanta put him out yourself," Shorty said, "call the sheriff. Ernie'll take care of him. He don't like that guy nohow."

But Sinclair shook his head. He got into a nervous tramping. He circled the corral half a dozen times, then came back and said, "You don't understand. The man's got a damn bad look in his eye. He helps himself to my groceries, cooks up my grub—and *eats* it; and leaves all the dirty pots for me. Everytime I say something about him moving, he gets out that shotgun and sits there fiddling with it. And now, this morning, before I got up even—before seven o'clock! —he had that terrible Crowsnow in visiting him. They sat there swilling down my good coffee and laughing about what Crowsnow was going to do when he takes your ranch away from you—"

"Oh, is that so!" Shorty blared, getting riled again.

"Yes; and Crowsnow said he was going to turn your place into a chicken ranch. He's going to kill off your mares to feed his chickens—cheap feed, he called it—"

"I'll cheap feed *him!*" Shorty shouted. "I've a mind t' go over there an' push his face in! Kill my mares! I better not *ketch* him!"

"Crowsnow and Fritchet are talking of going in pardners on it; they've got it all fixed up how they're going to pull down your buildings and use the material to make brooder houses," Sinclair said, scowling.

Shorty scowled, too. He swore in a passion. "They better not bust so much as *one winder* or they'll wake up t' find theirselfs laughin' in the Hot Place! Ahr—they're jest tryin' t' git you worked up," he told Sinclair. "Don't pay no 'tenshun to 'em."

Rose called just then to say lunch was ready.

"Come along," Shorty said, "an' git a good meal under your belt. Don't let them polecats git you rattled."

AFTER LUNCH Sinclair went back home and Shorty and Hellbound went back to their mares. Mr. Dunne came out after awhile to watch them and, after mulling it over a bit, Shorty said to him, "Any chance of you passin' out a loan, Mister Dunne? I could sure find a use fer about five hundred right now."

Mr. Dunne kind of squirmed in his clothes for a minute. He might have been recalling the unfortunate episode of yesterday when Shorty had left him to wrastle with the skunk. "I would like to oblige you," he said finally, "I really would. But as it happens I've only got one of my checkbooks with me and it would be an inconvenience to let you have that much cash. Now let me see," he said, casting back in his mind, "tomorrow I'll be owing you another week's rent; I could give you that now, if it would be a favor to you."

"I expect that's better than nothin'," Shorty grunted; so Dunne passed over the hundred and twenty dollars and went sauntering off toward where he kept his scooter.

"Gittin' money outa dudes is like tryin' t' git hair off a frog," Shorty grumbled; and Hellbound grunted complete agreement. "What did he do with them clothes he was wearin'?"

"I dunno. He still smells a little whiffy on the lee side," Shorty said.

Hellbound said, "Thet wood pussy smell is plumb hard t' git off you. I onct knowed a feller— Psst! Yere comes Saint Clair ag'in."

And sure enough; it *was* the bean expert, come back with another load of woe, by the look of him. Sinclair got dispiritedly off Kerley's crowbait and came scowlingly over—as Hellbound afterwards said, "Like Sodom after the fall of Gomorrah."

"For just two cents," Mr. Sinclair said bitter like, "I'd give up that place and go back to Santa Fe!"

"What's the matter now?" Shorty asked, looking up. "Ain't put you out, has he?"

"He's sicked the Pipesley's police dog on Smoky! That poor little kitten is clean up at the top of a sixty foot pole! And I can't get her down. She's scared to death!—scared to turn round, even! I've tried everything—"

"Didja try climbin' the pole?" Hellbound asked him.

"No. I can't climb poles— Anyway, I haven't any climbin' irons. What am I going to do? Smoky'll *starve* up there!"

"Try callin' the fire department?"

"Yes. They refuse to go outside the city limits."

"Why'n't you call the S.P.C.A.?" suggested Hellbound. "They'll git her down fer you."

"I suppose I *could* do that—I hadn't thought of it," Sinclair said, kind of hopping around like he had new shoes on. "That beast of a Ben just stands around with that shotgun, grinning. Says he'll be glad to move out if I still want him to. Says he can't abide people that will have cats around them. He's got the building bug now—says Mr. Pipesley, my neighbor, will let him build over there. Just the other side of my fence, more than likely!"

"Let him go. Good riddance."

"But he won't move a step," complained the thrifty Sinclair, "till I've paid him for all the work he has done."

"What work?"

"He claims he's got a week's wages coming, at a dollar an hour—"

"He never worked two hours hand-runnin' in his life!"

"Well, he's claiming a week's wages. He wants the cost of the seeds he's planted. I've got to reimburse him for the light bill. And pay him for his labor and those horrible turkey shacks he's put up—he says they're improving my property. Oh, I can't remember the half of it, but the bill comes to more than *fifty dollars!*"

"I'd see him in hell before *I* paid him anythin'."

Sinclair said: "But I've got to do something. He tells me the most awful stories about the things he's done—about how he's got even with people who thought they were putting something over on him. He's a *beast!* A nasty little beast!" Sinclair shuddered. "It's got me so upset I can't write, I can't eat, I can't sleep or anything!"

Shorty said, "Call up the sheriff an' fergit about him."

"Do you know the number of that Cruelty to Animals?"

"I ain't got no phone. You'll hev to call from the Crossin'."

"Well, thanks anyway. I'd better hurry back before Smoky catches cold up there. That Crowsnow fellow was back again. He says—"

"Yeah. It's too bad about him! Him an' Fritchet's sufferin' from the same kinda trouble—diarrhea of the jawbone," Shorty said, and snorted.

But just the same, Shorty was a heap more worried than he let folks know about. The idea of them tearing down his good buildings to make brooder houses for a bunch of fool chickens filled him with bitterest fury; and it would be just like them to do it, too! Fritchet, especially! Sometimes he felt like strapping on a sixgun and seeking them out to demand a settlement; but he knew that wasn't the answer. That would only involve him more deeply than ever. Going gunning for them would just get him locked up, which was the last thing he wanted—a fate to be avoided at any or all costs. He had all the outdoor man's instinctive distrust of being cooped up inside of a building. It made him squirm just to think of it.

He did not reckon he could be jailed for the trouble he had so far been having with Crowsnow. But unless he could scrape up that five hundred dollars, the Court's decision looked bound to effect his hold on the ranch. It would be just like that Tucson bunch to take it away from him and give it to the Earl. Or force him to sell it to settle the Earl's claim!

He saddled Blood of Kings thinking a ride might help him; but it didn't. The only thing he got out of the ride was the firm conviction that the Quarter Horse Speed Trials was his only chance to get that money in time to do him any good. And even the Speed Trials might not save him —not even if he won. There were to be twelve races, including the big one—the Open Championship; and the purses would be made up from the gate receipts. The Championship purse might not be large enough to do him any good. And his case came up the same day as the race; about the same time, in fact. What would they do if he didn't show up? Give Crowsnow the verdict, probably. Would the judge order his arrest—maybe throw him in jail? He'd be pretty well bound to slap a hefty fine on him, and where was he to dig up the money for *that?*

It was a dreary black picture any way you looked at it.

But, desperate or not, that Championship race was his only chance.

It all boiled down to that. Shorty shook his head glumly. Blood of Kings was a plenty smart mare, but it took more than smartness to win a championship race. The odds were all stacked up against her. So far as Shorty knew she had never been run—never even been started. Who, indeed, would be fool enough to race an *albino!* To be sure, Mr. Dunne appeared to think highly of her; but what, if anything, did Dunne know about racing? He probably knew just about enough to bet. Just the kind, Shorty thought, to line the pockets of the bookies.

Even granting Blood of Kings both speed and savvy, she would have to match these with the very best. She'd be up against the cream of the Quarter Horse breed—horses that, according to Ernie, had been bred from away back in 1665 for the one prime purpose of winning short races. It was not a heap likely Blood of Kings could outstrip them.

But she should have her chance. Her chance and Shorty's being just now synonymous. She did have some Quarter Horse blood in her veins. Shorty wished Mr. Coyle could have been more explicit.

He decided to try her out. Running out here on the desert was not too comparable to running on a track, but it might give him some kind of notion.

He had never really let her out before, had never had any occasion to. He gave her her head and she lunged away in a quick easy gallop, all her muscles coordinating, mane and tail streaming out in the wind. She seemed to be running with an effortless ease, kind of floating along, hardly touching the ground so smooth was her stride.

Shorty pulled her down after a couple of minutes. She looked back at him with her ears cocked enquiringly. She didn't seem to be panting much; she was warm, of course, but she did not seem at all tired or over-exerted. And she was fast, all right; or it seemed so to Shorty. But he knew how deceptive such a trial could be. Lots of horses seemed fast on the open range, but the ultimate test was a track and a stop watch. And these were things Shorty did not have. Fritchet had a stop watch, but Shorty was danged if he'd ask Fritchet for it. Nor would he ask that bustard to clock her for him. "What—the little white daisy?" Fritchet would sneer. "You don't need to clock *her*. She's the fastest thing out of Mexico City since Blue Jacket beat Little Joe down there!"

Nope. He wasn't asking Fritchet for anything.

SINCLAIR dropped around again just before supper. His long Scots face looked morose and gloomy. "I've got a notice from the Express Company," he said. "I guess my stuff's come from Lincoln. Have you got any way you could bring it out for me?"

"How much hev you got?"

"Thirty-five boxes—"

"What you need's a truck!"

"Maybe George Provencher would haul it out in his trailer," Rose said.

"That would be swell!" Sinclair said, brightening up a little. "That's the very thing—I'll ask him. Would you take me to town so I can call him up, Hammock?"

"Sure," Hammock said. "Grab your hat and let's go."

"How are you an' Mister Ben makin' out?" Shorty called.

"Oh, the beast is calm this evening. He ate a good supper from my groceries. I left him smoking up my pipe tobacco. He says he will leave now anytime I want to make the adjustment. He's started his house—a two-by-four frame shack—over in back of Mr. Pipesley's. He's been hammering away all afternoon."

"If it was *me*," Shorty growled, "I'd *throw* him out, an' he dang well wouldn't come back again, neither."

"Well . . ." Sinclair said. "I'll see you later."

18

THE OPEN CHAMPIONSHIP

THAT WAS IT, all right. The race was his only chance.

Supper over, Wild Horse was sitting gloomily hunched on the porch when a truck pulled up and stopped by the gate. A four-horse van. But Wild Horse didn't even turn his head; he was too wholly wrapped up in the miserable prospect of losing his ranch. All for the lack of a paltry five hundred!

The driver unclasped himself from the wheel, climbed out of his vehicle and opened the gate. It was the screak of the gate hinge which finally roused Shorty.

He looked up, scowling; and there was Buck Fletcher in his blue jeans and Stet hat.

Buck waved him a greeting and Shorty half-heartedly hoisted a hand. Then he sank back into his morose reflections. It all went back to that polecat, Tranch. If he hadn't tried to buy that horse from Tranch he would never have been in the fix he now found himself. Everything went straight back to Tranch.

Buck came striding over. "Hi there, Shorty! What are you asking for that mare of yours now?"

Wild Horse looked at him.

Buck explained. "That one you brought over to sell me the other day."

"Not the little white daisy!" Shorty said sarcastically.

"Huh?" Buck stared. "For that white mare, sure. How much?"

"I don't want to sell her."

"Come, come," Buck said, getting down to business. "A man will sell anything if he can get what he wants for it. Here's what I'll do. You been wantin' a good stud for as long as I've known you. I've got a damn good stud—a registered *A*rab. I'll make you a swap."

Just like that, Buck said it.

"My *A*rab stud for that little white mare. How's that strike you?"

"No soap."

"You don't want to trade?" Buck's eyes narrowed. "The other day—"

"Yeah. But this here's *today*. I've done changed my mind."

Buck said thinly, "I'll give you five hundred dollars, cash money, for that mare."

Shorty jumped to his feet. Then he sat down again. This was not as good an offer as the swap, but it was cash. Cash money! Five hundred dollars for an albino mare! And five hundred dollars would square things with Crowsnow.

Shorty scowled, sorely tempted.

Across temptation came a vision of the mare, and he shook his head.

"I guess not, Buck. I reckon I'll be keepin' Blood of Kings," he said.

HE WAS OUT in the corral, fooling around with the mare, when Ernie rode over and climbed from the saddle. "You got that money?"

Shorty shook his head.

"Then you better be gatherin' up your belongin's. Crows-
372

now's all set to take over this place. He's going to force you to sell it to satisfy his claim. Been telling all over how he'll bid it in cheap—and I guess he'll do it. He's got 'em *all* bluffed. You won't get another bid."

Shorty patted Blood of Kings. He didn't say anything.

Ernie came over, put a hand on his shoulder. "It's tough luck, Shorty. I wish I could help you." He eyed Shorty thoughtfully. He didn't like this quietness. He started to say something and changed his mind. He said instead, "Buck Fletcher passed me headed back towards town—he was drivin' that truck like hell couldn't catch him. What do you reckon he was so frothy about?"

"He come out here to buy Blood of Kings," Shorty said.

"You mean you didn't sell her!"

Shorty jerked his thumb at the barn. Ernie saw it then; a big new sign, home-made but readable. It said:

BLOOD OF KINGS AGAINST THE WORLD

Ernie snorted. "You talk like a numskull!"

"That's the way I feel about her," Shorty said. "Buck had his chance. I went out there to sell her to him and he turned her down cold. Didn't want no white mares. Now he wants her—even offered t' swap me his good *A*rab stud for her. What you reckon's got into him?"

Ernie chuckled. "It's that Oregon Oriole. That movie bunch is gettin' in Buck's craw. They've changed her part again. Way they've got it now she has to ride a white horse in one of the sequences. Buck's got the contract to furnish all the stock and you've got the only white mare in five hundred miles. You had the chance of a lifetime!"

"Would you of swapped *your* horse?"

"For that pure-blood stud horse? Don't be a nump! You're damn tootin' I would!"

Wild Horse shrugged. "I reckon you an' me is built diff'-rent," he said, and changed the subject. "I've entered the mare in them Speed Trials."

"You have? Which race?"

"The Open Championship."

Ernie shook his head. "You haven't got a chance. Queeny and Squaw H both are running. You won't get to first base."

"Prob'ly not," Shorty said.

THE DAY OF THE RACE dawned slightly overcast. There was a cool wind blowing, but the grounds of the Rillito Track were packed and jammed with a milling, vociferous, gesticulating crowd. Rich dudes and cowpunchers rubbed elbows without noticing. Papago Indians in all their finery were there with their squaws and papooses; Mexicans, race touts, policemen and soldiers. It seemed extremely doubtful if there was one trade or union which was not represented. Hot dog and pop peddlers were lost behind hordes of customers; and no place were folks packed tighter than just back of the grandstand northeast of the wire.

Curious, Shorty rode Blood of Kings over there. Then he snorted, disgusted. He might have known it would be Hellbound Hank. Lounged on a barrel the old man was grinning around encouragingly as he unwound a spiel to drag in the unwary. He had a .22 rifle in the crook of his elbow, and in his high cracked voice he was whining enticingly:

"Right yere, folks, fer the easiest way t' double yer money! Try yer luck with the rifle—only ten bucks a shot! Simplest thing in the world—somebody allus wins! Anybody with a lick o' sense ort t' be able t' drive a hole through a barrel! Thet's all you got t' do—step off ten paces an' shoot through the barr'l. Ef yer shot comes through the back end you git twenty bucks without any argyment. Twenty silver dollars!

374

Now who'll be the next t' lug home a whole month o' my wages?"

While Shorty was watching, a tall skinny guy stepped up, handed over ten bucks and picked up the rifle. He backed off the required distance, drew a bead and let go. The rifle barked. Hellbound put the dude's money in his pocket. "Who's next? Must be *some*body in this bunch kin shoot! How about you over there— No! Thet mealy nosed guy in the new straw shingle! I been listenin' t' you do a heap o' talkin'— Why not step right up yere an' show these folks?"

The embarrassed dude, with the laughs of his friends prodding him over to the rifle, gave Hellbound ten dollars and stepped back the prescribed paces. "Jest aim it in the open end o' the barr'l," Hellbound told him. "Ef yer shot comes through you git twenty dollars. Jest like fallin' off a log!"

The dude looked the rifle over. "These sights all right?"

" 'Course they're all right! What kinda flimflam d'you think I'm pullin'?"

"How about you doin' it first just to show us?"

"I ain't out yere t' do no shootin'. You're the one what thinks he's so good. Shoot or git off the pot."

The crowd guffawed and the red-faced dude pulled the trigger.

Hellbound put his money away. "Next! What about you, soldier? Wanta try yer luck?"

The burly-looking sergeant scraped up ten dollars from the grinning guys with him and picked up the rifle after Hellbound loaded it. He jerked back the bolt and took a look at the cartridge. It was loaded all right. It showed no sign of tampering. Somewhat chagrined the sergeant slipped it back in and drove home the bolt. He took careful aim.

"Now—by the numbers," Hellbound said. "The flag is wavin'—"

The sergeant fired, with no better luck than the ones preceding him. But he wasn't taking Hellbound's word for it. He went and examined the butt end of the barrel. It was really wood and no hole showed in it.

"I don't see how you ever got them stripes—or thet medal," Hellbound said, and the sergeant looked like he was minded to do something, but his hoorawing friends led him off toward the hot dogs.

"Never in all my borned days," said Hellbound, "hev I saw so many pore shots in one gatherin'. Betcha there's a fortune in fittin' spectacles! Hi, Saint Clair! Wanta try yer luck?"

"Not *me!*" Sinclair grinned. "I'd rather watch."

"Wal, it don't cost nawthin' t' watch," Hellbound said. "Who's next? Shucks, ther' ain't a feller in this bunch c'ld drive nails in a snow bank!" He peered around tauntingly. "How about *you*—thet feller in the new shirt! Wanta bet thet shirt you kin hit the bottom of this barr'l?"

Shorty'd seen all he wanted. He turned Blood of Kings through the milling crowd. He bored through the mob toward the saddling paddock. The first race entries were now being led in. It was a 220-yard course, for two year olds only. He saw Joe II, a handsome chestnut colt by Painted Joe out of a Thoroughbred mare, owned by the Mexican barber, Armenta; and Red King, another good chestnut by a stud named Texas from over around Benson. Those were the only ones he could recognize by sight, but they were all good lookers and each one was groomed to perfection.

Shorty rode Blood of Kings over next to the rail, proud of her behavior in all this excitement.

Everybody and his uncle had turned out, it looked like. There was Sidney P. Osborne, the state's fine governor, a friend to the ranchman, who had come down from Phoenix in honor of the occasion. Ma Hopkins, who edited the Cowboy's Bible (*Hoofs & Horns*), was talking with laughing Nick Hall and Jazbo Fulkerson; and yonder, John Lindsay, the famous rodeo clown, was loping around in his tent-sized overalls, rolling his eyes at every girl who would look at him. Ma spied Shorty and waved. And, just at that moment, who should strut by but the Oregon Oriole with the Earl of Clank who was wearing a monocle screwed in his eye and looked sourer than swill with the top off the bucket.

Shorty's mare was attracting some notice, especially from dudes—the pop drinking variety. One smartly dressed lady came dragging her anemic looking escort over. "Say! Isn't he a beauty!" she exclaimed, all smiles. "Such a noble profile—such an elegant build! And such color! Just look at those lavender spots, Wilfred— Did you ever see anything like it? What do you call him?" she smiled up at Shorty.

"Blood of Kings, ma'am—an' she ain't a he," Shorty said. "She's a filly."

"Well, she certainly is a beauty. Are you going to race her?"

Shorty said, "I'm kinda plannin' on it. Goin' to race her in the Open Championship—Sixth Race." He touched his hat and steered Blood of Kings off toward Melville Haskell who was near the judges' stand talking with Jelks. Haskell was local inspector for the Quarter Horse people.

"Howdy, Mister Haskell," Shorty said, reining in. "What do you think of this mare? Reckon I could git her corralled in the Quarter Horse book?"

Haskell looked at the mare. "Kind of light, isn't she?

377

Then, of course, there's that eye. We don't give papers on a glass-eyed horse."

"She's got some pretty good breedin'—"

But Mr. Haskell had gone back to his talk with Jelks; and Shorty, mouth tightening, kneed the mare away. He rode her over toward the section reserved for the entries. Among the welter of vans, trucks and trailers, trainers were leading their blanketed charges around. Several studs nickered and tossed their heads but Blood of Kings showed no interest in them. She had been raised right and catcalls and jibes were beneath her notice.

Shorty saw Old Man Cheeney and got down to talk with him.

"That's a nice looking mare," Cheeney said, rasping a gnarled hand against his cheek. "That the mare you're en-terin'? How much trainin' has she had?"

"I don't guess she's had any," Shorty said, reluctant like, "but I been doin' a lot of ridin' on her lately. I don't s'pose she'll stand no chance."

"Queeny ain't gettin' much trainin', either, but the wise lads are sayin' she's going to win the Championship. Shue Fly's down with a cold, you know. Queeny might win at that. You see some mighty odd things around the race tracks, Shorty."

"What do you reckon counts most in a race?"

"You mean, how does a feller get the most out of his horse? Well," Cheeney said, "a whole lot depends on the rider. A good jockey, one that understands his horse, will know when to call for that last bit of energy. A good jockey can sometimes come in with an inferior horse. There's a lot in the rider. Time and ag'in I've seen better horses beat."

Shorty said, "I was figgerin' to ride this mare myself."

"I don't know as there's any rule against it. What's your weight?"

"Oh, I ain't so dang heavy. This mare kin carry weight. Nice track they got here."

"One of the best," Cheeney nodded. "Well, there goes the first race. Goin' over and watch it?"

"Reckon I'll jest look around fer a spell. Kind of hanker to look over some of these horses," Shorty said.

He climbed back in the saddle. He spent better than an hour riding around and looking. There were a lot of crack horses on the ground today. He saw Mrs. Haskell's four-year-old chestnut mare, Ready, that Ernie liked for her smooth, trim lines and fine carriage. He saw Effie B, a four-year-old brown by Flying Bob; and Nettie Hill, by Dodger. Dolly Dimples was led past by her trainer, and Texas Lad by Monte. Mr. Nail's sleek mare, Gallant Maid, went by.

And then Shorty saw a man leading around a blanketed chestnut whose fine head and proud bearing drew his eye at once. "What horse is that?" he called; and the fellow grinned back appreciatively. He said, "Pardner, you're lookin' at the next World's Champ, the best quarter-miler from hell to breakfast. This is Squaw H by King, owned by J. O. Hankins of Rock Springs, Texas."

"Would you mind slippin' off that blanket a second?"

"Not a bit," the man said, and did so. He chuckled when he saw Shorty's eyes bug out. Squaw H seemed to know she was on display and pranced all around in fine shape. Her wide nostrils flared. There was fire in her eye and she pricked up her ears when Shorty spoke to her. Shorty longed to get down from the saddle and run his hands along that smooth, arched neck. But he stayed where he was, remembering Blood of Kings' temper; she was not of the kind to

379

stand calmly by and watch while some other mare fetched Shorty's praises.

"She's a beauty," Shorty said.

"You bet!" the man grinned, replacing her blanket. "And smart! She does everything but talk."

Blood of Kings pawed the ground impatiently. She blew through her nostrils, shook her head and stamped. She just couldn't stand hearing another horse praised.

"Well," Shorty sighed. "I guess I better git along."

"Not a bad looking hide you got there— Who's she by?" the man said.

"Gammill's Rainy Day— He's a Oklahoma horse."

"Yeah? Ever race her?"

"Got her entered in the Open Championship."

The man stared at her closely, then his grin came back and he said "Good luck." He did not seem at all worried, Shorty thought.

It made him kind of mad in a way. There wasn't nothing wrong with Blood of Kings but her color.

Prejudice—that's what it was! When had *color* ever won a race? What good was color if the colt wouldn't trot? They were all against her on account of her hide—her hide and those china-blue eyes that she had.

They didn't ever notice the expression of her eyes—they just looked, saw the color and lost all interest. Just the fact they were blue was enough to condemn her!

Personally, Shorty had some pretty strong notions on the way by which horses ought to be judged; notions which his own mares did not back up. He placed individuality first. This, to his mind, embraced both conformation and temperament, and with individuality he usually included the qualities of strength, stamina, disposition and soundness.

380

A good stock horse, to Shorty's notion, should be pretty well built, compact and close knit, deep through the flanks and inclined more to roundness than to angularity. The good stock horse should be close to the ground, not dumpy, but with his hind legs longer than his front ones. He should have plenty of muscle, but it didn't have to bulge like a bad place in a tire. He should be short backed and long of belly. Should have flat bone and wide knee joints with hind legs set well under him. His tendons, below hock and knee, should stand away from the bone—this, Shorty thought, was very important.

Another thing Shorty strongly believed was that the index to ruggedness could be found in the eye and hoof. Disposition could be gauged by observance of the head, by its shape and expression. Blood of Kings' head, by current standards, might be judged too small, but it tapered sharply to wide open red-lined nostrils and a sensitive muzzle. She was full in the face and wide between the eyes which, although of that hated blue, were both large and bright. These, together with her small alert ears, gave to her countenance a lively expression—a *bold* expression almost. Especially when her interest was roused. When bored she sometimes did not show her spirit.

She was bored right now.

"Never mind," Shorty said, reaching down and giving her a slap on the shoulder. "Never you mind, old girl—we might fool this bunch after all, you know."

SHORTY LED Blood of Kings to the saddling paddock, to the little pole corral spoked off like a wagon wheel. The Sixth Race was coming up—that race of all races, the Open Championship. This was the race that would tell the story, that would decide whether Shorty lost his ranch or kept it.

There was an all-gone feeling in the pit of his stomach. His knees felt weak and a cold prickly chill ran along his spine, that had nothing to do with the wind that was blowing.

An edge of the sun licked through the clouds and cast weird shadows beyond the moving horses as their jockeys led them into the paddock. Then the blankets came off and the crowd cheered deliriously. Earl Hammock and Dunne were packed next the rail. Hammock flung him a wink, and Dunne gave Shorty an encouraging grin.

Shorty's big stock saddle had been left with Hellbound. He had another one now that Sally Fletcher had loaned him; a racing saddle like the jockeys used. Nothing to hold onto and the stirrups real short. Shorty's colors were red and white; and as he got the mare ready, he took a covert look round to eye the competition. It looked pretty rough as the blankets came off. Every horse looked outstanding. There was Club Footed Queeny, sleek Squaw H, that fast Jeep B, a horse named Blackout, and Lady Lee. They all looked good. Squaw H and Queeny looked *awful* good.

"There goes the paddock call!"

Shorty climbed up on the tiny saddle. He swung Blood of Kings in behind Lady Lee. He was trembling like a leaf—gritting his teeth not to show it.

Single file the field moved down past the judges' stand, cut a leisurely turn, came about and, passing by once more, strung out toward the stall gates a quarter mile away. They were all somewhat frisky on account of the wind, but the jockeys kept a firm hold on them and no untoward incident marred their arrival.

The untoward incident was biding its time.

The horses were carefully eased into position.

"They're off!" came the cry.

And they were, sure enough!

382

Lady Lee collided with Blackout, Squaw H and Queeny ran neck and neck with Blood of Kings off to half a jump the best of it.

Shorty, remembering McGee's advice at the time of the Sweepstakes, crouched low and did not use his whip. Blood of Kings was fully enjoying herself, scampering along at a fine rate, sure of her speed, sure of her ability to outrun those others.

But those others were thundering close behind; Queeny and Squaw H were creeping up. Their noses were even with the white mare's shoulders, with Shorty crouched tense as a coiled-up rattler, when Blood of Kings let go of herself and went into that stride that was just like floating. She drew away from the field, went skimming along like a bat out of Carlsbad.

Shorty flung a quick look across his shoulder. Pride almost choked him; pride in his mare, that she *could* run and *would* run.

She was running away from them!

THE CROWD WENT WILD.

And then it happened.

A black cat darted out from the rail. Blood of Kings saw it and turned her head. Wavered. Broke from her stride. She braked to a sudden and dust rousing stop with the field thundering past her and Shorty cursing. He pled with her, shouted, brought down his bat with all the strength of anxiety and desperation; but without avail. She paid no attention—seemed not even to notice. She stood with cocked ears, sharply watching the cat. Suddenly dropping her head she commenced to stalk it.

The cat crouched and turned, slunk back under the rail. Blood of Kings snorted and blew through her nostrils.

But the chance was gone. The crowd was yelling. Shorty

383

sat like a man struck completely blind while Squaw H and Queeny, racing neck and neck, flashed under the wire.

The race was over.

Shorty sat there stunned. He looked at the cheering crowd without seeing it. His hands on the reins were sweat streaked and trembling. Blood of Kings had been beaten. His ranch was forfeit.

Then a man jumped out of that milling crowd, ducked under the rail and came dashing forward, an outflung arm waving wildly at Shorty.

It was Tranch. He was yelling: *"Grab that feller! Stop him, I say! He's a goddam scoundrel! He paid for that mare with counterfeit money!"*

Shorty came to with a jerk, and cursed. He flung Blood of Kings clear around on her haunches, slamming her headlong up the track. Several guns cracked behind them. Lead screamed past them. Twenty feet from the stall gates he put the mare at the rail. She went over it cleanly and kept on going, headed for the brush-choked draws of the foothills.

19

GONE TO EARTH

IN A LONG winding circle Wild Horse swung to the west, carefully picking his way through the gullies that gouged and crisscrossed the Catalina foothills. He moved slowly now for they'd been going ever since they had quit the track and the plucky mare was beginning to show it. She wasn't used up but she was getting pretty warm. It was about four o'clock, Shorty judged by his shadow, and he decided it was high time to hit for his cache. If any of that bunch were still coming after him he guessed he must have lost them by this time. He would hunt up that cave he had used to call home and camp out a while till he could see how the wind blew. He had lost his ranch, not much doubt about that, but he sure didn't aim to give up his freedom!

It was the dangdest thing he had ever heard of, Tranch dashing out and yowling that way—calling him a crook and a dodrammed counterfeiter! What was the matter with the guy? Was he *whacky?* If there was going to be any talk about crooks, Tranch was the jasper to be rightfully called one!

"The nerve of that bustard!" Shorty muttered wrathfully, guiding Blood of Kings around an upthrust boulder. He just couldn't savvy Tranch's play to save him. Denouncing him that way didn't make sense!

Unless Tranch was out to get back his mare!

There might be something in that. Maybe Tranch hadn't realized the mare was so good—perhaps he had not known she could run. She *could,* by grab, if nothing distracted her! Maybe seeing her on that track this morning had made Tranch feel like he wanted her back. He had probably heard about the counterfeiter Ernie was hunting, and thought it a good chance to regain her for nothing.

And he might get away with it! There were people around who would be right pleased to see Wild Horse Shorty sent up for a counterfeiter—Halbert Crowsnow, for one! Probably Fritchet would, too. Shorty would not put it past Fritchet to bear false witness! Or some other guys, either!

A hard grin licked across his mouth. He said, "First, ketch your rabbit!" And the words were hardly out of his mouth when a rifle went *Bang!* and a bullet went *chunk!* into a cottonwood just ahead of him.

Shorty didn't stop to argue. He didn't stop for anything. He dropped down flat on the white mare's neck and dug in the spurs like all hell was after him.

"There he goes!" someone shouted; and Tranch's bull bellow came tearing after him, and Ex-Sheriff Potter howled: "Git him, boys—git him!" and the chase was on in deadly earnest.

You would not think of a neighbor trying to kill you, but somebody back there was trying to kill Shorty; and he was under no doubt but what they would if they could. Three times rifle lead went *whttt!* through his clothing and it was God's Own Mercy it didn't go through *him!*

It might have been Tranch who was trying to drop him. But they were all of them back there—all his enemies, all those who hated him, or envied him, or had any other cause to bear him malice. Tranch, Potter, Crowsnow, Fritchet and that bald-headed toad of a dang hotel leech—a quick squint back through the trees had disclosed them. There might have been more. He was sure of those five.

This was not any time to pick posies, and Shorty drove the mare full tilt until the sound of pursuit grew dim behind. Then he changed his course and made for higher ground, because only a fool would ride the gulches and maybe get stuck in a blind box canyon.

But there was danger up here, too. A guy had to be careful not to skyline himself.

But Shorty felt pretty confident he could lose them. They had caught him asleep this last time; but that wouldn't happen again, by godfreys! He would shake them. It was just a matter of time and time, right now, was bound to play in his favor for it would soon be dark. Once darkness came, he could thumb his nose at them. Nobody knew these hills like Wild Horse. He knew every creek, every spring and catclaw. He hadn't hung out in these hills for nothing!

They cut over to a spring Shorty knew about and had a good drink, then pushed on. He kept the mare going at a steady walk while the sun dipped lower and lower before them. Because of the direction he wished to go it was going to be necessary to cross a few highways; and Shorty kept his eye peeled, alert for trouble. Not until they'd crossed the Maranna Road dared he draw his first real breath of relief. Then he turned in the saddle and waggled his fingers.

Tomorrow they would have all these highways posted, but tomorrow it would be too late to catch him for he'd be at his cache ere the dawn came around, and there he could hide for weeks without danger.

They were into the edge of the Tucson Mountains when dark finally came.

Shorty climbed down and loosened the saddle. He let Blood of Kings take a rest for a spell while he smoked up a couple of hand-rolleds and cogitated.

There'd not be much chance of anybody finding him once he got to that hidden cave. He had not been there in a long long while, but he'd left it pretty well stocked with canned stuff; and if he remembered aright, there'd be a rifle there likewise and cartridges to fit it. That was where he had lived while he was hunting wild horses; and nobody knew of the place but Ernie.

Shorty wasn't much afraid of Ernie. Ernie was his friend —even Rose had said so. Ernie was the kind you could ride the river with. He would know dang well Shorty wasn't a counterfeiter.

But Shorty had to sigh whenever he thought of his ranch. All that work gone to pot! Plumb wasted! Twelve months of scrimping and scraping shot to hell. That blasted Earl would take over the place and pull down his buildings to make brooder houses and maybe kill off the mares to feed his durn hens!

"It jest ain't right!" Shorty cursed in a passion. With a scowl he jumped up and tightened the girth again. Then he patted Blood of Kings and climbed into the saddle.

It was blacker than a black cat's overcoat now. But the moon would be up pretty soon, he thought; and anyway Shorty could have ridden this country blindfolded.

There wasn't any sound up here in the hills but the steady clop-clop of the white mare's hoofs, and occasional gusts from the vagrant wind. There was a good clean smell to these mountain passes, and it reminded Shorty he was getting hungry.

Above them, dimly limned against the stars, rose the jagged crests of the Tucson peaks. But Wild Horse knew his way every minute. He left the choice of footing up to the mare, content to trust her sharp eyes and judgment. A horse will sense trouble long before a man will.

Up and down they toiled through jumbled rocks and catclaw thickets that thrust out thorny arms to snag them, on and on through the whispering night while the white moon rose and flung its silver round them. There was a ring around the moon tonight and the wind was become a little more gusty, blustering shrilly through the mesquite tangles and swaying the ghostly fronds of ocotillo as the game mare took them higher and higher.

All about them now in the night rose the tall, fluted columns of the giant sahuaro, those greatest of all cacti that thrived nowhere else as they did around Tucson. It was odd, Shorty thought, how they could grow so well here where everything else seemed to pindle and shrivel and could hardly get enough moisture to live; even down in the desert they grew. This was a bold harsh land, but a fine one too, rolling away in great spaces, in desolation and silence. It was the kind of land to fill one with awe. Once let it claim you and there'd be no leaving.

AT THE FOOT of the trail leading up to his hideout Blood of Kings came suddenly to a snorting stop. She went up on her hind legs and whirled clear around, and Shorty had all he could do to hold her. She trembled like an aspen leaf and blew through her nose with loud snorts of terror. Shorty faced her around but she would not stand there. She kept backing away, throwing her head around and fighting the bit.

"What the hell!" Shorty growled, trying to peer through the blackness of the canyon's deep shadow. He gave her a taste of the spurs and she danced around on her hind legs, but she would not go another step on that trail. She had her ears laid back and the whites of her eyes showed when Shorty gave up and stepped out of the saddle.

He could not see anything that would scare her. But she was scared all right—she was plenty scared. He stood holding the reins, carefully probing all the brush patches round them.

Maybe someone was living in his cave, he thought. Some saddle tramp or prospector. It might pay to be careful.

He took another long look at the trail. The most of the trail was bright with moonlight and there certainly wasn't anyone on it.

Shorty cuffed back his hat and gave a hitch to his chaps; then, holding the reins, he started forward. But when the reins drew taut in his hand, he stopped. He had to. The mare wouldn't budge. She stayed where she was, very firm like, and snorted. When Shorty looked at her, mad like, she gave him back a reproachful stare.

Shorty flung down the reins. "Then stay there, durn you!" he said, and went forward.

He stopped right sudden at the first patch of shadow.

Blood of Kings had been right—absolutely! There was Death on that trail with a capital D! It was all coiled up just inside the shadow, its bright little eyes glittering wickedly. A green tiger snake like the Hopi Indians used in their dances; they seldom rattled if it did not suit them and, most of the time, it did not.

Shorty picked up a rock and bashed its head. He wiped the cold sweat off his own head, and with a long forked stick poked the snake off the trail. Even so, Blood of Kings did a lot of dancing and considerable snorting before he got her to go past the place.

With such a close call bulking large in his mind Shorty

did not move into the cave that night. Moving into that cave in the midnight dark seemed a heap too much like trying to commit suicide. Fooling around with snakes was bad medicine; and where there was one there was apt to be another.

And there was, sure enough.

When Shorty, next morning, cautiously entered the cave, there was the dead critter's pardner coiled up comfortably on Shorty's bed. Shorty went to the corner and got his shovel. Then he looked around for something to throw. There was a weather-cracked boot lying under the remains of his rickety table. Shorty grabbed it up and let it drive at the snake. The snake uncoiled and slid off the bed. It headed for the door and Shorty crept along after it, stalking it gingerly in fear lest it turn. When they got outside he brought down his shovel and the snake's head went one way and his tail went another. With Blood of Kings dancing around him and snorting, Shorty shoveled the writhing remains into the canyon.

When he had made sure there were no more snakes on the premises Shorty looked around to find some oats for the mare. But the rats had cleaned up everything in sight. So he took her up the trail a ways to where there was a little mountain meadow with a fine stream purling through it and the whole enclosed by a snug pole fence. This was where Shorty had kept his wild horses. There was plenty of pasture and it would be a good place for Blood of Kings to rest up while Shorty was debating what the next move should be.

He stripped off his gear and left her there and went back to the cave where he ate a cold breakfast out of some cans and washed it down with a dipper of spring water. Then he got his hair rope down off the wall and stretched out on the bed and went to sleep.

It was plenty dark when he awoke. For the first few minutes he could not think where the hell he had got to. Then remembrance came and he scowled through the blackness with ears cocked, listening. But all he could hear was his own thumping heart and the wind outside as it swooped through the canyon.

Still lying on the bed he struck a match and looked carefully around before he reached for his boots. One at a time he up-ended them—and lucky that he did! A good-sized scorpion dropped out of one and Shorty brought down a boot heel on it.

He dropped the burnt out match and pulled on his boots, hung a strip of tow sack across the entrance and lighted a candle he dug out of his cache. Then he thoroughly went over the whole place again, just to make sure some inordinately bold reptile had not come in across his hair rope. Then he dug out a couple more cans and had supper.

He was just getting up to sand off his dishes when hoofs rang out on the rocks below. At first he thought it was Blood of Kings gotten loose, then remembering the labor he had put into that fence he reached for his rifle and snuffed the candle.

Those were hoofs all right and they were coming closer up the canyon floor.

But the night was too black outside to see anything.

He crouched by the entrance with his rifle and waited.

"Hello up there!" came a sudden hail, and Shorty mighty near collapsed with relief.

It was Ernie.

"WELL, HOW goes it?" Ernie said, sitting down on a packing box and shaking out some Durham. "I see you made it all right."

Shorty sat on the edge of the bed and braced himself. "Let's hev it," he said, eying Ernie uneasily. "What has that bustard done to my ranch? Is Rose all right—an' how are my mares?"

"Rose is all right," Ernie said reassuringly. "Sinclair got rid of that feller, Ben, and then got discouraged and rolled his cotton. Pulled his picket pin an' went high-tailin' it back to Santa Fe. Where the real people are! Couldn't stand the 'commercialism' of our little oasis. Says he just couldn't get his mind down to writin' here; sold the place off to some feller from Houston."

Shorty said, "Not enough beans around here, mebbe." He gave Ernie's face a searching glance. "You ain't said nothin' about the ranch or my mares."

"I expect you better forget that ranch. Crowsnow hasn't waited for any court order—but he'll be getting one all right. He moved in this morning. Dunne an' the Hammocks have gone to the hotel and Rose is stayin' with my wife for the moment—"

Shorty said, alarmed: "She ain't figgerin' on leavin'—"

"Going to try and get a job in Tucson—"

"What does she wanta go rantin' up there fer?"

"She's got to make a living. Can't get anything decent at the Crossing—"

"Won't that White woman give her a job at the *hotel*? Anyway," Shorty growled, "she oughta know I'd take care of her. All's—"

Ernie said bluntly: "You ain't in a position to take care of anything. You got the law on your trail, boy—you better keep hid if you know what's good for you. You stay hid anyway till I see what's cookin'."

Shorty hung his head. "Reckon I ain't much account, am I, Ernie. Guess Rose ain't t' be blamed—she's took a lot off me. All's I kin think of, it seems like, is horses." He shook his head sad like. Then he scowled and said drearily, "I expect Rose is right. I'm jest another damn Hellbound."

"Well," said Ernie, "you're kind of shaping that way, for a fact. Foolin' around all the time with that bunch of scrub mares, throwin' every cent you make into feed for 'em— Anyone but Rose would've quit you long ago. But look here," he said, speaking straight from the shoulder, "you've got a damn good chance now to start over right. If you scrape loose of this counterfeitin' charge, I mean. You won't—"

"You don't think I've been counterfeitin' do you?"

"*I* don't think so. No," Ernie said. "Takes a pretty smart guy to make *that* racket profitable. Like I was sayin', you got a good chance now to start over right. You'll be startin' from scratch. You've lost your ranch. Crowsnow has got rid of that bunch of broomtails—"

"He's got rid of my *mares?*"

"Sold 'em all to the glue factory. Good riddance, I say. You've had them mares round your neck long enough. He's got rid of them all, and those two broken-down studs. You're right down to bedrock. All you've got to worry about now is the shirt on your back an' that albino mare. Maybe, *now,* you can get some place!"

Shorty didn't say a word. He was bogged down in gloom.

Ernie didn't give him much time to feel sorry for himself. He said, "What you need now is a good job of work—

and I mean *work*. When this business blows over you hunt up Dink Parker or Haskell or some other good breeder an' hook yourself up with 'em; get on their payroll. Work around with them for a couple of years. Then, if you've kept your eyes open and hung onto your money, you'll be in a position to get started off right. Maybe."

"But—"

"There ain't no buts about it. You don't want to be another Hellbound, do you? That's a hell of a distinction— the town's bad example! You see if you can't make a man of yourself. Make Rose proud of you—give her somethin' to *be* proud about! Now," Ernie said, having preached his sermon, "have you any ideas about this play Tranch made?"

It took Wild Horse a while to pull himself together. He finally said meekly, "No. I reckon he was jest tryin' to git the mare back fer nothin'."

"It's a lot more likely he wanted to sell her to Fletcher for that picture outfit. What I meant was about that counterfeitin' angle. Tranch has got five hundred dollars in nogood currency; he *claims* he got it from you when he sold you that mare. That doesn't make you a counterfeiter, but it gives you a heap of talkin' to do—or it would if I wasn't sheriff of this county. It looks damn peculiar. You see that, don't you?"

"I see I oughta go down there an' bash his brains out!"

"Now here!" Ernie said, "you keep away from that guy! Jumpin' on *him* ain't goin' to help you any. You stay hid till I get to the bottom of this—"

"Hell's fire! That's apt t' be till I'm old as Hellbound!"

Ernie said, kind of scowling, "It won't take me *that* long. You've got to have a little patience. Restrain yourself. Rome wasn't built in a day, you know. I'll get to the bottom of it. You stay up here where I'll be able to find you. Here —I brought you some smokin'."

Shorty eyed the sacked Durham without much enthusiasm.

Ernie said, "You'll be all right here for four-five weeks anyway. Maybe by that time I'll have you cleared."

Shorty shrugged and sank back on the bed again. Gloom had him completely. He saw no light anywhere.

"Well, take care of yourself," Ernie said, and left him.

20

A LITTLE MATTER OF ARCHITECTURE

SHORTY felt lower than a snake's belly.

He sat on the bed with his chin in his hand and thought the world might be as well off with him out of it. Luck had turned its back on him. Anything he tried was bound to go haywire.

He knew just how Job had felt in the Bible. Or, maybe, it was Lot.

Nothing ever went right for him.

He recalled his anger with McGee and felt mean.

He thought of Rose, of all she had had to put up with, feeding his dudes and doing up dishes and cooking and cleaning, and having all the time to apologize for him; trying to make ends meet with such an almighty little to make them meet with. She had stood a lot from him, worrying her heart out and all the time trying to keep the place going; trying to humor the dudes so they'd come back again next year. Oh, Ernie had the right of that matter! Nobody else would have stood it this long.

Shorty thought of some things he might have done better, and quite a few other things he might better not have done

—like buying that no-good palomino stud horse; throwing his money away like water.

But, mostly, he just sat there, miserable.

Gone, all gone. Rose, the ranch, his mares and everything.

Nothing to keep him around here longer.

Might as well cut his string and leave the country.

He would probably been a lot better off if he never had gotten that ranch in the first place. All it had brought him was grief and more grief. He had worked like a mule and not a thing to show for it. The less a guy had the easier it was to get along in this world. When he hadn't had nothing he had got along fine. All his troubles had come with that ranch.

Maybe he *had* better quit the country. Maybe Sinclair had the right idea.

A WHOLE WEEK passed, and still Shorty had not got his mind made up if it were better to go or linger on in this country. It was mostly pride which had kept him stalling. Not that he had anything to *be* proud of—Ernie had shown him the straight of *that!* But he hated to admit he was beat that way. Quitting the country was a heap too much like tucking his tail.

Shorty had not come of a tail-tucking family. His forebears had mostly been a loud swearing lot, equally ready for a fight or a frolic. One had been hung for a little brand doctoring, another had been shot while stopping a stage; but none had ever tucked tail and run, and Shorty sure hated to smirch their record.

And he hated to think of slinking away with that dadburned Earl comfortably fixed on his property. And Tranch had rimmed him—twice Tranch had rimmed him; and there had ought to be something done about that. But it was that yellow-shoed Halbert who had finally ruined him. That Crowsnow bustard!

Shorty's dander rose every time he thought of him. If he could only think of some way to get even! He could think of all kinds of dire fates for the Britisher, but he could not dig up any way to encompass them.

Then he suddenly stopped pacing. "Clank!" he said, and stopped in his tracks, almost floored by remembrance. He staggered to the bed and sat down heavily.

He sat there, moveless, for a long long while.

"Holy cow!" he ejaculated finally; and got up and went out and soaked his head. But the remembrance stuck. He could not dislodge it. The wonder was it had not struck him sooner. All this time it had been right under his nose.

As Hammock's wife, Ethel, would have said—"Um-hmm!"

Back and forth he tramped, face puckered with thought. Then he went outside and talked it over with the mare. Blood of Kings nodded in entire agreement.

Next morning, after breakfast, Shorty scribbled a note and left it on the table to be sure Ernie found it. Then he went up to the meadow and saddled Blood of Kings.

Half an hour later, with the white mare under him and a couple tins of canned meat rolled up in a slicker behind the cantle, Shorty jogged down the trail headed out of the mountains with Blood of Kings' nose pointed south by east.

THE MARE was in fine fettle this morning, eagerly scanning the countryside round them, alert ears harking in all directions, glad to be on the move once more.

She seemed always at her best when there was work to be done, always ready and willing, seeming always to know what her rider required and doing it well without fuss or foolishness. Running loose in the wind she showed her spirit; under saddle, in service, she kept a disciplined calm, observing all with a knowing eye. Yet the spirit was there, held in leash but always ready to leap forth like a flame the instant the call came down the reins. She would turn for a knee, for the slightest flexure, or break into rollicking head-long speed. This was the heritage of her Quarter Horse blood; and she carried her head with a gay defiance that acknowledged no shame for the color of her coat.

They passed the Mission in mid-afternoon. Under great yellow straw sombreros a handful of Indians drowsily hoed their fields. Shorty waved to a couple, swapped greetings with another; and by four o'clock he was pulling Blood of Kings up into the shade of a crumbling, half-fallen adobe wall which was all that remained of the old stage station on the Helvetia trail. Rope cactus, cholla and ocotillo grew here in abundance, with now and again clumps of prickly pear raising their spiked pancake leaves like a bunch of tortillas set neatly on end. Shorty got a cool drink from the hidden spring, and a hatful of water for his thirsty mare. Then he led her back into a mesquite thicket and pulled off the saddle and turned her loose to browse for a while.

He hadn't been there more than a couple hours when Ernie rode up and climbed out of the saddle. "You sure do believe in givin' me exercise! What's the big idea? Thought I told you to stay hid—"

"I'm hid here, ain't I?"

"This place is no good. Too close to home. Potter's scourin' the—"

"Ain't you sheriff of these parts no more?"

"Sure I'm sheriff. But I can't be in more'n one place at a time! An' I can't very well tell Potter to lay off you! Tranch has swore out a warrant for your arrest. Him an' Obe Potter has been riding all over. Potter says he'll find you or bust a button. I wisht I could think where I've seen that guy—Tranch, I mean. Him an' that Crowsnow is gettin' right chummy. There's talk Tranch is going to be Crowsnow's foreman. Crowsnow's changed his mind about those hens; going to stock your place with Hereford cattle now."

"That's all right with me," Shorty said.

Ernie stared at him sharply. "You take it well!"

"How else kin I take it?" Shorty shrugged, and then stiffened as a quick phut-phutting came out of the distance.

"What the hell!" Ernie said; and they peered through the branches.

"Beau Dunne!" Shorty grinned; and Mr. Dunne it was.

He pulled off the trail and stood peering around. Then he mopped his red face on a handkerchief. "Hey!" he spluttered. "Where are you, Sheriff?"

Ernie said, "In here—an' bring that contraption with you."

"Well, well!" Dunne said, eyeing the pair triumphantly. "I thought if I followed you around long enough—But I got to admit I was about ready to give up."

Ernie eyed the binoculars' case Dunne had slung to his shoulder. "Been spyin' on me, have you?" And Wild Horse said, "Must have a good reward up fer you t' take all that trouble—"

"I haven't heard of any reward," Dunne said. "But I've got some news I believe will interest you. That Tucson crowd is going to stage a Mountain Race with a thousand dollar purse for the winner!"

"He can't get in no race," Ernie said. "The Law's after him—"

"I know," Dunne assured him, "but if he could win that thousand dollars he'd be able to get his ranch back; and I'm willing to bet he could win it."

"They'd grab him the minute he showed up at that race—"

"That could be fixed. You're the sheriff, aren't you? You could hold them off. It isn't as if Shorty could get away again—his horse would be too tired. You could point that out—"

"You must want awful bad to see him caught!"

"Not at all," Dunne said. "I want to see him save his ranch. Also, I'm figuring to win some money on him. Tranch is entering a palomino stud called *Sangre de Cristo*—"

Shorty swore.

Dunne said, "Anyway, him and Crowsnow are offering to bet any taker three thousand dollars that this stud will win. If Shorty'll ride the white mare I'll call that bet, and I'll split the winnings with him fifty-fifty. And here's another good reason why he should want to try it; the winner gets to pick and *keep* any other one horse that survives the race."

"You're on," Shorty growled. "Jest count me in!"

"Now don't be a goddam fool!" Ernie snarled. "You might just as well cut your throat an' be done with it! Racin' a horse down the side of a mountain!" He scowled at Dunne. "Where they havin' this slaughter?"

"Down that second biggest peak in the Tucson Mountains."

"That's a six hundred foot drop!"

"So what?" Dunne said. "At Williams Lake, up in British Columbia, they pull that stunt and drop *seven* hundred feet. Down Couger Mountain. They have one every year—"

"If a horse ever fell in a thing like that—"

"Lots of them do. Lots of guys get killed. What of it? Lots of guys get killed in automobiles too, but that don't scare people out of them, does it? If Shorty can win, he gets his ranch back. He gets a thousand dollar purse, fifteen hundred from me, out of Tranch and Crowsnow, and he can have his pick of the surviving horses."

"If any!" Ernie said.

Shorty laughed. "Jest keep that crowd offa me till it's over an'—"

"That's the spirit!" Dunne grinned. "I'll put up your entrance fee and send your name in."

"You dadburned fools!" Ernie swore. "This is the nuttiest damn thing I ever heard of! I wouldn't even sit in the saddle of a horse that so much as thought of *walkin'* down that mountain!"

"Yeah," Shorty said. "But you an' me is built diff'rent, pardner. Jest rig up that bet an' leave the rest t' me!"

21

HELLITY LARRUP

WILD HORSE SHORTY had always been a good bet with the newspapers—but now he was the scoop de luxe. Every day they wrote him up and sometimes even ran his picture with it; but whether they had a picture or not, he was always front page copy. And when Dunne tipped them off he was going to ride Blood of Kings in the Mountain Race all the newspapers got out their biggest type, and even Bernice Cosulich got down off her high horse to notice him. They rehashed Tranch's denouncement of him, and Shorty's wild flight from the race track. They ran stories about his horses and somebody recounted the great pala-moosa hoax. The most preposterous speculations concerning his present whereabouts found their way into print as gospel, and Deputy Sheriff Potter made a scathing statement and declared *"if that saddle tramp so much as shows his nose"* it was going to be too bad for someone. The sob sisters dramatized Shorty's life and the People's Forum printed letters about him; and the bets got to flying thick and fast as to whether or not he'd have the nerve to show up when the time came.

The Tucson Citizen ran a number of articles on mountain racing, preparing the public for the coming spectacle.

It was being staged, they said, by the Southern Arizona Horsebreeders Association who had got the idea from Jo Flieger, a ranchman up around Winkleman who had twice won the race at Williams Lake—the only white man ever to have that honor. They recounted in full the Great Canadian Mountain Race of 1925 which Flieger had won on a horse named Grey Eagle, carrying one hundred and seventy-five pounds. Distance one mile. Drop seven hundred feet. Time one minute, thirty seconds. They said nothing about the casualties.

But it made good reading and everyone talked of it, what time they weren't arguing about Wild Horse Shorty. Dunne's wager with Tranch and Crowsnow came in for considerable attention, as did Crowsnow's acquirement of Shorty's ranch—there was a lot of hard feeling stirred up about that. And the Oregon Oriole quit appearing in public with Crowsnow out of fear for the eclipse her popularity might suffer.

Potter, egged on by Tranch, threw out more guards and redoubled his efforts to capture Wild Horse until Ernie began asking himself if it were not perhaps best to sack Mr. Potter. But he did not do it. Potter, sacked, would stir up more talk than ever against Shorty, and he might become downright vindictive.

There was a lot of wild betting being done about the race. A good many persons figured Tranch to win, being quite taken up with his stallion's fine looks. Others, more in the know about this kind of racing, were putting their money on a Papago Indian, picturesquely named Lorenzo Mountain Sheep, who had been in a few of these things before.

As the Great Day approached Potter flung out a cordon of special deputies all along the foot of the mountains, and the bets on Wild Horse dropped to zero. The experts said he would never show up. Tranch said if he did, Potter would have him in irons before the race ever started. But Tranch and the experts both were wrong, though it looked like they weren't till the very last moment; and Beau Dunne all but pulled out his hair.

At last the Great Day arrived.

The race was scheduled for two o'clock. By noon the hills were black with people. They came in every kind of rig imaginable—buggies and spring wagons, ox carts and buckboards; automobiles of every make and condition; by bus, by horseback, mule and burro. Some even walked. And the schools all closed so the kids could go.

By one forty-five the better part of eighty thousand spectators had assembled on points of vantage. The entries— minus Wild Horse of whom nothing had been heard—had all lined up where the race was to finish and were parading their mounts back and forth for the judges. Mostly, at Tucson livestock events, one judge gave the prizes and made the decisions; but this show was different. The S.A.H.A. had gathered together three eminent persons to do the honors; Jo Flieger himself, Melville H. Haskell, and that popular man about town, Nick Hall. Doc McQuown and Doc Courtright were genially present to give equine casualties the *coup de grâce,* or to stitch them up where stitching was possible. Ma Hop was on hand with the newspaper crowd, and three top hands at action photography, Messrs. Levitz, Helfrich and Striker, stood off at one side with their heads together, talking. Charlie Schuch, that weasel of the conde crayon, was loping around in an old straw hat—even Nick Eggenhofer had flown in from Jersey. And Porter's—Sporting Wear & Leather Goods—was giving away a brand new saddle of his *very own choice* to the man who should win this breakneck tournament.

With fourteen minutes to go, the contestants started

walking their broncs up the slope—no mean feat in itself, by the way. At the crest, by order of the judges, the horses were to have a four minute rest. The starter, having meticulously set his watch to correspond with the timepieces of the distinguished judges, now rode off after them.

There were not as many contestants as the crowd had expected. Even around Tucson crazy galoots were the exception, not the rule. Fourteen men had got their names on the list, but only a mere six were now climbing the mountain: Tranch and five *Indios*. Mr. Tranch was riding his glorious palomino, *Sangre de Cristo*. Of the Indians, two were mounted on thoroughbreds, two on part-breds, and the fifth, Lorenzo Mountain Sheep, was disdainfully perched on the withers of a paint.

There was a lot of hard talk about Wild Horse Shorty.

But when the sweating six reached the crest of the climb, there was Shorty, comfortably settled and waiting for them. He looked to have been settled there quite a good while. Blood of Kings, all saddled, was browsing beside him.

The starter looked bug eyed. Then he aired his lungs. "How'd *you* get up here?"

Sangre nickered. Blood of Kings nickered back.

"Potter's looking for you!" Tranch growled; and Shorty said, "Is that so?" politely. And then "Potter!" he sniffed, and smelled of the air. "That guy couldn't find a skunk in his pocket!"

Tranch said like he was Moses: "You can't ride in this race—you're an outlaw!"

"Dear me," Shorty clucked; then he winked at the starter. "You got any orders to that effect?"

"Not me!" the man said. "Your name's on the list, you can ride if you wanta."

Shorty looked at Tranch. "Your move, ain't it?"

Tranch eyed him and shrugged. "It's not up to me. But if I was in *your* boots, I'd light a shuck out of here! They'll grab you soon as you finish the race—"

"Mebbe," Shorty grinned, "I'm goin' t' want to git grabbed," and Tranch's grip on the reins suddenly showed white knuckles.

The starter said, "Get mounted. Get in line an' get ready."

He looked at his watch. He walked out to the edge and raised his flag.

The Indians pitched away their empty extract bottles.

Tranch's cheeks looked worried. There was sweat on his hands and Shorty knew he was rattled. Deep down inside him he exulted fiercely.

The starter whipped down his flag.

"Let's *go!*" he yelled; and Tranch and Shorty left the crest together.

Lorenzo Mountain Sheep, on the pinto, was scarcely half a jump behind. And he was coming fast— They all were! He had a switch in his hand and he was burning the pinto at every jump, screeching and yelling like all hell was after him.

Blood of Kings' powerful legs were driving like pistons, every sinew and muscle was brought into play. Sparks tore from her shoes and you could see the red lining of her distended nostrils as she bounded down that breakneck slope, ears back and eyes bulging.

Mountain Sheep's pinto was even with them now—a crazed horse, maddened with fear, running blind with terror.

But Shorty had no time to watch Mountain Sheep; he had all he could do to stay with his own horse. He expected any moment to be shaken clear loose or to get scraped off on some passing tree.

Down, down, down and ever down they went, tearing through brush, past trees and great boulders, sometimes hurdling the things in their path. There could be little swerving at that headlong pace. There wasn't enough time. They were traveling like a bullet, and the wind was a steady rushing screech around them.

Suddenly Mountain Sheep's paint lost its footing. Horse and rider went end over end, over and over, rolling on and on. Tranch's face showed gray all around his whiskers. He was doing his utmost to hold the stud in, but he might as well have tried to hold back a whirlwind. There was no holding back on that crazy pitch. Horses were falling all over the mountain.

Shorty let the mare go and she went like thunder.

The wind sang round them like it was blowing through wires.

Shorty got kind of scared of a sudden on his own hook. They were well in the lead and going like blazes, but a five pole fence suddenly burst into view and Shorty could not see how they ever would clear it. He hated like sin to think of losing out now, but he sure wasn't hankering for a harp or a halo! He reared way back, trying to pull up the mare, feet braced in the stirrups, every muscle strung taut; but he might just as well have barked at a knothole. Blood of Kings wasn't slowing one dadburned bit!

Twenty yards from the fence she kicked loose of the ground and it was just like being astride of a buzzard. They sailed through the air like a bolt of lightning, and Shorty let out one long scared yell. Then they landed. But he kept his seat and the mare kept her feet and they went pelting across the line—first in!

The crowd went wild with a mighty roar. Never in their lives had folks seen such a spectacle. They stood up and yelled their dadburned heads off; and it was lucky for Mrs. Potter that she wasn't around, because sure as heck she would have lost her bonnet. Ten seconds later one Indian came in on a wild-eyed thoroughbred. Only God could tell you what had happened to the others.

The judges crowded round to congratulate Shorty—the whole bunch, it seemed like, wanted to shake his hand; and Ma Hop waved with tears in her eyes.

Then Potter dashed up and grabbed Shorty's shoulder; and Halbert Crowsnow was right along with him. There wasn't any love light in Crowsnow's eye.

Potter snarled, "You're—"

"Just a minute," Ernie said. "It still happens I'm sheriff—"

"An' there's yer dang counterfeiter!" Shorty blared. "Right *there!*" he said, and jabbed a stiff finger into Crowsnow's belly. "This bogus Earl is the guy you want—it was *his* dang money that I give t' Tranch!"

"An' there goes Tranch right now!" someone shouted; and he was, sure enough, trying to make his getaway off to the left along the flank of the mountain.

"I'll take care of *him*—an' you, too!" Ernie growled, making a jump for Crowsnow who was trying to get clear. Ernie knocked the gun right out of his hand and exploded a fist on Crowsnow's chin. The Earl gasped once and folded over.

AT LAST it was over. They were back on the ranch, and Blood of Kings and *Sangre de Cristo* were comfortably recuperating in adjoining stalls in the great horse barn Luther Dickerson had built when he'd owned the place before

Shorty got it. Two great individuals bound to make history and to start Shorty off in his yellow horse breeding.

Shorty, with a pocketbook stuffed full of bank notes, sat with Rose on the porch drinking juleps with the dudes and grinning at Ernie while they listened to the guests still riding the Mountain Race.

"What I can't seem to get," Mr. Dunne repeated, "is how you ever got onto Crowsnow, Shorty."

"Jest like fallin' off a log," Shorty said, "once it hit me. I remembered it was *his* money I had used to buy that mare off of Tranch. He gave it to McGee. McGee gave it t' Rose. I got it from Rose when I went after that stud horse. An' I remembered, too, how that bustard of a Earl was always flashin' his roll— Why, he gave that Ben a *thousan' dollar bill* jest t' git him a knockdown to the Oregon Oriole!"

"We've got him dead to rights," Ernie said. "He broke down and confessed— That guy ain't got no more guts than a rabbit."

"But how was Tranch mixed up in the mess? And how did Shorty get Tranch's horse?" asked Dunne. "I thought Tranch got clear?"

"*He* thought so, too," Ernie grinned, "but I was watchin' for that. I had some deputies scattered round that mountain myself. They grabbed him before he could get out of sight. I knew all along I'd seen that bird before, an' last night it come to me. There was a jail break over to Yuma a while back and yesterday afternoon I gets me a circular. Phil Cinch, Lute Dickerson's former foreman, got away in that break. Tranch was Phil Cinch with a wig on an' whiskers. He's on his way back to the Pen right now."

"He wasn't mixed up in the counterfeitin'," Shorty said; and Hammock asked, "But what about those horses—Blood of Kings and the stud? Won't—"

"No. He had a perfectly good title to those horses," Ernie said.

And just then Shorty remembered Rose's letter that he'd been carrying around with him all this time. It was a little mite crumpled and looked kind of grimy, but he gave it to her anyway.

Rose tore it open. "It's from Coyle," she said. "I wrote him again about your horse, Shorty."

Over her shoulder Shorty read it wide eyed.

As it happens, Coyle said, *we did go a little into the white mare's background; we were acting as agents for another party. On the distaff side she goes back to King Herod, by way of Dan Tucker and Barney Owens. Through Zebra Dun and a sorrel mare called Lasca she goes, via Joe Hancock, once again to Herod. This is very good blood. Unfortunately, from the viewpoint of a high class breeder, there are too many unknowns in her pedigree. Of course, there is in horse history such a thing as mutations, or sports. Perhaps she is one. I would not worry too much about those glass eyes, because I think she would be ideal for your purpose. On her sire's side, she goes to Waggoner's old yellow Rainy Day, a most commendable stallion.*

Shorty read it aloud and slapped his thigh. "I knew dang well she had good blood back of her!"

"She's plenty good in herself," Ernie said. "The race proved that— It takes a damn good horse to stand up to that stuff." And Hammock's wife, Ethel, said "Um-*hmm!*"

Hellbound, coming up round the corner just then and spying the drinks, said to Shorty: "What you celebratin' anyhow? You fixin' t' git hitched up, or somethin'?"

Rose said, "I swear I'm not going to marry him in *those* things. Just *look* at those clothes— Why, they're all tore up from that crazy ride!"

412

FOUR FAST-ACTION NOVELS OF THE FRONTIER WEST

THE SPIRIT OF THE BORDER   (318, $1.75)
by Zane Grey
Lewis Wetzel was an Indian hunter, a self-styled avenger and the
right arm of defense to the settlers of Fort Henry. To the super-
stitious Indians he was a shadow which breathed menace from
the dark forests. . . .

THE HERITAGE OF THE DESERT   (328, $1.75)
by Zane Grey
Jack Hare was faced with a desperate choice: Either gun down
the son of the man who had saved his life—or be killed himself!

THE TROUBLE AT PENA BLANCA   (330, $1.75)
by Nelson Nye
The ad read: "Wanted—A Tough Hand for Trouble!" But for
Bendigo to do the job, he'd have to go back to Mexico where the
Durango Militia, hot on his heels, had almost got him at the
border. . . .

THE CISCO KID   (338, $1.75)
in "The Caballero's Way"
by O. Henry
Meet the *real* Cisco Kid, who was as heartless as he was handsome, who killed for the love of it and who escaped capture because he could shoot five-sixths of a second sooner than any sheriff or ranger in the service.

*Available wherever paperbacks are sold, or order direct from the
Publisher. Send cover price plus 35¢ per copy for mailing and
handling to Zebra Books, 21 East 40th Street, New York, N.Y.
10016. DO NOT SEND CASH!*

SOMETHING FOR EVERYONE—
BEST SELLERS FROM ZEBRA!

THE SOUL   (321, $2.25)
by Ron Gorton
Possessed by an angel, a man named Rebuck came out of nowhere—a maverick, a rebel—to found the Church of Michael,
which threatened to destroy the foundations of organized religion, plunging the world into chaos, terror, and religious war.

HITLER'S NAVAL WAR   (300, $2.25)
by Cajus Bekker
Based on secret, just-released documents, this is the incredible
story of the underrated, undermanned German naval force that
nearly won World War II.

THE LIAISON   (325, $1.95)
by Maria Matray and Answald Kreuger
The rich and beautiful Princess Louise von Coburg embarks on a
reckless flirtation with a lieutenant in her husband's army that
rapidly grows into a grand passion. The true story of one of the
most romantic and powerful love affairs of all time.

COLLISION   (326, $1.95)
by Spencer Dunmore
The nerve-shattering novel of a sky crash—and the horrifying af-
termath when two giant aircraft are joined by a tangle of tortured
metal high above the clouds. Spellbinding!

DOLLY PARTON: DAUGHTER OF THE SOUTH (295, $1.95)
by Lola Scobey
Meet the South's Cinderella, and get to know the woman behind
the sequined jeans and "Carvel" hairdo as Dolly talks about her
family, her faith, her future, and her favorite thing: her music.

Available wherever paperbacks are sold, or order direct from the
Publisher. Send cover price plus 25¢ per copy for mailing and
handling to ZEBRA BOOKS, 521 Fifth Avenue, New York, NY
10017. DO NOT SEND CASH!

**DON'T MISS THESE SUPER SCIENCE FICTION/
SCIENCE FANTASY BESTSELLERS!**

THE BLAL   (351, $1.75)
by A. E. Van Vogt
Space pioneers are met with unearthly resistance from blobs and
sleep creatures when they disrupt the serenity and balance of new
unexplored territories in the outer limits. Plus other short stories.

THE GRYB   (331, $1.75)
by A. E. Van Vogt
Journey to Zand at the end of The Ridge where a desperate trav-
eler is willing to sell a pair of very special glasses, or travel to the
land of the blood-sucking thing known as The Gryb. It's a non-
stop trip to the star worlds of tomorrow and beyond.

200 MILLION A.D.   (357, $1.75)
by A. E. Van Vogt
Cross the barrier to a new unearthly dimension when a man of
the present and a man of the future, inhabiting the same body,
battle to rule the world. He is the great and mighty god they wor-
ship as Ptath.

CHRYSALIS   (287, $1.95)
edited by Roy Torgeson
The greatest anthology of original stories from the pens of the
most talented sci-fi writers of this generation: Harlan Ellison,
Theodore Sturgeon, Nebula Award winner Charles L. Grant,
and other top storytellers.

*Available wherever paperbacks are sold, or order direct from the
Publisher. Send cover price plus 35¢ per copy for mailing and
handling, to Zebra Books, 21 East 40th Street, New York, N.Y.
10016. DO NOT SEND CASH!*